Madness Bound

Book 1 in the Madness of Kanaan Trilogy

Karina Fabian

I0634081

**LASER COW
PRESS**

Laser Cow Press

MERRITT ISLAND, FL

Laser Cow Press
Merritt Island, FL
https://fabianspace.com

Cover art by 100Covers
Laser Cow Logo by Allen Oaks

Book Layout © 2017 BookDesignTemplates.com

Madness Bound/Karina Fabian -- 1st ed.
Print ISBN 978-1-956489-18-7

Dedication

To my husband, Rob, who tolerates my own craziness and taught me to believe in myself.

Contents

Prologue

Ydrel threw himself into wakefulness with such force that he sat up in bed. Still, the nightmare images clung to his mind: the beat of a hundred hearts, the smell of sweat and fear. He clutched his stomach and fought the urge to scream.

A hundred bodies crowded around him, crushing him against the splintered wood of the boxcar.

No, this isn't real!

No room to move. No air to breathe. Suffocating. Drowning.

No, this isn't me!

Confusion and fear. Fear the trip would never end. Terror of what waited at its completion.

No! These aren't my memories!

Ydrel threw up shaky mental barriers. The visions faded, just slightly. He forced his eyes open, drinking in reassurance from familiar objects.

He sat in bed, an oversized twin, backed up against pillows rather than splintered wood. Pre-dawn light shone softly through the blinds.

On the nightstand, Descartes regarded him with one button eye. The only thing left from before his mother died, he'd slept with that bear until an orderly commented on his "abnormal attachment." Since then it had stood watch over him instead, braced against the lamp. Even now, without any orderlies around, Ydrel resisted the urge to clutch it close to his chest, but he reached out to touch one tattered foot.

On the shelf beside the window sat a portable boom box, a gift from his first birthday here—his thirteenth. Five years ago, today. The maintenance man had disabled the volume control after Ydrel played it too loudly. Thereafter, he'd found other ways to block out the moans and occasional screams that penetrated the closed door. Happy birthday.

The stereo held up several books. He was studying them in case *it* called. He both dreaded and longed for the calls. Each episode only gave them more reason to keep him there, yet there was something as familiar and comforting about *it* as his old bear.

He turned his gaze to the far wall and the framed pictures of a nebula and the solar system by his half-empty closet. On his sixteenth birthday, he'd been allowed to decorate his room, and he'd chosen those posters and a mild blue paint to replace the still–lifes and the institutional burgundy-and-pink color scheme. While it had been a relief to his eyes, it was also a constant reminder that they never intended for him to leave.

This is my room, he thought. *In the asylum.* Even after five years, he'd never call it home. He'd never give Malachai the satisfaction.

Calmer now, his mental barriers in place, Ydrel allowed himself to examine the vision that awakened him.

Hundreds of bodies packed into a train car not suited for twenty. Most had traveling clothes, but had shed them against the heat. No room to move. The air was stifling and stale. No one knew where they were going. Some suspected, but said nothing. The destination was worse than the trip.

Ydrel sighed. Isaac was on the train to Dachau again.

Ydrel threw off the covers and dressed quickly in a blue T-shirt and jeans, socks and generic sneakers. Already Isaac's projected fear was breaking down his mental defenses; Ydrel's fingers trembled as he fumbled with the laces.

Once out in the corridor, he hastened to the old man's room, forcing himself to keep his pace smooth, his face composed. Someone would stop him if he hurried or looked distressed, and any delay would be unbearable. As he walked, he got into character. His stride lengthened; his face hardened. He held his hands relaxed but ready by his hips. When he got to Isaac's door, he cast a wary look down the hall, then slipped in.

The old man lay on a standard hospital bed, his wide, wild eyes staring at the ceiling but focused on his inner horrors. His hands fluttered helplessly on the thin coverlet. He labored for each ragged breath.

Ydrel sat beside him and composed his own vision.

The train stops so suddenly that people would have been thrown down if they hadn't been so tightly packed in. The sound of gunfire and shouts in German. The boxcar door opens with a rusty screech. Someone yells in Yiddish, then German: "Out! Now! Quickly, to the woods—to the south!" Relief from the press of bodies, then a new pressure as the flow of people pushes him through the door. Someone grabs his arm—

Ydrel grabbed Isaac by the arm as he pushed the new vision into the old man's mind.

Isaac blinked, twisted toward Ydrel, then smiled, his eyes bright with tears. "Gideon! Old friend. Thank God!"

Chapter One

Joshua Lawson gave his name to the receptionist and sat in a high-backed gilt chair in the waiting room.

"Swanky place," he muttered to himself, and again tried to quell his nervousness. The furniture, the thick carpet, the subdued walls with tasteful art, all spoke of a society he'd never been part of and money he'd probably never see unless he became a rock star like he'd dreamed. He crossed his legs, uncrossed them quickly as the sole of his shoe bumped the carved tiger on the chair arm, leaned forward, then back, then crossed his legs more carefully.

Relax, you want to make a good impression.

He was glad there wasn't a mirror in the room. He knew what he'd see. His rich dark skin meant he didn't flush with nervousness, but it would be apparent around the eyes and the tightness of his mouth. His hair was cut short in a style more conservative than he usually liked—last year, he'd had LaTisha's initials shaved in the back—as was the new gray suit he wore, a going-away gift from his parents. He fingered the chili pepper tie tack he wore, a going-away gift from his best friend Rique Martinez. "So when you're with all your *Rhode Island* colleagues you can remember your obligation to Chipotle."

Like Joshua could forget their band. Momarosa would have a fit, too. She was the one who pushed them to join the parish choir when they were kids, and then volunteered their garage band to play at the Holy Family Parish carnival.

Now they had an audition in New York City in July. Momarosa was over the moon, and Rique had warned him not to let her or the rest of them down. After the way Josh had nearly blown things with the band during his relationship with LaTisha, there was no way he'd do that on the eve of what could be their big break.

Besides, if the agent liked them, he could lose the suit and make his money doing what he really loved.

He turned his attention to one of the paintings—it was like something he'd expect to see in a museum rather than a hospital—and told himself how lucky he was to have such a good summer job when most of his classmates were trying to convince people to "biggie size" their order.

Meanwhile, I'm interning under a respected psychiatrist—one I'm actually not related to, for once—and I'll make enough this summer to pay my expenses next year. I've got it made.

When Dr. Sellars walked into the room, he rose quickly and shook her hand. "Joshua Lawson, ma'am." Rique would have teased him for that.

She smiled. "Edith. I prefer to keep things informal. Are you all settled in?"

"Yes, ma'am—Edith. I drove up a couple of days ago and got moved into my apartment. Not like I had much to do; it's bigger than the dorm, but not by much."

'Course, not as big or nice as this room.

She seemed to pick up the thought, and indicated the room with a wave of her hand. "So, what do you think?"

"Pretty swanky. Kind of how I'd imagine the Betty Ford Clinic." He could have kicked himself, but fortunately, she laughed. She pointed to the door with an open hand, and they headed to her office.

"Well, our clients aren't always the rich and famous, but they can afford some luxuries. The low intensity wings have a full gym, a pool—locked unless an employee is present, of course. But you'd have read all that already. Incidentally, you're welcome to use those facilities in your off time. I'll introduce you to Jean, the facilities manager. The medium intensity wings are more restricted, of course, and the high intensity is more like what you may have seen at the Colorado Mental Health Institute in Pueblo—with better quality, of course."

"Really." He tried not to sound miffed. He'd done a lot of volunteering at the psychiatric ward there, and knew the care was sound, despite the clients' not rolling in dough.

She paused at a door with a wood plaque bearing her name, opened it, and let him in first. The office was as big as his living room, and boasted a couch nicer than the daybed in his apartment. More comfortable, too, he realized as he sank into it. Edith sat in the matching Queen Anne chair.

She continued. "You'll need to keep in mind that this isn't just a mental care facility. It's a for-profit business. The families of our clients—and the clients themselves—expect a certain level of comfort, and we deliver that. That means top-quality care. That means a high standard of professionalism, including a strict dress code. It also means that though we're on a first-name basis, you'll address others by honorific and last name until invited to do otherwise. And it means swanky facilities."

She paused a moment, as if not sure how to phrase what she wanted to say next. "I think that's one reason your father asked me to sponsor you. This is a side of the psychiatric world he felt you needed to see. What are your feelings on that?"

Joshua had to stop and consider his next words. True, he regarded his father's few wealthy clients as high-society whiners, but he'd promised to hold off on forming opinions of the clients here until he'd gotten to know some.

He sidestepped the issue. "I hope my father isn't the reason I got this job."

"You're nineteen years old," she said flatly. "Your father is the reason I'd even consider someone so young, college senior or no. Your mother did an excellent job homeschooling you; you've had opportunities most people never get, and you've done an impressive job of taking advantage of those opportunities. Your experience at the CMHIP and with your father's practice convinced me and enabled me to convince my superiors. Your papers were impressive, too. I'm frankly quite curious to see if the Neuro Linguistic Programming you and your father practice is as effective as you seem to portray it."

"It is," Joshua spoke with complete confidence.

Neuro Linguistic Programming was a decades-old process around a simple concept: study your patients, discover their thinking process, then use their own tools to help them find their own cures. Joshua's father was one of the pioneers of the method, and Joshua himself had been learning both from his father and from attending seminars with him since he was eight years old. He'd always been a very observant child, and it was easy for him to pick up people's thinking styles by watching the eyes, listening to their words, noticing patterns in posture and tension. He'd been scurrilously practicing (on friends, sometimes on his own family) since he'd attended his first seminar.

Now, it was almost second nature to him; in fact, as they sat talking, part of him was studying Edith—her reactions, how she processed a thought before vocalizing—not intending to use the information in any way, just recording how she acted in an environment where she was calm and in control.

"So, you're following in your father's footsteps?"

She'd asked this during their phone interview. For a moment, he thought about telling her he actually wanted to live up to his nickname, Josh-a-ham, and be a professional musician, preferably a rock star, but psychiatry was steadier and more certain work. Instead, he gave her the same answer he did then: "My choice, not his."

"Good. Come on, then, and I'll explain your schedule as we go. I want you to meet someone, one of my special clients. We'll get you a passkey card and a combination before you leave today, so you won't have to do this again."

"Isn't all that security a little extreme?" He regarded the electronic lock and cameras as they passed the foyer.

"It actually is very handy. We once admitted a client for delusional fantasies that Mafia assassins were trying to kill him. Turned out he wasn't hallucinating—the guards caught them trying to get in, impersonating friends of a client. They gassed them in the foyer."

"Wild."

"Mmm-hmm. Ydrel tipped us off. His name is really Deryl Stephens, but never call him that. He goes by Ydrel. He says it means 'The Oracle,' but I haven't found a language yet it matches."

"Sounds Jewish or Eastern European or something."

"It's not. He claims it's his father's language, so I thought maybe, but I checked with a linguist friend at Brown, and it's just an anagram as near as he can tell. Anyway, Ydrel has been here more than five years. He's eighteen today and we're having a little party for him."

"And he's been here since he was thirteen? Man."

"Don't start feeling sorry for him. He's got an uncanny ability to read people. That's part of the reason we can't break him of his illusions. And until we do, he's just not safe outside."

They entered a small room similar to the reception area, but with the addition of bright balloons, crepe ribbons and a banner: *Happy Birthday, Darrel!*

On yet another comfortable-looking couch, a middle-aged couple sat nervously. Across from them, a young man leaned over the arm of a chair, talking intently to an old man in a wheelchair.

As Josh and Edith stepped into the room, however, the young man leapt to his feet, for all the world acting like he was reaching for a gun. The couple jumped, and the old man gasped with panic. When he saw Edith, he rolled his eyes. "Don't you ever knock?" he scolded.

Edith did her best to look chagrined. "Sorry."

"Yeah, sorry. Someday you'll be sorry with a hole in your head." And he leaned back to the old man, speaking quietly in some foreign language. Slavic, Joshua thought, and decided he'd do his own internet search on "Ydrel."

Then the young man glared suspiciously at him. "Who's he?" he demanded. "You know the rules."

"A friend," Edith said.

The young man seemed doubtful, again glaring at Joshua. "All right," he said after a moment. Then he called to a tall, thin black man—an orderly, Joshua guessed from the simple white uniform—and said, "Ishmael, would you?"

He spoke a last time to the old man as "Ishmael" wheeled him out. When the door closed behind them, the young man flopped into the couch opposite the couple and buried his head in his hands.

The woman reached for him, then pulled her hand back and leaned a little closer to the man, who looked at Edith, askance.

"Ydrel, how long has he been like that?" Edith asked.

"Since about five-thirty this morning. He's been kind of fading in and out for a while, though. It's okay."

Looking at the way the couple all but huddled together on the couch, Joshua thought it was far less than "okay." Was this party their idea? If so, they weren't getting the happy bonding time they'd probably hoped for.

"Mr. Goldstein is a Holocaust survivor," Edith explained to Joshua and to the couple. "He has Alzheimer's, and it takes him back to the memory of those days. Ydrel's found that if he plays the part of a freedom fighter trying to help him escape, it keeps him focused away from the worst of the memories."

"Really?" Josh was impressed. It wasn't much different than the work he and his father did.

"More like psychic self-defense," Ydrel retorted hotly. "*Really*. Do you know what kind of fear that man feels? What he projects? It hides in the shadows and behind doors and if I drop my guard for a second, it pounces. Then I'm the one living his fear, feeling his tortures. Do you know where he was this morning? In this boxcar, packed in with all these people and children were crying and there wasn't enough air to breathe and people were passing out, only they couldn't fall down because we were packed in so tightly—"

His eyes widened and turned inward and he started to wrap his arms about himself.

The woman leaned her head into the man's shoulder and he pulled her closer. Joshua saw a ring. Husband and wife, then. Ydrel's parents? He wished he'd gotten more of a briefing than just "Ydrel's turning eighteen."

Edith sat beside Ydrel and laid a hand on his arm in a gesture both reassuring and restraining. "It was his life, Ydrel, his memories. And he survived it. And he has lots of happy memories, too."

"Why can't he project those?" Ydrel sighed, then shook himself and stood. He circled Joshua slowly, scrutinizing him from head to toe. Josh stood calmly; he'd had this happen before. "So, Joshua Abraham Lawson," Ydrel drawled the name, "welcome to the land of the rich and loony, minimum security. Hope you'll find we're not all whiners using our money to buy attention. Did Edith tell you what it means to be working in a swanky facility like ours?"

Josh bristled. Crazy or not, this guy's attitude stunk. He took on a parody of a Jersey accent. "You want I should call you 'sir'?"

"Ooooh. Found a witty one, didn't you, Edith? It means, at least to me, that as long as there's money to be made off me, I never get to leave."

He continued to circle, just enough inside Joshua's personal space to make him feel edgy. Even though Ydrel stood a couple of inches shorter than Joshua's six feet, he seemed to loom. Joshua forced himself to relax, to move outside himself and stare ahead laconically, studying Ydrel with his peripheral vision.

Edith watched, her face neutral, but did nothing. The couple shifted nervously,.

Meanwhile, the young client continued to circle. "I'm a prisoner here, Joshua, as long as the money holds out and they can manipulate my family into fearing me—"

"Ydrel, that's enough!" Edith scolded. She didn't raise her voice, and in fact, sat down and regarded the client with stern gaze and crossed arms. She tilted her head toward the seat on the couch.

Ydrel stopped his menace and regarded Edith with a sad smile. "Not you, Edith. You've been nothing but kind. You just think I'm delusional. Malachai knows better."

Joshua spared a glance at his "family." Not parents, then? Or was Ydrel including others—siblings at home, maybe? They were silent through the exchange, but they watched Edith intently, waiting for some signal from her to tell them what to do. Maybe Ydrel wasn't so far off in his assessment. Great.

Ydrel gave the last of his smile to the couple, then turned back to Joshua and resumed his circling. Edith merely watched. So much for "that's enough"—or was she testing Joshua already?

Ydrel continued his monologue. "*Doctor* Malachai knows I have paranormal abilities—good words, eh? His words. He's studying me, like a lab animal, until he finds a way to duplicate my talents in normal humans. Until then, he'll keep using me. If I resist, I get punished. If I cooperate, he gets that much closer to his goal. Either way, I'm stuck here."

Then, Ydrel stopped. Joshua glanced sideways at him. He had a faraway look, as if he was seeing something that surprised and scared him a little. When he spoke, his voice matched his expression. His pupils seemed unusually contracted for the light.

"One day, I'll learn to do something Malachai can't control. He'll find some way to get rid of me. He'll convince everyone I'm really psychotic. Violent. And he'll drug me, take away my will..."

Joshua watched the man stiffen and the woman start to twist her hands in her lap.

"You know," Joshua cut into his reverie, "I don't think anyone has to convince your family of anything. You're doing a first-rate job of scaring them yourself." He wasn't sure if he'd overstepped his bounds. He didn't know Ydrel's case, but he trusted his instincts.

Ydrel blinked, then looked at Joshua with surprise and some respect. "You're right. Sometimes, I get a little caught in my Gideon persona."

He brightened and settled down on the couch next to the psychiatrist. Edith's expression didn't change, except that she arched her eyebrows and tilted her head slightly in the direction of his family.

He looked at them, then his head turned sharply away, as if he'd been struck. He paused like that, eyes squinted as if in pain, then let out a shuddering sigh and looked back at them.

"Some party, huh? I'm sorry. He's right. I scared you and I, I'm sorry. Please, can we start again? Joshua Abraham Lawson, meet my family: Aunt Katheryn and Uncle Douglas. Aunt Kate, Uncle Doug, meet Joshua Abraham Lawson, the new intern come to study me. He's my present from Edith—an unusual gift," he said, smiling at Joshua, then Edith. "Couldn't you have at least found a girl?"

"Darrel!" his aunt spoke for the first time, pronouncing the "a" like "ah" and emphasizing the "e," which struck Joshua as weird.

Almost atop her scolding, her husband commented, "Hell, if that's what you wanted, you should have said something!"

"Douglas!" his wife reproved.

Laughter broke the tension in the room. Edith motioned Joshua to sit, so he pulled a chair over from the table and sat on it backwards, his arms draped across the back.

Douglas reached into his inner jacket pocket. "I did bring something else appropriate for one's eighteenth birthday." With a flourish, he pulled out a transparent flask. Dark amber liquid caught the light from the florescent lamps.

"How did you sneak that in here?" Katie demanded.

"Plastic flask. Happy Birthday, Darrel."

"It's Ydrel. I'm eighteen. I can choose my own name. It's not like you ever spelled or pronounced my old one right, anyway." But nonetheless, he reached for the flask.

Edith was quicker. "I'll hang onto this. It's against regulations—and in any case, you're still underage."

"Legalistic crap. If the boy's old enough to vote, he's old enough to drink."

"Can the committed vote?" Ydrel asked.

"Hell, how do you think Clinton got elected?"

"Douglas!" Katie rolled her eyes. "Republicans," she said to Joshua, as if it were a bad habit she couldn't quite break her husband of.

"At least my party wouldn't put up a womanizing, draft-dodging, bureaucratic—"

Edith started to interrupt what was apparently an old argument, but Ydrel stopped her with a raised hand. "It's been a long day. Let them have their fun." Then he looked over at Joshua. "Feeling vulnerable?"

"What?"

Ydrel indicated Joshua's backwards-turned chair with a lazy wave of his hand, then shrugged. "It's okay. We all need barriers. Most of mine are up here." He tapped his temple.

"It's comfortable," Joshua bristled.

"Mine are, too. When they work. Hey," he turned the arguing couple. "How about we shelve the politics and have cake instead?"

The men sat in silence as Katie and Edith prepared the cake with candles. Douglas shifted uncomfortably and watched his wife gather paper plates. Ydrel, too, seemed to focus on his aunt, but then seemed to focus through her, then not focus at all, lost in dark thoughts. He smiled but didn't seem to listen as they sang "Happy Birthday"; when the song died, he was still focused elsewhere.

"Darrel, honey, make a wish."

Ydrel suddenly glared at his aunt. "Why? I wish for the same thing every year. It's not like it'll come true. I wish for my freedom. I wish to find someplace where people will believe me and not think I'm crazy or a guinea pig or—I wish I could go—"

He bit his lip, stared down at his hands.

Silence.

Finally, he looked up, met his aunt's sad eyes. "Tell you what: I'll make a wish for you." He made a great show of closing his eyes to wish hard then blowing out the candles in one long puff.

"So, what did you wish for?" Her voice quavered a little and she drew in a breath.

Ydrel smiled, this time a genuine happy smile. "Oh, you'll find out in about six months."

Douglas turned to his wife. "Katie?"

Edith smiled. "Kate, are you pregnant?"

She smiled and nodded, but more nervously than Joshua would have expected. "I, I wasn't going to tell anyone. I've lost so many—"

"Not this one." Ydrel spoke confidently. "This one will be strong, beautiful and healthy. I *know*." Again, he met her eyes and smiled.

The smile she returned was shaky, and full of hope and fear.

Chapter Two

"Here we are." Dr. Bartlebort stopped at a door whose fancy nameplate declared "Office of Dr. D. Randall Malachai" with an accompanying alphabet of credentials. He smiled at Joshua. "Time to meet the big man himself. Dr. Malachai is head of the institution— but don't worry; he's just like any of us."

You mean he'll treat me like I'm fourteen? Joshua kept his face schooled into polite neutrality. Most of the staff, while curious, had treated him with respect, but with the exception of Edith (and now Bottlebort), the psychiatrists seemed suspicious of this "kid" one of their own hired as an intern. He wondered how many had even bothered reading his résumé.

He didn't want to come off as an uppity intern, especially his first day, so he bit back the urge to finish sentences for them and settled for asking questions that displayed a depth of knowledge.

Apparently, his strategy worked, because Dr. Bartlebort introduced him to Dr. Malachai as "Edith's project, though he seems to know his stuff" and didn't bother to hide the surprise in his voice. He left Joshua at the door.

Joshua walked into an office that was tasteful, professional, and completely devoid of humor or warmth, despite the rich colors of the décor.

A large cherrywood executive desk dominated the view as he first walked in. On the left corner was a pen and pencil nameplate with "Dr. D. Randall Malachai, MD, PhD," and a slew of other initials in smaller print. A slim, black 21-inch computer monitor perched on the right corner. A small notebook with a pen sat with studied neglect among a stack of files.

Behind the desk, the wall was plastered with framed professional certificates, guarded on either side by the matching cherrywood file cabinet and a bookshelf filled with professional books and journals. Those with Malachai's name on the spine were on the perfect shelf to be noticed by someone sitting in the visitor's chairs, Joshua noted.

To the left of the desk were a low sofa and a higher quality version of the wing-backed chair Joshua had used in the waiting room, with a coffee table between them. The room was so large it also held a small conference table; Dr. Malachai's spot at the head was readily apparent by a small butler's table, also in cherrywood.

No expense spared here.

"Sit." Dr. Malachai indicated one of the two leather chairs in front of his desk, then stood and pulled his executive chair from behind the desk. His was slightly higher than the others.

Dr. Malachai leaned back, ankle resting on one knee, arms crossed lightly. He smiled a patronizing smile that made Joshua's hackles rise. Joshua had automatically put on the polite but distanced aura he always wore around people he disliked. He was usually successful at hiding his feelings, but something in Dr. Malachai's smile said he saw through the facade.

"So, you've met Deryl, or Ydrel, as he prefers to be called."

It was not a question, but Joshua answered anyway. "Yes, sir."

The smile quirked smugly. "It shows on your face. Tell me, did he describe me as a Nazi madman or a modern Dr. Strangelove?"

"Uh, neither, sir, really, though he did give the impression you and he did not get along." Joshua kept his answer as neutral as possible while he tried to figure out where this was leading. He'd only known the senior psychiatrist for a minute, yet he already had the impression that Dr. Malachai never did anything idly.

The psychiatrist chuckled. "All right. Keep your confidences if you feel you must. Just remember that there's a line between developing trust and endangering an employee or client."

Then he looked away and sighed. "You know, there was a time when Deryl confided in me. I like to think I was a father figure of sorts. Perhaps that explains some of his behavior to me now; developmentally, he's at an age where he needs to define his identity, establish his independence, and of course, there's only so much independence he can have due to his condition. Therefore, he seeks to make that 'break,' as it were, by rebelling against the closest thing to parent he has. Surely, you can identify with such teenage rebellion?"

As Malachai spoke, Joshua caught himself leaning forward, a student listening to the wise words of a mentor. Deliberately, he changed his posture to match that of the psychiatrist's, replying peer to peer.

"Actually, I never went through that, meself; my parents were strict, but gave me a lot of room to make my own decisions. I did witness it in some of my friends, however." He did not add that those who rebelled the most were the ones whose parents were the most controlling.

"Then you are lucky, indeed. At any rate, Edith believes Ydrel is at a stage where he may respond more openly to a peer rather than a parent. However, let's talk about the rest of your internship: What do you intend to accomplish?"

The rest of the conversation went smoothly, even pleasantly. Soon Malachai rose, saying he had some appointments, and led Joshua back to the nurse's station, where he would be passed on to the next person on his agenda. Dr. Malachai spent a few minutes chatting with the nurses before going back to his office.

"He's so nice," one nurse commented as he left.

Somehow, "nice" was not a word Joshua could associate with Malachai. Charismatic, yes, and such charisma set his teeth on edge. Hitler had such charisma—

Hitler? Wow. Maybe Ydrel made a bigger impression on me than I thought. He had no reason to think so ill of the senior psychiatrist, yet his instincts clamored.

Nonetheless, he thought of his mother. "Trust your feelings, Joshua," she often told him, sometimes mimicking Obi Wan Kenobi, sometimes in complete earnest. She was a firm believer that there was more to humans than intellect and emotion, something she called "body knowledge," so part of his education had been biospiritual focusing, intuitive medicine, and other "hocus-pocus hippie stuff" as some of his friends—and even one of his professors—called it. Rique called her "Mama Kenobi" when she said those things to him.

Joshua knew that his mother would tell him to trust those instincts; they'd tell him more than his intellect. Even when in opposition to what his intellect told him, his body knowledge was most often right.

I wonder if Ydrel just has an abnormally strong inclination himself, so strong he can't ignore—

"Joshua?"

He realized he'd been woolgathering about his encounter with Malachai and snapped back to the present. He turned to smile at Edith, and they returned to her office.

She closed the door and opened the blinds to let in the late afternoon sun, then motioned for him to sit while she finished notes and pulled out other files in preparation for tomorrow.

Finally, she asked, "Well, what do you think?"

While he thought, he leaned back and let his eyes wander around the office. He hadn't looked at it closely earlier, other than to note that it was large, expensive and full of plants and photos. Now he saw that the photos were of horses, some with her astride them, some framed with ribbons. The obligatory bookcase housed books on horses as well as a wide variety of fiction: *Black Beauty, The Red Tent, The Nanny Diaries: A Novel.*

"Where's your DSM?"

Edith laughed. "On disk. I keep the rest of my books in the library or at home. I'd rather have my clients here thinking about other things than how I'll diagnose their pathos."

Josh grunted. "Do a lot of riding?"

"Did. Dressage. Went to Nationals twice. But that was a long time ago. Now, I just ride for pleasure. My husband's a trainer, and we have a small horse farm. I'll take you sometime. But you haven't answered my question."

"I'm the first intern here, aren't I?"

"Was it that apparent?"

He gave her a half-smile-half grimace in answer, and she sighed.

"I think we have a lot to teach, and an obligation to do so. I finally convinced the board to give it a try, and you're our trial run. Does that bother you?"

He shrugged with a nonchalance he didn't quite feel. "I guess I should be honored. I've been the guinea pig before, so no, it doesn't bother me. Besides, I'll learn a lot here."

It was a neutral answer, but one he meant. Edith had asked one of the therapists to show him all three facilities, then had taken him along on her afternoon rounds. He'd met a few clients he automatically pegged as "high-society whiners," seen a few cases that were similar to those he'd helped with in Colorado and encountered a pathos he'd only read about. He had three or four he was dying to study, and he hoped they would work them into his schedule. He would spend most of the summer in the minimum intensity care ward but would be allowed to work with a few more serious cases in July or August—if he proved himself.

With study, he'd probably be working twelve hours a day, but the knowledge he'd gain would be worth a semester of courses. And the experience, not to mention how it'd look on a résumé. Just in case the agent didn't work out.

He shifted into a less comfortable position on her comfortable couch. "So what's the deal with Ydrel? How much does he have to do with my being here?"

She didn't answer immediately, but pulled out a large file—it took two hands to carry—and set it on the table in front of Josh. "I really should put it on CD. This is a summary of the highlights of Ydrel's time here. I have an entire drawer on him, and Randall has even more, I'm sure.

"He's incredibly difficult to pin down, diagnostically. Medicating him is a disaster. I won't tell you his current designation. I want to see what you come up with. Regardless of how we label him, the key lies in what keeps him here: He's hooked on this delusion that he's psychic, and what makes it worse is that he's such a good reader of people, he can make it seem true."

Joshua shrugged. "Lots of people make money using 'psychic' abilities. Some of them probably even believe they have powers."

"Ydrel doesn't stop at 'reading' someone. He internalizes what he picks up, and not just emotionally, either. We have to be careful who we put in the rooms next to him. Twice we had someone on suicide watch in the next room, only to find Ydrel trying to kill himself. Several times, he's begged me to move someone. Once, he said the girl was 'making him' violent—and in fact, she did attack several clients in the common room—and another time, he said his neighbor was thinking suicidal thoughts. Again, Ydrel was right. You've seen his reaction to Mr. Goldstein."

"So how is he around, well, regular people?"

Edith smiled sadly. "The one time he left on a family visit, it...didn't go well. He's not been out since. No one knows how he'd react to a crowd. His family is afraid he'd hurt himself, more than anything. The staff is concerned he'll encounter someone really troubled—whether a street person or a criminal—and pick up that persona. More and more, too, Dr. Malachai and some of the others on the board are concerned that, if given a chance, he'd try to escape."

She shook her head sadly.

"But he won't escape," she concluded. "He doesn't think he has anywhere he can go. I've been working his case for the last three years, and every year, I see him becoming more and more hopeless. He's being convinced he's a freak with no place in the outside world.

"That's where you come in, Joshua. I want you to give him back hope."

Joshua felt his jaw drop. He tried to hide it by smiling. "Really?"

She sat on the couch opposite him. The file sat on the table between them and she idly ran her hands over the cover as she collected her thoughts.

"Ydrel has spent some of the most formative years of his life surrounded by mentally troubled clients and the mental health staff—hardly a typical cross-section of the population." She quirked a smile, then turned serious. "Most of the clients are in their late twenties or older. He hasn't been around a single mentally healthy person his age since he was first committed. But given his situation...I was discussing his case with your father—with Doug and Kate's permission, of course—"

"—and he suggested me." Joshua couldn't keep the disappointment out of his voice. He'd thought they'd come to an agreement on that sort of thing.

But Edith looked up sharply in a way that he'd learned meant he was insultingly off-base. "Your father suggested an intern, and when I told him the resistance I've met in starting such a program, he suggested you might be able to change some attitudes. I meant it when I said you're good—even exceptional. Some of the staff already knew you by reputation from papers you'd published with your father—and were amazed to learn your age. If you prove yourself here, it will benefit you and help future interns. Nonetheless, setting up this program has been a lot of headache for me, and frankly, I did it with Ydrel in mind.

"I know that's not what you were expecting. Your internship is more than just his case. But he needs someone his own age, someone he can relate to. If you could make him believe he can have a life outside those gates..."

She let the sentence hang. He met her eyes for a moment, then studied his shoes. Silence stretched out between them.

Finally, he broke it. "Any ideas?"

She smiled and let out a breath. "The usual psychological methods won't work. That's certain. Ydrel was right when he made the crack about my giving him a friend. He needs someone to simply be a friend. Not a doctor, not a mentor, not an intern. Don't study him. Treat him like you might treat a new roommate, maybe a foreign-exchange student who's suffering from culture shock. Help him understand that he can adapt if he tries. If you come up with any ideas, run them by me. I'll give you as much leeway in this as I can."

"And Dr. Malachai?" He was Ydrel's primary caregiver.

"You let me handle Randall."

So he's not too keen on your plan. He'd guessed that from their conversation earlier. That only motivated Joshua more. He thought carefully about his next words. Edith, he'd learned, was a person who thought in feelings and visuals, and he knew to convince her, he'd need to meet her on that level. "I'm excited about this internship—I see it as a clear chance to both learn psychology and practice it, outside my father's influence. I can't promise not to do that when I'm with Ydrel. I'll see what I can do about befriending him, though frankly, if we'd had a run-in like that in the dorms, I'd be looking for a new roommate."

He smiled, and she smiled in return.

"I'll try," he promised. "I'll clear what I can with you, but if I see an opportunity to help him, I'm going for it. I can promise not to use the 'usual' psychotherapeutic methods, though, and I can promise to try to make him feel he has a life outside these walls."

"Fair enough." Edith rose and handed him a binder from atop the cabinet. "This is your first study assignment. I'm going to call it a day. You're welcome to stay; just lock up and sign out with the guards when you leave."

She hung up her lab coat, grabbed her purse and started for the door. Then she stopped, and with a thoughtful look on her face, reached into the pocket of her lab coat and pulled out the plastic flask. She regarded it wistfully.

Joshua stopped flipping through the case studies in the binder to look at her.

"You know," she mused, "this is probably one of the few times someone's tried to treat him like any other teenager, and I had to take it away from him."

"It's the thought that counts?" Joshua ventured.

"Perhaps." She crossed to him and set the flask in the desk drawer beside him. "Still, it's such a shame." She met his eyes expectantly.

He glanced at her, at the drawer. "Kind of a wasted opportunity."

She smiled. "Just lock the door when you leave."

"Will do."

Chapter Three

Two hours later, Joshua sighed, stretched and looked at the clock. Almost 8 p.m. He'd read through a couple of the cases he was immediately interested in, but not Ydrel's file. He had no intention of wading through that mess unless it was absolutely necessary. Besides, Edith said not to study him.

Still, he wasn't tired and he certainly didn't have anything to go home to. Idly, he opened the desk drawer.

It would probably be quiet on the floor, especially in "minimum security." He slipped the flask into his pocket and headed to Ydrel's room.

Everything did seem quieter, more muted, in the evening. The corridor lights had even been dimmed slightly. *This place has class,* Joshua thought, then sighed slightly. *This place has money.*

He wondered how much it cost to "stay" here.

They certainly didn't stint the staff if his internship pay was any indication. Still, he wondered what could be accomplished with the money that had gone to the "little touches" if it were allocated to a public facility instead.

Then he smiled as he heard Rique's voice in his head, "Yeah? You tellin' me when we hit it big, you just gonna give all your money away?"

He stopped at Ydrel's door. A heavy-set orderly passed by and eyed him suspiciously. Joshua smiled at him. For a moment, Joshua thought the other man might stop and challenge his presence there, but the orderly just nodded once and continued on his way. Joshua raised his hand to knock, but Ydrel's voice interrupted him.

"Don't bother knocking. The door's open and it's not like I have any say, anyway."

"It's your room," he replied as he walked in. He whistled at the sight of it: posters, books, a ragged stuffed bear leaning against a lamp—and the dirty clothes on the floor, the shoes lying askew in a corner as if flung in that particular direction, the dirty dishes on the headboard. "You've made sure of that, I see."

"A gilded cage is still a cage." Ydrel was reclining on his bed, propped up with pillows, reading. He didn't look up, but he snorted. "Never mind. Just a passive-aggressive response to my incarceration. So, you going to make me your pet project?" His voice held venom.

"Yeah," Joshua said, taking the chair by the door. "And the first thing we're going to do is give you an attitude adjustment. You'll never have any friends if you keep acting like a jerk."

"Any 'normal' friends, you mean, and I won't have any 'normal' friends anyway. Just addicts and crazies and do-gooders who'll make me their 'cause.'"

No use trying to deny it right now. Joshua rubbed two fingers together. When Ydrel didn't look up from his book, Joshua said, "Hear that? The world's smallest violin playing your pity-me song. Probably 'It's My Party and I'll Cry If I Want To.'"

Ydrel set down the book with a thump. "You always treat patients this way?"

"No, and that's the point. Listen, I'll try to find the number for Jerks Anonymous later—we can both go. In the meantime, I brought you a birthday gift." He pulled out the flask.

Ydrel sat all the way up and scooted to the edge of the bed, crossing his legs and smiling a genuine smile this time. "Bless that Edith. Sometimes she can surprise me. I didn't think she'd give it back."

He reached for the flask.

Joshua pulled it out of reach. "*She* didn't. No one did and don't forget that. And we'd all get in trouble if you got sloppy drunk, so I'll keep charge of the flask, okay?"

"Okay, okay. Half a loaf." Ydrel stopped reaching, but still leaned forward, his eyes shining with curiosity. "So what's in it?"

Joshua unscrewed the cap and sniffed. Not like it helped. "Darned if I know."

"Well, here's our chance to find out. Come in and shut the door!" Ydrel called suddenly, although no one had knocked.

Sure enough, the door opened and a short, black-haired nurse stepped in. "You know I can't do that," she scolded.

"We're chaperoned," Ydrel countered and pointed to Joshua, who stood to introduce himself.

"Hi, I'm—"

Whoa, what dark, exotic eyes.

"I'm Joshua Lawson," he finished, his voice a little quieter and deeper than when he'd started.

She smiled and nodded coolly. She had a smooth round face with slightly flattened cheeks. She was slight and short—he stood a full head taller, and she had to tilt her head to meet his gaze—yet there was an easy confidence in her stance that said size did not intimidate her.

And those eyes. He could drown in those eyes.

"Sachiko Luchese," she said, her tone cool and professional, but Joshua heard violins, low and mellow. He fought the urge to close his eyes and bask in the tone. He realized with a start that she was watching him expectantly. Tongue-tied, he just smiled at her.

She sighed and took on a long-suffering look. "My father was Air Force, stationed in Misawa Air Base Japan, and my mother was a local civilian working with the housing office. Obviously, I take after her in appearance. And no *La Familia Luchese* jokes."

She seemed to expect a response, but he was having problems concentrating past the music of her voice. "Really? Okay."

"So you're the new intern?"

"Yes, ma'am." Mentally, he kicked himself. He finally remembered his manners, then he treats her like she was an old lady?

She didn't seem to notice. Her gaze slid down his arm and she raised an eyebrow. "And is this some new treatment they're teaching in college these days?"

He was still holding the flask where anyone could see. He started to shove it behind his back, realized how stupid that would look, aborted the move and tried to speak instead, "Uh..."

"Yes!" Ydrel exclaimed before Joshua could embarrass himself further. "It's called 'treating Ydrel like a normal person.' Now, are you in or not?"

"And who knows about this?" She regarded each of them with crossed arms and a stern look. In an effort to retrieve some of his dignity, Joshua spoke before Ydrel could.

"Edith—Doctor Sellars— is turning a blind eye..."

"And Malachai doesn't know a thing!" Ydrel finished, smiling wickedly at Sachiko. "Can you imagine how he'd react if he ever found out?"

The stern look slowly faded from Sachiko's face, replaced by a slow, lopsided smile. Joshua had to look away before he said or did anything even more stupid. It was such a cute smile.

She stepped a little further into the room and shut the door. "So what's in it?"

"No idea!" Ydrel replied almost gleefully. "Edith swiped it and the conversation changed before my uncle could tell us. You know, that's got to be the nicest thing he's ever tried to do for me. I know it's the thought that counts, but I'm kind of curious about the gift. So would you tell us?"

He turned to Joshua. "Sachiko's father owns a restaurant in Newport, so she grew up a connoisseur. Joshua, of course, hasn't handled anything more than sacramental wine."

Now it was her turn to reply, "That so?"

He shrugged. "I grew up in a dry house and just never saw a reason to acquire a taste." He didn't add that he was underage, and when he was little, he'd seen someone jump into the Arkansas rapids and drown because a couple of beers had impaired his judgment.

He handed her the flask and watched as she took a small sip and rolled it on her tongue. She smiled appreciatively.

"Scotch. Not imaginative, but nicely aged. Smooth. It'll have a kick you won't notice until it's too late. I'll be right back." She stuck the flask into her lab coat pocket and left. Joshua couldn't help following her with his eyes.

No sooner had the door closed than Ydrel sprang up, grabbed Joshua by the shoulder and whirled him around.

"Sit down and put your tongue back in your mouth!" he growled.

"What?"

"You heard me. And you listen close to this." Ydrel stood on the edge of the bed so he could glare down at Josh. "Sachiko is one of the genuinely good people in this place. She acts tough, but she's fragile as a Ming vase and if you so much as think about hurting her, I will be on you like a disease. You understand?"

"What's wrong with you?" Joshua somehow managed to keep his voice low despite the anger rising in him like lava. "There's no way I'd ever dream of hurting an incredible woman like that, got it? Sit down and chill."

Ydrel glared at him wildly for a moment, and Joshua belatedly wished he'd read at least enough of the files to know if the young client ever got violent. Then Ydrel's expression changed, losing its hostility but remaining intense.

Joshua had read in fantasy novels how telepaths looked through a person, but Ydrel seemed to look into him, as if he could see past his skull and read his thoughts in the movement of his synapses. His pupils contracted almost to pinpoints, then moved, just very slightly, down-and-left, up-and-right, small jerky movements in a sea of blue. Joshua continued to glare at him, despite the crawly feeling it gave him.

Finally, Ydrel looked away.

"Okay, I believe you," he said as he sat back down. He squeezed his eyes shut and shook his head as though to clear it.

"I'm so relieved." Joshua's reply was sarcastic but truthful. He flopped back into the chair. Neither said anything.

It was into that uncomfortable silence that Sachiko entered.

"Did I...miss something?" she asked.

Ydrel's affirmative answer came almost atop Joshua's negative one. Sachiko glanced first at Joshua, eyebrow raised. Despite everything, his heart fluttered. To cover it, he turned a raised eyebrow at Ydrel, who said nothing, but stared hungrily at the bakery box the nurse held in one hand.

When it became obvious she wasn't going to get any answers, she sighed in exasperation and set the box on the bed. Ydrel cheered as he pulled off the top. Inside were half a dozen small pastries, a pretty shade of green with a delicate icing leaf on each. Ydrel took one of the napkins also in the box, set a sweet on it and handed it to Sachiko. Reluctantly, he handed another to Joshua.

"I doubt you'll like it," he grumbled.

Sachiko explained as she handed him a Dixie cup of the scotch. "They're a Japanese sweet made with green tea. Don't worry if you don't care for the taste. Most Americans wouldn't. You driving soon?"

"I won't drink much," he promised her, then looked at Ydrel. "No more than communion wine on Sunday. How'd you know that, anyway?"

Ydrel rolled his eyes as he took a bite of his treat and followed it with a sip of his birthday contraband. "Don't really go together, does they? Sake would be better. Still, that makes three thoughtful presents in one birthday—that includes you, Joshua."

Ydrel took another bite, smiling blissfully. "Oh, this is so much better than that awful cake."

Joshua set his pastry aside. Sachiko had been right. "I thought the cake tasted great."

"I hate chocolate. It was all I could do to choke it down."

"So why didn't you say anything?"

Again the rolling eyes. "Normal people like chocolate."

Joshua had noticed Ydrel's eyes moving up and left, the way most people accessed visual memories, and played the hunch.

"Where'd you read that?" he asked and fought down a smile of victory as both Ydrel and Sachiko glanced at him in surprise.

"There's a comment in my record. 'Almost pathological avoidance of chocolate,' whatever that means. How did you know?"

"You're the psychic. Read my mind and figure it out for yourself."

Ydrel flushed hotly and leaned forward. For a moment, Joshua thought they were going to have a repeat of their earlier confrontation. But Ydrel just snatched up another sweet and took a large bite.

"I've read you enough for one day," he said through a mouthful. "Besides, Sachiko can't read minds."

"Well in that case," Joshua said, turning his most winning smile on the beautiful nurse, "I'd be glad to answer any questions you have."

Did she flush just a little? She ducked her head, her silky hair covering her face for a moment, and Joshua was aware only of her. He could hear the exotic music of a Japanese Koto, see her hands move over the instrument and cherry blossoms fell around them, filling the air with their delicate scent. She looked up, met his eyes—

—and broke the illusion with a cockney accent: "What is the approximate air velocit-yy of the unladen swallow?"

She'd caught him off guard, but the reference was too obvious to miss. "African or European?" he replied in the same accent, then joined her. "I don't know—aaah!" They fell into giggles.

"What?" Ydrel cut in sharply.

"*Monty Python's Holy Grail*!"

Ydrel sighed. "A movie. I can't watch videos. Epilepsy, or so they say. The flickering screen triggers seizures."

Now it was Joshua's turn to be confused. "I never noticed the screen flickering."

"My mind processes information faster than humans."

Joshua decided to let that comment slide for now. "So you've never seen any movie? Or TV? No Python? No *Star Trek*? That stinks."

"You like Trek, too?" Sachiko cut in.

"Uh-huh. There are only two things I have to do every year: go to StarCon in Denver and RenFest in Larkspur."

"I love the Renaissance Festival! We have one in Massachusetts. I go every year—costume and all."

"Warrior, wench, or noble lady?" Even as he asked, he was imagining her in outfits for each. He hoped it didn't show on his face.

Maybe it did, for she smiled coyly. "Depends on my mood. You?"

"Oh, wench, definitely!" Laughing, he turned to Ydrel, who was staring at them, mouth open, a line forming between his brows. "You have got to get out of here. You're missing out."

The look of surprise turned into a glare, and through the corner of his eye, he could see Sachiko wearing a similar look.

"Don't worry about it," he told her in a stage whisper. "It's part of the therapy."

She turned to Ydrel, seeking his reaction. *She really cares for him*, Joshua thought, *Not just as a nurse. There's something else there. Not romantic, just...tender.*

Despite the insight, he felt a flare of jealousy that confused him. He set his paper cup under his chair. Maybe that Scotch was stronger than he'd realized.

Meanwhile, Ydrel had reassured Sachiko that things were okay. "We're going to join Jerks Anonymous together," he quipped.

"Ri-ight. Well, speaking of therapy, I'd better go do the rounds once more before the shift ends."

She started through the door, then stopped, her hand on the knob. "You sticking around for a while?"

Joshua nodded. "Another half hour or so. I won't have any more to drink, promise."

She nodded. "Still, come by the desk before you leave. Good night, Ydrel. Happy birthday."

He lifted his cup in salute. "Thanks to you."

Chapter Four

Even after she'd left, Sachiko's smile seemed to linger, and for a while, the two sat silently, each in their own thoughts. Joshua simply replayed the conversation with Sachiko, hearing her laughter like bells, light but just a touch mellow. He'd never liked tittering, giggly girls. The more he reviewed the last half hour, the more he noticed her reserve, how she never really answered or asked questions, keeping the conversation friendly but not personal.

He shook himself mentally. For crying out loud, they'd just met, and it was Ydrel's "party."

And what was this protectiveness Ydrel has for her? The feeling was certainly mutual. There was something more going on there, some dynamic he was missing...

Well, he had all summer to discover it.

Slowly, he focused his attention on the young patient in front of him. Ydrel remained cross-legged on his bed, eyes resting on a patch of nothing on the bedspread before him, just the sort of non-stare that Joshua had probably been wearing earlier. In one hand, he held his plastic cup of Scotch, rhythmically rolling it between thumb and middle finger. It was still nearly full; he'd done a good job of pacing himself.

Joshua started moving into a complementary position: one ankle on his knee, elbow on knee and chin resting in hand. His cup remained on the floor, but the chair swiveled, and he moved it gently to match the rhythm of Ydrel's cup. It was something he'd been training himself to do since he attended his first Neuro Linguistic Programming seminar. Match postures, match breathing or rhythm, establish rapport on a nonverbal level. Observe and react. Then decide what you would do with it.

He decided to start easy.

"If you're trying so hard to be normal that you'd choke down chocolate cake, why do you insist on being called something as unusual as Ydrel?"

"It was supposed to be my name," he responded quietly and took a rather large swallow of his drink. "My mother said the name came to her in a dream. But she was trying hard to keep on good terms with her family, so she named me Deryl, D-E-R-Y-L. After she died, my aunt and uncle insisted on writing it the conventional way. For convenience, they said."

He glanced around the room resentfully. "Guess what happens when you're not 'convenient' in my family?"

"How did you know I was Catholic?" Joshua challenged gently instead. "And don't give that 'I'm psychic' crap. I want to know what process."

"Big on process, aren't you?" The words were harsh, but his posture hadn't changed much. Certainly not to the tensed-up straightness Joshua had noticed when Ydrel was feeling defensive.

Ydrel sighed and thought. Again his pupils contracted and moved as he reviewed the memory. Joshua leaned forward. That was so weird.

"There was music," Ydrel started, then in a high tenor, sang, "*Panis Angelicus, fit panis nominum.* You were kind of sad because you weren't playing for the choir. There was this lady holding a gold cup—a chalice, I guess it's called. I don't think she was a nun or anything, but she was old. She said, 'Blood of Christ' and her voice shook. And the wine—I don't know, is it good stuff? It was awfully strong and sour. A little...spicy?"

Ydrel made a face. He shut his eyes. When he opened them, his pupils were back to normal, slightly dilated against the light of the room.

"Good enough for you?"

Joshua's reply was hoarse. "Great." It was, in fact, a frighteningly accurate account of last week's communion—in Pueblo, Colorado. He began to understand the way Ydrel's aunt had looked at him today.

He took a slow breath, trying to cleanse himself of the thoughts and feelings inside. He could sort out his internal signals later; right now he needed to be aware of the externals. "Uptime," Bandler and Grinder called it; being wholly aware and reacting to what was going on outside you, rather than listening to the internal messages.

He noticed Ydrel had leaned forward, head in hands. His shoulders were tight and hunched. His breathing was shallow and a little fast. "You all right?"

"Yeah. I will be. I don't usually go into someone else's mind like that—not willingly, anyway. It makes me dizzy being in two bodies at once. So, do you believe me now?"

"No idea." It was a totally unconsidered, completely honest answer. "But does it really matter? My belief isn't going to get you out of here—nor, for that matter, is my friendship."

"So hope isn't the cure?"

"Do you believe it is?" When he got no answer, Joshua continued. "I think hope helps, but it's neither necessary nor sufficient."

"So how do you cure a psychic?" Ydrel challenged, eyes still buried in the heels of his hands. The tension in his wrists seemed less, so Joshua met the challenge with a direct and honest answer.

"Same way I'd cure a schizophrenic, or someone with Dissociative Identity Disorder or phobias, or whatever: give them the tools they need to make it in society despite their condition. You can do it, and I can show you how."

Now Ydrel laughed. "Talk about arrogance! I've been here five years and no one's been able to—quote—break my illusion. What makes you so special?" His voice had a snide tone, yet he sat forward, and his face was alive with interest.

Joshua felt a spark of excitement but ignored it, instead leaning forward himself. For a while now, he'd been matching Ydrel's breathing, using the rapport they'd established to calm him. Now he increased the pace of his own, bringing some enthusiasm into his posture as he did to his words. He sat up, waving a hand before him and setting it on his lap as he spoke.

"I'm not trying to break any illusion. It doesn't matter if you're psychic. It doesn't matter if you think you're Joan of Arc. What matters is being able to effectively handle yourself around people so they don't get this urge to toss you into an institution. I mean, there're lots of people who claim they're psychic. They have conventions and everything. So why is it they're out there and you're in here?"

"They're fakes!" Ydrel suddenly exploded. "You have no idea what it's really like, when somebody's thinking or feeling something really strongly or you have several people feeling the same thing and you get so overwhelmed and you find yourself acting out their desires—only they can keep control and you're—I'm—just lost!

"Like Isaac?"

"Ha! Isaac is child's play. You want an example? There was this new teacher—gorgeous, really incredible—and on the first day of school, she comes in wearing a tight blouse and mini-skirt... I tried to kiss her because that's what all the other guys were thinking about doing. That's what being psychic is."

"Really." Surprised, Joshua dropped the posture and breathing, but he managed to pay attention to the eyes. It happened so fast, but yes, it was there: that pinpoint contraction of the pupils. What was that?

Ydrel looked down, ran a hand through his long blond hair and pulled. "I was twelve. I didn't even know if I liked girls. I still don't.

"And it just got worse. I couldn't be around happy people without laughing hysterically. And if people were angry..."

He took a deep breath and let it out in a gust. "After I—I tried to kill myself, my aunt and uncle brought me here." He gave a short laugh. "I guess I should be thankful. At least Malachai was able to teach me to put up some barriers."

"But they're not enough?"

"Obviously. Did Edith tell you about the one time they did release me? The first thing I did was smash all the bottles in my uncle's liquor cabinet because the butler—yes, Joshua, they have a butler—is an alcoholic and was obsessing on it, had been obsessing on it for years. It was that or drink myself stupid, just because *he* wanted to. That was nothing. My aunt took me shopping. All those people, all those thoughts…It was like ants crawling in my skull. I was just managing to ignore them, and I felt this woman screaming—"

"'Felt?'"

"Yeah, felt. Inside my head. I couldn't help it. I snuck away from my aunt, followed the thoughts—she was so scared!—I found her in a part of the mall that was being renovated. This guy had her pinned. He was going to—" Ydrel broke off.

"What did you do?" Joshua asked.

Ydrel shivered. "Beat him unconscious. Then I tried to knock myself out, too. See, he was so full of hate, and he wanted to— So I did, too. And the girl tried to stop me and I yelled at her and scared her all over again and I tried to run but the police showed up. So I ended up back here, where the environment, at least, is controlled, even if it isn't exactly normal. Even then, it's not always safe for me. Sometimes, Malachai puts someone in the room next to me…to study my reaction, sometimes to punish me."

He looked up and his eyes were wide with fear. "I've got to get out of here, Joshua. You're changing the dynamic. It's not safe for me anymore."

Joshua was beginning to think it wasn't safe for him either. The last thing he needed on his internship was to get caught up in some problem between a patient he wasn't supposed to be taking on, and the head of the institution—a friend of his father.

Still…

Earlier, when Ydrel had laughed at the idea of Joshua helping him, Joshua had moved his arm in a very deliberate way. Now he used that same motion to recall those feelings of hope and interest Ydrel had expressed. He waited as Ydrel calmed, watching him take a shaky breath and release his hold on his hair, his fingers running through the length, before he spoke again.

"We'll work on it, Ydrel. In the meantime, I'm not going to let anyone hurt you."

Whether he believed him or not, Ydrel nodded.

"Okay. You have some barriers. You've said that they work sometimes. I want you to think about one thing that keeps you here that your current barriers don't protect you from." He couldn't see Ydrel's eyes, for the patient had shut them, but waited for other cues.

"When my barriers work sometimes, or not at all?"

"Your choice."

"The Miscria."

"You don't have to tell—the what?" Curiosity got the better of him.

"The Miscria. It calls me, and when it does, I can't help it—I fall into this trance. I can be doing anything, even walking, and just—boom. Then I have to tell it everything it wants to know before it lets me go with some new assignment, and for weeks I'm studying God-knows-what until it calls me again."

"You've lost me."

"Information, Joshua." Ydrel opened his eyes and waved impatiently to the pile of books on his desk.

Joshua walked over and examined the covers. "The Miscria wants to know military history?"

"Tactics. Sword smithing. Triage. Medieval fortress architecture. So I go cra—I have to learn everything I can about the subject, and it just wants more. At least we have a good librarian. He humors me, you know."

Joshua set down the book he was leafing through: *Eye in the Sky, A Warfighter's Guide to Space Reconnaissance*, by Felix Monroe.

"So this 'Miscria' calls you, you pass out in your oatmeal, and you tell it everything you know about whatever subject it's told you to study? Huh. Ever refuse?"

Ydrel blinked. "I— But it needs to know."

"Why? Ever ask it?"

Now Ydrel sat forward, dumbfounded. "I...It never occurred to me to ask."

"How about going inside yourself and asking it now?"

Ydrel shut his eyes, furrowed his brow. Joshua stayed standing by the desk, watching the young man first tense completely, then seem to relax every muscle, much the way someone under hypnosis would relax while remaining straight in their seat. Several minutes passed in silence before Ydrel shook his head. "I can't. It has to call me."

"Then that's your first assignment. When it calls you, try this: First, see if you can establish some kind of arrangement so that it doesn't call you at inconvenient times—you decide together what that means. Second, find out more about it, like why it needs this information so badly."

"What if it refuses?"

"That's really up to you. Myself, I'd hold out. Blackmail can work wonders."

Ydrel met his eyes in a steady gaze, not challenging and not trying to see into him, yet searching. "You don't believe me about the Miscria, do you? You think it's some weird part of my unconscious. You don't believe it's an outside entity."

Joshua moved his hand as part of a shrug. It was a visual anchor he'd used many times and it was a natural movement for him. "It doesn't matter either way. The process works the same. Just give it a try. You don't have anything to lose."

A yawn escaped his mouth, surprising him. He hadn't realized he was so tired. "I'm sorry, but I'm beat. Finish that drink off, if you want it, and go to bed. I'll see ya in the morning."

He started for the door when Ydrel called him back. "Are we going to be friends? I mean, regardless of what Edith asked you to do?" he asked.

He regarded him for a moment, a spoiled and snarky kid dealing with something he didn't think he could control. Josh could help him; he knew that. But be friends?

Then he thought about how this spoiled kid had jumped up to protect the nurse he considered the one good person in his life. There was definitely more to him than met the eye.

Joshua smiled. "Yeah, Ydrel. I think we are."

When Joshua got to the nurses' station, Sachiko was deep in conversation with another nurse, so he parked himself at the counter and waited. He got lost in appreciation at the way her hair caught the light and tried hard not to stare.

She approached, a slight frown on her face. "What are you doing here? I thought you'd gone home."

Joshua blinked in surprise. "You asked me to come by first."

"That was two hours ago."

"Really?" How did he lose track of time so badly? "Really," he repeated softly.

"Un-huh. Shift's over and we're just heading out. How do you feel?"

Now Joshua smiled. "Wiped. Ydrel is one intense kid." The comment earned him some snickers, not only from Sachiko but from the other nurses. He wasn't sure if they were in agreement or in amusement—he wasn't much more than a kid himself—so he let it pass. Sachiko introduced him to the others: Monique Jones, a 30-something black woman with a matronly smile, and Kelsey and Keith St. Claude, both tall and blond, close enough in looks to be twins, but actually a married couple.

They chatted for a few minutes, then Kelsey excused herself to make the rounds. Joshua offered to walk Sachiko and Monique to their cars, again earning amused looks. They stopped at the locker rooms to pick up their stuff, showed Josh how to clock out, and headed into the dark parking lot.

Sachiko was silent most of the way, but Monique, who had family in Denver, kept up the conversation about Colorado until they dropped her off at her car. As she drove off, Sachiko turned to Joshua.

"You can just leave me here. I don't need you to hold my door." She started toward another part of the lot.

"Huh?" He hastened after her, confused, until he realized he'd taken charge of opening every door from the locker room to Monique's car. "Oh, that. It's habit, something my mother trained me to do. I didn't mean to offend you or anything."

"No, no. It's just I don't have a door." She stopped at a motorcycle.

Not just any motorcycle. A Harley-Davidson FLSTC shone in the lamplight. The gas tank and saddlebags were custom painted with dragons.

Joshua couldn't help it—he gaped. "Really," was the only thing he could say as she reached into her gym bag and pulled out a leather jacket with long fringe on the sleeves and a helmet with paint job to match the bike.

"Okay. Out with it."

"With what?"

Sachiko sighed in exasperation. "Whenever you have something else on your mind, you cover it by saying 'Really.'"

"Really? I mean, I do? I never noticed."

"Don't change the subject. Out with it."

Joshua just looked at her for a minute; the skeptical look on her face, the jacket zipped over her uniform, standing hipshot in front the Harley with her helmet balanced on one hip. He sputtered a moment before blurting out "Women with motorcycles are so sexy!" and fought against flinching at the storm he was sure would follow.

Instead, she stared at him blankly a moment, then a small, almost wicked smile spread across her face. It was just barely visible in the dim light, but nonetheless enough to make him weak in the knees.

"Play your cards right, and I might give you a ride sometime," she said in a low, warm mezzo.

He could listen to that voice forever. He let his own smile and tone match hers. "Deal."

She rewarded him with a flashing smile and the honor of holding her helmet as she mounted the bike.

As soon as she was out of sight, he glanced back at the building. The windows were darkened, the curtains drawn. No one was up and watching. He let out with a joyous whoop.

It was going to be an incredible summer!

Ydrel sighed and let the curtain fall back into place. His window overlooked the commons, not the parking lot, and sometimes he liked to look out over the neatly manicured lawn with its old oaks and pretend that it was just his yard. That was easier to do at night, when the grounds weren't used by clients with white-uniformed orderlies and nurses milling about, making sure everyone was comfortable—and controlled.

Not that they really needed to. Most of the time when people went outside, it was to sit quietly in the sun, lost in their own thoughts. Occasionally, a client with a passion for fitness and nature would shun the gym for jogging the fence line, and there were conversations among clients or between them and visitors, but mostly the commons was a quiet, brooding area, and it always felt darker to Ydrel, as if the moods themselves blotted out some of the sunlight.

When he'd pulled himself out of his initial depression after being admitted, Ydrel had tried to get some people involved in a game of football or catch or...anything. An orderly would usually oblige him, but their minds were always on the other clients, watching, anticipating. After a while, Ydrel gave it up and spent his requisite sun therapy time quietly reading or brooding along with the others.

Maybe I could get Joshua to bring a football. No, a Frisbee.

He remembered diving for the ball, missing utterly and falling face-first into the dirt while his friends alternately groaned or laughed. Joshua's memory, along with the knowledge that Joshua was on the unofficial college Frisbee golf team.

His head swam for a moment, and he wondered if it was from the alcohol or from the double-life effect of probing someone else's thoughts. He had meant it when he told Joshua that he seldom consciously entered another's mind; in addition to the vertigo it gave him, it made him feel dirty.

I had to do it. For Sachiko. When Ydrel had sensed Joshua's attraction to his friend—one of the only friends he had—he had to be sure this intruder could be trusted. Ydrel had forged an initial link after she left the room to fetch the sweets and had found Joshua's surface impressions confusing, but the intern had been honest enough in intentions that he backed down.

Nonetheless, when Joshua lingered after Sachiko left, Ydrel took the opportunity to probe deeper, guiding him gently into a daydream while he delved, seeking to absorb the essence and motivations of this person who was already threatening to have a major impact on his life—and Sachiko's. He'd sensed the interest in her too, deeply guarded even from herself, yet ready to come crashing to the forefront with the right provocation.

I had to do it. I had to be sure she could trust him. Last time, I didn't step in until it was too late and it almost killed her. I won't let that happen again.

He knew that was only half the story. He had to know if *he* could trust him. As lonely as he was, he'd misplaced his trust before, too. But what he'd found was that Joshua Abraham Lawson was one of the most genuinely genuine people he'd ever encountered.

Genuinely genuine, he chuckled to himself, suddenly realizing he was a little drunk. One of the other advantages of his little probe was that Joshua didn't notice when Ydrel had poured the other's Scotch into his own cup.

"Genuinely genuine. Genuflect. Genouillere. Genu—"

He'd run out of words, so he kept repeating *genu, genu* in a singsong way as he rinsed out the paper cups then tossed them into the trash. He didn't want to get his genuinely genuine friend in trouble, after all.

He had made it to the edge of his bed, the alcohol in full effect and making the room seem to tilt just so, when the Miscria called him and he fell face-first onto the mattress.

Chapter Five

I am the Miscria. I am the Seeker. I bring my Questions. I call the Ydrel. Hear me.

The words surrounded him, echoed in his mind and pulled at his soul. He was the Ydrel; he was needed.

Not this time. He fought against the sense of well-being, pulling with all his stubbornness. It was like when Malachai tried to hypnotize him. He'd resisted then. He'd resist now.

Normally, the Miscria's calls were shrouded in darkness and need. This time, he imagined himself opening his eyes and looking around. Everything was gray and misty, like a fog-filled gymnasium. His heart pounded. It was like when The Master used to call him. Could they be...?

No. The Master's visits meant pain and humiliation. The Miscria wanted something from him, sure, but all it ever did was ask. It has to be coincidence.

As if sensing his distraction, the Calling came again.

You are the Oracle. As I ask, so you shall answer—

"I don't think so," he said into the fog.

The Miscria hit his statement like a wall.

In the pause that followed, he felt a momentary thrill of panic. What if it gave up? How would he get back to himself? Could he end up stuck in this gray netherworld, his body comatose until he gave in?

No. I'll figure it out. I have to if I'm not going to remain a slave to this thing. He wondered if the alcohol was making him brave, or was it Joshua's words.

It doesn't matter. I'm here and I'm resisting. I've committed himself.

The pun made him giggle and the panic yielded to mirth. Meanwhile, the Miscria was trying again.

I am the Seeker. You are—

"The Oracle. The Ydrel. Yeah, I know. Listen, I don't know about you, but I'm getting tired of this routine. Can we try something different?"

He felt a wave a confusion from the Miscria that made him laugh. Things were already as different as they could get.

"Well, for starters, how about showing me what you look like."

Look like?

"Yeah. I mean, we're obviously sharing a reality, but it's awfully dark and misty on my end. How about a little scenery? Can you do that? And you—what are you? Human? A green-skinned Martian? An iguana? What?"

Again, he felt its confusion, flickering with testiness. He almost heard the complaint: *Why does it always speak in riddles?*

Then the scene shifted and he found himself in a small clearing surrounded by trees he didn't quite recognize. The pines seemed too soft, the maples too broad in leaf. He didn't hear any animals or birds, and the trees cut off any distant views. He didn't mind. At least there weren't any walls.

Walls?

He turned to where he felt the thought, and gasped. "You're a girl!"

He didn't need to be psychic to guess her reply. The look on her face told him she thought that was a ridiculously obvious observation.

He sat down hard on the mossy ground. "They're going to have a field day with this," he groaned.

They? There are others like you?

The ground distracted him. He pushed on the moss and it sprang back like the memory foam pad on his bed. With a grimace, he started digging at a piece with his fingers.

The Miscria squatted down beside him and watched curiously.

"If there's a hole in my bed when I wake up, then you're a figment of my imagination," he mumbled.

Are you the Ydrel?

"That's what you keep telling me," he snarled. He kept his focus on the growing hole in front of him; he did not want to see the long black hair that swallowed the light instead of shimmering, or the lean, hard muscles of her arms. Besides, if he glanced up now, he could see partway down her shirt and he was definitely not going there.

Then he felt that funny warm comfort that always accompanied her call, and questions began to fill his mind, questions he really should answer...

He flicked the feeling and the questions away like they were bothersome insects. He didn't feel buzzed anymore, he noted. He wondered if that meant he was outside his own mind. Assuming any of this was real, of course.

We are in the Netherworld, the Miscria finally offered. *It is a safe place for both of us. And my name is Tasmae. I am real.*

With a sigh, he gave up his project—he had a sizable hole, anyway—and looked at her. She had marvelous cheekbones and the darkest eyes he'd ever seen. "So what's Miscria mean? And can you talk, or do you have to put thoughts in my head?"

She sat back, her brows knit. "I can talk, if that's what you wish."

Her voice was warm and strong, like the Calling. He wondered if it was really hers.

"Of course it is my voice!" she responded, annoyed. "Who else's would it be? Are you the Ydrel? Why do you not answer my questions? Why are you playing these games with me?"

Again he felt a thrill of panic, but recognized it as hers, and he suddenly felt very ashamed. "Look. I'm sorry. But I don't think you realize what effect your questions have on me. You're ruining my life."

"You are the Ydrel. You came to our people in our greatest need. You bring us the knowledge we need to survive. That is your purpose, just as mine is to ask the questions, and learn the answers. I am the Miscria." He felt her shoving aside her fear and replacing it with determination, and he realized she could be as stubborn as he was.

He held up his hands in fake surrender. "Okay. I'm the Ydrel. Fine. But up until now, all that's meant is I pass out for no reason at all, whenever and wherever, because *you* find it convenient. Then I wake up with a weird compulsion to study some bizarre topic that no one on my world cares about anymore, and I never know why. And it makes it hard for me to live a normal life, whatever that is."

"We need your knowledge."

She's scared, he thought. She thinks I'm going to abandon her.

Suddenly, that was the last thing he wanted to do.

He made himself speak gently. "It's okay. I'm not saying I won't help." He felt a wave of relief that almost made his eyes water. "But we need some ground rules. Because I can't continue like this. And maybe, maybe, if we actually talk to each other instead of this compulsion-thing you do, I can help you better?"

Comforted, she settled herself cross-legged in front of him. "The Miscria haven't always understood your answers," she said. "Explain your riddles, and I will find other ways to contact you."

Chapter Six

Joshua was nodding over his latte—his second of the morning. He'd bought an extra-large on the way to work, but it had barely cleared away the cobwebs.

And staff meetings sure don't help, he grumbled to himself. Well, that's what I get for staying up most the night.

Not like he could have helped it. He'd been keyed up, and the radio had accommodated his mood with upbeat love songs so that he had sung all the way home. Once there, he fought off the urge to call his parents. (What could he have said? His first "session" with Ydrel had been inconclusive but promising, but there was this nurse with the most awesome bike?) So he had puttered around his little flat until he was tired enough to doze.

Even then, his sleep had been light and fitful, full of dreams of Sachiko. They were on her bike, but it was parked in a meadow, up on some kind of double kick-stand that held it steady while they—

"Well, Mr. Lawson?"

Josh snapped out of his reverie. He took a long sip of coffee to cover his confusion as he scanned his short-term memory for Malachai's question, while the rest of the staff stared at him expectantly. Something about what he was doing last night?

"I'm not sure what you're asking, sir," he finally confessed.

It actually seemed to be the answer he was hoping for. With a slightly smug look on his impassive face, Dr. Malachai reached under his mammoth Day Planner and pulled out a sketchbook. Joshua got the impression that he wanted to fling it in his direction, but he simply passed it around to Joshua—the long way, so that as many people as possible could see its contents as it was passed. Whatever was on the pad elicited some smirks and a few raised eyebrows. When it finally got to Joshua, he understood why.

The top page held a sketch of the face of a young woman. Dark, wide-set eyes shone intently in a narrow face. With high cheekbones and not-quite-full lips, she was more interesting than beautiful, though there was something indefinable about her that captured Joshua's attention. Across the top corner were the words THE MISCRIA and in a lower corner, TASMAE.

"As you can see, Deryl's delusion now has a face," Dr. Malachai announced.

"More than a face," Joshua murmured as he turned to the next page. This was a full-body drawing, and the one that elicited the most reaction.

Although slight and fully clothed, she was obviously a bodybuilder's dream. Her sleeveless tunic showed off broad shoulders and heavily muscled arms. Her pants were tight—she had runner's legs—and although her tunic bloused, one surmised that the rest of her body was just as well-toned.

"My point," Dr. Malachai continued above the snickers and coughs, "is that we have spent the last five years trying to rid young Deryl of this 'Miscria' delusion. You spend two hours with him and suddenly 'it' is a 'she.' What do you have to say for yourself, Mr. Lawson?"

How about "Score one for Joshaham"? Joshua bit back his caustic reply and instead put his energy into looking thoughtful. He let the silence hang a moment, then leaned back, a trick he'd learned from his father.

"There's this woman in Manitou Springs, a real favorite of the local radio shows. Claims she's psychic. She's got not one, but four spirit guides: an angel and a devil who were apparently best friends before the Fall, a Native American spirit whose nature she doesn't know or won't disclose, and a deceased plumber named Harvey.

"Now these spirit guides, they sometimes help her, but sometimes, they just take over. She'll be in the middle of an interview on some morning show and all of a sudden, there's silence and she'll start talking in some ancient tongue—or maybe she's just babbling, who knows? Afterwards, she'll say one spirit or the other 'called her away'—"

"Your *point*, Mr. Lawson?"

"My point is she has a nice house in Manitou, a condo in Vail, and a beach house in the Bahamas. And she's been carrying four delusions—faceless and otherwise—for twenty years."

"So you plan to offer Deryl career advice?" Dr. Hoffman asked. His comment drew chuckles, but Joshua didn't take offense. Hoffman was always making jokes.

Joshua leaned forward and spoke earnestly. "I'm offering him *survival* advice. Isn't that what it's all about? Yesterday, the Miscria was an undefinable horror beyond his comprehension. Today, it—she—is someone he can negotiate with. If he can't rid himself of this Miscria—whether she's a delusion or spirit or a real woman—he can at least learn to live with her."

"So to speak?" Again from Dr. Hoffman.

Joshua shrugged, acknowledging the double entendre with a smile. "But like any relationship, communication is key."

"So you think these sketches are a positive sign?" Edith asked.

"I don't think of them as any sign," Joshua replied cautiously. "From what Ydrel told me, the biggest problem is that she calls him 'out of his body' at inconvenient times. I'm more interested in finding out what they said to each other, whether they set some ground rules for that."

They were listening to him, some even nodding, accepting his analysis as that of a peer. Although he kept his outward appearance professionally neutral, inwardly he was basking in the respect.

"Well," Dr. Malachai's voice broke the moment. He spoke in a fatherly but patronizing tone. "You've done an adequate job of defending yourself. However, in the future, if you wish to try any of your tricks, you will be sure you are accompanied by a qualified member of the psychiatric staff. I trust I make myself clear?"

Joshua glanced at Edith. They'd discussed this yesterday; would she back him up?

She appeared to be studying some notes.

"Am I clear, Mr. Lawson?"

No one else intervened. Malachai expected a response. It seemed Edith's single question was the best defense he could expect.

"Clear, sir."

The psychiatrist smiled. "Excellent. Now, if we turn to the next item on the agenda."

Forty-five minutes later, they were on the last item of the week. Joshua had to admit he was impressed. Dr. Malachai was ruthlessly efficient with the agenda yet managed to make everyone feel they'd had their say. Maybe there was something he could learn from the chief psychiatrist after all.

Yeah, like how to be a jerk without anybody noticing, he thought waspishly. While part of him chided himself for childishness, another part agreed that it was a useful skill, and still another part of him justified his hurt feelings. *"Tricks." I got your tricks...*

With all the internal dialogue, he lost track of the final comments and found himself blinking in surprise as people shut their organizers and started getting up.

"You ready?" Dr. Hoffman smiled. "You'll be joining me in group this morning."

Joshua stifled a groan. He hated group therapies in institutions. Let's toss a bunch of strangers together and see if they can solve each other's problems without infecting each other with their own psychoses.

Well, at least he'd learn more about the patients, and Dr. Hoffman.

I am feeling hostile. What's the matter? Too much caffeine?

"Okay if I hit the john first?" he asked as he stood and picked up his coffee cup. Only ice-cold dregs left.

"Sure." Hoffman jerked his chin toward a mahogany door at the far end of the room.

Joshua ducked into the bathroom and took a quick look around. Swanky. Private. Soundproof.

Joshua hissed and paced, walking off his anger. "Sanctimonious, self-serving, pompous—! Where does he get off? I did good work, made a real connection, and he has the nerve to call it 'tricks'?"

When he found his thoughts circling, he stopped and took a long cleansing breath, then faced the mirror, and reality. "You're an intern. You're here to learn. Put it behind you."

Nonetheless, he took a childish pleasure in imagining Malachai's smug face in the toilet bowl as he emptied his bladder.

Hoffman had been a therapist before getting his psychiatric degree, and he loved group therapy sessions enough to keep leading them even though they no longer fit his job description. Patients were given their choice of session times, so the resultant groups had little in common except an affinity for 9:30 or 10:30 meetings.

Carter Doleson preferred the second session. He sat in the cushioned but not particularly comfortable chair, arms crossed, with his expression even more cross as his eyes roved from the six people in the semicircle to Dr. Hoffman and Joshua, to the walls, windows and ceiling. The more Mr. Starke talked about the pressures he'd felt working on Wall Street, the more agitated Doleson got—not that Joshua blamed him. Personally, he was feeling sorrier for the stockbroker's clients. Joshua tried to follow Doleman's gaze, but it never focused on anything in particular but seemed to be searching instead.

"So, I'd have something when I got home—to relax, you know. But then I needed something in the morning to give me back that edge. It just became a cycle—"

"Will you shut up?" Doleson burst out. "They are listening!"

Five other clients groaned and shifted in their seats, and Starke exploded, "Dr. Hoffman, do we have to put up with this every week?"

"Carter," Dr. Hoffman chided, his voice calm, but his body language showing signs of barely contained annoyance. "You may wait your turn—"

"What turn?" a young woman in pajama bottoms and a sequined tank-top asked. Joshua tried not to look at her too often because when he did, she'd smile at him in a way he would have enjoyed under different circumstances. "He never talks. He just comes to tell us to shut up."

"Because they're listening. Why can't I make you people understand that? They are listening and you people go on with your trivial weaknesses and your—"

"It's not your turn," Hoffman repeated. "You may share your thoughts then."

"They can't hear my thoughts, thank God! But they are listening—"

"Why don't you shut up, then?" the girl growled.

"Roe, that's not very helpful..."

"None of this is helpful—except maybe to them!" Doleson responded and kept talking over the renewed protests.

Joshua cleared his throat and cast a "may I" glance at the psychiatrist, who shrugged indulgently.

"Why are they listening?"

Carter stopped mid-tirade. "What?"

"Why are they listening? What do they want?"

He looked at Joshua as if the intern were crazy. "They're studying us."

"Why? What are they going to do with this knowledge?" Joshua leaned forward. "C'mon. This is important information. Share it with us."

Carter leaned forward, too. He shrugged, yet his eyes had lost some of their nervous jitteriness. "They...they just want to learn about us. It's their job, to learn. We're their experiments, their subject of interest."

Joshua nodded. "So what happens when they think they've learned everything they can about us? What then?"

Carter's eyes grew wide, and he actually trembled as he spoke. "They'll kill us. All of us. The study ends. The experiment is over. The subjects disposed of."

Roe made a rude noise, but Joshua ignored her, and with his focus on Joshua, so did Carter.

For a moment, Joshua reflected the client's fear, then turned thoughtful. "So the key to our survival, then, is to keep them interested? Make them think there's always something more to learn about us?"

Carter opened his mouth to speak, then stopped. He leaned back into his chair, his eyes up and to the right, lost in thought.

The rest of the session went pretty smoothly.

"Carter has never taken to anyone like that before. You've got a gift for reaching people," Dr. Hoffman said afterwards, on the walk back to his office.

Joshua smiled his thanks. *Yeah, I got tricks, Malachai.* "Sir, could I join you in Carter's private sessions? We planted a seed today and I'd like to help it grow."

"I like that idea. We might make a good team, eh?"

"Think fast!" a voice called as a brown object hurtled toward them. Dr. Hoffman ducked, but Joshua, who had just spent the last year living in the dorms across the hall from a quarterback-wannabe, instinctively caught the football before it hit the wall.

Ydrel whistled, leaning against the open doorway of his room. "I'm impressed."

Dr. Hoffman unfolded himself with as much dignity as possible and turned sternly. "Deryl, you know better than to throw that thing inside the building."

Ydrel did his best to look chagrined. "I'm sorry, sir. So...can Joshua and I go out to play?" He looked at the psychiatrist pleadingly through his long lashes.

The older man's expression softened and he glanced at his watch. "Well, it's almost lunchtime, anyway. Just get me your notes by morning, Joshua, and remember to be in Dr. Weaver's office by 1:30 this afternoon. And don't forget what Dr. Malachai said at the staff meeting."

"Yes, sir!" Ydrel answered for him. "Woo-hoo. You're the best!" He grabbed Joshua's sleeve and dragged him toward an exit that led to an inner courtyard.

Joshua pulled his arm free once they were outside and handed the ball back. "'Woo-hoo. You're the best'? I thought I was going to be sick watching you."

"It worked, didn't it? Hoffman thinks he's some kind of indulgent uncle to me or something. Where'd you learn to catch a ball like that, anyway?"

"What? You think that's a new trick? Live in the dorms a year and you get used to it. Whoa! It's hot out here!" Joshua stripped off his jacket and laid it and his tie carefully on a chair before following Ydrel out to the open grass.

"What? Doesn't it get hot in Colorado?"

"It's a drier heat. Besides, you're not dressed in a professional monkey suit." Ydrel had on an oversized jersey and long loose shorts and looked enviably comfortable.

"It's just for a few minutes. We need to talk." He tossed Joshua the ball and backed up.

"Why can't we talk inside under the air conditioning?"

"Because they're monitoring us."

What is this? Theme du jour? "Well, let them monitor this." He tossed the ball as hard as he could, so that Ydrel had to jump for it—and even then, it slipped through his fingers. He landed, stumbling, then retrieved the ball.

He moved closer and gave Joshua a dirty look before throwing the ball. "I'm not talking about Carter's fantasies. I mean that Malachai has turned on the surveillance equipment in my room. We can't talk there anymore. And if you're going to be so cranky, I'd suggest you lay off the double lattes."

"How'd you—?"

Ydrel just rolled his eyes. "Malachai is not going to let you really help me get out of here. He's going to keep you—and me—under observation to make sure you get back safe to 'dry heat' Colorado and I stay trapped here."

"And there's surveillance equipment in your room?" Joshua couldn't keep the skepticism from his voice.

"Don't believe me. Ask Sachiko. It'll give you an excuse to talk to her. Alone, even."

"Speaking of," Joshua again tossed the ball, this time an easy throw that kept them within conversation distance. "Dr. Malachai showed us your sketches. I take it you talked to the Miscria last night. Good for you. So, what's TASMAE mean?"

"That's her name. The Miscria is like a job title or something." Ydrel caught the ball and tossed it back. "Yeah, we talked. That's why Malachai is so mad at you. You managed to do in one hour what he couldn't accomplish in five years."

"Really? So she's going to leave you alone from now on?"

Ydrel caught Joshua's return, then held the ball between both hands, studying the laces. "She, well, she promised to knock first."

"Knock."

"Yeah, so to speak. Sort of a psionic check to see if I'm asleep or busy or whatever. It was kind of funny, actually. All this time, she's thought I was some kind of cross between angel and supercomputer. She was awfully surprised to discover I'm flesh and blood like her."

"'Flesh and blood,' huh? So, what *else* did you do?" Joshua asked with a suggestive waggle of his eyebrows.

Now it was Ydrel's turn to scowl and throw the ball hard—at Joshua's stomach.

"Hey, easy! Now who's uptight?"

"Why is it psychiatrists always think there's a sexual motivation to everything?"

"Oh, and you didn't make a similar if less pointed suggestion to me a few minutes ago? Besides, if your sketch is accurate, she's kind of attractive, if you like muscle-bound Xena types."

"You mean xeno, like xenophile."

"I mean Xena, like *Xena, Warrior Princess*." He paused to study Ydrel's blank expression before throwing the ball. "You don't know Xena?"

Ydrel caught the ball. "No." Toss.

Catch. "You don't know about *Star Trek*?" Toss.

Catch. "No." Toss.

Catch. "Piers Anthony? Harry Potter? Sherlock Holmes? Really, you've got a library here. Don't you ever cruise the fiction section?" Toss.

Catch. "Why?" Toss.

Catch. He stopped to wipe the sweat from his eyes. "Brother, we've got to broaden your education. Listen, you may be cool, but I'm not dressed for this. Can we get back in under the A/C?" Catching Ydrel's disappointed look, he added, "I'll bring some shorts, and next time we can even schedule it in. I think Edith would approve. And we'll find a way to talk away from prying ears."

"Yeah, okay."

"Cool." Joshua tossed the ball sideways to him. Ydrel winced as he caught it. "You all right?"

"Uh, yeah. I must have slept wrong or something. Let's go."

They headed back to where his jacket and tie waited, with Ydrel walking so slowly that Joshua had to concentrate on holding back his pace. He seemed to be gathering his nerve to say something, so Joshua let the silence build until Ydrel had to break it.

"I. I— Look, I don't know what you did yesterday, but you're the first person who's really helped me in a long time and I, well, I want you to do it again."

"That's what I'm here for." He slid the tie back on, but decided to wait on the jacket until they were inside and the fabric had a chance to cool off some, too.

"It's not that easy. Malachai's watching us now. You're a threat to his pet project. He's a dangerous man, and there's not a person in this facility who'll stand up against him."

Yeah, I noticed that. "Tell you what. Let me think on it." Then he shrugged in the same manner he had when he'd built Ydrel's confidence the night before. "We'll find a way to work it out."

The anchor was still in place. Ydrel relaxed into a smile, which he kept even after they were back inside the building and among the surveillance and scrutiny.

"Okay. Hey, can you bring a Frisbee? They don't have one here, and since you're so good at it, you can teach me."

"How did you know?"

Ydrel rolled his eyes, and Joshua mimicked the gesture and laughed.

Chapter Seven

Joshua peered into the nurse's lounge and smiled. Sachiko was eating dinner and studying. Alone.

Earlier in her shift, he'd spent about half an hour with her and Monique, learning about their routine: shift change procedures, when and how they made their rounds, how they handled emergencies, what they did for dinner breaks. He'd asked Rita Sanchez similar questions about the housekeeping staff and planned to get to know the orderlies tomorrow or the next day. His father had impressed upon him the importance of meeting the support staff and learning how they worked.

Today, though, he had to admit to an ulterior motive.

"Mind if I interrupt?"

He took her preoccupied flick of the head as assent and sat down across from her with his tray. It was already 6:30 and the smells from the cafeteria had enticed him to try the "institutional" food. Besides, it gave him a good excuse to join Sachiko.

Sachiko was reading a medical text, occasionally pausing to close her eyes and repeat something silently, committing it to memory. While he waited, Joshua tried his venison stew and bit back a hum of appreciation. The staff could get their meals from the same cafeteria as the patients and, as with everything else, the patients were paying for the best.

Sachiko came to the end of a section and used a napkin to mark her place, putting the book aside. "What are you still doing here?"

"Writing up notes for Dr. Hoffman, studying up on a few cases."

"You a workaholic?"

Yes. "No, just new in town and enthusiastic about the job. Besides..." He paused to pick at his food. "I have some kind of stupid questions..."

"And you don't want to look foolish to your mentors?"

"Well, yeah."

"But a nurse is okay?" Her wry grin took some of the venom from her words.

"Actually," Joshua grinned back, "I figured after last night, nothing I could say could make me look more foolish to you."

Her grin softened to a genuine smile and he felt his heart skip. "I like your honesty," she said quietly.

He was finding it hard to look into her eyes and still breathe. He turned his gaze to her book instead. "What're you studying?"

She sighed. "Procedures in the Reproductive System."

"Pardon?"

"You know—cancer screenings, Paps..." She smiled wickedly. "Vasectomies."

He gave the expected wince. "So is this continuing ed, or are you working on a medical degree?"

Her smile disappeared. "An MD, but only if I pass this time. I've taken this stupid course three times already. If I fail again, I'll have to drop the program."

Now Joshua's wince was genuine. "Listen, if you want some help studying, I know a lot of memory tricks..."

"Thanks. This is summer session. I'm hoping the change of professor and the faster pace will help." She picked at her salad a moment, then said, "So, what are your questions?"

"Ydrel made this comment today about Dr. Malachai having turned on some surveillance equipment in his room—"

"Oh? There's nothing in the logs about it."

"Really, I know it sounds paranoid, but he—what?"

"I said if he has, he hasn't informed the nurses' station."

"You mean it's true? The rooms are bugged?"

She glanced at him with raised eyebrows. "I take it that wasn't in your orientation?"

"I didn't think it was even legal!"

She shrugged. "Every client signs a release giving us permission to monitor them 24 hours a day if we have reason to believe they may be a danger to themselves or to others. Surveillance equipment in the rooms is more efficient than a 24-hour bodyguard, don't you agree?"

"But even in minimum care? I mean, these aren't criminals." He knew he was scowling and tried to force his face into a more neutral expression.

"You met Dr. Weaver today. Notice the ugly scar over her eye? Years ago—before my time, before we had the system—a client came in for alcoholism. His wife warned the staff that he sometimes turned violent; nonetheless, he responded well to detox and treatments, so they put him in minimal care. They figured the violence was directly related to the alcohol, I suppose.

"Dr. Weaver went to check on him one day when he didn't show up for a session. He ambushed her in his room. Beat her with a lamp. She still gets dizzy spells from that head wound, I understand. Apparently, there had been clues about his abusiveness, but not enough to warrant transfer to medium care. If they'd had the equipment, though, we would have heeded his wife's warning and he'd have been monitored—and Dr. Weaver might have been spared a great deal of pain."

Joshua didn't say anything for a long time, and the two ate in silence. Finally, he spoke. "Okay, but what did Ydrel do to mark himself as dangerous all of a sudden?"

"I don't know. As I said, the nurses on duty are usually informed when the surveillance equipment is turned on."

Joshua noted that she didn't suggest Ydrel might be lying or imagining things. "So why else would he bug Ydrel's room?"

She looked up in annoyance. "Maybe he found out about Ydrel's birthday present, or maybe it's because of what you did. I heard you got quite a dressing-down this morning in the staff meeting."

Joshua snorted. "What I 'did' was teach Ydrel to cope with a situation Dr. Malachai has spent the last five years unsuccessfully trying to repress. What I 'did' was sound psychiatry, and he took it as a challenge to his power base. Called it 'tricks' because I didn't mother-may-I."

He stabbed at his meal viciously. "Who does he think he is, anyway?"

"He is the senior psychiatrist of one of the most respected institutions in the nation—and your boss. You are an intern. You'd better remember that and find a way to deal with him, or you're not going to make it through the summer."

He looked up in surprise and found her staring at him with an expression as cold as her tone.

She held his gaze for one scolding breath, then reopened her book and again focused on her studies. If she noticed his hurt reaction, she gave no sign.

Joshua gathered up his tray and left, holding his tongue and his anger.

He didn't hold back with his parents, however.

"I thought you'd be on my side!" he snapped into the phone.

"Of course we're on your side, honey," his mother soothed. "And that means when you screw up, we need to call you on it."

"But I did good work!"

This time his father, who was on an adjoining line, replied. "What you did with Ydrel sounds promising. We're not arguing that. But you're not a 44-year-old psychiatrist with a PhD and two decades' experience. You're a teenage intern without a degree or a license. If anything had gone wrong—or goes wrong—it could open up a big can of worms for the institution."

Joshua made a pained sound. "I never thought of that. I'm surprised Dr. Malachai didn't bring that up."

His mother snorted. "I'm not. You showed him up pretty badly. He wanted to put you back in your place."

Now, Joshua smiled. That was more the reaction he'd hoped for. "So what do I do? I really want to help this kid, and I can. And you know I can, Dad, or I wouldn't be here. The point is, I get the feeling that Dr. Malachai doesn't intend to let me have any real impact with Ydrel or anyone else for that matter. And Edith doesn't expect me to do more than be his buddy. That's not what I came here for."

"You went there to learn, and not just about working with patients," his father said. "Find a way to work with Edith and Randall. All those skills you've learned aren't just for clients, you know. Find the best way to approach them with a plan that's palatable to both of them."

"Yes, sir."

"And remember, my maverick," his mother added, "talented though you are, you are a 19-year-old undergraduate intern. Dr. Randall Malachai is a top-rated psychiatrist, administrator of an important mental health care facility, and your boss. If you're going to survive the summer, you'd better find a way to work with him."

Joshua sighed. "That's what Sachiko said."

"Sachiko?"

"Yeah," he sighed again. "She's this nurse."

When he didn't say anything more, his mother prompted, "And?"

And she's smart and funny, and the way she smiles— "Well, I don't know, really, she's the swing shift supervisor, and really close to Ydrel...and when I talked to her tonight about all this, she just said about the same thing, that's all. Really." *Only she got ticked and I got mad and I've probably blown any chance with her and why am I even thinking about that?*

Now he heard a different set of sighs from his parents: the worried *can-we-protect-you-from-this?* kind.

"Sugar, you just picked yourself up from a really hard break-up," his mom reminded him. "That's one of the reasons you decided to intern so far away—"

"Mom, it's okay. Really."

"Whoa." Joshua picked up the 4-inch binder Dr. Malachai had dropped onto the table in front of him. The cover page, slipped neatly into the plastic front, had the SK-Mental logo with the motto "Providing Optimal Care for Optimal Mental Health." Printed over the logo was "Internship Schedule: Joshua A. Lawson, Book One" and dates for the next two weeks in bold blue letters.

Two weeks? He'd had year-long courses that looked less intimidating.

"I've decided that we'd underestimated your ambition, so I adjusted your course load accordingly," Dr. Malachai said, taking a seat at the small oblong conference table. Across from Joshua, Edith shrugged and gave him an encouraging smile.

Joshua grunted noncommittally as he flipped through the schedule. This week, he was finishing his orientation; then in addition to the more in-depth mentoring from the psychiatrists who had volunteered to take him under their wings, he would be working at least a half day with most of the other aspects of institute, from the orderlies ("bedpan duty," he thought) to their lawyers. Plus, there was a guided reading list with real cases to study and draw parallels...

It was beyond anything he'd imagined. It was exactly what he'd hoped—a real-world education and a workload heavy enough that he could drown in it for a summer.

It also left him with a scheduled forty-five minutes "recreation" time with Ydrel three days a week after lunch. Less, since he'd have to change clothes if they were playing outside.

Malachai guessed his thoughts. "We thought it'd be best if you kept your interactions with Ydrel to structured activities."

"What if he wants to talk?"

"By all means talk, just no..." The Chief Psychiatrist let his voice trail off.

No NLP "tricks." Joshua forced a smile. "Yes, sir. So when do I start?"

Edith escorted him to a small office they had set aside for him. It was just big enough for a desk with a computer, a bookshelf and a locking file cabinet. He swapped the back-breaking binder for a notepad and followed her down to payroll, thinking he'd rather have bedpan duty.

By his scheduled time with Ydrel, he was sure he'd rather have had bedpan duty. He was equally certain that he was going to work extra hard to not mess up his audition with Chipotle in July. Then he could spend his days singing and playing music and let his agent deal with the numbers hassle. With his head swimming with numbers, tax codes, and profit margins, he headed to Ydrel's room.

"Performing's just a different sort of hassle, you know," Ydrel greeted him at his door, then started toward the grounds without bothering to see if the intern followed. Joshua bit back a sigh and followed.

"Aren't you going to be hot in that?" he asked. Ydrel wore a long sleeve T-shirt and sweatpants despite the fact that the temperature had already passed 95.

"I'm fine," Ydrel snarled. "Don't change the subject."

"Sorry. What exactly is the subject?"

Ydrel huffed. Joshua half-expected him to straight-arm the door open, but he opened it gently. Maybe he was learning to control his temper after all.

"I don't feel like games, so let's just walk." He led him to the path that wove along the fence line before speaking again. "Being a rock star. Don't know why you think it will be easier."

"How'd you know? Never mind. First off, I don't think it's easier so much as it's what I'd rather do. But at least I don't have to worry about liability insurance."

"No. You have to worry about contracts and whether your agent is cheating you and how it will affect your family. You're naïve."

Joshua snorted. "Considering I don't have a girlfriend—"

"She likes you."

"What?" Joshua stopped.

Ydrel paused only long enough to roll his eyes. "You're an idiot." He started back toward the building.

"Hey!" Joshua grabbed his shoulder. Ydrel flinched.

Josh pulled his back his hand quickly. "I'm sorry. Will it make you feel any better if I tell you marriage trumps fame?"

Ydrel squinted at him, and again Joshua experienced the crawly feeling like he'd felt the night before.

"You know," he said to cover his shudder, "I'm getting tired of having to pass your little tests."

"Tough." But Ydrel broke his gaze and started back to the building. Josh fell in beside him.

"What's with you, anyway?"

"Nothing. Bad night. I'm relieving you of your obligation today."

"Oh, are we going sing that song again? You haven't told me what's up with you and Tasmae."

"I didn't see her last night."

When they got to Ydrel's room, the housekeeper was in the middle of making his bed. She looked up and smiled. "*Buenos días, señores.*"

"You finished in the bathroom yet?"

"Oh, yes. I did it first."

Ydrel turned to Joshua. "You'd better get back to work. I'm going to get a long shower before I have to face my afternoon session with Malachai and Edith. Talk to you later. And...sorry."

"Sure."

Ydrel brushed past the housekeeper, grabbed a change of clothing and disappeared into the bathroom. Joshua loitered by the door, watching the middle-aged woman finish the bed, pick up clothes and sort them, re-folding clean ones and putting dirty ones into a bag. She put away the papers, books and pencils, even give the ratty old bear a fluffing. When he heard the shower turn on, he spoke.

"*¿Es él siempre tan grosero a usted?*"

She glanced up from where she was pulling a sock from under the bed. "*¿Habla español?*"

"*Sí. Soy de Colorado y tengo amigos chicanos.*"

"*Ay, sí. Fue de Puerto Rico.*"

They chatted a moment about the island and how she missed its beauty and her family but not the crowds or the politics, then he returned to his original question. "Is he always so rude to you?"

She just shrugged.

"Do you always have to pick up after him like that?"

"He is sick, no?"

Joshua snorted and folded his arms over his chest. "He's spoiled."

In the shower, Ydrel adjusted the water to the hottest temperature he could stand, re-pointed the showerhead, then squatted in the tub. As the water beat on his sore and bruised back, he curled into a ball of misery and gave himself to tears.

Oh, he hurt! His body was a mass of aches and stings. He'd have spent the morning in bed, whimpering, if it hadn't been for those stupid mikes.

Does Malachai really think I don't know when he turns on the surveillance equipment? he thought, then corrected himself. Of course Malachai knows—and he wants to make sure I know he's got a close eye on me. Or ears, I suppose. But I'm not giving him the satisfaction of a show.

When Josh had grabbed his shoulder, he'd wanted to scream. He hadn't checked, but he knew he'd find an arch of bruises across the back of his shoulder to match the ones on his front. The monster had done its best to rip off his shoulder before he'd managed to kill it.

Just as he was making headway with the Miscria, the Master had returned, and his training was more relentless than ever.

Chapter Eight

The Master had been coming to Ydrel long before the Miscria. Before he'd been able to read minds and sense emotions, even. In his uncle's house, not long after his mother's death, he'd cried himself to sleep and the Master had called Ydrel away to a land of mists and shadow, given him a sword, and started to instruct him.

At first it had been wonderful. Working through the moves with the Master, he had been able to escape the pain of losing his mother. He'd reveled in the attention. He awoke feeling tired and sore, but remembering everything, and he would practice in anticipation of the next dream.

His uncle had noticed his interest and had arranged with the boarding school for him to have lessons in fencing and martial arts. He'd flourished under the praise of both his teachers and the Master.

Then, some two years after the first dream, everything changed.

The Master became more aggressive. Mistakes were no longer met with verbal correction, but with physical blows that sometimes left bruises visible in the waking world. When he did something right, he was rewarded with a tangible sense of pleasure. Soon, he was fighting with a mixture of fear and anticipation.

Those feelings transferred to his regular lessons as well. His coach praised his newfound "competitive nature" and even though he was only 12, put him against the stronger and more skilled high school students. Ydrel responded to the challenge with pride and a fierce sort of joy.

Until the day he ripped the foil from his opponent's hand, tearing off his own point guard with it.

"Darrel, hold!" the coach called, but caught in the rush of adrenaline, Ydrel followed with a slash that ripped through his opponent's jacket and scratched his chest. He felt a wild elation at the sight of the blood.

The boy jumped back with a shout.

"Darrel, *stop*!" The coach ran between them.

Ydrel blinked, saw what he'd done, dropped his sword and fled.

That night, the Master scolded him. "You didn't follow through."

"What? I hurt him! I could have killed him!"

"That is the point." Then he struck the boy hard enough to send him to his knees and drop his sword. When he could see again, the Master was before him, holding a sword to his throat.

"If I had been the enemy, you would be dead."

"That hurt!" he managed to blurt. "Besides, it was an illegal move."

"Illegal? This is not a game, child. What I'm teaching you is survival: kill or be killed. You have the skill. It is time to develop the instinct."

"But I don't want to kill anyone!"

"Then you will die." And with horrifying calm, he beat Ydrel so fully that the boy awoke coughing blood and barely able to move. He spent a week and a half in the school infirmary recovering.

Since he insisted none of the students had hurt him, and no student came forward to confess or accuse, school officials assumed he's done it to himself. The school psychiatrist came to talk to him. His fencing instructor reassured him he just needed to learn a little self-control, and that came with age and experience. Even the boy he'd injured tried to console him, telling him that mistakes happen and even praising his skill.

Ydrel knew better. It was neither a mistake nor a loss of control. The Master was trying to turn him into a killing machine.

He refused to touch a sword or weapon of any kind.

A month passed without any nighttime visits, and Ydrel began to believe the Master had given up on him. He relaxed, reveling in the first normal life he'd had since his mother died. He tried out for other sports, though he wasn't very good, and began to excel in his studies. By the end of the school year, he'd actually made a few friends and didn't even mind when his aunt and uncle decided to keep him at the boarding school for the summer sessions.

One hot July night, he fell asleep to find himself again in the land of mists and shadows.

He glanced about wildly. *Let it be a dream, just a nightmare—*

The Master stood before him. "You should be rested now. We'll resume where we left off."

"No! No, please, just leave me alone!"

To his surprise, the Master smiled and threw down his sword. "Is that what you want? All right. Kill me."

"What?"

"Kill me. Run me through. You know how. It is your final test—and your only way to be rid of me."

Suddenly, a sword was in Ydrel's hands. He clutched it, feeling revulsion and desire. "I hate you!"

"Hate does no good unless it is translated into action. Kill me!"

Ydrel started toward him, imagining every way the weapon could kill his master. He saw every vital organ, every major artery. It would be so easy.

"Yes. Be rid of me. Forever. Kill me."

Revulsion overcame desire. Ydrel dropped his sword and fell to his knees, sobbing.

After a moment, he heard footsteps and felt a hand gently lift his chin. Through tear-blurred eyes, he saw the Master's tender expression.

"I've tried to make this as easy on you as possible." He gazed pityingly into Ydrel's eyes, then looked away thoughtfully. "Perhaps, a change of target?"

Ydrel followed his gaze. And screamed.

The monster that was making its way through the mists was vaguely humanoid, but with arms ending in blade-like appendages. The rest was so hideous, his mind refused to focus on it or recall any details. Ydrel skittered backward, bumped into the Master, looked at him with wild, pleading eyes.

The Master's face was again a cold mask. "Kill it or it kills you." He disappeared.

Ydrel scrambled to his feet and ran.

Suddenly, the thing was before him. It swung, knocking him down. Ydrel rolled, got to his feet, and ran again.

Again, it appeared before him. Again, it struck him. This time, Ydrel fell near his sword. Without thinking, he picked it up and swung, cleanly slicing off one arm. The thing moved to strike him with the other arm, but he got in under its swing. His blade pierced through its belly and tore its heart. The monster fell back, ripping the blade from him. It convulsed once, then was still.

"Good!" He heard the Master's voice. Then he was engulfed in pleasure so intense that it wiped out all pain, all thought.

He awoke to cold, wet sheets and an overwhelming sense of shame.

His roommates teased him. The school psychiatrist gave him a long lecture about the facts of life, then called his uncle. His uncle laughed sympathetically. "Welcome to puberty!" was all he said.

Ydrel gave all the expected replies and tried to bite back his panic. How could he tell them the truth?

The next night, he pleaded with the Master. He would do anything, just no more "rewards."

Twice a week, the Master "trained" him. Sometimes, they practiced technique; sometimes he pitted the boy against monsters.

Somehow, he managed to hide his bruises and avoid serious injuries, but there was hardly a day he didn't feel sore or exhausted. Teachers began to look at him with concern, and once or twice he lied that he had a cold coming on.

That was just the beginning. At least once a week, the Master called him to the dream world to lecture him about the manifest destiny of his people, who eschewed all advancement and most technology, but would somehow conquer worlds based on their faith alone. Any argument meant severe punishment, so Ydrel sat and listened until the words became a buzz in his head and sometimes invaded his daytime thoughts.

About the same time, he found himself having visions and sudden insights. Thoughts that clearly weren't his would suddenly pop into his head, so that he had to be careful not to speak too soon or raise his hand too quickly, lest he respond to a question not yet asked or a thought not meant to be expressed. Taking summer finals was a nightmare; several answers would come to his head, and he wasn't sure which were right or even his own. He started catching the moods and feelings of others around him, so that it was hard to be with more than one person at a time.

As fall approached and the rest of the faculty and students returned, the problems multiplied. The thoughts of others became a confused static in his brain, giving him constant headaches. Crowds were unbearable, as was being near anyone with strong emotions. Then came the first day of class and the horrible episode with a new teacher.

Again, he was sent to the school psychiatrist, and desperate for help, he told him the truth. Dr. Wells scheduled him for weekly sessions and called his uncle to discuss Ydrel's "psycho-sexual and social maladjustments." Ydrel tried to make him understand that he wasn't crazy, that he really was hearing other people's thoughts. He took careful notes of the thoughts and feelings he picked up, where he was, who was around, the time and circumstances.

The notes were filed away and he was put on chlorpromazine, a medication commonly used for schizophrenia. It made lightheaded and nauseous, and even more vulnerable to others by day and the Master by night. One morning, about a week after starting treatments, he didn't show up for class. The faculty finally found him in an empty room in an abandoned wing of the school: curled up in a corner, blinking away tears and unable to form a coherent thought.

After that experience, the burden he carried seemed easy. They took him off the medication. He stopped complaining and simply tried to cope on his own. He tried to read up on psychic phenomenon, but a proper school like his didn't encourage such frivolous pursuits. The books he was allowed to get from interlibrary loan had little about the mechanisms of ESP and even less about control.

So he found hiding places where he could be alone, and tried to stay near people who didn't seem to "radiate" as strongly. When he had to be with others, he took ibuprofen or whatever painkillers he could get, buying them from other students or stealing them from the infirmary when his supplies ran out.

With all of that, the visits from the Master had come as a relief; in the land of shadows and mists, he was shielded from others—more and more, his regular dreams had been filled with the nightmares and images of other people. The monsters, however, were mindless. For all their violence, they were without emotion, and the Master was a blank slate.

He tried to talk with the Master about his problem, but he was dismissed as if he were a child complaining about being able to hear well.

"If this is unusual for your people, then use it to your advantage," he finally advised.

"But, how?"

"Treat it as you would any other weapon."

And that was just what the Master taught him to do.

Chapter Nine

The steady spray of hot water continued to pour on Ydrel's back, but lost in misery and memory, he didn't notice.

Ydrel hadn't thought life at school could get more hellish. He'd been wrong.

Perry Harvey transferred to the school and almost from the first day, decided to make Ydrel's already miserable life worse. Perry, a senior, was tall, swarthy and athletic, with a ready laugh that hid a quick judgmental streak. Although he entered the school a month into the semester, he had the family, finances, and general charisma to make himself instantly popular with teachers and students. He professed to like everyone, but he took an immediate dislike to the reclusive Ydrel.

Former friends shied away from him. Homework or personal items went missing, only to reappear days or weeks later. Then there were "accidental" trips and shoves in the hallway or in gym class, usually timed just right to send him careening into a locker or the bleachers or another person. He wasn't sure which was worse: one gave him bruises atop the bruises inflicted by the monsters, but the emotional abuse from his classmates added to his already pounding headaches.

In desperation, he told Dr. Wells about it. Even though he wasn't a good psychiatrist, he was school counselor; surely, this was something he could help with.

The counselor suggested he and Perry "discuss their differences" with him as mediator.

Remembering the meeting made Ydrel curl up into a tighter ball in the shower. What an idiot he'd been to think the counselor would have any sympathy for his side.

He shouldn't have walked into the counselor's office once he saw that Perry had brought his cronies with him. He should have walked out as soon as one said, "I don't know where this kid gets off spreading lies." Instead he stayed, and tried to stay calm and reasonable, and prayed the counselor would see through them.

Instead, the counselor listened sympathetically while they accused him of setting Perry up as a scapegoat. It was Ydrel, they said, who pushed people then claimed to have been bumped. It was Ydrel, they said, who accused others of stealing his homework so he could turn it in late. It was Ydrel, they said, who was trying to make Perry, the "new kid," look bad.

There was no discussion. There was no mediation. Just his tormentors firing accusations like bullets while he sat there too stunned to defend himself. Not that he could have said or done much anyway. Not only was he outnumbered, but Perry was older and popular, and Ydrel was the one with the "psycho-sexual and social maladjustments."

When he was finally released, he was barely able to hold back the tears of rage, shame, and helplessness. He tried to flee, but Perry and his buddies intercepted him in the hall to gloat. At least, the two cronies did; Perry was the epitome of innocent sincerity.

"I had to do it," he said rationally. "I had to defend myself. Surely you can understand."

Something in Ydrel snapped. Rage clouded his vision like a red mist. He could hear the Master's voice, hard and imperative: KILL HIM.

The boys were snickering as Perry asked his forgiveness.

Ydrel clenched his fists. His hands itched. God, how he longed for a sword, a blade, any weapon—

YOU HAVE A WEAPON, ONE NONE OF YOUR PEOPLE HAS. USE IT. KILL THIS MONSTER BEFORE HE HURTS YOU AGAIN.

He felt power burning through him. He could do it. He could see himself reaching with psychic hands into Perry's chest—

YES. USE YOUR ADVANTAGE.

"Drop dead, Perry."

"Come on, now Darrel—"

Taking his heart into his hands. Grasping. Squeezing.

YES. FIGHT BACK.

Perry smiled patronizingly. "Now, Darrel, I'm sure you can understand the situation here."

His buddy nudged him. "Hey, Perry, maybe we ought to tell Dr. Wells about this development."

Squeezing. The heart struggling.

Perry gasped.

YES. KILL THE MONSTER.

"Die, Perry."

All four chambers stopping.

"Perry? Yo, Perry, you okay?" His friends stopped their taunting as they noticed Perry fighting to catch his breath.

The look of fear and surprise on Perry's face as he'd fall to his knees. So sweet—

YES. FEEL THIS VICTORY. KILL.

"Perry?" his friend shouted. "Someone help!"

Ydrel blinked and the mist and rage were gone. Perry lay sprawled at his feet, eyes wide with surprise— just as Ydrel had imagined. The other boys were standing, open-mouthed with shock.

"Perry!" Ydrel hastily knelt and laid his head on the older boy's chest. He didn't hear anything. Oh, God, he didn't hear anything! "Perry! No, Perry, don't be dead! I didn't mean it! I didn't mean it!"

"Dead? Holy—" One boy flew into a stream of invectives. Both boys backed away.

Ydrel placed a hand on Perry's neck. He didn't feel a pulse. "Please, Perry! I didn't mean it!"

IDIOT. LET HIM DIE. FOLLOW THROUGH. SAVOR YOUR VICTORY.

"Shut up!" He glared at the two boys. "Don't just stand there! Get the doctor. Call 911! GO!"

They ran. He hoped they were going to do what they said but couldn't go after them. He tilted Perry's head back, blew into his mouth. He felt along the chest, seeking Perry's sternum, trying to remember the CPR course he'd taken that summer. Was it two fingers or four? He guessed, placed one hand over the other and rocked. "C'mon, Perry! Don't die. I didn't mean it! I'm sorry! Don't die!"

FOOL. The Master left his mind.

How many rocks was it supposed to be before the next breath? In his panic, he couldn't remember, and he'd lost count of how many he'd just done, anyway. He stopped, blew into Perry's mouth, then started with heart massage again. The whole time he babbled, begging the senior to get up, to live. When a hand touched his shoulder, he shrugged it off wildly. Someone grabbed him by both shoulders and pulled him back. It was the school physician.

"Darrel. You did fine. We've got it from here."

Already another teacher was giving Perry breaths. The doctor released Ydrel and took over heart massage, counting in a calm, even tone. Perry lay, head cocked back, mouth open and just a little blue, eyes staring unblinkingly at the ceiling. Teachers were trying to keep back curious students while trying to assuage their own curiosity. They kept looking from the dying boy to Ydrel.

Ydrel gave them one wild look and ran.

He hadn't known where he was heading until he found himself in the upperclassmen's bathroom, retching into a sink. His stomach churned. His arms and chest ached. His throat was raw. His lungs burned as his breath came in racking sobs. His mind was on fire with panic and pain.

He'd killed him. He'd killed another person.

NOT QUITE.

Ydrel whirled. There, leaning against a stall door, was the Master. He was short but heavily muscled. His orange outfit gave his narrow face and wide-set eyes a satanic glow. His thin-lipped mouth was curled with disdain. He was a real, physical manifestation, yet he spoke to Ydrel within his mind as he always had.

YOU HAVE FAILED. YOU DIDN'T FOLLOW THROUGH.

"But I didn't mean it! I didn't want to kill him. Not really!"

The Master rolled his eyes with impatience. YOU STILL DON'T UNDERSTAND. YOU ARE NOT LIKE

THESE PEOPLE. YOU ARE SET APART, ALONE. IF YOU ARE TO SURVIVE, YOU MUST FOLLOW THROUGH. KILL. OR BE KILLED.

With that, the Master disappeared. Ydrel felt him leave his mind, too, taking what little support he had. He sank to his knees, throwing up on the tile floor. The Master's words echoed in his mind. Kill or be killed.

When his stomach had at last emptied itself, he pulled himself up, and saw his face in the mirror. The face of a weakling.

The face of a murderer.

A sob rose in his throat, became a scream, then a force—

He ducked as the mirror shattered.

He sank to the ground, crying amid the broken glass. Trembling, he reached for one long, narrow piece. His first attempt missed the vein and hurt so bad that he almost dropped the shard. Then the Master's words came back to him: He hadn't followed through. He was apart, alone. He must kill or be killed.

His second try left him seeing stars but sliced neatly through the vein. Oddly, the second wrist, done with his left hand, cut more easily and with less pain. He dropped the bloody piece of glass and leaned against the wall. He was too tired to cry anymore, too tired to think. He had just enough energy left to sit and wait and die.

Whether from fatigue, loss of blood, or simple relief, he did not know, but he actually felt calm and mildly euphoric. He relaxed into it until he heard footsteps and realized he hadn't locked the bathroom door.

YOU DIDN'T FOLLOW THROUGH.

He jumped up to correct his error, but blackness overcame him and he collapsed.

Ydrel's back had numbed from the heat and steady pounding of the water. He unfolded himself, washed quickly, then turned the water to an icy blast just before turning it off. He thought that would shake out the memories, but as he dried, he found himself staring at the long scars on his wrists.

The two months after his suicide attempt were still just a hellish blur of fear and confusion. He still didn't know how he fought himself back to sanity, but when he had, he'd found himself in the High Intensity Ward at SK-Mental under the care of Dr. Randall Malachai.

Malachai, who believed him.

Malachai, who with a combination of biofeedback and meditation, helped him gain a rudimentary control over his telepathy.

Malachai, who then turned on him, demanding he "stretch" his abilities, and who punished him when he didn't perform. Was Malachai really so different from the Master?

And Joshua wondered why he had trust issues.

Chapter Ten

For the next week, Joshua took his parents' advice, lying low and observing Dr. Malachai with the same intensity he'd give a new client. He noted his eye movements and listened to his speech patterns, trying to determine his cognitive orientation. He listened to how things were presented to the senior psychiatrist—what approaches worked for whom. Above all, he paid close yet emotionally distant attention to how Malachai treated him: How did Malachai view him and his role, and where and how far would he let Joshua stretch that role?

In the meantime, he finished his orientation with the facility, having shadowed each psychiatrist and spending time with aides and specialists.

Sometimes, it was a challenge just to sit quietly and learn. On Thursday, he was invited to witness a "rebirth therapy," where the client was made to re-enact his own birth—a radical New Age therapy he would never have expected in so conservative an institution. He sat behind a one-way mirror with half a dozen other interested people, including a reporter doing an article for the local newspaper. After half an hour of watching the client try to wriggle his way out of a blanket (the womb) while the therapist alternately pushed on him with pillows and urged him to keep trying, he wondered aloud when they would call in the surgical team for Cesarean section, sending the entire room into laughter.

Fortunately, the room was soundproofed, and the reporter was gracious enough to promise not to print the comment, but he was sure his remark would make its way back to Malachai.

Later that day, while shadowing the art therapy specialist, he got a chance to talk to Ydrel. He saw the young client at an easel, putting the finishing touches on a kind of dinosaur-lizard with wings. Like his sketches of Tasmae, it was detailed and amazingly life-like.

"That's really good," he ventured when Ydrel stopped to clean his brush before changing colors.

"It's an everyn."

"You mean wyvern?"

Ydrel gave him a don't-be-stupid look. "Does it look like a wyvern? It's an everyn. Tasmae showed me one last night. They use it for reconnaissance."

"Oh." Joshua decided to let it pass for now. "So how's ol' She-Who anyway?"

"Sheehoo?"

"Yeah. She-Who-Must-Be-Obeyed?"

Ydrel grinned. "She'd hate that, though she'd probably agree."

"Then she's got a lot in common with my mom. So? Is she sticking to your deal?"

"Yeah." Ydrel sighed.

"What's the matter? Miss passing out in your oatmeal?"

"Of course not. It's just that before, she'd ask me a question, I'd do some research and give her an answer, and that was it. Kind of memorize and dump, you know? Now, I have to give these endless explanations: What's this mean? How's that work? I didn't even realize that I'd been giving technological answers to a non-technological society this whole time. How do I explain a satellite when they don't even have light bulbs? It's a wonder they've accomplished as much with what I've given them as they have. Tasmae has this incredible imagination. Now, though, she wants direct answers, and I can't give them. Not to mention there's so much about her world I can't figure out."

"What do you mean? I'd think it'd be easy to figure out her world if we're so much more advanced."

Ydrel grunted and turned to a page in his sketchbook. In it was a long list of questions. "It's not just her world, it's the world she's fighting—Barin. If they're so advanced—and they have space travel—why haven't they wiped her people out by now?"

He started to hand Joshua the pad, then pulled back. "This is between you and me. If one of the psychs sees this, I don't even want to think about what wild assumptions they'd make."

Joshua crossed his arms and thought for a moment. He couldn't make that promise. Nonetheless, he needed to build some trust if he was to help Ydrel; besides, he was curious. "Listen, I'm just an intern. I can't go guaranteeing confidentiality as if you were my patient.

"I can do this much: I won't bring it up unless directly asked--unless there's anything in there that indicates you're a danger to yourself or someone else or that you are indeed on the path to true Looneyville, Then, I have to tell someone. But I'd tell Edith first, in confidence, and let her decide what to do. Good enough?"

"I guess that's the best you can do." He handed him the book and Joshua scanned the questions:

- Why do the Barins have spaceships, but use shotguns and rifles and swords?
- Why do their guns only fire once, and never work again?
- What do the Barins want from Kanaan?
- Why does the Season of War increase each year?
- Why do earthquakes, tidal waves, and other weather-related disasters precede the Season of War?

"Weird," was all he could say as he handed the book back. "She's asking you these?"

"No, these are the things I don't understand, and to her, it's just the way it's always been. But I can't help feeling they're important. I—" He shrugged. "Maybe I shouldn't say any more."

"I'm interested, though," Josh said.

Ydrel snorted and turned back to his painting. "Let's pretend I'm writing a story, then. By the way, any ideas on achieving my eventual release?"

"Actually, I have, since you're willing to put in the work. I need to talk to Edith and Dr. Malachai, but—"

An orderly—Floyd, Joshua remembered; he'd talked with him the day before— interrupted. "Mr. Stephens? You have a visitor. Says he's an old friend of your mother's. I'm to escort you to the front desk so you can identify him."

The look on Ydrel's face said he had no idea who the visitor might be, much less why he'd come to visit after so many years, but he stuck his brushes in a can of paint thinner and wiped his hands. "Well, let's go then.

We still on for Frisbee, Josh? I can't imagine this taking long."

"I'll catch you after lunch."

After lunch, Joshua found him outside at one of the umbrella tables still with his visitor, a lawyer or business-type from the suit. They were leaned together. Ydrel was writing something in one of those leather-bound legal-sized folders, after which the man gave him the yellow copy and put the rest in his briefcase. Ydrel put his paper into his sketchbook. Joshua waited until he'd left, accompanied by Floyd, before approaching Ydrel.

He sat down across from the young man, who was leaning on the table, one arm protectively over his sketchbook, an iced tea in the other hand. "So, who was that?"

"An old client of my mother's. He followed her advice and made a fortune, and he finally came back to thank her, found out what happened and decided the least he could do was look me up instead."

"Uh, huh," Joshua replied skeptically. Although Ydrel spoke easily, the movements of his eyes were wrong. "Listen, you don't want to tell me, that's fine, but just tell me it's none of my business and change the subject, okay?"

Ydrel blinked, then scowled. "Fine. It's none of your business. What's going on with you and Sachiko, anyway?"

"You really change a subject. Really, um, nothing that I know of."

Ydrel snorted. "Well, what *I* know of is that whenever the two of you are together, you pussyfoot around each other like you expect the other to explode, and when you're apart, you're brooding over the other. No one else may notice, but you're making my brain itch. Whatever is going on, would the two of you just apologize and get over it?"

"She doesn't have any reason to apologize. I was the idiot."

"Fine. Tell her, not me. But do it soon, before I get a full-blown migraine. Hey, I asked Edith about setting up a Frisbee golf course. She said she'd ask you about what we'd need."

"Really?"

Ydrel shrugged. "Yeah, really. She just wants me to be happy."

"And Dr. Malachai?"

"He wants to keep me here. If I can amuse myself, it's that much easier to control me."

Ydrel closed his drapes. The "bugs" in his room were still active, so he was careful not to make a sound when he shut the door and braced a chair under the doorknob. He pulled out the yellow legal papers Bill Renier had given him, then folded them carefully until he had a small yellow rectangle. Using the mending kit Floyd had found for him, he pulled out the stitching in Descartes' side, slid the papers in, and sewed it back up. Then he hugged the ragged bear in triumph.

Mine Mine Mine! He could have jumped for joy. His mother had left him a sizable trust fund when she'd died, one that was to be turned over to him when he turned eighteen. Of course, that was before all of the *(say it, Ydrel!)* insanity that brought him here.

Since then, his uncle, as legal guardian, had been tapping into the account to pay Ydrel's "medical" expenses, but he'd never made any changes to ensure Ydrel couldn't access the account. Perhaps he hadn't expected Ydrel to be committed for so long, or maybe he didn't consider it an issue. After all, Ydrel was a teenager—and crazy, to boot. What could he possibly do from inside an asylum?

Very little, actually—except for saving the life of a Mafia accountant. "Renier" had been committed for paranoia after he'd stormed the regional FBI office insisting that the Mob was after him. Only Ydrel had believed him. When the hitmen tried to reach Renier in the asylum, Ydrel had made certain they would fail.

The accountant had mostly gone straight, but he still wasn't above a few tricks. Renier secured a numbered bank account, and now that Ydrel had turned eighteen, all the funds from Ydrel's trust had been transferred to that account, leaving just enough to pay for a few months at the asylum. He'd even arranged to have the bank statements sent to a phony address.

Ydrel closed his eyes, envisioning the dollar amount typed on those yellow papers. He could live comfortably on his own for some time. Now he had to find a way to get out, and soon, before the money left in his trust ran out or his uncle wondered about the statements.

Ydrel put the chair back in its proper place, then curled up on the bed. After going to all the trouble of making it look like he was napping, he might as well actually get some rest. As he set Descartes down in his usual spot and closed his eyes, Ydrel had one fleeting, disturbing thought.

How had Josh known he was lying?

Chapter Eleven

Joshua knocked on the door of the nurse's lounge with a certain amount of déjà vu. Once again, Sachiko was eating dinner alone and poring over her medical text. Once again, he was feeling just a little nervous, though for a completely different reason.

"Uh, Sachiko...?"

She spun around and got to her feet. "Joshua!" Her smile was hesitant but not unwelcoming, so he went in. They stood face to face, yet not quite looking at each other, and their words tumbled over the other's:

"Listen, I don't mean to interrupt, but—"

"I was hoping I could talk to you sometime—"

"I just wanted to apolo—"

"I'm sorry about—"

They both stopped and laughed, and Joshua felt the tension drain away. "I think this is really a case where the guy goes first." As she crossed her arms and waved one hand for him to proceed, she gave him an amused half-smile that made his heart beat a little faster.

"I'm really sorry about the other evening. My pride was hurt, I was mad, and even though I said I was looking for advice, I guess I mostly wanted to gripe. It wasn't fair of me—we just met and all, and I put you in a bad position because I was looking for some sympathy. Then when you gave me sound advice, I got mad because it wasn't what I wanted to hear. Anyway, I was really out of line, and I apologize."

"Accepted. I'm sorry, too. I knew you were upset; I could have been more diplomatic, at least. My only excuse is this dang class. It already has me in a bad mood. You're not the first who's had a bad experience with Dr. Malachai. You find a way to cope, or you leave."

"So you had problems with him, too?"

"We have a good working relationship now." She shrugged, then winced.

"Something wrong?"

"It's nothing. I strained a muscle or something this afternoon."

"Well, here," he turned a chair around so she could sit in it with her arms draped across the back. "Sit down and let me see if I can help. C'mon. Consider it part of my apology."

After she sat, leaning forward on the cushioned back and burying her face into crossed arms, he gave her a massage, starting just below the hairline, then working down over her neck and shoulders. "So what were you doing to pull your back?'

"Lifting Mr. Goldstein into bed. Used to do that stuff all the time when I worked at South County, but I guess I lost the knack."

"Mr. Goldstein? Isn't he the gentleman Ydrel hangs around with? Pretends he's in the resistance with him?"

She hummed assent. He worked her shoulders gently, then with growing strength as he felt her tension melting away. "He's taken a turn for the worse, physically. I don't think he'll be with us much longer. He really ought to be in a nursing home, not a mental institution. Have you had training at this?"

"Nope. It's kind of a choir-drama thing. You know, someone's always giving someone a backstage backrub before a performance. You just pick things up. I'm not licensed or anything."

"Hmmm." She sighed and sank a little deeper into the chair. "Well, you should get licensed," she murmured. "Those hands are too skilled to be legal."

"Thank you," he said in a low, deep voice, "I aim to please."

Some of the tension returned to her back. He wanted to say something to reassure her, but he didn't know what to say without making it worse.

Instead, he followed the tension up to her neck. Her hair was caught in a bun, and he had to resist the urge to undo it. He knew it would feel as silky as it looked.

"So," she asked with a chuckle. "Is there anything you can't do?"

He worked a knot he found under her shoulder blade. "I can't diagram a sentence. I can't speak French with a proper accent. I can't make my checkbook agree with the bank statement—"

"You been asked this before?"

"A time or two...I can't swim."

"You can't?"

"Sink like a stone. Feel better?"

She stretched and stood. "Terrific. What do I owe you?"

How about we do this again at my place? He quickly banished the thought. How much trouble had that line of thinking gotten him into last year? *This summer is all about work and the audition. Head in the game, Josh!*

Fortunately, her pager beeped, saving him from answering her. She sighed. "I'd better get back. Somebody needs a nurse, and even if Monique answers before me, I'll need to man the nurses' station."

"I'm sorry—I mean, you didn't even finish dinner."

"Don't worry. I feel much better. I can always finish this at my desk. But you—" She flung her backpack over her shoulder, then turned to poke him in the chest. "You should be out having fun, meeting people and making the most of your summer. Got it? Go to Newport. There's always a festival or something going on there."

Without waiting for an answer, she left.

"Festival. Right." Music, food. Beautiful women he'd want to dance with. That was the last thing he needed.

With a sigh, he headed back to the office. He'd read another case study, then go home and take a cold, cold shower before hitting the sack. He'd promised his parents. He'd promised Momarosa—*ora et labora.* Pray and work. He promised Rique and the guys—no distractions. Even if she was someone he thought he could talk to all day and kiss all night.

You just had to touch her, didn't you, Joshua?

Chapter Twelve

It was just after two in the morning when Ydrel awoke—although "awoke" was the wrong term.

The Miscria had just released him from a Calling.

For a moment, he lay blinking in the darkness, as the world of air conditioning and man-made comfort replaced the natural beauty of hers. Before it all faded into dreams and compulsions, however, he snapped on the lamp on the side table and reached under the bed for his notebook.

It'd become his habit this past week: write down what she'd told him, memorize the pages, then sneak them into the cafeteria trash can before breakfast. He'd realized after showing his list to Joshua the other afternoon what a risk he was taking. No one would believe he'd suddenly decided to become a fantasy writer.

It took him ten minutes to scribble it out: what he'd taught them, where he'd learned it, what they did with his knowledge. Ten minutes to summarize four hours of conversation. Ten minutes. Four hours.

Five years of his life.

Five different Miscrias over several hundred of their years.

That's what he'd learned last night: that her people had been relying on him for generations; that certain Miscrias were gifted with the ability to contact him with questions; that they contacted no one else. At first, she'd been surprised to discover he was the only Ydrel, but she'd brushed off the knowledge with a casual acceptance that irritated him.

"If God has arranged it so, then that is how it should be, though I do not understand this newest development," she'd said.

"Your people believe in God, then? Never mind," he'd added when he felt her confusion. *What's not to believe, right?*

He tried to hide his bitterness.

Fortunately, her attention was elsewhere. "You've saved my people. Your knowledge, even couched in riddles, has given us the tools we need to survive. Why do you withhold it now? Why do you insist on questioning me about the past instead of helping me prepare for the future?"

"Look, I just want to understand. Maybe, maybe if I know your world better, I can give you better answers. Just, show me your world."

So she had: a beautiful world without pollution, without machines. Huge buildings made of immense living plants woven together. Sentient animals working in concert with humans. Food growing in abundance. Healers who cure by encouraging the body to heal itself. And at the center of it all, the Miscrias, who could sense the changes of Kanaan—their world—as easily as Ydrel could read a book.

There had come the time of the second sun, when Kanaan was nearly torn asunder, and the Miscria's mind as well—but the Ydrel came to her, soothed her, taught her the mysteries of the changing weather so that she could heal her world.

The second sun moved on and the world calmed, but a new world shared their sun, and its people hungered for Kanaan's abundance. The invaders came in metallic ships and brought guns, but anyone who fired a gun found himself denied breath by the very air of Kanaan. They soon switched to more primitive weaponry. They fought while their planet, Barin, loomed large in the Kanaan sky—weeks the first time, then longer with each successive orbit, then months. When Barin grew smaller in the sky, they boarded their ships and fled in thunder and flame. They'd destroyed nearly a third of the Kanaan.

Again, the Miscria turned to the Ydrel for protection and defense. And the Ydrel taught them to design their cities so the people would be safe. A new race of Kanaan was born, bred for war and able to kill without succumbing to the mind sickness of watching another die, and the Ydrel provided them with the knowledge of the sword. Healers, by their nature, had to join the minds of their patients, but too much pain or too many minds and the healer would lose his sanity; the Ydrel taught them alternate means of caring for the injured and how to quickly assess battlefield injuries.

Each Miscria brought new questions to the Ydrel and each time the Kanaan learned from him how to better handle the invaders.

"Now, it is my turn," Tasmae concluded, "and I no longer wish to merely defend. I wish to destroy them utterly or deal them such hurt that they do not return."

Deryl had crossed his arms. "That's bloodthirsty."

She shrugged. "The Miscria talent manifested late in me. I am trained as a warrior. My mentor was killed before I was half-trained, shot through the throat by a traitor who rotted the city walls with his touch. He was my father's best friend, driven insane on the battlefield while trying to heal both Kanaan and Barin. I am sick of war. I am sick of killing and I am sick of seeing people die—my people and the Barin. Teach me to end this war."

"Can't you talk to them?"

She shivered. "Their minds are chaotic. To communicate with them is to share their insanity—only healers dare try."

"So *talk*. Don't they have language?"

"We know their words. Some have tried. The Traitor..." Her thought trailed off, replaced by sadness. "They believe we are demons. They believe God intends our world for them, if they can prove their strength by annihilating us. They are relentless. Teach me to stop them."

And he'd awakened with an overwhelming desire to do just that.

Only he didn't know how.

Ydrel rubbed his eyes. They felt hot and dry. His mind felt dry, too. He wished he could go back to sleep, but he was afraid. He knew where he'd learned the skills he'd passed on to the warriors. The Master.

He didn't want to hurt anyone. Why would God pick him for this stupid calling, anyway?

He wanted to help Tasmae. He wanted her people to go back to the peaceful time she'd shown him. Maybe, if he got her through this, she'd release him, and he could get on with his own life. Never see her or her kind again.

Suddenly, that didn't seem as attractive as it had a few days ago.

He ran his hands through his hair, pulling at the roots. *What kind of idiot am I? First, I'm desperate to do anything to block her from my mind, now I'm enjoying her company? I enjoyed the Master's company, too, until he tried to turn me into a killer.*

Tasmae isn't like that, a part of him said. She said herself she's sick of war, sick of killing.

She also demanded I teach her how to destroy her enemies or hurt them so bad they'd never come back.

Did Perry ever come back? Had he learned anything from what happened?

Ydrel sighed and released his hair. There was no way he'd get to sleep now. Besides, what if the Master came to him? No. He'd wash his face with cold water and stay up drawing for the rest of the night. He could get a nap later, then see what he could do for her.

He ripped the page out of his notebook and took it with him to the bathroom to flush it. Standing in front of the toilet, he looked the list over once more, feeling his heart sink at the brief summation of his life.

Even if he got out of the asylum, what could he possibly do with himself? All he knew how to do was fight ancient wars.

Chapter Thirteen

At 11:00 Monday morning, Joshua stood at Ydrel's half-open door. Instead of his usual suit, he wore jeans and a T-shirt. He had a backpack of books across one shoulder and a bucket of cleaning supplies in one hand. He raised the other hand to knock.

"Why do you even bother, Joshua? Just come in."

Joshua rolled his eyes and did as he was asked.

Ydrel was leaning against a pile of pillows on his unmade bed, his nose in a huge, black-bound book with the title *Air War* in gold letters on the spine. Scattered across the bed and floor were dirty clothes, books and sketchpads, and a tray of something half-eaten and dried. Oblivious to Joshua's attire or the things he carried, Ydrel continued to read, flipping through the pages at an uncanny rate.

"You engrossed in that book or can you put it down awhile?"

"Just let me finish the chapter."

Joshua kicked aside a pair of shorts, set the bucket in a corner, then sat on the edge of the bed and idly picked up one of the sketches: the same winged dinosaur-creatures he'd seen Ydrel painting earlier. This time they were flying, some carrying things and others dropping objects on the people below. He only had time to think, *There's a happy scene*, before Ydrel closed the book and tossed it aside. It landed badly on a lopsided pile of notebooks, which toppled off the desk.

Ydrel glanced at the spill, then shrugged with annoyance. "What's up?"

"You really read that fast?"

He nodded. "Photographic memory."

The intern grunted. "Well, that'll make things easier. I brought you presents." He pushed the sketches into a neat pile, then placed the backpack in front of Ydrel. With a quizzical smile, Ydrel upended the bag. Books spilled out and he picked up the largest: *Preparing for the GED*.

"What's a GED?"

"High school equivalency test, in lieu of a diploma. There are lots of practice tests in it you can take. I figured we'd try a test or two first just to see what subjects you need to work on. Then we can arrange a study schedule. I took this test when I was fifteen. If you have a photographic memory, it should be a piece of cake. What's wrong?"

Ydrel was staring at him oddly. "I...nothing. Does Malachai know about this?"

"Sure. Edith, too. I had to discuss it with them; this could become a major part of our new routine. The test prep, I bought for you. The rest of these books are from the library. You don't have to read them all the way if you don't want to, but at least give them a try. You need to expand your horizons."

Joshua watched while Ydrel looked them over: a book by a humorist named Dave Barry, *Phule's Company* by Robert Asprin, *The Idiot's Guide to Dating* (Ydrel rolled his eyes) and *Arrows of the Queen* by Mercedes Lackey.

Joshua tapped the Lackey as he spoke. "Some are just fun, but a few might have useful information." *The main character's an empath like you, and it over-whelms her, too,* he thought hard, feeling slightly foolish as he did so.

Nonetheless, Ydrel nodded slightly and put the book on top of the pile, which he placed on the end table, pushing aside a half-full glass of juice to do so. "Okay. And the bucket?"

"That's one of what my great-great-granpappy called 'The Pillars of Survival.'"

"Your great-great-grandpappy?"

"Yeah. Survived slavery, the Civil War, life as a cowboy, even clawed his way out of a cave-in of the silver mine he worked. Lived to be 110 and was lucid to the end. Used to say all the fancy schooling in the world didn't amount to much if you didn't know the four pillars of Survival: reading, writing, ciphering, and keeping yourself clean and fed. Now, I know you can read and write. I don't know how you are with finances, but we can work on that later. I'm guessing you can't cook. And you obviously don't know—or don't care—about keeping your room clean."

"I've got housekeepers for that!"

"Sure. Here. What about when you leave? Think the staff is going to come and clean your house out of the goodness of their hearts? Believe me, you have not endeared yourself to them that much."

Ydrel snorted. "Do you know how much money I have?"

"No idea. Do you know how much a good live-in housekeeper costs?" Into Ydrel's silence, Joshua added. "Listen, if you can prove you have the money for it, along with everything else you need or want, for the rest of your life, we'll skip the cleaning. Personally, I can do without looking at your toilet."

He waited, trying hard not to laugh at the sullen look on the teen's face. He was sure he'd worn that look when his mother pulled the same challenge on him.

"I thought you were going to help me get out of here."

Joshua sighed. "You know I can't do that. But I can teach you some skills to help you handle life on your own when you do get out. And as you learn, you'll be showing people around here that you are ready to live on your own. That could make a difference in how people look at you."

"I'll bet Malachai thinks this all rather amusing."

"He supports the idea," Joshua said neutrally, then played his trump card. "As does Edith. She was actually a little embarrassed that no one had thought of it earlier. Especially the school part."

Ydrel's expression softened, and Joshua knew he'd won. "Once I prove I can do this, do I get my housekeeper back?"

"We'll see." Joshua rose. "But first, we're going to the kitchen. I'm going to give you weekly cooking lessons—unless Mr. Moneybags is sure he can afford a full-time chef?"

Instead of rising to the bait, Ydrel said, "I'm surprised they'll let me near all those knives."

"I'll be with you at all times. Besides, you're not planning on running amok brandishing one, are you?"

"Only if necessary." Then, more loudly: "That was a *joke*, Malachai."

Ydrel looked at the empty, stainless-steel kitchen as if it were heaven. "This is so great! We can talk freely here, too. How did you talk Malachai into it?"

"It wasn't easy." In fact, the display of mother-may-I he'd had to show still had his teeth on edge. Even harder had been convincing Malachai that his humility was genuine without looking like he was trying to convince him of anything. But he'd done it. *Score for the Joshaham.*

He noticed Ydrel giving him an odd look. "Never mind. Let's see what they got, then we'll decide what to make."

What they had was an abundance of everything. Overwhelmed, the two finally decided on grilled cheese sandwiches and tomato soup. While Joshua sliced cheese and buttered the bread, Ydrel set a pot of water and milk on the gas range to boil.

"Thought we were making tomato soup. Where are the tomatoes?"

"We'll use tomato sauce, but you get the water and milk boiling first. Then you put in some baking soda. *Then* you add the tomato. This is an old family recipe. No messing with the order, got it?" When the intern looked up, he found him staring intently at the flames. "Something up?"

"What kind of plant doesn't burn?" He didn't seem to be addressing the young intern, but Joshua answered anyway.

"All things burn if you get them hot enough. Why?"

"So it's a matter of density?"

"I'm not good at hard science, but I think it has to do with chemical composition, too. And green wood is harder to burn than dry wood. Why the interest?"

"Something Tasmae said this weekend, about growing fortress walls...Does that sound cr—odd?"

"Crud?" Joshua teased, then answered more gently. "It's not as odd—or as crazy—as you might think. There's a *Star Trek* episode where an alien culture grew its starships. And look at what we're doing now, stuff our ancestors would've never imagined. You know, totally fireproof materials would be really useful. If you could figure out how to do it, you and I could make a fortune. We could even afford our own housekeepers."

"'You and I'?"

"And what were you going to do with the idea except brood that someone might think you're hallucinating? Someone's got to be the moving force in this duo. And you may as well get used to the word crazy. People say it a lot; it's not a bad word, you know."

"It is here. But thanks for at least pretending to take me seriously. The water's boiling. What do I do next?"

Joshua reached into a drawer. "Half-tablespoon of baking soda, then the tomato sauce. This is a measuring cup. Use this kind for liquids. There's another kind for flour and dry goods."

Ydrel snatched the cup from his hands. "I do know some stuff. My mother used to let me help her."

"Okay. So, um, when did she die?"

"A long time ago."

Joshua waited, but Ydrel didn't elaborate, just grabbed a large can of tomato sauce from the back shelf.

"And your dad?"

Ydrel answered with an annoyed tone. "No idea. Aunt Katie and Uncle Douglas are my guardians. okay? Now, how much tomato sauce do I add?"

Despite the safe surroundings, Ydrel didn't seem to want to talk. They made small talk through lunch. Finally, while they were doing dishes, Joshua took the initiative. "How are things going with "She-Who.""

"Tasmae." Deryl glanced at him sideways with mild annoyance.

"Okay. The Tasmae-nian She-Who Devil," he said, and Ydrel laughed. "So? No more calling you at odd times or making obscure demands?"

"Well, every answer just breeds more questions, so we're going back over the stuff I already taught her, tactics and weapons and stuff." He dried the last dish and put it on the rack. "So what's next?"

By his tone, Joshua knew he wasn't talking about chores. "Why don't you read that Lackey book first?"

"The one about the empath? Oh, come on, you practically shouted it at me. What's a fantasy novel going to do for me?"

"In that one, and in the sequel, she's learning to control her ability and block things out and such." The intern shrugged. "I just thought there might be some hints in there you could use. I mean, really, psychic abilities are a little beyond my experience."

"What?" Ydrel sneered. "You can't just apply that NLP you swear by? I thought it was one-size-fits-all-psychoses."

Joshua could hear the hurt under Ydrel's sarcastic tone and paused to choose his next words carefully.

Screw it. The world doesn't revolve around him. "Yeah. I could use NLP. We could do it right now. And if we got caught, I'd lose my internship—maybe even any chance of getting my license. You tell me: Is Malachai that influential?" He barely paused. "Even if he isn't, I need this job so I can pay for college next year and have time to concentrate on my grades. I'm here for two and a half months. Why don't you give me a couple of weeks to convince the staff I know what I'm doing, and maybe I can broach the subject professionally and we can do it right. okay?"

"Yeah, okay."

Maybe I overdid it. "Here," he said, handing Ydrel the knife he'd used to cut the sandwiches into triangles. "Second drawer to your left."

"You're trusting me with a knife?"

"Any reason I shouldn't? Put it in its sleeve; it's in the drawer."

Nonetheless, Joshua watched him. Ydrel pulled open the drawer. Then he stopped, staring at its contents.

"Uh, problem?" Joshua asked.

For a moment, Ydrel didn't answer. Then, "Just how many knives does one kitchen need?"

Joshua laughed. "Who knows, here? A bachelor needs four: one for cooking, one for bread, and two for eating."

"Why two?"

"Gotta have one for your date. Women are funny that way. C'mon. I've only got an hour before I have to meet with Edith, and your room is a mess. Most women don't go for that, either."

"Like that's ever going to happen," Ydrel groused as he put the knife in its sleeve and shoved it into the drawer. "Let's go tackle my room. You're going to help, aren't you?"

"I said I would, didn't I?"

Cleanup went quickly, although Joshua's idea of "helping" was little more than bossing Ydrel around as he did the folding, dusting and sweeping.

"Big help you are," Ydrel complained as he scrubbed the toilet. At least Joshua wasn't making him use a toothbrush.

Joshua shrugged from where he leaned against the bathroom wall. "It's how my mom 'helped' me. I showed you how to fold a shirt, but you're a big boy—you should know how to handle a rag. And don't forget to wipe behind the back."

Because of the microphones, they kept the conversation casual, mostly about life in the real world. Joshua told him about college and life in the dorms.

"Aunt Kate and Uncle Doug sent me to boarding school. I'd hate the dorms," Ydrel declared.

"But you can't judge one based on the other," Joshua said as they cleared, then made the bed. "For one thing, everyone's starting to outgrow those cliquish games. For another, you have real freedom. You can come and go as you please, no curfew, no one telling you what to do. Last year, I spent more time at my girlfriend's apartment than I did in my dorm room."

"That how you lost your scholarships?" Ydrel asked.

A wave of sick fear struck him suddenly, like a punch in the stomach.

"How'd you know I—? Ydrel, what's wrong?"

Ydrel braced himself against the bed, his eyes shut tightly in furious concentration.

He and Ruth. Standing in a line. Silent. Scared. Gripping each other's hands for strength. A haughty, sneering blond man in uniform approached. Cold blue eyes looking Ruth up and down, undressing her in his mind. She looks down but stands her ground, squeezing his hand to keep him from moving. The soldier's smirk grows and he speaks.

"Ydrel...?"

"Shut up!"

"Diesen." Another soldier grabs her arm.

"Nein!" he yells, and grabs for her with both hands as the soldier pulls her away.

No! This isn't me!

Her hand rips from his.

"Ydrel?"

No! These are NOT my memories!

Two soldiers hold him back. She screams for him. "Isaac!"

Come on, Ydrel. This isn't you. Open your eyes. You're safe. In the asylum. Joshua is here. Open your eyes, focus on him.

Ydrel forced his eyes open. Joshua stood before him, a hand gentle but firm on his shoulder, his eyes full of concern. Slowly the vision dispelled, though it didn't quite leave.

"Ydrel, what is it?"

"Isaac." Without another word, he strode from his room. He barely registered Joshua's exasperated sigh as the intern followed.

The mini blinds in Isaac's room were slanted against the afternoon sun, casting the room in a kind of twilight. The old man lay in his bed, a frail figure thrashing weakly against nightmares, moaning softly.

Ydrel stepped beside him. Joshua took a spot to one side, where he could closely watch them both. Ydrel looked at the man with a mixture of anguish and pity. He took several deep breaths, like a swimmer about to dive deep. Then he squinted, and Joshua could almost imagine him throwing some kind of mental energy at the other man. Abruptly, Isaac stopped his struggles.

Ydrel reached out and shook his shoulder roughly and started jabbering at him in a language Joshua didn't recognize.

Chapter Fourteen

By the time Ydrel reached Isaac's room, he'd all but forgotten Joshua's presence. This was a new memory, with new pain. He hadn't thought the old man's memories could get worse, yet the anguish, heartache and humiliation as he saw his *(Isaac's, not my)* wife torn away from him still threatened to overtake his defenses. The phantom ache in his solar plexus from when the guard struck Isaac was pale by comparison.

He wanted to run, to curl up in a ball and hide from this new onslaught, but he knew that wouldn't do any good. Isaac's pain was just too strong. As he paused near the old man's side, he wanted to cry. For Isaac. For himself.

Instead, he composed a new scene.

We're in a broken-down shack. The setting sun sends thin shafts of light into the room, the only light we can afford for fear of detection. Still, we're safe, if not especially comfortable. You're lying in a thin cot, exhausted, but dreaming.

He fixed the scene in his mind and pushed it into the mind of the old man. Then, he shook him.

"Wake up, Isaac," he hissed. "You're having a nightmare. Do you want to tell the world we're here? Wake up!"

Isaac started, blinked at the psychic. "Gideon! Ruth. They took her. We have to find her. We must!" He tried to sit up, but Ydrel pushed him down firmly.

"You're not going anywhere. You are too weak, and they are still looking for you. My men are working on it. You have to trust us."

Isaac let out a shuddering sigh. "Who's this?"

Ydrel blinked, remembering the intern beside him. "The American I told you about."

The old man glared suddenly at Joshua and spoke in accented English. "When is your country going to help put an end to this insanity? How many must die?"

Caught off guard, Joshua managed to sputter, "We're...uh...working on it. Really."

"And right now, there's something else he should be working on. *Right*, Joshua?"

The young client turned to face him, and Joshua got a good look at his eyes. Despite the dimness of the room, his pupils were contracted to mere pinpoints, and—were they jittering? Or was that a trick of the light? No, there it was again. Just like the other night.

"*Right*, Joshua?"

"Oh. Yeah. Right. You'll be okay?"

But Ydrel had already turned back to Isaac, brushing back the old man's hair as he whispered to him in what Joshua now realized was probably Yiddish or some German dialect.

Joshua left the room, shutting the door gently behind him. He stood for a moment blinking, disoriented as much from the change in mood as from the change in lighting. He had the feeling he was supposed to be doing something but couldn't think what. His thoughts kept returning to what he'd just witnessed.

What was with those eyes? Serious weirdness. He loitered at the door a moment longer, trying to remember if he'd ever seen or read anything about a person's eyes reacting like that. *It was almost like he wasn't seeing the real world at all but looking at something in his mind. Or like his mind was (unconsciously?) trying to block out outside stimulus.*

He remembered reading, somewhere, about predatory birds whose eyes did similar things. Pinning? Pinpointing? Where had he read that, and did it apply? He shook himself and headed toward the nurses' station. He at least needed to tell them about Isaac and Ydrel, and maybe if Sachiko was on duty, he'd ask her if she'd ever noticed anything like that before.

He found her looking over logs at the duty station. Just the sight of her improved his mood. He leaned over the high desk and gave her his most winning smile. "Hi."

She barely glanced up. "Hi, yourself," she snapped. "You'd better work on keeping track of time."

"Pardon?" He glanced at the clock. 2:15. Memory hit. "Oh, no! Edith!"

Sachiko scribbled her initials on a page. "She called just a minute ago to see if we'd seen you. Better be glad it wasn't Dr. Malachai; he's a stickler for punctuality."

"I'm on my way. But first..." He told her about Ydrel and Isaac, omitting his observations for now. He could ask her about the eye thing later when they had more time. Maybe he'd stay past dinner.

Sachiko set down the logbook and listened. When he was done, she sighed and murmured a couple of words in Italian. "I've been expecting something like this. I don't think he'll be with us much longer."

"Who? Mr. Goldstein?" Monique asked as she came from the glassed-off office. "I thought he was getting better. We had a great conversation just yesterday. He played a mean game of hearts, too."

"Brief periods of lucidity often precede death," Sachiko replied, her mouth a thin line. "I'm going to talk to Dr. Malachai again about contacting the family. It's been over a month since they've visited."

Monique sighed. "Not that he recognized any of them the last time. Alzheimer's. What a rotten way to go."

The door to Edith's office was open, but he knocked gently anyway. "I'm sorry I'm late, but something unusual happened." He launched into his story, starting with Ydrel's odd behavior in his room and ending with the strange movements of his eyes.

Dr. Sellars listened intently. Only after he'd finished did she seem to notice he was still standing, and she waved him toward one of the chairs. Even after he took a seat on the couch, she sat quietly thinking for a few minutes longer. "He hadn't been with Isaac earlier?"

"I don't know. Not since noon when I was with him."

"He couldn't have heard anything?"

Joshua shook his head. "We were in the kitchen, then in his room with the radio on."

"How could he have known? He must have picked up on some clues."

Joshua shrugged, then grinned. "Makes you wonder if there isn't something to his psychic abilities after all."

Edith returned the smile. "Don't let Randall hear you say that. It was a stretch just to get him to agree to the extra time. But I like the idea of cooking and cleaning lessons for Ydrel, and your work last week was exemplary. I never noticed that thing with the eyes. You're the closest thing we have to an expert here, with your NLP training. What do you make of it?"

"I don't know. I've never seen or read anything like it. With your permission, I'd like to talk to some people, mentors in the field, about it."

"Just remember patient confidentiality. We take that even more seriously here than elsewhere, given our clientele. You know, Joshua, I think we made a good decision with you, especially as far as Ydrel is concerned."

Joshua waved off her comment, bringing in a "good feeling" anchor similar to the one he'd built with Ydrel. He had also established it with Edith some time ago. It was a matter of habit with him, one that made him easy to get along with—even though it annoyed his mother, who often caught him in the act.

"Ydrel is an independent learner," he reassured the psychiatrist. "I doubt he'll have much trouble with the GED. He can probably CLEP a bunch of college classes, too. Any chance of arranging driving lessons?"

Now Edith laughed. "Now who's talking crazy?"

Hours later, Joshua had to admit he was feeling a little crazy. He'd just sent off several e-mails to people he knew in the field, describing the incidents with Ydrel and asking if they knew anything about a correlation between the unusual eye movement and supposed psychic abilities. His father would know whom he was talking about, but he thought he'd been general enough that he didn't violate any of the confidences.

Next, he'd done a web search with no luck. Maybe he'd ask his friend Taylor to do one for him. Taylor was majoring in journalism and had taken courses on finding information on the Internet. Of course, how could he ask his friend without sounding like an idiot?

I'll worry about that later, he decided. He stretched and looked at the clock. Almost 6:00. Just enough time to grab some dinner from the dining hall and head over to the staff dining area. Sachiko had long since established the dinner hour as her study time, and for the most part, the staff honored that by letting her have the room alone.

Suddenly, Joshua felt like a little like a heel for interrupting her studying, but after that uncomfortable week when they hardly spoke, and the way she'd snapped earlier, he wanted to make sure she wasn't mad at him again.

"If you don't mind, I'd rather be alone," Sachiko said as Joshua pushed his way through the door carrying a tray with dinner and two cappuccinos.

He almost turned and left, but something in the way her voice caught made him hesitate. She was hunched over the table, shoulders tight and curled in, no book to be seen. She hadn't even looked up to see who the interloper was. He walked in and set the tray down.

"I said—"

"It's okay," he interrupted, moving behind her and setting his hands lightly on her shoulders. "I got your back."

"Josh!"

She hissed tightly, and he braced himself for an on-slaught of fury. But it never came. Instead, she dissolved into silent sobs.

He stood behind her, saying nothing, just letting his hands rest gently on her shoulders. Finally, he felt her breathing begin to calm, and she sniffled. "Can you bring me a tissue, please?"

He fetched the box from the counter, then rummaged around for a clean dishcloth, which he dampened with cold water. Wordlessly, he passed it to her. She turned away from him, so he took the hint and sat down to eat while she composed herself.

"Thanks," she murmured as she pressed the cool cloth against her face. She took a couple of deep, cleansing breaths. "You know, this is why I'll never go into geriatrics."

Joshua stopped in mid-bite. "You mean Isaac?"

"No, no. I'm sorry, I'm not being very clear. No, he's fine, as fine as can be expected, anyway. For now, but..."

Again her voice caught, and she paused to swallow back tears. "He's not going to live much longer. I'd say a week. And there's nothing we can do about it."

"Has anybody contacted the family?"

"I spoke to Randall—Dr. Malachai—after he took that bad turn last week. He said he spoke to them and they were aware of the situation."

"But they aren't coming up," Joshua concluded.

Sachiko nodded. "And Dr. Malachai didn't want to disturb them again. So I called. I thought maybe they didn't...understand the immediacy of the situation."

Joshua grunted and took a bite of chicken before he said anything. He wouldn't trust Malachai to convey the full message either, not if it somehow might look bad for their institution. "And?"

Her already red eyes flashed with anger. "'I've been appraised of my grandfather's condition and am confident you're providing the best of care. I am a member of your board after all. I've penciled in a date when I can get away for a visit.' His grandfather is dying and he's penciling in dates. I'm sure he'll be calling Dr. Malachai to complain that one of the nurses is interrupting his oh-so important day."

"Will you get into trouble?"

She waved away the thought. "I can handle Randall. What I can't handle is watching that poor man just die."

Joshua shrugged, laid a hand on hers. "It's kind of an occupational hazard."

She jerked away. "No! Nursing—medicine—is about fighting for life. Before I came here, I worked in the ER. Yeah, I know, people died. But we always did everything we could to save their lives. What can we do for poor Isaac?"

"We give him comfort. Give him the respect and dignity he deserves. And, when the time comes, we make sure he doesn't have to die alone. If his family can't do that for him, we can."

"That easy, huh?"

"No. That simple. It's never easy."

"You sound so sure of yourself."

He shrugged. "My best friend's mom is a hospice nurse. And my grandfather died at home. So, you know..." He shrugged again.

For a moment, they were silent, lost in their own thoughts: he, imagining her in the ER, cool yet intense as she worked over some desperately injured victim, saving his life, and only afterward surrendering to the heebie-jeebies. She'd make an amazing doctor.

She's just amazing now.

He's pretty amazing, Sachiko thought. In her mind's eye, she saw him at someone's deathbed, gentle, reassuring, holding the person's hand and telling him it was okay, something wonderful was ahead. He would believe in that something wonderful...

She caught him looking at her with a funny half-smile and quirked a brow. He looked away, pursing his lips, a sign she'd learn to recognize in him as embarrassment.

"That cappuccino sure smells good," she ventured to distract him.

With a genuine smile, he handed her the second cup.

She blinked in feigned surprise. "What? You taking mind-reading lessons from Ydrel now?"

"Not really." Joshua laughed. "I...thought you might use it, considering what's going on with Isaac and all."

"He's a dear man." She took a sip and sighed. "But I don't want to talk about that anymore, or I might cry again. Tell me about your weekend. Did you have fun?"

"I guess so. Sunday, I went to church, then found a Barnes and Noble. Got Ydrel some stuff to study for his GED. Saturday I mostly cleaned my landlady's yard. She's getting on in years and can't do a lot around the house, so she said she'd cut my rent if I did the garden and fixed things up. Shutters and stuff. Not real complex, but expensive if you hire someone."

"Aren't we paying you enough here?'

Once again, he pursed his lips and looked away before answering. "I...let my grades slip last year and lost my scholarships. I'm really hoping to make enough money over the summer that I can pay for college and just concentrate on studies this year. Really."

The last "really" let her know there was a lot more to this story, but he wasn't ready to disclose it yet. She let him off the hook. "Fair enough. So. How do I look?"

He gave her a look that would have been more appropriate on a date than at work, but all he said was, "Uh, kind of blotchy around the eyes and nose," and she was glad she couldn't read minds.

"Okay. Drastic measures time." After another quick swallow of coffee, she went to the freezer and pulled out a bag of frozen vegetables. She pressed it to her face. Joshua noticed there was white tape across it that said: ICE PACK. DO NOT EAT.

Joshua laughed. "I thought my mother was the only person who did that."

When she spoke, her voice was muffled. "Oh, it's an old nurse's trick. Frozen peas make the best ice packs. Are you free this Saturday night?"

Saturday night? He was glad that her eyes were covered by her cold pack so that she didn't see his jaw drop. He took a second to compose himself, hoping she would think he was mentally running over his schedule. When he spoke, he did his best to sound casual. "Sure. Evenings are free. What did you have in mind?"

"I'm having a dinner party at my place. I've invited nine people; you'll know most of them from here. Dress is Newport casual: slacks, nice shirt, but not too fancy. It'll start at 6:30, with dinner at seven. Want to come?"

She turned to put away the peas, which gave him a chance again to compose himself before answering.

"I'd love to. Should I bring anything?"

She sat down again and took a long sip of cappuccino. "No food. I love to cook big, fancy meals. I used to help out in my father's restaurant before I started med school. However, all my guests must provide the evening's entertainment."

"O-ho. Sing for my supper?"

"You've got it, although we've had a lot of different things: board games, comedy. Dr. Malachai will probably do magic tricks. He's actually rather good. Do I look better now?"

"Mm-hm."

"Hope so. I've got to get back. I'll e-mail directions to you tonight. Thanks for the coffee. And..." She set her hand on his. "Thanks."

"I thought I might find you out here," Sachiko said as she came up behind Ydrel. Her shift had just ended, and she'd gone to check on the young client before she went home. Finding his empty room, she'd headed for the inner courtyard, where she knew she'd find him reclined on one of the lounges, brooding at the stars.

She took a seat next to his. "You okay?"

He shrugged. "Yeah. I guess. My head hurts, still. Sach—is it...okay...to wish that, that..."

"That he'd die? I don't know. It is, and it isn't. It's not fair that he should suffer."

Ydrel spoke in a whisper. "We hurt so bad. It's not anything you can drug him against, either. I can't shield myself. I'm not sure I want to. If I did, he'd be hurting and alone."

"You've been a good friend," was her only reply. She hadn't doubted his psychic powers for years, since the night he'd caught her in the supply room stealing medicines with the intention of killing herself.

She'd been on the midnight shift then, and everyone had been asleep. Even her coworker had been nodding off at the desk. Ydrel had been awakened by her acute anguish and had run to the usually locked room where they kept the medicines, where he'd found her mixing herself a deadly poison, pulling a little of several narcotics so that the loss hopefully wouldn't be noticed until it was too late.

He'd known exactly what she'd been thinking: *Not that anyone notices what I do, anyway*. For two years, she'd been carrying on an affair with the chief psychiatrist and no one had noticed, much to Malachai's satisfaction. Last month, when morning sickness sent her running to the head at four o'clock in the morning faithfully for two weeks, no one noticed. No one noticed anything unusual in her sudden absence, nor in her change in demeanor when she returned to work; they were all content to attribute it to the "flu" Dr. Malachai had mentioned she was getting over.

"I noticed," he'd said, and she whirled, nearly knocking down the cart with its many bottles.

"Ydrel, you shouldn't be here." She had tried to sound stern.

"Neither should you," he'd responded, and bit back a sob. "Sachiko, I'm sorry! I know what a manipulative monster Malachai can be, and I didn't say anything. I was, I don't know, scared. I swear, I didn't think he'd talk you into—"

He couldn't say it. He looked at her stomach instead.

"What are you talking about?" she whispered.

"I'm sure you'll make the best decision for yourself," Ydrel said, in a perfect imitation of Randall's voice. "I do love you, Sachiko dear, although I think it's in our best interests that this not happen at this point of our relationship."

Sachiko slid to the floor.

"Sachiko!" He knelt in front of her and took her hands.

"He dumped me," she whispered. "He took me to the clinic." She laughed a bitter, angry laugh. "He took me to the clinic, and then his mother called and he left. He spent the whole weekend with her in Boston. Called me once. Told me I had acted responsibly, and if I could take my shift, he'd arrange for someone else to finish the week. Like it was a big favor."

He felt the bile rising in her throat as if it were his own. Her self-hate bombarded his senses until he was dizzy. Her words swam in his mind: *stupid, selfish, worthless—*

"No, you're not!" Ydrel cried. "You're wonderful and compassionate and the best thing that's happened to this place in a long time! I trusted him, too, Sachiko. I'm psychic, and I believed his lies! And he's just doing the same thing again, manipulating you, trying to make you leave. You're not useful to him, so he wants to get rid of you—just like he'll try to get rid of me if I ever stop being useful to him.

"Please, please don't let him win. You're too good a person, and you've done so much for us here. You have no idea what that orderly Roger used to do to us before you took over the shift. And you always take time for us, and you always know what to do. And—and you're my friend. The only one I've got in this whole damn place."

He bowed his head and sobbed openly. "I'm so sorry I didn't warn you. I was stupid, scared of Malachai. Please don't kill yourself. If you do, I will, too, I swear. I can't live knowing you'd— it'd be like I killed you."

"Stop it. This isn't your fault."

"Maybe not." He looked up again. She stared past his head, and he sat up so that she had to look him in the eye. "Maybe not all of it. But it's not all your fault either. Don't let him make you believe that."

"But I—" she started and hadn't been able to make herself finish. Then the tears had come, and they'd leaned into each other and cried together.

Between sobs, he promised to use his abilities to protect her. And he had. And he would.

"You know," Ydrel ventured suddenly, "you should tell Joshua."

"You've lost me. Tell Joshua what?" The "I-don't-believe-this" tone of her voice said she knew quite well what he was saying. Still, he answered.

"Everything. What you're feeling. What happened before. Everything."

"And just what am I feeling?"

She knew as well as he did, and knew he knew. He sidestepped the issue. "I trust him, Sachiko."

The realization hit, and he laughed. "I haven't trusted anybody except you since, I don't know, since before my mom died, I guess. Except Malachai, of course, but that was blind trust, and I learned my lesson. It took a year to truly trust even you. And here's this teenage intern who only half-believes I'm not some deeply disturbed person, and I trust him right off the bat."

"He has that effect on people, doesn't he?"

He could feel as well as hear her mind's suspicions vying with her heart's desires. He decided to tip the balance.

"Sach, he's not like Malachai. I could never read Malachai. I don't think anyone can. So I took him at face value, like an idiot."

"You weren't an idiot. You were desperate for help, and he was offering."

He waved the reassurance away. "It doesn't matter. The point is, I can read Josh. *Have* read Josh. He's genuine. He says what he means and believes what he says."

When she didn't reply immediately, he knew he'd won his point. Finally, she stood up. When she spoke, it was with annoyance, but he could see her smile in the dim light from the windows. "How'd we get on this tangent, anyway? I'm almost thirty, and he's just a kid, and even if I was thinking about it, I'm trying to get my medical degree in my time off. I don't have time for this. Put your matchmaking away and let's get you tucked in, *capice*?"

Italian. She hardly ever spoke Italian anymore. He bit back his smile. "Yes, ma'am."

Chapter Fifteen

"Well," Joshua said as he handed Ydrel back his graded practice test, "I don't think you'll be having any trouble with the GED."

It was Friday, and that morning, Ydrel had announced that he'd read the GED book and, if that was all there was to it, he was ready for the test today. So Joshua arranged for someone to monitor him—Floyd volunteered—while he took a timed practice test. A little more than half the allotted time later, Floyd had quietly called Joshua out of another group session (much to Joshua's relief) to show him the test.

"I don't think he got one wrong," the orderly commented, and he'd been right.

Ydrel snorted and leaned back in his chair, a smug smile across his lips. They were in his room; Joshua was seated at the clean desk, and Ydrel was in the comfortable sitting chair, his back to the door. "How hard can it be with a photographic memory?"

"Photographic memory, eh? You didn't happen to look at the answer keys, just by accident?"

Ydrel didn't answer and Joshua purposely didn't look at the young man's face. "Anyway, I'll bring a couple more tests on Monday for you to try. The practice never hurts. In the meantime, rack your brains and write down everything you've ever learned, or projects you've ever done, like your art. Books you've read, stuff like that. We'll put it into a transcript/résumé you can use for college applications or job hunting. How are you at writing? Real writing, reports and such, I mean."

Ydrel thought for a moment, then smiled in bemusement. "I don't know. I haven't really written anything since I was...fourteen, maybe? Wow. I used to write long letters to my Aunt Kate, but I stopped *that* pretty fast."

"Really? How come?"

"Oh, I found out the psychs were reading them and putting copies in my file for further analysis. So much for privacy, eh?" Although he spoke lightly, the young client's eyes were dark with anger.

Joshua couldn't help agreeing. "Man, that stinks. Let's start with something easy, then."

He scanned the books Ydrel had lined up on the shelf and pulled down a thick hardback with a yellow cover and a Greek-sounding name: *The Landmark Thucydides.* He was taking History of Ancient Greece in the fall; might as well let Ydrel help him get a head start. He scanned the back cover and asked, "Finished this one yet?"

"I had some extra time this week."

"Smart aleck." *The Peloponnesian War. That was mentioned in the class summary. Score one for Joshaham!* "Okay, then, give me an eight-page summary by Tuesday."

"What? Are you cr—kidding?"

"Crazy. The word you are reaching for is 'crazy.' And, no, I'm serious. College profs just love eight-page papers. Don't ask me why. It's probably closer to sixteen longhand, unless you want to use a typewriter, double-spaced. Obviously, you summarize the main points, leave out a lot of detail—"

"The text's five hundred and fifty-four pages long!"

"Well, see there, Mr. Photographic Memory? There's one detail you can leave out. Unless, of course, you think it's germane, like 'This was five hundred and fifty-four pages of the most painfully narrated—'"

"Forget it. You can't expect me to condense the whole book into a few pages."

"Why not? The editors did it in one." Joshua held up the book jacket.

"Who cares?" Ydrel flared. "Playing school and writing stupid book reports isn't going to get me out of here, so why bother?"

Joshua sighed and laid the book down with great care. Then he turned to face the angry boy. Keeping half an eye toward the door, he looked at Ydrel and spoke in low, serious tones.

"Now, you listen to me. I came here to learn and practice psychology, not to play best-friend-nurse-maid-teacher to some spoiled patient who just happens to be close to my age. I'm putting in a lot of extra hours at night so I can devote a good percentage of my day to you, and in my off-time, I'm finding you books and materials I think you need to make it on the outside. I'm offering to build you a transcript and portfolio you can use for college or career—and believe me, that's no easy task."

Ydrel gaped at him. Good. He had his attention. He pressed on, one hand on his hip, using the fact that he was standing to look down at Ydrel without looming. Dominant, but not aggressive.

"Edith didn't ask me to do this, you know. I'm not sure what she had in mind, but I'd guess it was more like being a sympathetic ear or playing catch or something, and I'd say you've had plenty of that."

"Hey!" Ydrel protested, but Joshua wasn't about to give him a chance to say more. He held up his hand in the classic "stop" signal, and Ydrel pressed his lips together.

"You want to get out of here? Fine. It's time to stop whining and start working. Dr. Malachai is not the only person in charge of your fate. There are at least four psychiatrists involved in your case to some degree. There's the support staff. What about your aunt and uncle? They pay the bills; they can arrange for your release or transfer anytime.

"Are you telling me that Dr. Malachai can overrule all of them, all the time and in concert? Then maybe you ought to think again about your paranoia. I meant it when I said that no one needs to convince people you're nuts; you do a fine job of that on your own."

Joshua watched as Ydrel slouched and pulled his knees up—chagrined, sure, but Josh figured he'd felt like this before. Hadn't changed his behavior, though.

Joshua crossed his arms and put his weight on one leg. He gestured with an open palm, however. Skeptical, but willing to give Ydrel another chance.

"If you want people to believe you can cope out in the real world, then you need to act responsibly in here. I can help you with that. But if you want to treat this like some game, that's fine, too. Gnaw my ear off with your gripes while we play Disc Golf three times a week. That'll make you happy, that'll meet Edith's criteria, and that'll free up a lot of time I can devote to my studies and to patients who are serious about healing themselves."

He leaned back, bracing himself against the desk with his hands, giving Ydrel time and space to think about what he'd said. Nonetheless, he kept his gaze steady and his features neutral and open on his silent, downcast friend.

C'mon, he urged silently, though he didn't let his face reveal his thoughts, *don't run on me. Fight or talk, but don't run this time.*

When Ydrel did look up, his eyes were damp with tears. "I thought we were friends."

"We are," Joshua replied matter-of-factly. "That's why I'm being straight with you. I could have just given up on you instead, you know. So, what'll it be? Work or play? Or if you want time to think..."

"No. I, I want to get out of here." He sighed deeply, rubbed his eyes, then wiped his palms on his jeans before thrusting his right hand toward Joshua. "Let's try it your way."

Joshua smiled and they shook on it.

"But, Joshua, I don't know how to write a book report."

"Really? You never did one in that fancy private boarding school of yours? No wonder my mom home-schooled me." He turned back to the desk and Ydrel moved to look over his shoulder. "All right, first you need to decide what you think the most important part of the book is. There are a couple of ways to do that..."

"Sachiko, can I ask you a question?"

"Why not? You're overdue, anyway." Sachiko looked up from her books and smiled at the young man who'd made it part of his routine to join her in the nurse's lounge for dinner. Most of the time, he brought in a book or a case study and they passed the time in silence, but he'd obviously pegged her as someone he could count on for honest answers. It was flattering, but sometimes disconcerting. He could ask some real zingers.

From the way he tightened his lips and glanced away, this would be one of them. "I'm sorry. I don't mean to be a bother—"

"When you become one, I'll let you know. What's up?" She took the opportunity to open up her dinner of sushi and rice.

"What were you guys saying about me at the nurses' station this afternoon?"

She paused, California roll halfway to her lips. "Oh. Noticed, did you?"

"When you hear your name, then conversation stops when you approach, it's kind of a give-away."

"Don't worry about it. Just a couple of nurses acting immature. I was putting a stop to it when you came by." She took a bite, hoping he'd take the hint and be satisfied with that.

He wasn't. "I heard Ydrel's name, too. If people are saying things about my work with him, I need to know, if only to decide how to respond."

"Oh, no! That's not it. Everybody thinks what you've been doing with Ydrel is great. And not just Ydrel. Carter Doleson. Dr. Hoffman may be bragging about how he, with your assistance, has achieved a 'long-worked-for breakthrough,' but some of us know better. And what you did with Isaac. Oh, Josh, I don't think you realize what a load you've taken off us nurses, and I don't just mean workwise."

Joshua shrugged. "It wasn't anything big."

"Yes, it is." He'd set up a schedule for people to sit with the dying man. The staff—and some of the more stable clients—quickly rallied to fill the day, so that someone was always with him, whether playing games, talking, or just quietly reading in a corner of the room. The nurses had to give the volunteers a few instructions on what to watch for and, for those who were up to it, how to help him to eat and use the bedpan, but in the long run, it freed them from time and worry. Joshua had also printed out some information about Alzheimer's that he'd found on the Internet.

He smiled. "Everybody's pitching in, after all. I'm glad it's taken some of the burden off you nurses."

He'd almost said *off you*. She could tell by the pause in his voice. Maybe he tried to tell himself he'd done it for Isaac, but if so, he was lying to himself, and she knew it. What was she going to do with him?

What did she want to do?

"So what's the joke, then?" he asked.

Sachiko sighed. He wasn't going to let this go. She really wished he would. She'd overheard some of the nurses talking about the "Joshua Show," and had come to learn that they meant the hour when he and Ydrel played Frisbee golf outside, or, more specifically, how Joshua looked in shorts and a muscle shirt. She'd just begun to ream them for their unprofessionalism when Monique interrupted, "Like we haven't seen you admiring the view!"

She'd been searching for some appropriately scathing reply when Joshua'd shown up.

"All right. This is so juvenile, and I was putting a stop to it, but some of the nurses have noticed you playing that Frisbee game—"

"Disc Golf."

"Yeah, with Ydrel, and well... This is silly. It's just that's you're young and attractive, and anyway..."

"Is that all? okay." With a shrug, he went back to the file he was studying.

"'Is that all?'" Sachiko laughed, her embarrassment forgotten. "What? This an everyday thing for you?"

"Not every day. I'm in a band, is all. I'm used to being looked at." Then he added, in a quiet, sly voice. "So you think I'm attractive?"

She decided to ignore the question. "In a band, eh? You going to play for us tomorrow?"

"Mm-hmm. Got to sing for my supper." He turned back to reading silently, but the small, impish smile on his face said her lack of answer was all the answer he needed.

Standing in front of the bathroom mirror the next evening, that grin returned to her mind, interfering with her ability to concentrate on her make-up.

Could he have taken her comments as implying a personal interest? Did she want him to? He had a good body—*okay, say it girl, a great body*—nicely muscled without being overdone, his skin rich and dark and almost glowing in the sun. She shook herself as if to break a spell and, sighing, picked out a lipstick. Her guests would soon be arriving.

Worst part was, that wasn't even the most attractive thing about him. If it had been, she'd have been able to ignore it; she knew plenty of well-built guys. No, what set him apart was the way he looked at her, steady and intently, wholly focused on her.

It wasn't just her, she told herself. He treated everyone with that kind of intensity.

Still, there was something...more...about the way he looked at her. And that smile...

Stop being silly, she chided herself. He was just flattered. After all, you're attractive, and young enough for your opinion to matter.

She stepped back and appraised herself in the mirror. Her silky black hair was swept up into a neat roll, with a few ends artistically escaping from the top. Into it, she had stuck a couple of black lacquered chopsticks decorated with green dragons. Her make-up, though moderate, was done with effect, with green eyeliner accenting the exotic shape and tilt of her eyes. The jade dragon earrings she'd found at a Renaissance festival adorned her ears.

Her black dress had a high collar, and its folds of silk covered her collarbone and draped over her shoulders before plunging daringly to the small of her back, perfectly framing her tattoo. An Oriental dragon of green and gold twisted its way across her back, so that its head rested just over and between her shoulder blades and the tip of its tail curled at the base of her spine. It had taken her forever to find a dress that showed it off to its fullest, and she'd had to run next door to get Cindy to help her with body tape that held it in place, but as she twisted to watch the fabric fall softly around her dragon, she knew it was worth it.

The dress ended just above the knee. Her silk stockings—the kind with the seam down the back—and the leather heels with the "alligator skin" accents on the toes, finished the ensemble.

Tonight was for the dragon.

It'd been a long time since she'd felt like this: daring, happy. Alive.

The doorbell rang, and she shoved all the cosmetics into a drawer and hastened out of the bathroom to answer it.

Despite her suggested "Newport casual," Joshua was dressed to kill. Above subdued black pants that looked like some kind of soft suede and were cut a little baggier than his usual, he wore a dark, short-sleeved shirt with a reddish-bronze shimmer. Its priest-like collar wouldn't take a tie; he wore a simple gold chain. He also had a small gold hoop earring in one ear. She could just smell his cologne, something spicy and musky that called her to lean closer.

She wanted to lean closer. Instead, she said, "Joshua, you're early."

Joshua leaned against the doorframe. He carried a black rectangular case in one hand and held the other hand behind his back. "I left myself lots of time. Even so, I thought I might be late."

"Oh? My directions weren't clear?"

"Sure. Mostly. Your highways, on the other hand..."

Sachiko laughed. "Oh, no! Did you miss the exit? How far did you go?"

"Not far. I drove over the grass median to turn around, so I spent the next couple of miles watching my rear-view mirror, expecting a cop to flag me down. Speaking of cops, just how many Dunkin' Donuts are there in Wakefield?"

Her hands flew to her lips, but she stopped herself before she could touch them and smudge her lipstick. "I didn't even think! There's that new one at Tower Hill and Patton, but you were supposed to turn at the next one, on Old Tower Hill. I think Rhode Island has more Dunkin' Donuts per square mile than any other state in the union. I should have drawn a map. Sorry."

"Don't be. I stopped to check a map by this cool flower shop, so..." From behind his back, he pulled out a bouquet of oriental lilies, birds of paradise and red anthuriums.

"Joshua, they're beautiful!" She took them from him, ignoring the thrill that shot through her when their fingers briefly touched. The suspicious part of her said, *He gets lost and thinks about buying you flowers? He's either that sweet or that interested.*

Despite herself, she knew which option she wanted.

"They reminded me of you." He smiled shyly. "Graceful and exotic."

She looked at him over the flowers. Their gazes held. *That interested.* For a moment, she was very sorry she'd invited anyone else. "Come on in. I'll just put these in some water."

She backed up to let him in, then turned toward the kitchen, giving him a full view of her back. She hadn't taken a step when she heard a loud *thunk!*

She glanced coyly over her shoulder. "Yes?"

Joshua's keyboard lay leaning against one of his legs. He was staring, open-mouthed. He closed his mouth, opened it again, closed it, then finally burst out, "Tell me it's real!"

She tried not to let her swell of satisfaction show. The dress had just paid for itself. "Every painfully inked inch. And?"

She still had her back to him. His eyes moved over her with a mixture of awe and desire that seemed more suited for the bedroom. Maybe he realized what his face was revealing, for he smiled—an embarrassed, tight-lipped smile—and finally said, "You are full of the most incredible surprises."

She couldn't help it. She laughed. "Go put your keyboard in the living room and have something cool to drink! Want a Coke?"

"Sure. Diet, if you have it. Do you want me to set it up?"

"If it'll tuck out of the way somewhere."

A couple of minutes later, Joshua was perched on a stool at the kitchen counter, a glass of soda in his hands. The flowers were in a crystal vase at the end of the counter, except for one bird of paradise, which Sachiko had cut and placed in her hair.

He offered to help, but she refused—the kitchen was her domain. Besides, she decided she liked having the physical barrier of the counter between them until he'd calmed down some.

She turned from the stove to catch his gaze flickering over her tattoo, and there was such fire in his eyes.

I like that fire.

The thought unnerved her, and she turned back to the meal until she felt herself calm down as well.

After a few minutes of comfortable—if electric—silence, he asked, "So, why'd you do it?"

"The tattoo?" She gave the fish one last turn, then set the pan on a back burner to warm. She'd rehearsed and used a dozen different answers to that question over the years, but she found herself wanting to be a little more honest with him. She wiped her hands with a towel and pulled the antipasto out of the refrigerator. "I was at a low point in my life. Really low. I'd just gotten out of a horrible relationship with Ra—my ex-boyfriend. I'd done some horrible things, things I never thought I'd do, and I wasn't even sure why. It was like I didn't know who I was anymore. I wasn't sure I ever knew; I was just drifting, doing what others expected of me, being the good nurse, the good student, the good girlfriend.

"Anyways, I decided it was time to do what I wanted, find out who I was. Explore a little, you know what I mean? See what I thought of my wild side."

She set the tray on the counter.

"I like it." He snagged an olive and popped it into his mouth.

"Oh, yeah?" Suddenly, she leaned over the counter. "And just what's your wild side?" she asked in a low, throaty voice.

She'd expected to embarrass him. She had a brief image of him choking on his olive. Instead, he chewed slowly, swallowed, then leaned over the counter so that his face was only inches from hers.

"I meant," he replied in a similar purr that sent delicious shivers down her spine, "I like yours."

"Oh."

He leaned closer. She closed her eyes.

The doorbell rang.

Chapter Sixteen

They leaned forehead to forehead, both chuckling ruefully. Five seconds later, the doorbell rang again. Sachiko glanced at the clock, though she really didn't need to. It was exactly 6:30. "That'll be Randall."

"Dr. Malachai? How do you know?"

Because after all these years, he has that same annoying way of ringing a doorbell once every five seconds like he's timing how long it took me to open it. She remembered the times she'd rushed to the door: first in anticipation, then as a game, finally with resentment.

"I told you he was a stickler for punctuality."

She thought she heard Joshua mutter, "His timing stinks, anyway," as she hastened to the door, and she had to pause to wipe the smirk off her face before she opened it.

"Good evening, Randall."

He wore an expensive white suit and carried a long box tied with a red ribbon. No one was bothering with casual tonight. "Good evening, Sachiko. Roses for a rose of a hostess."

He presented her with the box.

"Well, this is my night for flowers. Come in." She backed away and turned just as she had for Joshua, but if the dragon had any effect on Randall Malachai, he didn't show it. Instead, he focused on Joshua. "Ah, our young intern, and early! Hoping to impress our hostess, are we?"

Joshua didn't rise to the bait. Or perhaps he did, for he glanced at the two-dozen long-stemmed roses in the box Sachiko had opened and set on the counter. "Nice flowers, sir."

Sachiko was glad she was busy pulling out her stepladder—it meant that she had her face in the closet. *Now, boys...*

"Randall, there's a bottle of Gemini chilling in the pail. If you'd like, do the honors and help yourself to a glass. I'll just be a minute; I need to grab another vase."

"Want help?" Joshua asked.

She was about to refuse when the doorbell rang. "All right, then. There's a tall vase lying on its side in the cupboard above the fridge. If it needs dusting, give it a swipe with the dishrag?"

"Will do."

She swept past Randall, pretending to be oblivious to the irritation she could tell he was pretending not to feel.

From the corner of his eye, Joshua watched as Malachai gave Sachiko one fleeting glance before giving the wine his full attention. Was he annoyed?

He's annoyed, Josh answered himself. But at what? Me, maybe?

The thought made him grin.

The rest of the guests arrived quickly, and Sachiko set them to work bringing dishes of tantalizingly aromatic food to the table while she arranged the roses in a tall crystal vase he'd fetched.

She must have been cooking all day. There was antipasto and bruschetta for appetizers, cabbage soup, roasted vegetables, eggplant stuffed with pine nuts, and two kinds of pasta—one with shrimp and one with a meat juice glaze. There were also two platters. one with tuna steaks with flavorful bread crust topping, and the other with braised beef. He could feel his mouth watering.

She handed Joshua a long match to light the candles on the already-set table. Her table was as elaborate as the meal: an old, sturdy antique that, with all its leaves in, stretched from her dining area into the living room and was set with full place settings for ten. The china was a simple design of white with a frosted green edge. The glasses, however, were a stunning combination of green glass with pewter handles carved in medieval and fantasy themes: kings and queens, dragons and fairies. Although no more than two seemed to match exactly, they did run in roughly three different sizes and one of each size stood guard at each plate. Each plate had a tag with a person's name on it.

Joshua found his and stared, bemused, at the complex table setting.

"You do know which fork is for what?" Dr. Hoffman muttered teasingly to Joshua as he set a large steaming bowl of linguini on the table.

Actually, the three different glasses had him a little baffled, and there was more silverware set out beside each plate than he had ever seen in his life.

Still, he whispered back. "Don't worry. Just follow my lead."

Hoffman laughed.

Edith went around the table filling the large goblets with water. That shed some light on the mystery of the glasses, at least. "Sachiko, the table settings are amazing," she said.

"Thanks." Sachiko brought another bottle of wine from the refrigerator and motioned for everyone to find their seats. "The china and silverware are actually hand-me-downs from my dad's restaurant, but the glasses I pick up at the King's Faire and Renaissance Festivals along the coast."

Randall sat at one end of the table, with Sachiko at the other. Joshua was to her right, with a lady he didn't know on his right and her husband on her other side. They introduced themselves as Grace and Brent Fletcher, friends of Sachiko's from their motorcycle club. Brent, a large, graying man with a huge handlebar mustache, was an orthodontist. Grace had blonde highlights in her brown hair and sold real estate. She also had a tattoo: a double heart with their names and a date. Brent, she explained, had one as well; they'd done them together on their honeymoon to cement their vows.

Across from Joshua sat Dr. Hoffman (Myles) and his wife Brenda. She was pouring soda into one of her husband's glasses, teasing him that she drew the line at feeding him, so he'd better figure out which fork to use, and fast. Then she caught Joshua's eye and winked.

"So, did you get these glasses to match your tattoo, or visa-versa?" Hoffman teased.

His wife smacked him with her napkin, but asked, "Dear, your tattoo is just so elaborate. If you don't mind my asking, how much did it cost?"

Sachiko ignored the first question, but grinned with mischief as she answered the second: "A tennis bracelet."

Several guests laughed, but Randall looked disgusted. "You mean you hocked your diamonds to purchase a tattoo?"

"Oh, no. It was a straight-across trade. He also painted my Hawg, so it was a good deal. Everyone ready?"

They began with a moment of silence for those who wished to pray, then Sachiko announced the rules: first names only, no discussing work. After the sodas finished their rounds, the wine was passed around; Joshua was offered and accepted a little in his glass.

Sachiko explained that it came from Newport Vineyards. Apparently, the soil and climate of Newport was quite similar to Bordeaux, France.

Joshua took a careful sip. It tasted strong and spicy, but overall he couldn't tell much difference between it and the stuff they used in church. He set it aside in favor of a Diet Coke. The food, however, was incredible. He'd guessed she was a good cook by the lunches she brought in, but when faced with delectable dishes hot from the stove... It was several minutes before he joined in any conversation.

"I remember when I used to eat like that," Myles sighed theatrically.

"You still do. You just show it now," his wife retorted. "Joshua, did I hear correctly that you're from Colorado? What a wonderful state. I've always wanted to visit. Do you ski?"

"Umm-hmm." He swallowed the last of his *melanzane a beccafico* and took a sip of water. "My dad has part of his practice up in Vail, so we do a lot of snowboarding there. And I cross-country ski on our ranch."

"You have a ranch? How exciting! Do you have a lot of cattle?"

Joshua laughed. "Not really. We let it out to other ranchers in the area for their herds. In return, they take care of our horses and pay us enough to cover taxes. My great-great-grandfather and a couple of his buddies claimed it during the silver rush of the 1870s and 80s, but they never had much luck. He bought them out when they moved on north."

"So he never found anything?"

"Just enough for this." Joshua held up his hand. On his third finger, he wore a simple silver band.

Sachiko took his hand and pulled it closer to look. The band was old and thinned in some spots. Any pattern was long since rubbed off. "I'd wondered about this. That's all he found?"

"Yup. Just enough to make two rings. This one was his; the other he gave to my great-great-grandmother when he proposed."

"How romantic." She smiled, and for a moment, that smile was just for him. He was sorry when she pulled her hand away.

"And how is it that a black man in the end of the nineteenth century would be able to purchase such a vast tract of land?" Randall asked with friendly interest.

It was a question often asked of his great-great-grandfather, and later of his grandfather and father; Joshua had the story memorized. "Luck and brains."

He told them how his great-great-grandfather, a cowboy for the Texas "beef barons," herded cows from Young County, Texas, up to Cheyenne, Wyoming. He'd risen up in the ranks until he was entrusted with the company payroll, something that wasn't all that unusual even for a black man of that time. A pretty barmaid caused him to stick around Pueblo one year after the company had done exceptionally well, and he won a worthless claim in Westcliffe in a game of poker, so he started a small homestead, where he searched for silver.

Nonetheless, he kept working the cattle runs, and gradually, he was able to buy out his neighbors as they used up their resources in a futile search for wealth.

"Then, when he found that little bit of silver, he took it as a sign he should settle down, so he had a couple of rings made, married the girl, and lived happily ever after," Joshua concluded.

The conversation turned to other subjects then, and soon the food was eaten, and people were pushing away from the table with contented sighs. Sachiko quickly organized volunteers to clear and shorten the table and set out the desserts—*biscotti regina, dolce delle Monache*, and brownies—and plates, plus another bottle of wine, as well as carafes of coffee and hot water for tea.

Those who needed to set up props for their portion of the entertainment set to work doing so. A couple of people who protested that they didn't have any talent were told, "You ate my food; you pay my price," and directed to the long table behind the couch, where they would find a small stack of books of jokes and poetry and a list of karaoke songs.

Everyone drew numbers to determine order of performance. Joshua was last, so he loaded up his plate with goodies, poured a cup of coffee, and found a spot on the floor near the pillow Sachiko had set down for herself. Since she would want easy access to the kitchen, she had picked a spot that was in the back of the room and to one side, which suited Joshua fine. When everyone was focused on the show in front of them, he might be able to lean back and casually touch her arm. Their legs had "accidentally" brushed a couple of times during dinner, and the feeling had been electric.

When Sachiko came in with her coffee cup, she slipped out of her shoes and sat gracefully on the cushion, her legs folded beneath her. She gave him the briefest of glances, but it was enough.

Grace, who had protested her lack of talent and was subsequently drafted by Dr. Malachai to be his magician's assistant, had drawn the first slot, so they opened the show. He turned out to be pretty adept at sleight-of-hand, though Joshua's favorite "sleight-of-hand" came when Randall announced his "fiery finale" and had Grace dim the lights. Sachiko shifted position just enough that their fingers touched, and she spent the duration of the trick tracing lazy designs on his hand.

Even though he was staring at the makeshift stage the entire time, he had no idea what the candle trick was and didn't even realize it was over until Sachiko pulled her hand away to applaud and Grace turned the lights back on.

Randall graciously directed applause toward Grace, took a bow himself, then quickly packed his gear and stowed it near the door. Then he pulled up a dining room chair right behind Joshua and Sachiko, forcing them to abandon their private entertainment and pay attention to the acts the others had prepared.

A couple of people read poems. Dr. Jody Weaver claimed to be too awful at telling jokes or singing to take a turn but was finally coaxed to the front. Embarrassment made her scar stand out fierce and red while she told a funny and touching story about how she had come to own a large orange tabby cat named Belle. Afterward she sat down, shaking but smiling.

"I hate getting up in front of people," she said.

Monique, who was in the choir at her Baptist church, sang "Amazing Grace." Grace's husband told dentist jokes, "Thus ensuring," he said, "that I'm never asked to provide entertainment again."

"Don't be so sure," Myles Hoffman countered. "My turn's next, and you haven't heard anything yet!"

Myles' act was to take suggestions from the audience and construct incredibly horrible puns. Within five minutes, he had everyone groaning, and when Randall criticized his awkward combination of cheerleaders and cults (he'd finally come up with the Hoo-Ra Girls) and he replied, "Well, religious jokes are so hard to work into a convert-sation," he was forced off the stage.

"I think that leaves you, Josh," Sachiko said.

"And may you be better than the last act!" Danny, an accountant and another of Sachiko's biker friends, added as Joshua moved his keyboard into place.

"Anything's better than the last act," Brenda added. When her husband feigned heartbreak, she gave him a playful shove. "The real question is: Are you good enough to drive the memory of those awful puns from our minds, dear?"

"I'll see what I can do." Joshua played a few notes, warming up his fingers. He adjusted the volume, then asked, "Anything in particular?"

"Oh, my! What do you know?" Monique asked.

"Try me. I'm in a band at home. We've played at proms, churches, *quinceañeras*, even the State Fair."

"Quit bragging and sing one of your favorites," Sachiko called out, so he picked Ricky Martin's "She-bang." Encouraged by the applause, he sang another current song, then a third. When he paused, a couple of people cried, "more, more!" so again, he asked for requests.

"Do you know anything other than love songs?" Randall asked.

Joshua blinked. He hadn't thought about the content of the songs, just sang whatever had come to mind. Now he paused, changed the settings on the keyboard to a country-western theme and started with a twang, "Oh, Lord, it's hard to be humble—"

"Self-love song!" Myles shouted over the laughter.

"Ow! You're right!" He changed the settings again, this time to woodwinds and flutes and Native American drums.

"My best friend Rique is our lead singer and song-writer," he explained as he let his fingers play over the keys, filling the room with the mysterious, haunting tones that always made him think of the prairie and buffalo. "He's Mexican and Pojoaque Pueblo Indian, and very into his heritage: the sounds, the themes, the struggle of tradition and lore with modern myth and contemporary society. Anyway, this summer, he's working at the Pojoaque Pueblo in Santa Fe and writing music based on their songs and stories, and the challenges they face balancing old and new. He just sent me this one a couple of days ago..."

He sang a ballad about a young dancer: Tired of what he feels is the hypocrisy of performing ceremonial dances for photo-mad tourists, he leaves home and disappears into the desert, where he stumbles upon an ancient ruin. He sleeps there and is haunted by dreams of his ancestors, who urge him to go home, take up the dance, and keep their memory alive.

Take up the dance
the song must be raised
One God unites the spirits we praise
take up the dance
the world is renewed
by efforts of muscle, bone and sinew
Take now the chance
Take up the dance.

The last notes faded into a silence that was more rewarding than the most thunderous applause. Joshua ducked his head and tried not to grin too much.

Finally, Monique broke the silence. "Wow. So when are you going to record it?"

"Actually, we're meeting with an agent in New York next month. Rique writes a lot of mainstream stuff, too. Including love songs."

"Play something else he wrote," Sachiko urged.

So he sang "Where the River Flows and the Eagle Soars," a love song of sorts. It was, he explained afterward, for a contest for the Pueblo Economic Development Council, and so the boyfriend tries to convince his girlfriend to stay with him by singing the virtues of their great hometown.

"Of course, no one ever completely loves his hometown, so to offset all that saccharine, we got together and wrote this." He sang "Where the Mill Workers Strike and the Birds Crap," a look at the less pretty side of his home.

It was actually a rather funny song, and with laughter and applause, he was allowed off the "stage." Sachiko put on some music and people broke into groups, talking. Joshua wasn't particularly good at small talk and found himself returning again and again to the dessert table. He wasn't alone; soon, many of the plates were empty.

"Bring a couple of those over here," Sachiko called to him from the kitchen. He brought in one empty plate and one with a single brownie left, which he took for himself on the way. He started to put them into the sink, but she gave him a "You've got to be kidding look" that made his heart skip.

"You don't think that's all I made, did you? Look in the oven."

He pulled out the pan of warm brownies, and she handed him a bag of biscotti. While he cut the brownies into squares and loaded the plates, she uncorked another bottle of wine. He couldn't help but admire how the fabric of her dress shimmered over the curves of her body as she twisted the corkscrew.

She must have mistaken his gaze, for she held up the label so he could see it: a shark with the title "Great White."

"Another local, but it's won international awards. A nice white. What'd you think of the Gemini?" she asked, referring to the red wine they'd had with dinner.

Joshua shrugged. "I'm not much of a connoisseur. It didn't taste much different from the stuff in church," he admitted.

"Maybe you didn't taste it right," she said as she filled a glass. "Now watch and learn." She held the glass under her nose, then took a lazy sip, eyes shut, and let it move slowly over her tongue before swallowing. "First, you want to smell the wine, let its bouquet tease your senses. Then you take a slow, easy sip, not too much, just enough to let it wash over your tongue and make sure it stimulates all those taste receptors. Got it?"

He was glad his dark skin didn't show a blush. "Sure. Really."

She handed him the glass, and he did as she'd instructed. It tasted better than the heavy red, but the real surprise came after he swallowed. He blinked.

"That is nice," he said as he handed the glass back. "There's an aftertaste, like a mist, just kind of washes over you."

She smiled. "You noticed, too? I just love the afterglow. Do you want some?"

It took him a moment to realize she was talking about wine, and once again, he had to smash his lips together to keep his jaw from dropping. He seemed to do a lot of that around her.

"Well, really, I'm not legal—"

She snorted. "We're talking one glass of wine, not a bender. I won't tell."

"You're not the one I'm worried about. Dr. Malachai, on the other hand, talks with my father regularly."

"And this concerns you, how?" Dr. Malachai asked as he walked into the kitchen. He was apparently after the biscotti, for he grabbed one and leaned one elbow on the counter as Sachiko answered.

"You're not going to tell on him if he has a glass of wine at my party, are you?"

Randall spoke sternly. "He is underage, Sachiko. You shouldn't tease him that way."

"I'm not teasing," she said as she handed Joshua the glass she held.

"I'm not teased," Joshua replied as he took it.

Randall gave them both a disappointed look and left. Sachiko took the plate of biscotti in one hand, the bottle of wine in the other. "He'll tell," she said ruefully.

Joshua grabbed the brownies. "That's okay. He'd have to bring it up in casual conversation during the week. I talk to my parents tomorrow. I'll tell them first."

Sachiko laughed. She dropped off her plate, then went over to where Monique was admiring her collection of Japanese wooden dolls. Joshua lingered by the table, munching on a cooling brownie. He took another sip of the wine, but it didn't taste nearly as good as it had at first, so he set the glass aside.

"Finished it already?" Randall suddenly appeared by Joshua.

"No, sir," Joshua showed him the nearly full glass before setting it back on the counter. "Doesn't go very well with brownies," he explained.

Randall nodded. "You know, you do not need to drink in order to impress our hostess."

The idea was so preposterous and the tone so much like his mother's that Joshua couldn't help it; he laughed. "Sorry, sir," he said, partly choking on his brownie, "but if you think that about me, you really don't know me very well."

"Hm, perhaps not," the senior psychiatrist said in a tone that, for a moment, made Joshua doubt himself. Why had he accepted that glass of wine?

You were flirting, he told himself. Any excuse to touch Sachiko, even just a quick brush of her fingers, is reason enough.

He must have been grinning, because Randall gave him another of those disappointed looks and wandered away. Yep, he was definitely going to have to catch his dad first.

He hadn't realized how late it was until the first of the guests were saying their goodbyes. Sachiko directed everyone to the counter, where she had set out the dishes of leftover food along with a tall stack of carryout containers and told people to help themselves.

Those with kids or those who had to get up early for work or church the next morning made their exits first, with Randall somewhere in the middle of that wave. Others remained and offered to help set Sachiko's apartment back in order, and since she needed to study the next day, she gratefully accepted the help.

Joshua grinned to himself. Sometimes the Pillars of Survival paid off in more ways than one.

Sachiko didn't comment when the last guests left but Joshua remained, dithering over the last leaf in her table. Instead, she asked him to dry the larger serving dishes and hand them up to her as she stood on her stepladder to put them away on the high shelf. When the last one was done, she carefully turned to hop down—

Only to find herself grabbed by the waist and swept off.

She yelped in surprise, then laughed as her feet touched the floor. She was about to say something teasing and cutting, but she looked into his eyes. He had that same look of awe and desire as when he'd first seen her tattoo. Up close, it took her breath away, and her words died in her throat.

Then his mouth was on hers and his arms tightened around her back.

They kissed until she was dizzy in the head and weak in the knees and warm in between, and she found herself thinking how they might be more comfortable somewhere else, like the couch, or maybe the bed.

Maybe he was thinking along the same lines: suddenly he broke the kiss and breathed into her ear, "Sachiko, I really, really—"

With her tongue, she teased his earlobe, the one with the earring.

"I've really got to go!" He pushed away and all but ran to the door. He snatched up his keyboard; then, with one hand on the doorknob, turned and gave her a longing, starry-eyed look.

"You are the most...incredible...woman I've ever met."

Then he was gone.

Sachiko stood there, blinking at the closed door.

She leaned over the counter and laughed.

Chapter Seventeen

She was still laughing as she stood in a hot shower, washing away her make-up and the residue of adhesive left from the body tape. She hadn't gotten that kind of reaction from a guy since...

I've never had a guy react like that. He's so intense.

She thought about that kiss, the way his hands played over the tattoo on her back, the way his tongue just caressed the inside of her lips. Oh, yes, intense was a good word for Joshua Lawson. She had to admit her own reactions were pretty intense, too.

"It's just been a while," she told herself and turned the hot water to cool until her thoughts cooled, too. Then she left the shower, slipped into a silk nightshirt and snuggled into bed. She had turned up the air conditioning for the party and it was still a little chilly, but she didn't mind. She loved the weight of blankets on her.

Tonight, though, it got her thinking about other weights. She rolled onto one side and stroked the other half of the bed, remembering when Randall used to share it with her.

Randall had insisted they conduct their affair in her bed, saying it was much more romantic than anything his apartment could offer. She had always found his bachelor's condo cold and impersonal, so she hadn't objected; but when it ended, especially how it ended, she hadn't wanted anything to do with this bed. She couldn't throw it out—it had been her grandmother's, brought from Italy and handed down to her when she got a place of her own—so she'd finally settled on changing the mattresses, sheets and blankets, and re-arranging the furniture. It helped bury the memories, but sometimes her traitorous body would call up those old feelings and she would run, crying, to the shower, as if she could wash them away with soap and hot water.

Maybe it was the wine, more likely it was Joshua's kiss, but tonight, she was able to look at those old feelings more objectively.

Randall had had a talent for knowing exactly how to touch her, had made her feel the most amazing things, and had always been ready with pillow talk afterward.

They never revealed their romance to anyone at work—a fact that had bothered her at the time, but for which she was now grateful—but when they were together, he had been charming and witty, attentive to her needs. He'd always bought her "love trinkets," as he called them, many of which were quite expensive. By all objective standards, he was the perfect lover.

Yet how many times did those little "perfections" leave her feeling somehow less loved? How many times, after a night of passion and intimate talk, did she lie awake feeling emptier than before, and then guilty at her feelings of emptiness? Why had those expensive gifts left her feeling cheap? He had given her that tennis bracelet after their first night together.

"To celebrate the deepening in our relationship," he'd said.

She'd worn it, many times, but it always made her feel like a whore. Later, it had paid for her entire tattoo.

At the time, she thought something was wrong with her, and had been grateful for his understanding patience. When she realized she was pregnant she felt no joy, just horror over all the careful plans she'd ruined. Her first impulse had been to run crying to her parents, but shame held her back. She had been a 27-year-old nurse. How could she have been so careless? So she had run to Randall without thinking about what she wanted, only seeking his comfort and his advice.

He'd had the advice, all right. And cold comfort afterward.

Even when he was so horribly callous after the abortion, she'd defended him. Even though she'd tried to kill herself—thank God, Ydrel had stopped her—she stayed silent, and took Randall's offer of a few days off.

She didn't tell her parents, or even her twin cousins when they happened to drop by just as she was heading to the trash with the first box of things he'd given her. She only told them that it was over, and that she didn't want anything to do with him. She was even ready to quit school and her job, but her cousins quickly put a stop to that.

"You're going about this the wrong way, ya know what I mean?" Liz said. Vinny took the box out of Sachiko's hands and returned it to her apartment. "He's already treated you like dirt. Why you gonna go punish yourself? Sit down. We're gonna give you a little lesson in revenge, Luchese-style."

They'd spread everything out on her living room rug and sorted it according to value and how easy it would be to sell. Over pizza and wine, they brainstormed how to get rid of each item in a way Randall would hate.

Sachiko remembered him complaining about an abandoned building that had been taken over by squatters, not far from his parents' home in Boston; all the clothes and linens would go there. Liz wanted to give the lingerie to some streetwalkers, but Sachiko had a better idea: they spent half an hour cutting the fine silks and satins into rough squares for the quilting guild at Liz's church.

"I've never understood the lure of quilting," Sachiko said, mocking Randall's voice. "Spending hours over scraps when modern manufacturing produces superior products. Simply a matter of needing an excuse to gossip, I suppose."

They convinced her to stay in school but switch her degree from psychology—chosen so that she could go into private practice with Randall—to medicine, which was what she really wanted. And they kept her laughing for hours with their outrageous ideas for getting rid of her stuff. Somewhere past two, they started talking tattoos, and she'd known what to do with the bracelet.

Lying in her bed, she smiled, remembering Randall's horrified expression when she'd let it drop just how she'd used that particular "love trinket." Revenge, Luchese-style, was sweet.

Yet there had still been times when she had wondered if maybe, somehow, she'd just read him wrong.

Now, she knew different. The problem was in Malachai, not her. One kiss from Joshua had convinced her of that.

Randall was an accomplished lover. Accomplished. That was a good word for him. Sex was just another goal, and I was some kind of long-term— semi-long term—project. Joshua, on the other hand...

She lay on her back, reliving that kiss. Physical feelings aside—and it was pretty difficult to think past those physical feelings—that kiss left her feeling happier, more whole, than she'd felt in a long time. She could get used to kisses like that.

Then again, maybe I shouldn't. He's only here another, what? Two months? Then, he'll be back in school, surrounded by all those beautiful undergrads, and I'll be—hopefully—finishing med school and working 36-hour days in my residency. Two months isn't long enough to build a relationship. Is it really fair to tease him?

Then she remembered the wine and Randall's accusation. And Joshua's words: I'm not teased.

All right, Mr. "I'm-Not-Teased," we'll just play this by ear and see where it leads—as long as it doesn't keep leading out my front door. She chuckled, remembering his hasty exit. He was so pitifully cute!

"Pitiful. You're pitiful!" Joshua glared at his reflection in the bathroom mirror. "What kind of idiot runs like that?"

His reflection glared back, not offering any explanation.

He'd driven home in a kind of elated panic, hardly aware of anything other than the pounding of his blood and the memory of her lips on his, her tongue on his ear. He wasn't even sure how he'd made it home in the dark without getting lost. It was only by sheer reflex that he'd grabbed his keyboard before he left. He'd stowed it in the corner before throwing himself into a cold shower. It was several minutes before he was chilled enough to think clearly.

Oh, how he wanted her! He'd thought LaTisha had cooled some of those reflexes, and in fact, he hadn't really reacted to a woman, any woman, in over a month. Then, one kiss with Sachiko and it was all he could do to keep from sweeping her off her feet and carrying her to her bedroom.

Even worse, though, was what he'd wanted to say—what he'd almost said.

I'm so in love!

His reflection was grinning. He threw a towel at it.

He could still feel himself grinning like an idiot as he lay on his bed, and no amount of biting on his cheeks could stop it. He finally gave up and lay there, smiling into the dark. Even with his eyes open, he could see her face just before their kiss, the way her impish grin faded into the most beautiful mix of surprise and attraction. And when he shut his eyes and remembered her body pressed against his—

Easy, Josh. You'll need another cold shower.

But he was used to that. He could handle those feelings. What panicked him was the rightness of it, like someone had handed him a sheet of perfect music, and there they were, played in harmony.

Well, you can't sing it yet, Romeo, or it'll be the minute waltz. There is no way: you'll scare her; the lovesick pup routine would just about kill any semblance of professionalism you've got going at work; and Rique, he'd be livid! You told everyone you came here to drown yourself in work and forget about women. And what about Mom and Dad? No, you just don't say anything about—oh, man!—being in love. So you're just going to take it easy, play things by ear.

Madness Bound ✸ 175

He rolled over and punched his pillow. *Right. If she even wants to see me again after tonight. What an idiot I was! Oh, God, please let her want to see me again. She is so incredible, please let this be real!*

He was just starting to nod off when the phone rang. Out of reflex, he picked it up.

"'Bout time you got home!"

"Mom! Dad!" Joshua jerked fully awake with a shock. He glanced at the clock. 2:05, just past midnight, Mountain Time. He'd been dozing only a few minutes. "What's wrong?"

"Nothing, but we've been trying to reach you since midnight, your time. I can't sleep until I know how the party went."

"And your mother wouldn't let me sleep until she knew," his father added teasingly.

"You two're never asleep before midnight, anyhow," Joshua retorted. It was true, and they often said the best part of being self-employed and homeschooling was that no one had to get up before nine. It had also come in handy when *Chipotle* started getting gigs. They had no problem acting as roadies, with the added benefit of chaperoning the teenage boys.

"Really, I'm a grown man. You don't need to check up on me. Besides, I've been home for about half an hour. You must have called while I was in the shower. Buuu-uut, if you must know, the party was great."

He told them about the food, and the entertainment, how he'd enjoyed "going solo" and that everyone had liked Rique's latest song. He told them about the wine, and Dr. Malachi's disapproval.

"I expect he'll bring it up when we talk Wednesday," Mr. Lawson chuckled. "Did you drink much?"

"Not really, just a couple of sips. She made these fantastic brownies, and they just didn't go, you know?"

His mother laughed. "That's my choco-boy."

He told them how he stuck around to help clean up, then came home. "That's about it, really."

"Oh?"

His mother's voice was skeptical and he found himself responding. "Well, really, the only other thing is that I was kind-of the last person to leave and well, we, uh, we kissed." The stupid grin and happy panic were back in force, and it was all he could do to keep from giggling like a 12-year-old. Pitiful!

"What else?" his mother urged, an edge in her voice, but his father cut in: "Now, Maggie."

"'Now Maggie' nothing!" he heard his mother snap at his father. "Last year, I gave him his space and look what happened. Maybe if I'd asked a few more questions... So this year, I'm nosy, and you can—both—just deal." Then her voice turned gentler. "Well, Josh, what else?"

Suddenly, Joshua had the urge to be six again, and curled up in his mother's lap, sharing secrets. The feeling was so strong, it actually choked. *It's too soon don't say anything.*

"It's stupid. Really. I—Forget it."

"Joshaham..."

The childhood nickname undid him, and he asked in a small voice. "How, how did you guys know?"

"Know?"

"That, that you were in love? That you were meant to be, you know, forever?"

His father whistled. "That must have been some kiss."

"*It was!*" His parents laughed, but the intensity of his feelings had made him sit up and the words poured from his mouth. "But it's not just that. I feel so stupid! And happy, and panicked, and I don't know! It's like there were parts of me missing, like I was an incomplete song only I didn't know it until she came in and filled in the silences."

"Joshaham, what a beautiful thought!"

"Oh, yeah, son. That was some kiss."

"Dad, I'm in love. I am so in love with Sachiko Luchese!" He moaned and flopped back against the pillow. "What am I going to do?"

"I take it she hasn't expressed similar feelings?" When Joshua didn't answer, he continued, his voice stern. "Then you have to slow down, young man. Get a better idea of what she's thinking and feeling before you go expressing your undying love."

"I know, I know, but how?"

"What did you do tonight?"

"Ran." It was several long moments before his parents could stop laughing, his mother muttering, "Oh, my baby!" and his father, "That *was* some kiss!"

Finally, his father spoke.

"You remember you have ten weeks. That's not enough to establish a permanent relationship, but it is long enough to lay the foundations for one. You have your whole life to tell her you love her. You can afford to wait a few weeks."

His mother took up the thread. "Get yourself a journal. Pour your feelings out there. In the meantime, if you get the urge to say, 'I love you,' say something else: 'I think you're wonderful,' 'I'm having a great time.'"

"'I think I should go now'?" Joshua suggested.

"If necessary," his father laughed. "I think it goes without saying that you should avoid letting things get too physical?"

"Forget it. I'm not going there until I have a ring on my finger and a blessing from God. But it's not going to be easy."

His parents had always been open with him about sex. In fact, he and Rique had received not one but three "talks": the technical and psychological side from Joshua's father, the emotional and "how we women see it" side from his mother, and the Marriage is a Covenant/Fear of God/Don't Ruin Your Soul or Your Life side from Rique's mother—none of which had prepared him for the real thing.

Even so, he'd never told them anything about LaTisha, and he could hardly believe he was saying anything now. "I mean, she's so beautiful and so right."

"It's tough when you're in love, even tougher when it is your soul mate," his mother said. "Believe me, we know. Ten weeks, Joshua. If she's the right one, you'll have a lifetime to explore every aspect of your love. And you have plenty to talk about before you start talking about love. For now, just relax. Have fun."

"I can do that. Really. I can." He let out a gusty sigh and took in a cleansing breath. "I feel better, now. Thanks, Mom, Dad. Love you." Their words strengthened him, and he hung up still feeling giddy, but calmer.

Chapter Eighteen

Sachiko dreamed she was riding a dragon, soaring and diving through the clouds, arms spread in delight.

Then with a lazy belly roll, it dumped her off. Somehow, that was okay too, and she thrilled at the wind rushing through her hair, the lurch in her belly. As the water rushed nearer, she contorted her body into a perfect swan dive.

She sliced through the warm water, the bubbles tickling her. She dove deep as any pearl diver, but the water was murky and she had to go up for air. She swam. And swam. And swam.

The more she pushed forward, the farther the surface became until she felt ready to explode for need of breath. Despite her desperation, her limbs slowed.

Then strong hands grasped her wrists and pulled her aboard a life raft.

Joshua.

He pulled her into his arms. They kissed. The boat rocked in a most provocative way.

The phone rang.

Groaning, she forced herself into wakefulness and picked it up. "Hallo?"

"Hi, Sachiko. Were you studying?"

"Joshua!" Suddenly, she was wide awake, the dream already a half-remembered specter. She glanced at her clock, groaned again. "No. I slept through my alarm."

"Well, you were up late last night."

"I could have stayed up later."

She could just hear a soft chuckle. "Yeah. I'd kind of like to make up for that—"

"Josh, normally, I'd be thrilled, but I have got to study today. I didn't do any yesterday, and this stuff isn't sticking, ya know what I mean?"

"No problem. I could come over this evening, like five, maybe. I'll bring dinner and help you. I know a lot of memory tricks..."

"This coming from the guy who lost all his scholarships?" she teased.

There was silence.

"Josh, I'm sorry. That was a catty thing to say."

"No, no. It's okay. It's not that I can't study; it's that last year, I didn't. If anything, all those tricks are probably what kept me from flunking out."

"Now I'm curious. What could have kept a workaholic like you from studying? I know you don't drink." Again, there was silence, and she got the feeling he was searching for the best way to begin. She settled back against the pillows, ready for a long story.

But he only said, "Her name was LaTisha, and I—really—I'm not ready to talk about it. But I can be a great student, and I'm great at preparing for tests. Trust me?"

She half-sighed, half-chuckled. "All right. You bring the pizza and I'll give you half an hour to prove you can teach me something I don't know."

"Oh, I could teach you a few things," he said in that same sexy low voice he'd used the night before. Then he laughed, as if embarrassed. "Um, but maybe that ought to wait for later. Much later. Anyway, I'll be by about five?"

"It's a date." She hung up, then nestled back down for a moment. Part of her wanted to go back to sleep, just a few more minutes, maybe find that dream again.

With a resolute sigh, she pushed off the sheets and got up. *Study* date or no, she wanted to get as much studying done as she could before the date.

Ydrel lay in bed, the covers pulled tight over his head, trying to block out the brightness of the morning sun. It had to be past 10:00, but he wasn't ready to face the day, especially not after the night he'd had.

The Master had again caught him in his dreams. This time was another lecture, and Ydrel had been forced to hold a kneeling position while the Master preached about his people and their Holy Mission.

For what seemed like hours, he stayed on his knees, fighting the seductive pull of the Master's words and the emotions he projected with them. An objective, distanced part of him knew he was being manipulated, but the more immediate, feeling part of him strained to take in each word, longed to believe there were such things as a brotherhood, and Manifest Destiny, and a Glorious Plan that was worth all sacrifice. He leaned toward his Master; a part of him screamed, "NO!"

"So what?" he suddenly burst out. "You may have a family and a noble cause, but I have to fight to prove my sanity by day and fight your monsters by night. I have no family, no brotherhood, no great destiny. Why do you bother telling me all this?"

He sank down, sobbing.

In a moment, he felt a strong but oddly soft hand cup his chin. His vision blurred with tears and his thoughts with confusion as he met the Master's compassionate gaze.

"You do not understand, do you? You have been called to further Our Cause. To be part of Us. That is why I train you, and so hard, and only abandoned you when my People needed me more. You will be our greatest asset if you just work and learn. When you are ready, I will call you away, forever, and *you will join us.* You understand now, do you not?"

With his words came a feeling of such warmth, and comfort and belonging that Ydrel had to blink back new tears. He didn't even notice the part of himself screaming as he nodded.

"Good. Then let us begin."

Suddenly, he was in the arena, weaponless. Five creatures advanced on him. They looked different from any he'd fought before, more human, yet just as lethal. In desperation, Ydrel spun, kicking up fog in hopes of seeing his sword.

The Master's voice echoed in the gloom. "You don't need that weapon. Use your mind! Kill with your thoughts!"

And he did. He took several wounds that sent pain lancing through him and tore at his concentration, but he eventually dispatched all five of the monsters. He fell to his knees, gasping. Then that warm sense of belonging washed over him again, and he curled up, as if he could somehow wrap himself around it.

Now, in the light of day, he realized how easily he was being manipulated, and what price he was being asked to pay for his belonging. *They don't want me; they want someone who kills at a distance, like a human SCUD.*

Shame and anguish made his stomach hurt. He shut his eyes and curled up tighter, hoping a little more sleep might take away the pain.

When he sensed Roger enter his room, he knew his hopes were in vain.

"Most people knock," he grumbled irritably. He was speaking more to release some anger than because he thought he'd embarrass the orderly.

Roger had a nasty streak. Most patients—those sane enough to care—learned not to cross him. He was particularly good at inflicting "accidental" hurts and little digs to fragile self-esteems. Most of the nurses disliked him; Sachiko actively hated him. She'd been watching him, taking careful notes of his behavior, until Malachai had her "promoted" to swing shifts where she didn't have a chance to check up on him.

After all, he couldn't lose one if his most faithful minions, could he?

Roger laughed as if he found such a courtesy funny. "Get up. Doctor Malachai wants to see you."

"Then let him come here." Ydrel pulled the covers tighter over his head.

"Doctor Malachai doesn't go to crazies' rooms."

"No, he just sends you to fetch them. Does it bother you to be treated like a dog?"

"Get up!" Roger growled, which Ydrel found funny, but then Roger grabbed at the covers and Ydrel knew he wouldn't be put off. Ydrel held fast to the thin blanket. Normally, he wouldn't have cared much, but he didn't know what new wounds might be visible past his pajamas.

"All right! Let me get dressed. Alone," he added irritably when Roger didn't move.

"What's the matter?" he sneered. "Shy?"

"No," Ydrel sneered back. "What the matter with you? Got a thing for watching young men dress?"

With a snarl to hurry up, the orderly retreated and slammed the door shut.

Ydrel rose slowly and went to examine himself in the bathroom mirror and stared with surprise at his uninjured body. His old wounds had been healed, and he didn't see any new ones, though he knew the monsters had scored on him more than once last night. Some reward, perhaps? Whatever the reason, he could actually wear short sleeves for the first time in weeks. Now if only his stomach would stop hurting.

He tossed on a T-shirt and jeans, put on slippers—he was not wearing shoes for Malachai—and followed the orderly to Malachai's office.

As usual, Malachai was seated behind his vast, orderly desk, like a king granting royal audience. Ydrel ignored him and scanned the room. The door to the cherrywood cabinet was closed, hiding the equipment it contained, but a straight-backed chair stood next to it. Ydrel knew what that meant—tests. An EEG, blood draws before and after doing some psychic something or the other, or trying to. All in Deryl's best interest, of course.

He sauntered in and plopped down sideways on a leather chair, one leg tossed carelessly over the arm. "What's up, Dolfus? Got an article due?" He bounced one slippered foot in the air.

"In fact," Dr. Malachai said evenly, "since the arrival of our young intern—"

"He doesn't belong to any of us. Least of all, you."

"—our time together has been somewhat curtailed," the psychiatrist spoke as if he'd not been interrupted. "So I've resolved to spend some of my weekend mornings with you. To work, yes, since the reason you're here is to learn to control those unusual talents so you can function on the outside, is it not? But also to talk."

"Talk?"

"We did do such a thing, not so long ago."

Yeah, before I figured out how you twisted my words and used my talents for your own gain. But he shrugged and settled down so that his head was pillowed on one overstuffed arm and both feet were up and nestled into the wing of the chair. It seemed to ease the ache in his stomach a bit. Malachai made no comment, but Ydrel knew he would note his behavior in his next report. Let him. "So. How was the party last night?"

"I didn't realize you were aware of the staff function last night. Joshua mentioned it, I gather?"

You'd like to think that, wouldn't you? In fact, for a moment, he had a vision—Malachai's vision—of Joshua, puppydog-like, chattering excitedly about his first adult party. If he hadn't been so irritated at the idea, Ydrel would have been surprised. Normally, Malachai was a blank wall to him.

"No," he said, glad to burst Malachai's bubble. "I heard some folks talking about it. They're happy to see Sachiko come out of her shell and entertain again."

"Indeed." Malachai's gaze actually wavered a moment. She had always made it a habit to throw a big dinner party once a month. After the abortion and her interrupted attempt at suicide, she had stopped socializing at work altogether.

"Yes, *indeed*. It's been a couple of years, they said. Some of them were wondering why she stopped in the first place."

"Well." Malachai paused a moment, looking at some papers. He tried to make it seem a deliberate move, but Ydrel could tell he'd knocked the senior psychiatrist off balance. Malachai didn't know how much he knew, nor how. Ydrel was fine with that—let him think it was his psychic powers. Better yet, let him think some rumors were starting.

Malachai cleared his throat. "Well, shall we begin with an exercise?"

"You mean an experiment, and no, we shall not."

"I beg your pardon?"

"I'd like that. I said, we shall not do an exercise today. I am tired, and my stomach hurts, and besides, we've been doing your 'exercises' for years and they don't work. If the best you can come up with is hooking me up to that machine"—with one foot, he pointed to the specialized EEG that waited behind the cabinet doors—"then perhaps I need to seek help elsewhere."

"Such as from your friend, Joshua?" Malachai spoke with a calm controlled voice, yet Ydrel knew he'd stepped over the line.

Well, nothing he could do about it now. "Such as with anyone who will treat me like something other than a lab rat."

Malachai spoke softly. "You are not a lab rat, Ydrel. You are a strong and caring person with a complex and fascinating condition. I can't help feeling that if we just knew more about what caused it, we could better bring it under control."

Ydrel might have believed him, had he not had a similar experience with the Master last night. Now, he just snorted and stared at the ceiling.

Malachai spoke again. "In all the years we've worked together, I've never tired of you. Indeed, you have become a primary focus of my practice. Young Joshua, on the other hand, is here to study psychology; his work with you is a favor for Edith, really, and I've seen indications that he's beginning to resent that."

Listened to that speech, did you? Anger burned away any feelings of uncertainty Ydrel may have had about Joshua. Intern Joshua had always been straight with him, even when irritated, while Doctor Malachai, concerned Doctor Malachai, was tapping his room. He stared at the ceiling until he had control of his features, then tilted his head to look laconically at the psychiatrist.

"You really believe an inexperienced teenaged intern is going to teach you to control your abilities enough that you can leave this place?"

Ydrel said nothing. The whole line of questioning was starting to make him sick again. He wanted to go lie down. "May I go now?"

"Very well." Malachai turned to his computer.

The royal audience was over.

When the doorbell rang promptly at 5 o'clock, Sachiko wanted to jump over the coffee table in her enthusiasm.

You're acting like a giddy teenager, she chided herself. Nonetheless, when she peeked through her peephole and saw Joshua standing there, smiling, she felt a thrill of butterflies below her sternum. She hoped it didn't show when she opened the door.

"Hi." His smile broadened. "You look beautiful."

She rolled her eyes. "I wasn't trying to."

In fact, she'd changed at least three times that day, trying to find something that was casual but not too grungy, nice without being provocative. She'd finally settled on a pair of soft cotton drawstring pants with a matching T-shirt. She had pulled her hair into a pony-tail and purposely refrained from putting on make-up. They were going to study or she was going to toss him out, she'd told herself each time she'd felt the urge to put on just a little blush.

Now, she wondered if maybe some make-up wouldn't have been a good idea, after all, if only to min-imize the flush she felt sure was showing on her face. "Come in. What have you got in the bag?"

"Study goodies," he said, handing her the bag. He set the pizza on the table while she rifled through it. She pulled out Oreos, a couple of candy bars, and Ding Dongs. "I like chocolate when I study," he said with a sheepish grin.

Also in the bag were three CDs.

"I don't study with music," she said, pulling them out.

"One has simple tunes we can put mnemonics to," Joshua said. "It's great when you have stuff you need to know by rote. The other two are for, uh, breaks."

She looked at the homemade labels: Break-fast, and Break-slow. Just looking at them ate at her resolve to keep this date limited to study, but she handed them to him and told him to put them by the CD player. Then she pulled out the last items.

"A plastic knife? And Play-Dough?"

"Well, I figured since you wanted to be a surgeon, you might be a tactile thinker. I thought we could make models and you could operate on them."

"You are too weird!" She laughed but didn't look up to meet his eyes. *And young! Play-Dough for study and romantic music for breaks? And he thinks I'm full of surprises. What am I doing with him?*

And why does it feel so right?

"I am not, I—whoa!"

"What?" At his exclamation, she looked up from the containers of brightly colored clay—how long had it been since she'd played with that stuff?—and saw him standing by the entertainment center, staring with horror at the roses Malachai had given her. "What's wrong?"

"They don't have any thorns!"

"Uh, huh. I think they're genetically engineered that way—"

"It's horrible!"

"You have something against biotechnology?"

"No, it's just..." He was breathing in short breaths. He paused, took in a deep lungful of air and said, "Roses without thorns are—are defenseless. Damaged. Nobody should ever think of you that way!"

She replied slowly. "Nobody does."

He continued to stare at the flowers as if he expected a snake to emerge from them.

Maybe surprises weren't always a good thing. Was he going to run again? "Joshua, you're starting to weird me out, here."

He shuddered, looked at her, then shook himself. "I'm sorry. I have no idea where that came from. Glad

I didn't notice last night," he added with an embarrassed laugh.

"Me, too." She went to him and took the vase. "Tell you what. Why don't I just put those in another room, and you get us a couple of sodas?"

"Yeah. okay."

When she returned from putting the vase in the study, he had taken the sodas and goodies over to the couch where she had her books.

He stood up as she approached. "Hi. Can we sort of do this again?"

"I don't know," she teased. "I'm not sure I want to repeat that scene."

He laughed.

"Maybe you ought to talk to someone about that? You do work with a bunch of psychiatrists, after all."

She expected him to laugh again, but he answered seriously. "Nah. I think I'll do some biospiritual focusing when I get a spare hour or so. If something doesn't turn up, I'll ask my mom. There's something about thornless roses..."

He shook himself, then moved closer, a different smile on his face. "Actually, I was thinking about something else," he murmured as he put his arms around her.

She'd thought that, recalling the evening before, she had built up their kiss into something more than it was. She was wrong, wonderfully wrong. When at last, they pulled apart, slightly breathless, she smiled. "Promise not to run this time?"

He smiled, too, and took her hands in his. "Promise, but you have to promise something in return." He kissed her hands but didn't meet her eyes.

Madness Bound   ✸   191

She waited. He was always so confident, even brash, at work, and now he was so shy. It was a side of him she hadn't expected.

Still not meeting her gaze, he said, "Promise me we won't go past first base."

Despite herself, she snorted. That was the last thing she'd expected to hear! "Awfully sure of yourself, aren't you?"

"No!" Now he looked up. "No, I'm not. That's why I need your promise."

The look he gave her was so vulnerable, so wounded, that she had the sudden urge to wrap her arms around him and protect him—from what? Slightly off balance, she answered more gruffly than she intended. "Sure. No problem. You're here to help me study, right?"

He smiled, and she saw the tension leave his shoulders. "Right. So what do you want to tackle first?"

Chapter Nineteen

Sachiko sighed and tried to focus on the log entry on the computer screen before her. It wasn't easy to do. Although she'd been able to concentrate fully in class—in fact, had actually anticipated part of the lecture, thanks to the silly ditties Joshua had made up for her—the routine of work at the institute made it all too easy for her mind to wander, and her mind kept wandering back to Joshua and the other part of their study date.

He was such a funny combination of contradictions. He had made her promise to keep things cool, but the first time she had stretched and called for a study break, he had run his hands up her sides from waist to fingertips, then settled her hands around his neck before letting his fingers slide back down her arms and over her back. He moved in to kiss her, setting her blood afire.

She'd wanted more, and it was obvious he had, too. Yet he had pulled away first. Once, as he had kissed a particularly sensitive spot on her neck and she had moaned his name, he'd actually pushed away, gasping.

"That was the most...erotic...thing I've ever heard. Please, don't do that again."

Erotic. He should talk, with those hands of his...

The computer had gone to screensaver again. With annoyance, she tapped the keyboard.

I wonder where he is today. He hadn't shown up at shift change, as he sometimes did, and she hadn't dared ask about his whereabouts. She didn't have a work-related reason to know and had made him promise to keep their romance private. He'd warned her he would not keep secrets from his parents or his friends back home, but agreed that at work, he wouldn't say a word—

"Boo."

Joshua's voice, low and close to her ear, made her jump and give a short "Ya!" of surprise. She spun. He'd already backed up several paces, his arms up, his face a study of childlike innocence. "Joshua!"

"Blame her!" he said, pointing to Monique, who was nearly doubled over with laughter. "It was her idea, I swear!"

"I'm sorry, Sachiko," Monique sputtered, wiping tears of mirth from her eyes and not looking sorry at all. "But you've been staring at that same entry for ten minutes. Do you even know what it says?"

"I—" Sachiko glanced at the screen, but the log entry had again been replaced with a picture of a beach.

Monique gave a knowing look to Joshua, which he returned. "So, who is he?"

"Who's who?" She forced herself not to look Joshua's way.

"Come on. You should have seen the goofy half-smile on your face. You don't think I know what that means? I've worn it myself on more than one occasion."

"I don't know what you're talking about," Sachiko answered coldly.

Monique would not be put off. "You may like to keep your home life secret, but this is one secret you aren't keeping. It's a man. I know it. Joshua, you're a perceptive guy, what do you think?"

"I think," he said slowly, "I'd be better off keeping my mouth shut." He glanced at his watch. "Dr. Malachai wants to meet with me in an hour, so I've only got about forty-five minutes to spend playing catch with Ydrel. Say, would either of you like to join us?" He glanced shrewdly at Sachiko, then Monique. "Or would you rather watch?"

Joshua left before he could see Monique's reaction, but he heard her "tu!" of shock, and Sachiko's calm reply, "You said yourself he was perceptive."

He chuckled to himself, ignoring the querying look a passing orderly gave him. He probably shouldn't have done it, but it might keep Monique off Sachiko's case for a while.

Of course, he probably shouldn't have done what he did to Sachiko, either, but it was just too good an opportunity to pass up. She really was in another world—one with him in it, he hoped—and besides, it was probably the only chance he'd have to get so close to her for days. She didn't wear perfume, but the flowery scent of her soap, enhanced so well by her pheromones, would sustain him for at least a day.

He let out a sigh as he opened his locker in the deserted locker room and started undressing. It was probably just as well she wanted to keep their romance out of the workplace. Many months of dating LaTisha had given him a taste for quick, illicit encounters in public but out-of-the-way places. Even now, he could imagine himself with Sachiko in some cliché of a storage room, her lips hot and urgent on his, her hands tearing at the buttons of his shirt. He'd kiss her neck and she'd moan his name—

He tossed off his shirt and changed, quickly and a little roughly, into his gym clothes, forcing the image of her out of his mind lest his body reveal his train of thought. Instead, he thought about Ydrel. *There is one person that I don't think either of us can hide this from.*

He knocked on Ydrel's door.

No one answered.

"Hey, Ydrel, you up?" Josh opened the door a crack, then wider when no voice objected. He walked in, amazed at what he saw.

The room was a mess, but not with the usual sloppiness he'd seen before. Papers looked like they'd been tossed in the air and allowed to fall like confetti. Descartes, the bear, was sitting atop a pyramid of books, a copy of *Arrow's Flight* upside-down in its paws. The bedspread and pillow were on the floor—on the side of the room bordered by a closet, Joshua noted. He poked his head into the bathroom. A big smiley face of toothpaste was sliming its way down the mirror over the sink. A gentle breeze caught his attention, and he went back to the bedroom. The window was open, its curtain hanging out on one side. The desk beneath the window was in curious disarray. The desk chair had been pulled out partway, and the books looked like they'd been pushed aside or stepped on. He glanced out the window into the courtyard, and what he saw made him head back to the nurses' station fast.

Sachiko was talking to one of the orderlies Joshua had only met in passing. "We don't have time to watch," she teased as he approached.

He ignored her. "Anybody know why Ydrel is up in a tree?"

The orderly laughed. "Who knows? He's been there since, like, eight o'clock this morning."

Sachiko frowned. "There was nothing about it in the logs."

The orderly—Paulie, Josh remembered—shrugged. "So? He's probably still in his pajamas, too."

"And this didn't strike anyone as unusual?" Joshua asked, his temper rising. "Something, that, I don't know, might be brought to Dr. Sellar's attention?"

Again, Paulie shrugged. "They do crazy stuff all the time." He lowered his voice conspiratorially. "This is an asylum, you know."

He apparently thought he was making a great joke, but it was clear Sachiko wasn't amused. "I think you and I and your supervisor need to have a little talk," she said with a deadly edge in her voice. Paulie looked bewildered. "Joshua, you want to get Edith?"

He considered. "I think I'll talk to Ydrel first, see what's going on and what I can do. Would you call Edith when you're done here?"

"This could take some time." She fixed the orderly with a glare Joshua hoped he'd never come under. Paulie paled slightly.

Good. "Take your time. I need a while with Ydrel, anyway."

Ydrel was about halfway up a huge oak tree at the far end of the courtyard, laughing and tearing leaves off a branch and watching them fall. It was a beautiful tree with thick boughs spaced just right. Most of the trees Joshua had grown up with were either too young or wrong for climbing, and for a moment, the intern considered going up after the errant client.

In the end, though, he decided one of them had better stay connected to the earth. "Hey, Ydrel! Come on down."

"Make me!" The boy's laugh was high and light, but a little forced. He tossed a handful of leaves in Joshua's direction.

He ignored them. "I'm an intern, not a fireman to rescue an idiot stuck in a tree. And I'd really rather not yell or get a crick in my neck. Besides," he added in sudden inspiration, "I've got a secret."

"You forget," Ydrel said. With a sudden crashing of leaves and small branches, he jumped. The boy landed on the lowest branch with his heels, slipped, caught himself at the knees and hung upside down. "I'm psychic. *I kno-o-ow all!*" He made a spooky sound, then laughed.

"Okay. Read my mind," and he thought hard. *You're acting weird, even for an asylum. Get down here before they come to get you with a straitjacket.*

Whether the young client read his mind or just the expression on his face, Joshua didn't know, but with a sigh, Ydrel grabbed a smaller branch and started to heave himself up. The branch broke under his weight and he fell hard onto his back. He lay there, blinking, the broken branch still clutched in his right hand. Then he began to laugh hysterically.

Despite himself, Joshua grinned. "Very smooth. Now—Hey!" He jumped back as Ydrel suddenly rose and swung the branch, sword-like, in his direction. "Watch it!"

"Don't worry," replied Ydrel, who now held the branch in both hands and was swinging it in what looked like a martial arts form. "I was on the fencing team in school, and I was good! There was even talk of me making the Olympics before I gave it up."

Watching him pretending to fight against one opponent—or more, from the way he swung in one direction and kicked out in another—Joshua thought it looked less like fencing and more like the jedi stuff they did in *Star Wars*. Still, he had to admit after Ydrel performed a helicopter move—two swinging kicks and a slash with his branch at the same time—he was good.

"So why'd you give it up?"

Suddenly, Ydrel stopped, his eyes wide, his chest heaving. He stared at the branch he held, then dropped it as if it were something poisonous. He looked like he was waking from a nightmare.

"Josh, you gotta help me," he said, his voice edged with panic. "He's out of control and I can't block him! And he's manic now, so we're happy—too happy. But when he gets violent, if I can't block him...Josh, you gotta help me! I don't want to hurt anybody!"

"Whoa! Slow down!" Joshua closed the distance and grasped Ydrel by the shoulders. Ydrel looked up at him with an expression of anguish. His eyes were pinning wildly, dilating and contracting as if someone were flashing a strobe. Joshua had expected something like that; he'd seen it before in him. But this time was wilder, as if Ydrel was fighting for control.

"Focus on me," he told Ydrel. "Use your other senses. C'mon, what do I look like?"

"Um..." Ydrel looked about, confused. He shut his eyes.

Joshua shook him gently but firmly. "Focus! What color is my skin?"

"Um, black." He gasped.

"You can do better than that. Get specific."

"Sure. Right. Specific. Brown, like somewhere between the color of my headboard and the frosting on that awful chocolate cake."

His breathing started to slow and his eyes to settle into a more normal focus as he scanned his friend's face. "And your eyes are darker brown, clearer, and your hair is black, short and flat on the top. Your nose is a little flat. You're—" he grinned a quick nervous smile, "really not my type."

He gave a nervous laugh, one that threatened to break loose into hysterics again.

Joshua spoke calmly and firmly. "You can do this. Focus on me, my face, my voice. Tell me what's going on. Who's out of control? Who can't you block?"

Ydrel swallowed hard. He was shivering from effort. "Greg McDougal. They put him in the room next to mine. He's manic-depressive, bi-polar, and he isn't taking his medication. But he's good at hiding it, and Malachai's not letting anyone check up on him. But he projects! Josh, he's so high, he wants to climb trees and jump and sing and he can't and I've been trying to block him, I have, all weekend I tried and I kept hoping Tasmae would Call me and she never did, and I'm having a hard time blocking other people too and it's happening all over again—"

"Ydrel, if he were half as gone as you're acting, there's no way he could have hidden it. Someone would have noticed."

"What, so you're saying this is my fault? Maybe I'm like some kind of buffer or sponge or something, picking up his mania while he acts all *calm* and *normal*. You think this is fun? You think I like feeling this way?"

Real or imagined, Ydrel's own happy mania was giving way to irritability.

Joshua thought quickly. Sachiko must have told Edith by now; if Joshua didn't find some way to bring Ydrel around, and fast, he'd probably end up in a straitjacket or medicated.

Here's hoping I don't get fired..."Ydrel, focus! Focus on my feelings. Let them in. Soak them in instead of McDougal's."

He concentrated on projecting calm, steady, determination—

"Who are you kidding?" Ydrel laughed. "You're so in love you want to go singing and turning cartwheels, yourself!"

Well, I was right about that, at any rate. Josh smiled but spoke sternly. "That's the infatuation. Look past that. Deeper." He filled his mind with thoughts of how centered and comfortable he felt. He let that quiet happiness fill him, and he watched Ydrel's breathing slow. Gradually, his trembling ceased.

"Better," Ydrel finally said. He took a deep cleansing breath. "For the moment, anyway."

"First things first, then. What happened to your shields?"

"Gone. McDougal's been next door since noon Sunday, and Malachai didn't let either of us leave our rooms. He's punishing me because I refused to do tricks for him—"

"We'll worry about that later," Joshua cut him off. "Right now, let's concentrate on rebuilding your shields, okay?" Ydrel nodded. "You ever meditate?"

"I'm not meditating!" Ydrel flared. "I tried that before. It opened a floodgate. Josh, I'm so tired, and I can't concentrate. I tried, honest!"

"Easy. I'm just thinking of ways to get you focused. You finish *Arrow's Flight*? How about *Myth Adventures* that I gave you Friday? Good. C'mon, we're starting to draw attention." He let go of Ydrel's shoulders and put a friendly arm around him instead, leading him out from under the tree to a flat sunny area. He let the client go, then stretched out on the soft, well-manicured grass. He jerked his head at a spot next to him that would place himself between Ydrel and the institute building. "Lie down. Pretend you're looking at the clouds."

Ydrel looked at his intern friend as if he should be the one committed but did as he was told. "I don't see how this will help," he said doubtfully.

"Maybe it won't, but unless you've got a better idea, try it my way a minute, all right? Remember when Talia and Kris were trapped in the blizzard and Talia's empathy got out of her control? We're going to try a little ground and center just like Kris taught her. So, I want you to imagine your power like an anchor, or maybe a drill, with a strong line tying it back to you. Go ahead. Let me know when you've got it."

He waited, and finally Ydrel muttered, "Maybe...okay."

"Good. That's your ground. You can use it to pull energy to steady you when you're buffeted by outside forces. Ready? Now plunge it into the ground." As he waited, he folded his hands behind his head and crossed his legs, trying to look as if they'd just decided to hang out and watch the clouds. Otherwise, he kept his silence, trusting in Ydrel's imagination to help him accomplish the task.

After a long moment, he heard his friend say, in a somewhat surprised voice. "Wow. okay. What's next?"

"Well, it seems to me you've picked up a lot of useless energy. See, we all give and receive energy from each other—everybody and everything, even plants and water and rocks. To plants and rocks and such, energy is just energy; they take in what they can use and pass the rest on. Humans, though, because we're sentient, emotional creatures, tend to translate energy into positive or negative: positive, and you feel happy and stable; negative, and you may feel initially stoked, but then irritated or nervous."

"So being in love is positive energy?"

"Oh, yeah. But do me a favor and keep that little gem of information to yourself. Sachiko wants to play things cool, and I don't want to scare her off."

"I don't remember this in any of those books."

"Oh, it's not. It's in some pop psych book I read, I don't remember offhand which, but it's still useful information. It works for me when I've had a rough day or I have to deal with someone I don't like. Back to you. You are full of negative energy; you're shaking with it. It's no wonder you're having trouble keeping things coherent. We've got to get rid of that energy so you can focus and load up on the good stuff. Make sense? You still with me?"

"Yeah, yeah, just...let's hurry." Ydrel's voice was strained and his breathing was starting to accelerate again. "So how do I get rid of it?"

"You've got your ground. Shunt it through there. What I do is imagine all that nervous energy flowing out my fingertips, like a river, washing out upon the ground—"

"But it's not 'nervous energy!' It's all these thoughts and feelings and—and they're not mine and they keep coming in. How do I deal with that?"

Joshua sat up and turned to face his prone friend. Ydrel lay stiffly on the ground, his hands at his sides, fingers slightly dug into the grass. Despite the muggy heat, he was barely sweating. Joshua wiped the sweat off his own face while he thought. This wasn't the first time he'd played into someone's fantasy, but it was certainly the most sustained and the most complex.

"Ydrel, I'm not psychic, and I don't know anyone who is, or even if there are any reputable books on the subject. I'm playing this by ear, and you're going to have to help me. One thing I do know, anything getting through your shields is obviously bombarding its way in, and you're so tensed up that nothing's getting out. You're so uptight, you're not even sweating. You look like rigor mortis has set in.

"It's like a dam in a flood, does that make sense? If you don't release some of the water, the pressure builds and the dam breaks, so you release it in a controlled way. So, if you relax, let all those thoughts and emotions and energy flow through you, even if more come in, you'll still relieve some of the pressure. Make sense? Okay.

"Start with a couple of breaths. Good. Remember your ground; you're not going adrift. Let your body get heavy. Feel the muscles get warm. Feel your pores open up. Each invading thought, each outside feeling is like a bead of sweat. Let them out, feel them seeping out your pores. Feel the tension leave through your grounding line, pulling the energy, the outside thoughts with it..."

He continued this way for a few minutes, guiding him through relaxation, watching as Ydrel's muscles loosened and went slack. Sweat began to bead up, then trickle down his face and dampened his blond hair. Gradually, his trembling eased and his breathing slowed.

When he spoke, his voice was closer to its normal timbre. "It's better. I can still feel all these thoughts coming in, but they're just sort of...passing through. It's kind of a crawly feeling."

"Well, you look more relaxed. Shake yourself out a little. Make yourself more comfortable. That's it. Think you can concentrate now?"

"I think so. For the moment, anyway." Ydrel put his hands behind his head, pillowing it, and bent one knee up.

"Good. Now let's work on your shields. Remember what Aahz said about ley lines in *Myth Adventures*? Use your abilities to sense around you. See if you can find a ley line around here."

"How?"

"Well, what'd Aahz say? Sort of, focus without focusing. I know." He lay back down so he could look at the sky. A few billowy white clouds graced the field of blue. "You ever look for shapes in the clouds? It helps sometimes to not look at them too hard, just let your mind and imagination take you where it will. Try that."

It was only a moment before Ydrel nearly shouted. "That's amazing! It's right there!"

He pointed to a spot to the right. "It practically goes over the building! And there's another one over there, like toward New York. How come I never noticed them before?"

"Never looked, I'll bet. Now what you need to do is tap the line. And no, I don't know for certain how. Imagine another ground line. Um, reach out with a psychic hand. But be careful. You don't know how much energy you're dealing with. Once you figure that out, start putting it into your shields. Tell me about your shields. What are they like?"

"Malachai helped me with them when I first got here, only he made me meditate and hypnotized me." Ydrel shuddered. "They're like big stone walls around my mind. They block out everything, but there are windows I can open when I need to. That was the theory, anyway. Even on good days, it doesn't work that well, but at least enough that I can cope." Again, he shuddered and gasped. "Joshua, I need to do something fast."

"Tell you what. Start with the walls. Translate the energy into stone. $E=mc^2$, right? Then, we'll try some other things—different materials, multiple walls. You're the military strategist; use that knowledge to your advantage for a change."

Joshua glanced at his watch. "Ydrel, I'm sorry to do this, but I have to meet Doctors Malachai and Sellars in fifteen minutes. If I'm late, they'll find us. You want to stay here and work on your shields?"

"Yeah. I don't think I can do this if I'm too close to people, especially McDougal. You don't have to tell Malachai I'm out here, do you? He kept me trapped in my room all day yesterday. He's trying to get me to use my powers for him, like some trained dog. He's going to be mad I slipped my leash."

"He probably knows already. The orderlies have seen you since you came out this morning and when I came out here, Sachiko was about to let Edith know. If it's any consolation, we've been out here nearly half an hour and no one's run you off yet. And, if I can, I'll go talk to this McDougal before I see the doctors. If he's off his meds, they need to know."

"Malachai knows," Ydrel snapped. "Why do you think he moved him next to me?"

"Right. Sorry. But if I talk to him, let him know I know...If others are noticing, he has to do something, right? Really, he's not going to risk his reputation or the institute's to punish you, is he?"

"I suppose not," Ydrel grumbled doubtfully.

"Just stay here. Take in energy. Build your shields. Shunt out the negative stuff. I'll catch you as soon as my afternoon appointments are over and we'll make dinner and figure out some improvements, promise."

Again, he glanced at his watch. "I have got to go. I don't know why Malachai called this special meeting but I've already been warned not to be late with him."

Ydrel watched his intern friend sprint across the compound with a pang of jealousy. Must be nice to have your biggest worry be whether or not you're on time for a meeting. That, and figuring out how to apply your favorite novels to a so-called "real" psychic.

He knew he wasn't being fair; Joshua's ideas had actually helped. He could feel the thoughts and feelings of others coursing through him, passing through his ground rather than bombarding his mind with images. It made him feel antsy, like he'd been given too many amphetamines or had too much adrenaline in his body, but at least he wasn't being overwhelmed. Nonetheless, he needed to rebuild his barriers and soon.

He looked again for the ley line. There it was: a wispy none-too-straight path where the air was a shade darker than the surrounding sky. He realized now he'd noticed it before but had passed it off as an optical illusion. What an idiot he was.

Just like with the books, he grumbled. *All the time I spent fruitlessly searching the school's nonfiction sections and I should have just boned up on my fantasy!* He felt the temptation to berate himself and forced it down. He knew where that would lead. Instead, he gazed up at the ley line until he could feel it as well as see it. Then he closed his eyes and imagined reaching up to it, gently—

"Wake up, Stephens!" The harsh voice broke Ydrel's concentration. It was Paulie, the orderly, and he was mad. "Get up. Dr. Malachai wants you back in your room."

"Joshua said I could hang out here a while longer." The words were out of Ydrel's mouth before he could stop them. The proximity of Paulie and the strength of his anger were threatening the last of Ydrel's already badly eroded barriers. Now, contempt was added to the offense.

"Oh, are we taking orders from the intern instead of the head of this institution?" he sneered, and Ydrel felt him resisting the urge to kick him. "Get up. Move."

I don't have to see the line. I can find it by feel. I've got my ground. I can do this. Nonetheless, he trembled with apprehension as he followed the orderly back to his room.

Chapter Twenty

Joshua paused at Dr. Malachai's office door and took a deep breath to ease some of his own apprehension. He'd managed to stop by Mr. McDougal's room, and it had only taken a couple of minutes to see that if he was taking his medication, it wasn't working. Then, when he'd taken the chance and asked him about it outright, the client had lied through his teeth.

Malachai wasn't stupid. He had to at least suspect. So why move him now? And why next door to the most sensitive person in the ward? And how could Joshua bring this up without sounding as paranoid as Ydrel?

Play it by ear, he told himself as he knocked and entered. You don't even know what this meeting is about. Maybe he's going to explain all this. Yeah, right.

His doubts were justified as soon as he saw Edith's face—disappointed, and a little sad. Dr. Malachai's expression was neutral but stern, and there was a hint of a glint in his eyes. Together, the two spelled trouble to Joshua, but he refused to jump to conclusions.

"Good afternoon, sir. Edith."

"Sit down, Mr. Lawson," Dr. Malachai indicated a seat near Edith. He did not take his usual spot behind the big desk, but rather perched himself casually on its edge, arms crossed. He stared at Joshua expectantly, as if waiting for him to say something.

Since Joshua had no idea what this was about, there was no way he was going to make the first move.

Instead, he met and held the senior psychiatrist's gaze, then waited. In his peripheral vision, he saw Edith look from one to the other. He felt a little bad for excluding her, but he was not about to look her way. It might look like he was asking her for help, and he wouldn't give Malachai that satisfaction. He waited.

The moment stretched.

Finally, Malachai broke the silence. "We wanted to discuss some concerns about your internship, specifically in regard to Ydrel Stephens."

"Yes, sir." He kept his tone and body language carefully neutral. *You'll have to give me more to go on than that if you want any admissions out of me. Of course, I haven't got anything to confess, really.*

"You've been spending a significant proportion of your day with him, and some weekend time, I'm told, acquiring educational and reading materials?"

"Yes, sir. Per my discussions with you and Doctor Sellars..." Joshua mirrored Malachai's formal words and tone. *If you want to be maddening, I can be maddening. At least until you tell me what this is really about.*

"And what is your assessment of the relationship you're developing with our young client?"

"Could you be more specific, sir?"

Whether in exasperation or simply to break the growing tension in the room, Edith spoke.

"Dr. Malachai is concerned you're feeling pressured to devote too much time to working with Ydrel. No one is criticizing your work with other clients," she added quickly. "Far from it; I've had nothing but the best reports. But you are putting in a lot of extra hours, and there's concern that you may be feeling the strain."

"Have I given any indication that I—" Suddenly, something clicked in his mind. He turned to Malachai with a sardonic smile. "Caught my little speech to Ydrel, did you?"

The psychiatrist looked away as if embarrassed. "I overheard some of it while passing in the hallway," he said.

So that's what you look like when you lie. Joshua filed the look on Malachai's face into his memory. He'd been very careful to keep an eye on the door while he was talking to Ydrel. The only way anyone could have heard the conversation unseen was to have snuck up and listened from the wall beside the doorway. Even then, he knew he had not spoken loud enough to be heard in the hallway. A sensitive microphone might have picked it up, however, which would also explain why Dr. Malachai waited until Monday to bring this up instead of hauling him in immediately afterward.

Aloud, he said, "I'm sorry you had to hear that, sir. Mother's Speech Number Three is really only meant for its immediate recipient."

"Mother's Speech what?" Edith laughed.

Joshua turned toward her with a smile; in his peripheral vision, he could see Malachai trying to cover his own confusion. Clearly, Joshua's answer had caught him flat-footed. Joshua's smile broadened and he hoped they would think it had to do with his explanation.

"You know how your mom always had the same themes she used on you over and over when she was mad? Well, when I was thirteen, I numbered them. Mother's Speech Number Three was, basically, 'I'm doing all this extra work because I love you, but if you really don't care, fine, throw your life away and I'll find something more productive to do with mine.' She used it a lot when I was surly and didn't want to do my assignments, so when Ydrel turned that attitude on me..."

He shrugged expressively.

Edith was torn between shock and amusement. "You used *guilt*?"

"It worked a lot better on him than it ever did on me."

"And this is your idea of sound psychology?" Dr. Malachai cut in disapprovingly.

Joshua answered, his voice completely deadpan. "I was told not to practice psychology without a chaperone, sir."

"I see. Well, that clears things up, and I'm relieved to know things are indeed well between you and young Ydrel. If there's nothing else." Dr. Malachai pushed himself off his desk.

"Actually, sir, there is something. I happened to meet Mr. McDougal, who's in the room next to Ydrel's. He's bi-polar, I understand?"

"Yes. We moved him to the basic care ward over the weekend."

Here goes. In for a penny. "Sir, he's not taking his medication. He was pinging—agitated, having a tremulous hold on his emotions—so I asked him how his medication was helping and he lied about taking it. Frankly, I doubt he's been taking it for a while."

"Indeed. And this is your conclusions based on, perhaps, two minutes' evaluation?" Although his voice and expression were neutral as always, there was a spark of menace in the senior psychiatrist's eyes.

Joshua refused to be intimidated. "I am very good at spotting liars, sir."

"Be that as it may, Joshua, Mr. McDougal has been my client for several months. I believe I am a bit better qualified to judge his state of mind. However," he added magnanimously, "I shall take your comments under consideration when I see him this afternoon. That will be all, Joshua; I believe Dr. Hoffman expects you. He seems quite impressed with your peculiar talents. Edith, if you'd remain a moment."

Dismissed, Joshua left alone and headed down the hall. When he came to the junction, instead of heading toward the common rooms, he started up the patients' hall.

"Hey. Where are you going?" Sachiko intercepted him as he passed the nurses' station. "Dr. Hoffman was asking after you. I told him you were with Dr. Malachai and—oh, oh. What happened?"

"There's a manic-depressive in the room next to Ydrel's."

She sighed. "I know. I don't like it, either, but as long as he's on medication—"

"He isn't." Joshua started again down the hall. She slipped around the desk to follow.

"What do you mean he isn't? How do you know—"

A howl of rage and the crash of furniture interrupted her question and together, they dashed to the source of the sound.

"Meddling little prick! You dare tell me what to do! I'll teach you!"

They found McDougal in his room, shouting obscenities and swinging a chair at a figure lying curled in the fetal position on the floor. Ydrel. Joshua dashed in to grab the chair before McDougal could land another blow on the boy's back.

McDougal swung backward and it hit Joshua across the side of the head.

He saw stars, but somehow managed to grip the chair and wrench it free. Sachiko flew in after, and in a few deft moves, had the raving client on the floor, his arm twisted and her knee positioned so that any move would cause great pain. It didn't stop him from doing his best to dislodge her or from his mad ranting.

"Get off me, yellow bitch! Interfering nigger! You have no right to tell me what to do! I'll be fine once I remove this poison from my sight! *Let me go!*"

He surged upward, nearly succeeding in throwing her off. He howled with pain and fury.

"Josh! Get Monique—tell her I need—!" McDougal twisted furiously, trying to get out from her grip. What she needed was drowned out in his roaring profanities.

"I'm not leaving you alone!" He didn't add that he was still dizzy and didn't think he could get up anytime soon. He settled for throwing himself on McDougal's legs.

"I'm here!" Monique shoved past Joshua, a syringe in her hand. Joshua did his best to immobilize the wild client's legs. He kicked sharply, catching him under the jaw, but he held on, trying to use his weight to pin him down. He could hear, almost from a distance, McDougal's yells and Sachiko's harried directions.

McDougal's screech told Joshua the meds found the right recipient's arm, but he continued to lean until a couple of orderlies bearing restraints took over. He didn't bother to stand up—he still felt a little dizzy from that kick—but turned around to check on Ydrel.

The boy still lay curled up in the fetal position, his arms crossed about his waist, his torso jerking spasmodically, his eyes tightly shut. Joshua shook his shoulder and spoke his name. He didn't respond. He shook a little harder. "Ydrel!"

Still no response. Joshua pried open an eyelid, the one that wasn't blackened from the attack. His eyes, staring ahead yet focused on someplace deeply inward, didn't even react to the change of light. With a sinking feeling of expectation, he sat the young man up. Like one of those dolls that closes its eyes when it's laid down and opens them when upright, Ydrel's eyelids snapped open, his eyes still unresponsive. He began to rock.

"Oh, my God, what happened?" Edith appeared at the doorway, accompanied by Malachai. She hurried through the door and knelt before the rocking boy, speaking softly and examining him.

"We heard yelling and found Mr. McDougal wailing away at Ydrel with a chair." Joshua tried to stand but sat down on the floor again quickly as an unexpected wave of dizziness swept over him. "Whoa!"

"Stay still. Your forehead is bleeding," Malachai said distractedly as he pushed past him to where orderlies were finishing putting the restraints on the raving client. With a tap on Sachiko's shoulder, he dispatched her to look to Joshua.

The restraints and sedatives were stopping McDougal from struggling physically, but he continued to yell and rant. "You!" he exclaimed when he saw the psychiatrist. "This is your fault! You promised no interference! I should kill them—all of them. No interference! I'll see to it they're dead and it'll be on your head! Your fault!"

His ranting dissolved into indistinct murmurs and howls as the sedative finally took effect.

Sachiko, meanwhile, had given Joshua gauze to press against the gash in his head while she checked the T-shaped bruise along one side of his face. "How many fingers am I holding up?" she asked.

Behind them, McDougal struggled to consciousness long enough to yell a few obscenities, and Malachai instructed them to take him to the advanced care ward. Edith continued to talk to the rocking Ydrel.

"Three, but they're blurry with this eye," Joshua answered, closing first the right eye, then the left. "Don't worry. I'll be fine in a minute. But I don't think he got like that from missing only one day of his meds," he added loudly as the orderlies dragged McDougal out of the room and Dr. Malachai joined Edith, standing behind her. Dr. Hoffman walked in at that moment and knelt next to her.

Malachai ignored the intern. "Well, Edith?" he asked softly.

"He's driven himself into a catatonic state."

Hoffman sighed. "Great. The last time, he was like this for two weeks. We never did figure out what triggered his recovery. Remember, Sachiko?" he said to the nurse, who was applying a bandage to Joshua's forehead. "You'd just started working here when it happened."

"It was my first day, in fact. What was Ydrel even doing in here?"

"Probably trying to convince McDougal to take his medication," grumbled Joshua. His head was starting to pound in time with his pulse, and he could feel his temper going. He rested his head gingerly in his hands, fingers seeking the pressure points that might help alleviate the pain.

"The important thing," Malachai interjected, "is what we should do about Ydrel's current state."

Edith's eyes were bright with unshed tears, but her voice was calm and professional. "Lorazepam?"

Dr. Malachai grimaced slightly. "I'd rather not. He reacts so unpredictably to chemical treatments."

"We could just let him be," Hoffman suggested. "He snapped out of it himself last time."

"Let me work with him."

All eyes turned to Joshua. Hoffman laughed shortly. "Work with what, exactly?"

Despite the aching behind his eyes, Joshua forced himself to meet the gazes of each psychiatrist as he spoke. "This is classic NLP. I find his rhythm, use it to get to wherever he is, then I lead him out." He looked directly at Dr. Malachai. "I've done it before; ask my dad."

"I don't need to; I've read the case study. I am not the proponent of Neuro Linguistic Programming that your father is."

"I understand that, sir, but what have you got to lose?"

Now everyone looked at the senior psychiatrist, waiting, hoping. He frowned slightly, never taking his eyes off Joshua. Joshua kept his own gaze steady.

Finally, Edith spoke. "Randall, let him try."

"All right, then, but you'll do this under observation and with recording equipment running. And I want commentary."

"No can do, sir. If I break rhythm to comment, I'll have to start over again."

"Indeed. You'll debrief later, then. Edith, will you see to the arrangements? I think the Small Room is available."

"I'll make some cancellations and meet you there in a few minutes," Hoffman said. "I want to see this."

"It could take a couple of hours," Joshua warned.

"I'll bring some reading."

"I'll get you some."

"Joshua, are you up to this right now?" Edith asked as she rose. A couple of orderlies came in with a wheelchair and loaded Ydrel into it.

"I'm fine," he said as he started to stand up, then winced as the motion brought a fresh stab of pain. He turned it into a sardonic smile. "I could use a couple of Tylenol."

"Come on." Sachiko led him out and toward the nurses' station. She took out her keys, unlocked the medicine cabinet, and pulled out a bottle of analgesics.

"Let me have three."

She frowned but did as he asked. "This may sound calloused," she said, "but Ydrel isn't going anywhere. No one would think less of you if wanted to wait until tomorrow, or even just a couple of hours."

Joshua resisted the urge to shake his head. It was pounding enough already. "No. I'm not giving Malachai any chance to back on this. I'll be fine, promise. Besides, I don't think I could go to sleep tonight with the thought of Ydrel rocking like that."

Or the haunted looks on Edith's face, and yours, he added silently.

She had that look again now. "Can you really do this?"

"Yes."

"Okay, then."

He walked to Edith's office to grab some of the articles he had on using NLP on catatonic or autistic people, including the case study he and his father had written for a psychiatric quarterly magazine. It also gave the painkillers time to work.

When he got to the observation room, they had set Ydrel up on the floor on a couch cushion with his back to the door and his profile to the one-way mirror that lined one wall. He continued to rock, completely unaware. Another cushion lay on the floor opposite him.

The observation room was actually four rooms: the room where the action took place, a small bathroom that led off of it, the room behind the one-way mirror where observers sat, and a smaller room that held the recording equipment. Edith and Dr. Hoffman were waiting for him at the entrance; Dr. Malachai, apparently, had more pressing matters.

"Here's some reading," Joshua said to Dr. Hoffman. He handed him a folder as he slipped off his shoes.

"Part of the therapy?" Hoffman asked wryly.

"I may be at this a couple of hours. I'd just as soon be comfortable. Edith, is there any way I can record something before I go in?"

She led him in and showed him how to operate the equipment. He sat in the chair, turned on the microphone and spoke the date, his name, and Ydrel's. Then he gave a brief description of Ydrel's condition and what he planned to do.

"This afternoon, Ydrel was complaining about feeling overwhelmed by the thoughts and emotions of others. He claimed that the proximity of a client with bi-polar one disorder—a client who he believed was not taking or responding to his medication—had broken down his defenses. He did not feel he had either the energy or the focus to rebuild those defenses in light of the onslaught he perceived.

"With this as his frame of reference, it's probable he's retreated into himself to someplace where the thoughts of others cannot touch him. Therefore, he will either be very easy or very difficult to draw out. A lot will depend on whether he feels this time inward has helped him renew his strength, and whether or not he trusts me to protect him while he rebuilds his mental shields."

He switched off the microphone and turned to Edith. "It's really important that no one disturb me while I'm doing this. It wouldn't ruin anything, but it'll make the process longer. I don't want anybody to come in after us, either. This afternoon, he expressed a lot of paranoia and feelings of defenselessness. He may have to work through some of that before he's ready to face anyone. We'll come out when he's ready. And Edith, thanks."

"Just help him if you can." She sounded more like a mother than a counselor. He gave her an encouraging smile and went in.

He sat down on the cushion facing Ydrel and spent a few minutes studying him. He was rocking at a steady 48 beats a minute; his breathing regular, as if he'd left his body in some kind of holding pattern. Joshua reached out and placed a hand against Ydrel's shoulder. "I don't suppose you'd make this easy on the both of us and just tell me what's going on?"

The boy stared through him, unseeing. He continued to push against Joshua's hand at a steady 48 beats per minute.

The rocking made things both easy and hard for Joshua. He didn't have to match Ydrel's motions to reach him; matching breathing and other less obvious signals would probably be enough. On the other hand, it might be the key to reach him. Either way, it provided easier access, if Joshua could keep it up long enough.

In the end, the cameras decided for him. They probably wouldn't pick up the subtleties of breathing well enough to show what he was doing. He took a deep cleansing breath, arranged himself comfortably, and entered uptime.

First, he began rocking, easy and small, in counterpoint to Ydrel. It took a few minutes to match him, and too soon, he felt his abdominal muscles start to protest. Ignoring them, he turned to his breathing.

It was no easy task to perfectly match another person's breathing pattern, but Joshua had been learning and practicing this since he attended his first seminar with his father at the age of eight. He was soon in synch with Ydrel's pace; minutes later, he matched its depth.

This much established, he simply kept pace until he thought they had rapport; occasionally, he'd introduce a subtle change in the pattern, to see if the client would follow. Twice, Ydrel started to break rhythm to follow, only to fall back into his own pattern.

Fine. Be difficult. I'm not giving up on you yet. Joshua now concentrated on the patterns of Ydrel's eye movements. Matching eye patterns was always harder for him—he seemed to need to blink more often. He usually avoided this step by sitting at an angle to the client, so that he wasn't in their direct line of sight. For some reason, however, he felt the need to be facing Ydrel. It took several minutes to get it right. He became very aware of the ache in his left eye and had to concentrate beyond it.

Rock, rock, inhale, rock, rock, exhale, rock, blink. Try a variation; return to the pattern when it failed to hold. Rock, rock, inhale, rock, rock, exhale, rock, blink. The ache in his side reached a crescendo and faded from awareness. His focus narrowed to just Ydrel.

Rock, rock, inhale, rock, rock, exhale, rock, blink.

He had lost track of time when the world began to go gray around him, and he felt himself enveloped in a kind of cottony fog. This was something that had never happened to him before, but he merely filed his surprise away and continued to concentrate on Ydrel and his patterns.

Rock, rock, exhale, rock, blink...

For a moment, even Ydrel faded from his awareness, but he couldn't seem to feel concerned. He felt secure in the clouds around him, like a child wrapped up in a big downy comforter. He followed the feeling, and the rhythm.

Rock, rock, breathe, rock, blink—

Then, he saw Ydrel, in the distance, enveloped by the same gray clouds.

Gradually, he changed the rhythm, rock, exhale, blink, rock, inhale, blink.

Ydrel followed. Each motion of the new routine brought them a little closer until once again, Joshua could reach out and touch him. He knew he was ready.

"So why are we doing this?" he asked causally.

"It's comfortable."

"Maybe for you."

Ydrel blinked, out of turn. "It's safe."

"Ydrel," Joshua reached out, gripped his shoulder. "Talk to me."

Ydrel stopped rocking.

Suddenly, the gray clouds were gone and Joshua was once again aware of the surrounding: the hard cold walls, the flattened cushion beneath him, the incredible ache in his sides.

Ydrel blinked, disoriented, then focused on Joshua. Tears filled his eyes and he threw himself sobbing into the intern's arms.

"Joshua, I tried! I swear, I tried! But they made me go in—couldn't find the line—and he was so mad. Angry at you, you were interfering. And I got mad, but it wasn't me, it was him and he wanted to kill someone and I couldn't let him feel like that. I'd feel it and I *could* do it—with a *thought*. Just a thought! I couldn't let it happen again. If he'd just have taken one pill, just given me a chance to breathe. He made me want to kill. I ran. I di-didn't know what else to do!"

He continued to babble while Joshua held him, murmuring reassurances. When at last, his cries turned to hiccups, Joshua pushed him away enough to see his face.

"Ydrel, look at me," he spoke gently as if to a child. "We're going to fix this right now, the two of us, okay? Look around. This room is ours for as long as we need it. No one is going to interrupt us, and you don't have to be near another human being except me until you've got your defenses in place and you feel strong enough to face others."

Ydrel sniffed and glanced around. "This is an observation room. That's a two-way mirror."

"Screw it," Joshua replied rudely. "You've been living in a fishbowl for five years. This way's just more honest. Now, if you want to wow your audience, you prove to them that you can solve this problem on your own with just some advice from a friend. okay?"

"But Malachai—"

"—is not here. One thing at a time. All right?"

Ydrel nodded.

Josh resisted the urge to nod back. He was starting to realize how much his head still hurt.

"All right. Will you be okay for a few minutes before we start? 'Cause I don't know about you, but my muscles are getting cramped. I need to stretch." As he spoke, he uncrossed his legs—it was more difficult than he'd expected—and moved his protesting body into a series of basic stretches, moving slowly in deference to the ache in his muscles and the dizziness in his head.

Ydrel replied, "I've still got my ground. That's all that's kept me from losing myself." He stood easily, bent forward, and touched his forehead to his knees. Then he bent the other way in a lazy back-walkover.

"Show-off. So what'd you do with the energy from your ground?" Joshua crossed his legs, one foot flat on the floor against the opposite knee, braced his arm on the bent leg and twisted. The stretch along his lats felt both painful and oh, so good.

"What do you mean, the energy I got? I thought I was supposed to use the ground to shunt energy."

"Works both ways, remember? The earth is full of energy—heat energy, magnetic energy, living energy—so you should just be able to tap into it, right? Why don't you try it now?" Joshua changed legs and twisted in the other direction. He hissed as the stitch in his side twinged, then resolved.

Ydrel settled into an armchair and closed his eyes in concentration. A moment later, he frowned and opened one eye to regard his friend. "Why didn't you tell me I could take in energy through my ground?"

"Well, really, let's see," he answered with annoyance. "I had about forty-five minutes. I had to find you. Talk you out of a tree. Watch you do an amazing Darth Maul imitation—"

"Darth *who*?"

"You are so missing out. Are you tapped in yet, or do you want to waste more time discussing movies?"

Ydrel growled but closed his eyes again.

Minutes passed in silence. Joshua finished his stretches and, feeling sore but better, replaced the cushions on the couch and lay on it. He was sure he looked totally unprofessional, but he didn't want to sit again anytime soon.

Besides, I'm just the intern. I don't practice psychology unchaperoned.

Nonetheless, if he didn't want Ydrel to be thinking about who might be looking on, he'd better not either. So he relaxed into the comfortable couch and ran through the notes and settings of the song Rique had sent him Saturday, working out the fingerings on an imaginary keyboard.

Ydrel made a sound of disgust and opened his eyes. "This isn't working. I don't know what I'm supposed to search for. I could be right on top of it and not even know," he complained.

Joshua lowered his hands, but otherwise didn't move. "Hmm. I hadn't thought of that. The books always talk about energy having a flavor or color or something...?"

Ydrel shook his head.

"All right, let's try a human analogy. You've said you can read some people more easily than others, right? And there are some you can't read at all? Good. Here's what I want you to do: pick one person on each end of the spectrum. Then think about the differences between them. Psychically, I mean."

"That's easy. One bombards me with images and feelings and thoughts. The other, nothing. It's like being around a wall."

"That's a start. Think again about the first person, the sender. Can you focus through all the sights and sounds and emotion to the—I don't know—the aura or energy underneath?"

Ydrel's brow furrowed in concentration, and Joshua turned onto his side so he could watch his eyes. The pupils contracted, as he expected. They moved one way, then the other, as he psychically accessed (and, Joshua suspected, discarded) first sight, then sound, memory, then thought. Finally, Ydrel smiled, bemused.

"Wow. There is something there, something...more. That's kind of cool."

"Good. Good job. Now see if you can find a similar kind of more right in the earth."

After a few moments, Ydrel laughed. "It's all over. It's different—I can't explain how—but it's there. So how do I take it in?"

Joshua thought for a moment. "Is your memory just photographic?"

"Why?"

"You told me once that your mom healed your hand with just a touch. Assuming she didn't use a psychic band-aid, she must have transferred the energy. See if you can remember."

"And if I can't?"

"Then we think of something else." Joshua let his head get heavy on the couch cushion, glad he was facing away from the mirror. He didn't think he would move for a week. He wasn't sure he could at the moment. He might throw up. Maybe he should have listened to Sachiko and waited.

I'm fine. Besides, I did it. Now all I need to do is sit, talk, and wait. And the couch is plenty comfortable.

"All right." Ydrel's voice woke him from a doze he hadn't realized he'd fallen into. "I figured that out. Now what?"

Joshua's thoughts felt like sludge. He sat up lest he fall asleep again but refrained from shaking his head to clear the cobwebs. "Defenses?"

"Yeah. $E=mc^2$. Build my walls again."

He again settled into concentration. Joshua did some more stretches, ran over the songs, and was just starting to wonder what he should do about dinner when Ydrel let out a great, relieved sigh.

"That feels so much better, better than I've felt in a long time."

"Got your old defenses back in place? Then, we're not done yet, but we could take a breather. Hungry? What say I poke my head out the door and order us some chow? You just stay there and take five."

He went out the regular entrance. Dr. Hoffman, who must still have been observing, was waiting for him. "That was the singularly most amazing thing I've ever seen," he said after Joshua shut the door.

Joshua tried not to grin too widely; it helped that his face was starting to hurt again. "Thanks. We're not done yet. Can we get some dinner, and maybe a bunch of munchies and drinks? Nothing too heavy, though," he added as his stomach gave an unexpected twist at the thought of food.

"What else do you have to do? He seems fine—well, fine for Deryl."

"Ydrel's big complaint is that he can't keep up his defenses against the onslaught of thoughts and emotions around him—"

"C'mon, Joshua. You're not buying into his 'I'm psychic' psychosis?"

"It doesn't matter. That's his reality, and it's preventing him from interacting with what the majority consider reality. Today, he couldn't even cope. All I'm doing is helping him acquire the tools in his reality that will let him live in ours."

"And once he can cope, we work on his delusions?"

"Once he's able to cope, there won't be any need. I'd better get back in there," Joshua started before Dr. Hoffman could argue. "Could you get someone to bring us some food?"

The older psychiatrist smiled. "Sure. Light main course and lots of munchies and things to drink. You like Diet Coke, I recall?"

"Yeah, thanks. I'll probably need the caffeine."

Chapter Twenty-One

"Are you going to lie on that couch all day?" Ydrel glared at Joshua's prone form with irritation. He knew Joshua was tired and his head hurt, but he also knew the intern was posing for their audience. *See? Psychology doesn't have to be hard...*

"Depends on you," the intern replied laconically. "We're here until you're ready to leave. Until then, we might as well be comfortable." He reached for his bottle of Diet Coke, peered inside with a half frown before swallowing down the last dregs. "Hand me another one, please?"

"*You're* comfortable. *I'm* working." But Ydrel got up and went to the table along the wall where sodas and bottles of water shared the space with plates of food. He grabbed a soda, shook it, then tossed it to Joshua.

"Funny." Josh twisted the cap until it fizzed just enough to let out the extra air. "You found that sky-borne ley line yet?"

Ydrel sat back down in his chair and crossed his legs. "I was working on it when you sent me to fetch your soda."

"You were griping about me lying down when I asked you if you'd hand me one. I figured you were looking for a breather."

"It's not easy, inside," Ydrel groused. "I can't see it."

Joshua sighed. "We can take this outside if you want, but you can't live in the Great Outdoors forever.

You need to be able to find it indoors as well. Can't you hear it or feel it?"

Ydrel leaned against the back of the chair. "I tried. There's too much noise. It's like swimming though mud. You can imagine what that's like, Mr. Sinks-Like-A-Stone." It was another tidbit he shouldn't have known about Joshua (he'd picked it up from Sachiko's mind), and a low blow besides, but the intern didn't rise to the bait.

"If I were drowning, I'd give it my best shot." He started playing some song on his imaginary keyboard.

"Fine." Ydrel leaned forward, elbows on knees, his fingers digging through his hair. He wasn't quite drowning anymore. The food had helped; the time "away" had helped; knowing Joshua was going to stay with him until they figured this out helped, too.

So had Joshua's idea of the ground and of letting things shunt through him. Now, however, he was finding that he had to get through that to sense anything beyond. It *was* like swimming through mud, but mud with a swift and dangerous undertow. He let out a nervous sigh.

Then he felt Joshua's attention on him, felt him wishing he could see Ydrel's eyes. Ydrel didn't understand NLP theory, but he knew Joshua took a lot of cues from eye movements and posture.

He'd know if I was drowning. He'd come after me. The thought strengthened Ydrel, and he sat back and let himself wade, then swim, through the wild, stormy sea of thoughts and emotions that threatened to overtake him. They terrified him, ate at his fragile defenses like water against sand, but he pushed on. If he stopped, he'd drown, and he didn't think even the Great Joshua Lawson would be able to bring him back.

Suddenly, he was no longer swimming but floating, surrounded by a dazzling clear light and exquisite silence that almost seemed to sing. All around him, he could—feel? Taste? He had no words. But whatever it was, it was there, refreshing him, filling him with a wonderful sense of power he'd never before experienced. A laugh escaped his throat.

"Found it?" Joshua prompted.

"It's...wow..." Ydrel squirmed in his chair and giggled. He felt so happy and excited, like he had that Christmas when he was five and he and his mom had gone to his uncle's and aunt's house and he knew he'd get some great loot. "This is so cool! There's so much, and you were right: there is a...a flavor or color or something to it. It's definitely different from what I got through the ground. So, what do I do with it now that I've found it?"

"Only three things to do with energy: use it, store it, or leave it alone. What do you want to do?"

"Shields, I guess. But what do I do?"

"I'm not the military strategist; you are. Why don't you take all that learning you've been passing on the Tasmae-nian She-Devil and use it for your own benefit for a change? Analyze the attacks, decide how you can defend against them, and build your defenses."

Ydrel closed his eyes and thought about the effect of people around him, how they wore away at his shields like an acid rain, or more like acid waves, and how a particularly strong attack battered through. It was painful; even as he thought about it, he could feel his barriers giving way.

Then, there was a gentle hand on his shoulder. "Ydrel, these are memories, right? You don't need to relive them. Examine them from a distance. Try putting them in a book or laying them out like a battle plan or something. Give me a report."

Speaking as dispassionately as he could, eyes still shut, Ydrel told him how the psychic emanations attacked his defenses.

"Good. It sounds like you have three different kinds of attack: the steady wearing down of your defenses by the everyday emanations of people around you—sort of like psychic white noise—the pounding attacks of blunt emotions, and the point attacks of specific impressions or memories. Sound right?"

"You sure you aren't a strategist?"

"Nah. Mom taught me how to summarize well, is all. Tell me what's wrong with your defenses in light of this analysis?"

Now that they had actually looked at it, the answer was clear. "I've got one single defense against multiple levels of attack, and no means to shore myself up as I'm worn down. I need multiple defenses with diversified materials and strategies, set up fallback positions, maybe have ready reserves of energy to build up my shields on the fly. I—I don't know if I can do all that."

"Why not? You've got a greatly enhanced source of energy, a safe haven for as long as you need it, and me to bounce ideas off of. If you need something more, let me know and I'll try to get it."

Ydrel opened his eyes and saw that the intern—his friend—was totally sincere. He also noticed the bruise on Joshua's face. Had Joshua gotten that rescuing him? He felt his eyes sting and mist. He pressed his knuckles into them hard.

"You okay?" Joshua asked softly.

"Yeah." He took a deep breath. "Yeah. I just, I've never had a friend like you before. No one's ever..."

Joshua shrugged it off. "You'll pay me back sometime. I get the impression the wall you have is a small, brick-type one, like around your mind or something?"

Ydrel nodded.

"Well, there are a lot of ways to think, not just with your mind. Some people think more with their bodies—you've heard of gut feelings, right?—and others with their emotions, which are as much tied into the nervous system of the body as the hypothalamus and limbic system. I'll bet you're getting a lot of 'Left Hook' attacks through your body. Why don't you work on building a personal shield that surrounds your body like a second skin or an aura—maybe an anti-aura, actually."

Ydrel spent the next few hours alternately eating and working. First, he created an ever-present shield of dull, impression-absorbing energy, which would capture the outside impressions and shunt them away through his ground. Things grew muffled but still present, like the sound of rain on a thinly insulated roof.

He tried making the shield stronger, but it blocked everything; for a moment, it was blessedly still, then he felt disoriented and scared. Everything seemed wrong, flat. Joshua stared at him with an expression he couldn't define, and when he spoke, his voice, though full of inflection, was oddly emotionless.

"Ydrel, are you all right?"

Hastily, Ydrel cut back the shield's strength. Color and impression returned. He found he was gasping with relief. He could now see Joshua's brow was furrowed with worry.

He told him what happened. "It was like suddenly being blind or deaf or something. For a minute, I wasn't even sure that you were you. I mean, it looked like you, but I couldn't be sure. It was weird."

"Interesting. That's an important lesson: you don't want to completely shield yourself from what's around you because you depend on it to recognize people. So how are you going to handle that?"

"I guess I need some kind of...radar screen to let me sense what's around me, and a way to determine what to let in and what to shield against. But how in the world can I do that?"

"That, I can help with." Joshua taught him about the "control room," a sanctuary inside his mind where he could have internal dialogues with himself. He taught him how to access his creative subconscious, set it to work on a task—in this case, his radar screen—and give it a way to signal him if it had ideas.

He followed Joshua's instructions. Then, with his subconscious working the radar issue, he set to work again on his defenses, building up several types of shields. Some, he would wear all the time. Others, he could call up in a hurry.

"There's one other thing we should think about," Joshua told him when he'd stopped for a break and to drink some water. "Reserves. You should have a way to store energy. After all, when you're out in the world, you may not be near a convenient ley line, right?

Ydrel nodded, polished off the bottle in a series of quick swallows, and turned his attention to the issue.

His first thought was to pile it, like batteries or ammunition, near his barriers.

"Your body stores energy in your fat cells," Joshua suggested. "Not that you should get obese or anything."

"No, I see what you mean. Make it an extension of my body."

"Yeah, like a sword," Joshua agreed.

A sword! Ydrel remembered his sword, the one from the land of mists. If he could embed it with enough energy, he might even be able to break free of the Master's spell! Could he find it and power it without drawing the Master's notice?

He resolved to try, but later. It was one thing he did not, could not, explain to Joshua. Besides, he felt better and stronger than he had in ages. He didn't have to accomplish everything tonight.

"I feel so...steady," he finally told Joshua. "I think I could take on anything."

"Really?" Joshua said thoughtfully.

Suddenly, a burst of anger flared across Ydrel's senses like a fireball. *I trusted her! How could she—!*

Ydrel blinked. "Hey! What was that about?"

As suddenly as the anger hit, it was gone, replaced by low-level surprise. "Thought you said your shields could take it."

"Well, it wasn't as bad as it might have been, but still, I wasn't expecting it. I've been concentrating on storing the energy, not putting it into defenses."

"You need to get used to doing both, plus whatever else you want to do, psychic and otherwise. Leastways, that's how they train them in the books. Or do you want to go around in life with a T-shirt that says: *CAUTION:*

PSYCHIC. PLEASE REFRAIN FROM USING STRONG EMOTION WITHIN 50 FEET?"

Despite himself, Ydrel laughed. "And on the back, I could put: SAME TO YOU, FELLA. You've got a point. Try that again."

"Oh, I will."

And he had, tossing out bits of emotion or memory at random, first making Ydrel block it, then block it but still identify it—part of the radar his subconscious was working on. Joshua returned to reclining on the couch, and talked to him a little about Colorado, about college, about books—about everything but the woman who had made him so angry.

"So, who was she?" Ydrel asked, reaching through his shields toward Joshua's emotions.

"Ex-girlfriend," Joshua answered. "Don't go there."

And the colossal wave of anguish and hurt that waited behind the anger made Ydrel retreat back to himself in a hurry.

They snacked until only crumbs were left—or rather, Ydrel did. Joshua stuck to crackers and water, with the occasional Diet Coke. Joshua would find some new memory or thought to toss at him. When Ydrel got good at identifying and deflecting emotional ones, Joshua turned to physical memories.

"Are you all right?" Ydrel asked after Joshua hit him with the memory of getting a chair to the face. "'Cause that really hurt!"

"I could use some more Tylenol, but I'll live," he answered. "What's next on the agenda?"

"Bathroom break," Ydrel said and rose to relieve himself.

When he returned, Joshua was asleep on the couch.

Chapter Twenty-Two

"Joshua? Come on, Joshua, wake up, please?"

For a confused moment, Joshua wondered what Sachiko was doing in his apartment. Then he remembered that he wasn't in his apartment; he was in the infirmary. He had fallen asleep working with Ydrel. Ydrel had actually cleaned up the room while Joshua slept, and then fetched Sachiko. She looked him over and declared he needed more than just Tylenol.

How he'd managed to walk on his own to the infirmary without throwing up or passing out, he'd never know. He was fairly sure he'd done both those things once he got through the infirmary doors.

The doctor took x-rays, diagnosed him as post-concussive. He remembered that. He thought he remembered the resident massage therapist coming to work on his abdominals and saying how everyone was amazed that he brought a client out of catatonia by doing crunches. It had hurt to laugh.

He must have fallen asleep during the massage. That was kind of embarrassing—as was the fact that he was only in his underwear, a fact he only realized after he sat up in bed.

Wordlessly, Sachiko handed him a shirt and he gratefully put it on. He didn't mind Sachiko seeing him shirtless, far from it, but it was cold under the air conditioning. "I'm so sorry! What time is it?"

"Ten o'clock."

"At night? I really sacked out!"

She laughed shortly. "Ten a.m. We weren't even going to wake you, but..." Her voice caught. "It's Isaac. He hasn't eaten in over 24 hours. He stopped breathing a couple of times. I don't think he's going to last the day."

He wanted to ask why she was there when this wasn't her shift—was she there for him or Isaac? Then he realized how selfish that would sound. Isaac needed her. Needed them.

"Someone called his family?" he asked instead.

Sachiko actually snarled. "His grandson will try to make it tonight—'important meetings' or some such bullshit. Ydrel's been with him since yesterday evening."

"How's he doing?" He finished buttoning his cuffs and took the tie she handed him.

"Remarkable. He's upset, naturally, but he's not lost, like he usually is around Isaac. Josh, I know you're still probably feeling awful, but you're the only one on staff who has any experience with this sort of thing, and you've spent a lot of time with him lately. Plus, I don't think Ydrel will leave his side for anybody else, and I'm not sure it's a good idea he be there when—"

"Hey, it's okay. I feel fine, honest." He started to get up, and remembered just in time that he had no pants on. "Uh, how about if I catch up?"

She smirked. "I'll meet you outside."

"Ko—?"

She paused with her hand on the doorknob.

"Has anybody called a rabbi? I don't know much about Jewish traditions, but he is pretty religious, I thought."

"I'll check."

She shut the door, and he hurried to finish dressing. Just as he shrugged on his suit coat, Dr. Caldwell came in and gave him a cursory exam and made him promise to return to the infirmary if he felt any signs of dizziness or nausea. Sachiko was hanging up the phone as he approached the infirmary desk.

"Rabbi Rosenbaum will be here in about half an hour," she said as they headed down the hall. "I'll need to talk to security and arrange an escort."

"I'll go on to his room, then."

She gave him a long sideways glance. "Are you sure you're all right?"

He wanted to put his arms around her and reassure her, but she'd made it clear that she didn't want any personal displays of affection at work. He settled on a smile. "I'm fine. And I appreciate your getting me up."

"All right, then."

He left her at the nurses' station and went on to Mr. Goldstein's room. No one had bothered to open the curtains or the blinds; despite the mid-morning sun, it was dark and dim, and kind of morbid, especially with the air conditioning cooling the room to a temperature more suited to tombs.

He went straight to the windows and pulled back the curtains, opened one enough to let in a little natural air in. Immediately, the place felt better. He pulled a chair next to Ydrel, who blinked owlishly at him.

"How you holding up?" Joshua asked.

"Fine, I guess. I just, I don't know what to do."

"You're doing everything you need to," Joshua reassured him, then took the dying man's hand from his. "Mr. Goldstein? It's Joshua. We've talked a few times. I wanted you to know your grandson is going to try to visit tonight. Also, Rabbi Rosenbaum is coming in a little while. Would you like to see him? If so, just squeeze my hand."

He felt the slightest pressure along his fingers. "Okay, sir, we'll have him come right in. In the meantime, though, you just do what you need to. Don't worry about us. You've done so much on this earth, you deserve to rest. Ydrel's here with me, and I know he feels the same way." He glanced at Ydrel.

"'Course I do." His voice was husky with unshed tears.

Joshua gave him the old man's hand back and they sat in silence. A few times, he took the opportunity to study Ydrel. Sachiko was right: although he seemed sad and even a little scared, he was nonetheless centered and certainly within his own mind. In the warm afternoon light, Joshua could examine his eyes. He didn't see any of the wild "pinning" he had come to associate with what Ydrel called his psychic abilities.

Nonetheless, Ydrel seemed to pick up his thoughts. "My defenses are holding pretty well," he said, "though I'm eating into my reserves."

"We've got some quiet time; replenish them now."

Ydrel nodded and closed his eyes. Joshua took the old man's hand.

A few minutes later, there was a light knock on the door and a man in a conservative suit but with a small round cap on his head poked his head in. Joshua waved him in. "Mr. Goldstein, the rabbi is here. Shall we leave the two of you alone? Squeeze for yes."

Again a slight pressure. The two got up to leave, then stopped as the elderly man spoke, "Ydrel," he breathed.

Ydrel rushed back, leaned close to his dying friend. "I'm here."

"Thank you."

"I—you're welcome." Gently, he kissed the old man's head, then hurried from the room.

Joshua lingered a few minutes with the rabbi. When he emerged from the room, he found Ydrel leaned against the wall near the door, hunched over so that his hair fell over his face, arms crossed, seemingly staring at a point on the floor six inches from his feet. Sachiko hovered nearby, looking helpless. Apparently, she had offered her sympathy and been refused. She gave Joshua a distressed look.

"Hey, Ydrel, when's the last time you ate?"

"I don't know. Dinner, I guess."

"Well, I'm starving. What say we go to the kitchen and grab some sandwiches or something?"

"I don't know," Ydrel glanced at the door, his face screwed up with indecision.

"The rabbi's praying with him. There's nothing we can do for a while. The best thing is to stock up on some food before you go back to him."

"Well..." Ydrel's looked up and right—visual construction, Joshua thought—and his pupils narrowed momentarily. Then he nodded sullenly.

"Good. Let's go. I'm starved."

Joshua waited until they got to the kitchen. "You okay?"

"Why'd you make me tell him it was okay to die?" Ydrel burst out in reply.

Joshua sighed. *Here we go.* "Sometimes, people are ready to die, but they...hang on. Sometimes, they're waiting for someone; sometimes, they're scared of what will happen; sometimes, they're more afraid of hurting someone."

Ydrel flopped miserably into a chair. "You think he's hanging on because of me?"

Joshua pulled up a chair, turned it around and sat with his arms draped over the back. "I don't know. That's why the rabbi's here now. Or he could be waiting for his grandson. If it makes you feel any better, this isn't the first time I've told someone something like that."

"How can you stand it?"

"Ydrel, Isaac hasn't really been living for a while now. And a lot of his days lately have been torturous—you know that more than any of us. It sounds cliché, but when he dies, he'll finally find peace, even joy again."

"You really believe that?"

"Yeah, I do. He was a good man, and very faithful. God will take care of him."

Ydrel pulled up his legs, resting his chin on his knees. "There were times, I wished he'd just die, so I wouldn't have to share his memories, anymore. But now, I—" His voice caught. He looked away.

He looked incredibly young and vulnerable sitting with his arms wrapped around his shins and his forehead resting on his knees, blond hair falling in wisps around his face. Still, Joshua made no move to comfort him. He'd refused Sachiko's comfort; this was just something he needed to work through on his own. Joshua gave him a few minutes.

"Ydrel?" he asked when the tension in the boy's hunched-up shoulders seemed to have relaxed a little. "You've got your radar focused on him, right?"

The psychic looked up, surprised. "How'd you know?"

"I saw you do it. That means you have a choice. We can hang out until after, or we can grab something fast and you can be with him through the end. You've done a lot for Isaac already, way more than anyone could have expected. Even Isaac knew that, or he wouldn't have spent his last energy thanking you. No one would think less of you for not being there. It's totally your decision."

"Would you stay with me?"

"Sure. If that's what you want."

He heaved a large sigh, then unfolded himself. "Then let's grab something fast and go. I don't think we have a lot of time."

Chapter Twenty-Three

Isaac died around 6:30 that evening.

Joshua waited by the door while Ydrel pressed the old man's hand to his forehead and whispered his goodbyes. Then he escorted Ydrel, white-faced and trembling, to his room.

At the door, Ydrel stopped to face him. "Listen, I just want a long shower and to sleep. That okay?"

"Absolutely," Josh said. "I'll probably hang around a while, and Sachiko's here 'till ten. But if you need to talk, call me, okay?"

Ydrel went into his room without replying.

Josh got to the nurses' station just in time to over-hear Monique telling an orderly about how Dr. Malachai handled Isaac's grandson. She waved him over and began her story again. It seemed his grandson was annoyed about making the trip for nothing—"'For nothing,' that's what he said!"—and demanded to know what arrangements had been made for the body. Dr. Malachai gave him a lecture about family responsibility.

"Dr. Malachai was furious! But he was so polite, and when he was done, was Isaac's grandson ever red. It was a beautiful thing to watch."

"Wish I'd been here to see it," Joshua said. "Where's Sachiko?"

"Taking care of Isaac's room—cleaning up, packing the personal effects, you know."

Joshua nodded, tried to keep his voice casual. "I think I'll go see if she'd like a hand."

"That won't be necessary."

Joshua turned at the sound of Dr. Malachai's voice. "It's okay, sir. I volunteer at a nursing home. I've done this sort of thing before."

"And Sachiko was a hospital nurse for several years before she came to work here. She's well-qualified to handle the situation without the aid of the remarkable Joshua Lawson." He smiled, but the comment grated on Joshua's raw nerves.

"I'm not doing this for an ego trip, sir." It was all he could do to keep his voice guileless, without the growl he wanted to express.

"And I'm not suggesting that," the senior psychiatrist answered just as smoothly. "However, you have had an extremely difficult few days. You've done remarkable work, been through a traumatic experience, and you've been injured. You've earned your pay—and your reputation. Now, it's time to go home."

Before Joshua could protest, he added, "I will meet you at the security gate in five minutes. You are to drive home, get a good night's sleep and return tomorrow ready to work. There are quite a few people asking about your performance with Ydrel on Monday, and I want you to prepare something we can show everyone. Do you understand?"

I understand you're taking me away from what little support I have right now. "Yes, sir."

After that, he had no choice. He went docilely to his car, but he didn't drive home right away. Instead, he took out his cell phone and left a message on Sachiko's answering machine. Next, he drove to the nearest Catholic church he could find, lit a candle, and prayed the rosary, twice. Then he knelt there until his knees hurt and his thoughts had spun down to nothing. After that, he went to a noisy restaurant and ordered the biggest chocolate dessert on the menu.

It was past ten when he did climb the stairs to his apartment. He heard his phone ring and rushed to grab it, hoping it was Sachiko.

It was his parents.

"Were you ever planning to call us and let us know that you're okay?" his mother demanded.

"Lay off, Mom," he said wearily as he tossed his keys on the table. "I just got home. I went to church, then went and got a big brownie cake with chocolate sauce." He knew she'd know what he meant. She knew his habits well.

"So your Alzheimer's client died? You poor baby. Are you okay?"

He sat down on the edge of the day bed. Homesickness hit him so hard he wanted to curl up into a tight ball of misery. "No," was all he managed to choke out.

An hour and a half later, he felt calmer and sleepy, so he hung up and went to bed. No sooner had he gone to sleep than the dreams came.

Isaac, lying in bed, crying. Crying for the wife he couldn't protect against the savagery of the Nazis. Then he became his grandfather, crying for the daughter he couldn't take care of if he died.

"It's okay, Grandpa. Dad and I will take care of her for you, promise."

His grandfather turning to smile at him, tears in his eyes.

Tears of blood.

Joshua woke, his own cheeks wet with tears. It was an old dream—a memory, really—but tonight it was too much. He didn't want to face sleep and a return to the dream, so he snapped on the light. His keyboard rested invitingly on its stand in one corner of the room, but it was too late at night to play with his landlady right below him. He went instead to the computer to check his e-mail.

Big mistake: Rique had e-mailed to report that LaTisha was in Santa Fe and had asked about him. *Not that I disapprove, but why'd you two break up, anyway?*

Joshua replied, asking Rique to tell her he was fine, but nothing more. Sooner or later, he'd have to tell Rique what had happened. So far, the only one who knew was Father Ron.

And maybe Ydrel. How much did Joshua give away, working with the psychic?

"Psychic." Like I really believe that. But do I?

Sachiko does.

Even though it was past three in the morning, his eyes kept straying to the telephone. If he could just talk to her—

You'll see her tomorrow, and if you want to make any kind of professional showing at work, you'd better get at least a few hours' sleep.

Sleep, when it did come, was filled with dreams.

Sachiko looked at the glaring red digital readout of her alarm clock and sighed. What was she doing awake at three in the morning?

Stupid dream. She couldn't even remember what specifically she had dreamed, but she still felt edgy and upset in its aftermath. She laughed bitterly to herself. It wasn't like she hadn't been feeling edgy and upset all week, as it was.

She'd been more worried about Joshua than she cared to admit; through her shift, she had had to fight the urge to check in on him as he lay unconscious in the infirmary. Mr. Goldstein's downturn had actually been a help then, for she could concentrate on him and on Ydrel who'd sat at his side with such dedication. Thinking about them, she'd hardly slept.

Then Edith called; Mr. Goldstein was getting worse, and with her emergency-room experience she was the best-qualified nurse they had for the situation.

When she came in at the start of her shift, she knew there was nothing she could do. He had looked so frail and afraid and all she could think was how wrong it was, that he didn't belong there, with no one but staff and one teenage boy.

Then Ydrel had asked in a small voice if she could please see if Joshua would wake up, and she had had to keep from running to the infirmary.

And he had known just what to do. He thought of the rabbi. He stayed with Isaac and Ydrel through the end. He knew how to comfort Ydrel when he'd rejected all of her attempts. He'd done everything.

Except comfort her.

Sachiko rolled over and punched her pillow savagely. *It's your own fault. You just had to tell him, "If we ever get to the point that we're getting married or something, you can go singing our love in the halls. But until then, we stay strictly professional—even if* we're alone." *Of course, he wasn't going to go putting his arms around you at work. Besides, Randall all but evicted him. And he did call...*

That call had left her with mixed feelings, too. Here he was, going to church in the middle of the week, actually seeking comfort there, whereas she hadn't darkened the door of a church since—

Since you started sleeping with Randall. Actually before. He never cared for "institutional religion," and you let that sway you. How could you let a man affect you so much? And are you doing it again?

She glanced at the telephone. She'd tried to call him as soon as she'd gotten home, but his line had been busy. At 11:30, she'd given up in disgust. He was probably cruising the Internet or playing some juvenile online game or something.

She thought about getting up and having a glass of wine but wasn't sure she'd trust herself to stop at one, and she needed to get up clear-headed in a couple of hours. Besides, opening a new bottle just seemed like too much effort. Instead she called upon the skills from her martial arts training and years as an emergency room nurse, did some relaxation breathing, and forced herself into a deep, dreamless sleep.

"Ydrel? Please wake up! Are you all right?"

Ydrel opened his eyes reluctantly. He was lying on a bed of moss and fallen leaves. For a moment, he was disoriented, then he realized where he was. The Miscria's netherworld.

He sat up and rubbed his eyes.

Tasmae, who had been kneeling over him and shaking him, now sat back on her heels with a gusty sigh of relief. "Are you all right? I 'knocked' and 'knocked' as you asked, but I got no answer, none at all. So I Called you, and it took all I had to bring you here."

"I'm sorry," he said, still a little confused. "A friend died today, and I was with him—"

"You were what?" She backed away, eyes wide, horrified at the thought.

Did they have some taboo about the dying he didn't know about? He was tired and raw, and his response came out more irritably than he intended. "It's something we do on Earth, okay? We're not going to let someone die alone. We sit with them, and we tell him it's okay, and sometimes, we say prayers and stuff—"

"Did you follow him?" she demanded. "Into death? Did you try to bring him back?"

"What? No! He was old, Tasmae. He was ready to die. I just... I held his hand..."

He stopped, suddenly angry. Only a day ago, he'd been so lost in his own mind that Joshua had had to retrieve him from his catatonia. He quickly squashed the thought. The last thing he needed was Tasmae picking up evidence of his instabilities. But somehow, it just made him angrier.

"Why do you care? It's not like you even knew him. Why would you think I'd chase his psyche or soul or..." He trailed off as he noticed her trembling. "What?"

"Sometimes, my people will 'chase.'" She paused and swallowed hard. He saw now how haunted her eyes were. "Sometimes, a healer tries too hard to heal, and they'll try to reunite the person with his body. Some say that is what happened with Alugiac, as he tried to heal a dying Barin, and a part of it returned and shares his body now. Now, he is both their leader and their slave."

She shivered suddenly and wrapped her arms around herself.

His anger vanished in the need to comfort her, but the most he could make himself do was set a hand over hers and speak gently. "Hey. Not me, okay? I'm on your side, promise."

She made the funny sideways nod of her people and let out a shuddering sigh. Then she wiped her cheeks and looked at her hand, surprised at the tears.

"Sounds like a ghost story," Ydrel commented.

"Ghost story?"

"Yeah, tales of the spirits of those who died but never made it to the afterlife. So they hang around Earth and cause lots of trouble. I've never seen one, and if anyone's qualified to see a ghost, it'd be me. But sometimes, they supposedly possess other people, too."

She looked at him with intense interest. "And how would you evict such a ghost?"

"Uh, an exorcism, I guess. A really holy person or priest calls upon God to force the demon soul out."

Disappointment covered her like a shroud. "Then he is not possessed, for I have called upon God, and Alugiac is no better than before."

Joshua was on the stage, this time with the mike and out from behind the keyboard. He was singing something hot and a little raunchy. He could see his audience: hundreds of beautiful women, all dancing and waving. LaTisha smiled up at him in a way that made him feel hot and a little raunchy, too.

Then someone threw a dead baby on the stage.

Suddenly he was running down a long backstage corridor—behind him a screaming, rabid mob of girls now hideous as they called to him and fought among each other. He dashed into a side room with a star on the door and leaned against it panting, safe. He saw Sachiko in the make-up chair and his heart leaped until he noticed she was curled in on herself, her head bowed. She looked up, tears in her eyes.

She held out her bloody hands.

Chapter Twenty-Four

Thursday was uneventful, but stressful in its own way. With a hot shower, two lattes and some eye drops, Joshua was able to fake his way through work. Dr. Malachai made such a big deal of Joshua's "miracle work" that nearly everyone focused on him and didn't bother to wonder how Mr. McDougal was able to fool such an experienced and observant psychiatrist when an intern had noticed, and one nurse had written in the logs, "Not sure McDougal's medication is working. Monitor him closely this pm and let Dr. Malachai know of unusual behavior."

Sachiko, he heard, was mad at herself for daydreaming when she should have been paying attention to the logs. He wondered if she was mad at him, too.

Edith asked Joshua to spend time with Ydrel, to make sure he was all right. So far, he'd rebuffed most offers of sympathy, although he did talk briefly with the rabbi, who had visited early that morning. He seemed to be handling things well, but Edith decided some alone time in a safe environment with Josh would give Ydrel the security to confront his feelings of grief.

So they absconded with a waffle iron and ingredients from the kitchen and took over the nurse's lounge for an hour. They talked about Isaac and death for a few minutes, in deference to her request, but Ydrel really wanted to talk about his newfound sources of energy. After assuring himself that Ydrel was indeed handling things well, Joshua told him what he knew about ley lines and magic and ESP, most of which came from a lifelong habit of reading science fiction and fantasy.

"I'm sure there are non-fiction books out there that treat the subject with more objectivity," Joshua said as he put a couple of the warm waffles on his plate. "Why don't you get the librarian to do a search for you?"

Ydrel laughed derisively as he sat down and thoughtlessly smeared syrup over his waffles, then handed the bottle to his friend. "Yeah, and get it put in my record: 'sudden interest in the occult after witness-ing the death of fellow patient.'"

"I see your point. Well, keep it in mind for when you get out of here." Joshua took the syrup and carefully filled each square. After a moment, he noticed Ydrel staring at him with a look of horror. "What?"

"Do you—do you always do that?" He pointed at the waffles with his fork as if they were something obscene.

"What? Fill the holes with syrup? Sure, for as long as I can remember. Why?"

"That's not, well, weird or obsessive or anything?"

Joshua shrugged and took a bite of his waffle. "Why would you think that?" He kept his manner casual but watched Ydrel closely.

"Never mind." Ydrel turned his attention back to his plate, but Joshua had seen it—that pining of the eyes, followed by a quick jerk left and up—visual recall. Someone else's.

"All right, who's sending memos saying that making sure your waffles are properly syruped is obsessive be-havior?"

Ydrel's head jerked up in surprise. "It's in my rec-ords. 'January 17th: Patient compulsive about ensuring entire waffle filled with syrup. Indicative of other obsessive behavior?' So I stopped doing that. Last thing I needed was another label." He looked down at his plate morosely. "I hardly ever have waffles anymore. There's either too little syrup or too much."

Joshua handed him the bottle. "Go for it."

They went back to Ydrel's room, and he hurried in first and went straight to his bed. He straightened out the covers, attempting as he did so to hide the old stuffed bear that normally sat on his headboard. Joshua bit back a sigh. "Let me guess," he said quietly, and mimed writing on a clipboard. Ydrel nodded glumly.

Joshua fought the urge to pull the bear out from under the blankets and formally present it back to his grieving friend. *Guess I'd better wade through Ydrel's records after all. What was one more thing to my schedule, anyway?*

On top of that, Joshua spent the day quelling rumors and jokes: "No, I didn't rock for five hours," "No, you don't need abs of steel to do Neuro Linguistic Programming."

In the afternoon, he had gone to the nurses' station to see Sachiko, only to overhear her telling Monique about her last class: "It was this litany of every mistake you could make in an abortion," she was saying, and Joshua decided to just walk on by.

"Joshua, come here," she called to him. "You might be interested in this."

"Thanks, but I've had enough death and pain for a week," he'd snapped and left the stunned nurses without looking back. He couldn't; the nightmare image of Sachiko with blood on her hands was still in his mind.

He was only too glad to follow Dr. Malachai's order to edit the tape they'd made in order to demonstrate the methods he used.

He and Floyd spent most of the afternoon and a good part of the evening in the editing room, reviewing and cutting out huge portions of videotape. At 8:30, they still weren't done. They'd called it a night, and Joshua went home, plopped straight into bed and slept fitfully until the phone woke him a couple of hours later. It was Sachiko.

"You know," she started acerbically, "you could have at least heard me out about why my class would have interested you."

"I'm sorry," he sighed. "It's just, I had a lot of nightmares about people dying: Isaac, my grandfather, babies—"

"Me?"

"You weren't dead."

She picked up his unspoken thought. "Ouch. No wonder you didn't meet me for dinner at the lounge tonight."

"No. No, that wasn't it. I—Malachai set me to editing that stupid video they took of Ydrel and me, and I had to work with Floyd. We were trying to get it done fast so he could go home, so we worked through dinner. When we finally quit, I was so wasted, I just dragged myself straight home. I wish there was some way I could leave you a note at work—"

"That's all right. I should have known it was something like that." Her voice was once again soft and sweet, and Joshua leaned into the phone, a warm feeling easing the tightness in his stomach.

"Are you all right?" she asked.

"Better now. You have no idea how much better. When can we see each other again—I mean outside of work?" He tried to keep the longing out of his voice. He wasn't sure he was especially successful, but for the moment, he didn't care.

"I don't have class Saturday. How's Friday night after work? Maybe we could meet somewhere—"

"Just come to my place. It's only a 10-minute drive. We can just hang out and relax. Unless you'd rather—"

"No. Your place sounds perfect! I mean, I don't think either of us is up for going out in public. By the way, the reason I wanted you to hear about my class is that, after listening to this awful list of every mistake and complication that can occur, I asked my professor how we go about repairing such damage. What I was supposed to do if I was the e-room surgeon who got stuck with some idiot's victim, you know what I mean?"

"Really?"

"Really. Floored him, too. He said he'd cover it next week, and a lot of my classmates caught me afterward to thank me for asking. But I never would have had the guts to speak up—and risk adding to what he might put on the midterm—if it hadn't been for you."

They talked a while longer, and when Joshua hung up, he fell immediately into a deep and peaceful sleep.

Joshua woke at five Friday morning, feeling completely rested and too excited about his upcoming date with Sachiko to just lie around. Because he had hardly been home all week, his apartment was in relatively good shape. In half an hour, he had it completely clean.

In the shower, he debated working on Rique's song over just heading in to work early. He decided on the latter: he had a case study he needed to work on for Edith, and if he could get some early time with Ydrel, he could catch Floyd as soon as he came on shift and get that ridiculous tape finished in plenty of time to get home and get ready.

As soon as he got through the security gates and heard the screaming, however, he knew he'd be lucky if he got home before Sachiko showed up at his door. With an inward sigh, he made a beeline for the common room. As he got nearer, the words became more distinct. "We're not like that! You...believe me!"

Two orderlies were blocking the doorway, holding a straitjacket. Nonetheless, they didn't seem to be trying to keep anyone in or out; rather, they were loitering, one actually leaning against the doorframe. Biting back his annoyance, Joshua looked between them to assess the situation.

Carter Doleson was standing on the sofa, yelling at the top of his lungs and gesticulating wildly. Dr. Rose Dover, the mid-shift psychiatrist, a small quiet lady only two months from retirement, was standing near the arm of the couch, trying calmly but ineffectively to get him to come down so they could talk. As with Dr. Hoffman, such soothing tones only made him more agitated.

"You don't understand! They have to know we're not like that!" He waved wildly at the TV, where the news was replaying live footage of a mob scene somewhere in Europe.

One of the orderlies blocking the door, who smelled vaguely of cigarette smoke and perfume and whose dishwater blond hair was slicked back, sniggered.

"Shall we give her a few more minutes before we jump in and rescue?"

Great. Wonder if this is the Roger that Sachiko is trying to get fired? What's he doing on the day shift?

"That won't be necessary," Joshua growled and pushed between them.

Dr. Dover continued to speak with fraying patience to the agitated Carter. Joshua snapped off the television, touched Dr. Dover lightly on the shoulder to alert her to his presence, then stood up on the couch next to the ranting client.

"Carter?" he asked softly.

"Joshua!"

Carter spun, nearly toppling off the couch, and grabbed the intern by the shoulders. "You've got to help me! We've got to make them understand! Humans aren't all evil or destructive or—"

"Carter, they have sensitive surveillance equipment, right?"

Carter paused. "Yes, but—"

"It can pick up the slightest whisper, right?"

"Right—"

"I think you've blown out their system."

"You're right, you're right," the older man sighed. "It's just that I can't stand their thinking we're all so evil, when there are so many good people, but all we ever see is the violence and the pain and—"

"Do you really think screaming is going to help? I mean, what would you believe—the evidence before your eyes or one man shouting to the contrary? Standing on a couch and shouting, no less?"

"But we have to make them understand!"

"Is this way working? Then you need to think of a better way. How about if we talk about it over breakfast?"

Together, they stepped off the couch and, after getting a nod of permission from Dr. Dover, turned for the door. Halfway to the door, however, they met the orderlies. One nodded to him and went to Dr. Dover. Roger just stood in their way and sneered.

Carter shrank back as the orderly held up the straitjacket suggestively.

"That won't be necessary," Joshua stated flatly. He was repeating himself, he knew, but he didn't trust himself to say anything more. He took Carter's arm to lead him past.

The orderly stepped in front of him and looked at him as if he couldn't be serious. "And let Carter have another screaming fantasy in the cafeteria? I hardly think that's acceptable."

"That's not your call."

"And you think it's yours, *intern*?" Blondie sneered.

"That's right." He'e conveyed in his tone and expression, *I can get you fired*.

"Think you're a big man, eh?" He glanced at Carter and gave the jacket a slight flick in his direction.

With a sudden movement, Joshua snatched it out of the orderly's hands. Then he folded it and handed it to Carter to hang onto.

"Now, I'm sure you can find something more productive to do?" Without waiting for an answer, he led Carter out of the room.

"Better watch it, intern," he growled as they passed by, "I'm on very close terms with Malachai."

"I don't need to hide behind someone else's authority, orderly." Joshua called back as they exited the room. He didn't bother to wonder where Dr. Dover had gone.

Later that morning, Joshua was heading to meet Dr. Hoffman when he saw Roger talking with Dr. Malachai in the hall, two doors away from Hoffman's office. He didn't know whether to laugh or sigh. *Guess some people can't take a hint.*

When Dr. Malachai called him over, he put on his blandest professional face.

"Good morning, sir."

"I understand you had a confrontation with Roger this morning."

Through his peripheral vision, Joshua could see the orderly smirking. He didn't acknowledge him, not even with a glance, and spoke as if he wasn't there, keeping his tone innocent and neutral.

"His and his partner's behaviors were not in accordance with the standards of this facility. They failed to help the psychologist on duty, then interfered when I tried to help. I let Mr. Ward," the senior supervisor of the orderlies, "know all about it. I figured they'd work out a solution, so I didn't think I needed to report it any higher."

He could see by the reddening on Roger's face that this was not the reaction he'd expected.

Nor, for that matter, did Malachai. "So, as *intern*, you felt it your duty to come in early to check on our orderlies, then?"

Such open sarcasm surprised Joshua. His first impulse was to laugh, but he'd gotten skilled at hiding his true feelings around his boss. He instead said, with some of the exasperation he felt, "Sir, I came in early to work on a case study for Dr. Sellars, but I certainly wasn't going to just ignore the shouting coming from the common room—"

"—And a good thing he didn't, either!" Just at that moment, Dr. Hoffman came out of his office. "Good morning, Randall. I just had a rather interesting conversation with Carter Doleson. Never have I seen such a dramatic change in attitude. If he continues like this, I wouldn't be surprised if we can discharge him before the end of the summer—and this, after a couple of conversations with our intern, here."

It took everything Joshua had not to smirk.

Fortunately, Dr. Hoffman was not finished and kept attention on himself as he turned on the red-faced orderly. "As for you—you will *never* approach one of my clients with a straitjacket or any other form of restraint without express permission of myself or the on-duty psychiatrist, do you hear me?"

"I was just being proactive, sir!" Roger managed to look stricken and innocent.

"Your actions were neither pro nor active."

He turned to Malachai. "Have you heard exactly what happened, or did you just get his version?" His tone indicated what he thought of Roger's story.

"I haven't heard all the details, but I'm sure we could discuss it at a later time," the senior psychiatrist said with stiff reserve. "Why don't we check calendars after your group sessions?"

"That'll be fine, Randall. Josh, you're with me. I want you to pick another client to work your NLP magic on, and this time lead me through it step by step."

The rest of the morning was a blur, with two group therapies, and an intense meeting with Dr. Malachai in which Joshua was grilled on the orderlies' behavior as well as his own.

Carter, also in attendance, got visibly angrier and angrier, but instead of standing and shouting, sat calmly until finally he interrupted, "Excuse me, Dr. Malachai. How you believe Joshua should have handled the situation is your business, but the fact remains that I was physically threatened by that orderly, and this is not the first time. What are you going to do about that?"

Afterward, as Joshua followed Carter out the door, he heard Hoffman say to Malachai, "See what I mean? No shouts, no panics, not a word of 'them.' And I would say he was plenty provoked, wouldn't you?"

Joshua managed to squeeze in an hour with Ydrel, in his room. He looked over Ydrel's book report, then taught him how to do a compare/contrast summary. "Why don't you try it out on two warfighting strategists."

"Strategists?"

"Yeah, you know, like Sun Tsu? *The Art of War*?" The names came dredging up from his memory. He'd never read the book, but LaTisha had studied it in a business class. When he'd laughed, she'd given him a particularly feral look. "Business is war," she'd said. He should have known then...

Ydrel actually looked embarrassed. "I...haven't read much theory. I'm usually trying to find specific information—"

"You mean, you've been laying all these tactics and tech on Taz with no overarching strategies? No wonder she's confused. Fine. There's your assignment for the week."

After lunch, Floyd found him, and they went to work again on the tapes, so he didn't get to see Sachiko. At dinnertime, he paused to stretch.

"Floyd, go home," he suggested. "I'm going to get a break, and I can continue on."

"No can do," Floyd said with his usual calm. "Dr. Malachai gave me strict orders to remain with you until the project is complete. I can get us something from the cafeteria."

Joshua clenched his jaw against the words he wanted to say. Then he took a long breath. It wasn't Floyd's fault, after all. "Sure."

Floyd went to get them dinner while Joshua scripted out a particularly telling section. He returned with a tray and an envelope, with Joshua's name in Sachiko's writing. As casually as he could, Josh opened it.

Hey, you,

I heard what you did to Roger—we all did! We just might get him fired this time. I could kiss you—and I will tonight!

-Ko

PS. Floyd knows and keeps more secrets than NSA. He's cool as a go-between as long as we don't abuse his generosity. See you around 10:30!

Joshua looked at the older man, not sure what to say.

He smiled. "She deserves someone good in her life," he said, then turned back to the tape he was queuing up.

Joshua smiled as he re-read the note, then put it in his back pocket. Then he wolfed down his food and turned back to the tapes, even more determined to finish as quickly as possible.

Chapter Twenty-Five

Sachiko guided her motorcycle into Joshua's driveway, glad that she'd decided to make a side trip to find it before going to work; it was much harder to spot in the dark. The modest little cottage was in a fairly good neighborhood but had definitely seen better days. The twisted shadows she passed attested to the wildly overgrown yard, with a few "tamed" areas. A swatch of neatly cut lawn, some ivy trained to the trellis, all told of Joshua's efforts.

The attic had been converted into a small apartment with a separate metal staircase on the side of the house leading to it. Despite the soft soles of her sneakers, it rattled as she climbed it.

Joshua opened the door before she could knock. He was dressed in one of those trendy yellow short-sleeved button-down shirts with dragons on each side, and a loose pair of black shorts. His feet were bare, and he had his cell phone cradled between shoulder and ear. He took her hand and led her in, saying, "uh huh" to whomever was on the line.

His apartment was much nicer on the inside than it seemed from the outside: one room held a small kitchen along one corner with a small refrigerator and stove and an apartment washer with a dryer over the top. The table, too, was small, but made of wood, as were the four chairs around it. A day bed doubled as a couch and had at least a dozen pillows of varying sizes and designs neatly lining the painted metal railings. A short bookshelf doubled as an end table and held a laptop computer.

Behind the couch/bed was a long closet, then the bathroom. Although the ceiling slanted in, it was at a shallow angle and the push-out windows with benches helped keep the room from being cramped. Both were open with fans to pull in the cool air. His keyboard and a small stool sat between them.

The walls were "apartment beige," but he'd added some framed photos of mountain scenes, and a large dream catcher made of branches and feathers. There was also a crucifix on the wall between the windows and copies of both the Serenity Prayer and the Prayer of St. Francis on the pantry doors in the kitchen.

She just had time to take all this in when he thrust the phone at her.

"I'm so glad you're here!" he said. "I really have to get something out of my car, so would you talk to my parents for a minute? Really, I'll be right back."

And he was out the door.

Dropping her backpack near the door, she put the phone to her ear. "Hello?"

"Hi, Sachiko. I'm Maggie."

"And I'm James," added a voice from what sounded like an extension. "Heard you've had quite a week."

"Well, not so much as your son," she said, as she peeked out the window. There was a light on in Joshua's car, and she could just make out his form leaning across the seat.

She let the curtain drop. "He's been spectacular, in more ways than one. People can't say enough good things about him."

"That's good to hear," his father said.

"And how about you?" his mother added archly.

"I think he's wonderful."

"He feels the same about you."

"Oh? Is that why I'm being set up here?" She winced as soon as the words left her mouth. *Great way to make an impression, 'Ko.*

But after a moment's silence, both his parents laughed.

"What gave us away?" his mother asked.

"What could he possibly have to get from his car for you?"

"Registration?"

"At nine on a Friday, your time? Plus, two 'really's in as many sentences is a dead giveaway."

"You noticed?" his mother shrieked. "Oh, you haven't told him—"

"Doesn't matter. It's a pretty ingrained habit."

"You need to understand," his father put in gently, "Joshua had a rather bad experience with a girl this last year, and it's made him unsure of himself. In fact, it's a testimony to your character that he's given his heart so readily."

At the words "given his heart," her own gave a happy little skip, but she said firmly, "James, we've only been dating a week—"

"Just a figure of speech, my dear. I mean he trusts you romantically."

Sachiko peeked out the window again. Joshua was leaning against his car, looking at his watch. He started for the stairs. "He's coming back up."

"You won't give him a hard time about this, will you?" his mother asked.

"'Describe Joshua in one sentence?'" Sachiko pretended to repeat as the door opened.

"Apparently so," she heard his father say to his mother.

Sachiko smiled at Joshua's surprised look and pretended to give the question some thought. "How about...He's as adorable as he is arrogant."

Joshua stared at her opened-mouthed. Then he rolled his eyes and thrust out his hand for the phone.

She sauntered away, causally putting the table between him and herself as she spoke over his parents' laughter. "Hmm, you want examples?"

"Oh, give me the phone," he said.

Eyes batting with exaggerated innocence, she pretended to not have heard him. "Well, he flirts with the nurses. It's true—he's shameless. And he's convinced one client that cleaning the toilet is therapy—"

"Give me that phone!" He started toward her.

She moved, keeping the table between them.

"He's one-upped his boss on more than one occasion—very innocently, *perhaps*, but nonetheless—"

"Give me that!"

"And what's this thing he has about roses?"

"'Ko!" He lunged over the table and yanked the phone from her hand. He put it to his ear, then pulled it away, glaring at it as if his laughing parents could see him.

He turned his glare at her, but she batted her eyes again, so he directed his attention back to his parents. "Mom! Well! They didn't have thorns—it was heinous! I— uh, huh. Uh, huh. Oh! No, I— uh, huh."

His expression went from annoyance to one of intent listening. She waited a couple more "uh, huh"s, then picked up her bag and pointed to the bathroom. Distractedly, he waved her on.

In the bathroom, she changed out of her T-shirt and riding leathers into a green silk skort with embroidered flowers and matching sleeveless blouse. She really wanted to take a shower, as she always did after work, but settled with washing her face, then re-applying some green eyeliner and lipstick. She brushed her hair until it fell smoothly over her shoulders.

Best I'm gonna do, she thought as she repacked and returned to the main room.

From the way Joshua's eyes shone when he saw her, she'd done well enough. "I think I'd better go now," he told his parents, then laughed. "She is, and I am! okay. Love you, too. Bye." He folded the phone and set it on the table.

"I am and you are what?" she asked suspiciously.

"You are as beautiful as you are perceptive, and I am in big trouble," he said. He cut off her chuckles with a kiss.

After a moment, her arms tightened around his neck.

"Does this mean I'm forgiven?" he murmured.

"Depends," she murmured. "You know what they say about paybacks?"

"Oh, oh." He pulled back to smile at her. "What do you have in mind?"

"Well," she coyly traced little designs on his chest with her index finger. It felt so good to be in his arms. *"If* I can get enough studying done and *if* you aren't too busy with that yard, I thought we'd take a drive down to Newport and you can meet my family."

"Really? I mean, oh-baby, you wouldn't do that to me—"

"Stop!" she shoved him playfully. "So what do you have in mind for tonight?"

"How do you feel about scrapbooks?"

Scrapbooks? "On a second date? Are you sure we're ready?"

"Now you stop! I just thought you'd like to see where I come from. That's all, really." Suddenly, he looked uncertain, and young. "If you'd rather do something else—"

She cut him off with a kiss. "I'd love to see your scrapbook."

Soon, they had settled on the couch with sodas, chips and Joshua's homemade guacamole and a large, 3-ring photo album. The first page was a large standard family portrait: His mother sitting, with him and his father behind, each with a hand on her shoulder. They all wore matching ski sweaters and black jeans.

Sachiko leaned into Joshua, intently comparing his face with those of his parents. His father had the same strong features as Joshua—the squarish jaw, the slightly hollow cheeks—and the same intent gaze, and a gentle smile. His mother's face was much rounder; from her, Joshua had inherited his eyes and sensuous lips. And—

"Look at your hair!" she exclaimed. Both he and his mother wore tight beaded braids: hers, styled elaborately on her head; his, hanging loose. "Was it really that long?"

"Some of it was extensions. I loved that style, but it's not exactly a professional image. At least, not in the psychiatric profession."

Madness Bound ❦ 271

"When was this taken?"

"I was 17. About a year and a half ago."

She groaned. "What are you doing with an old lady like me?"

He pulled back her hair and nibbled her neck by way of answer.

"All right! Next page."

"Here's my other family."

This portrait was of a Hispanic family. The mother, short and not fat, but pudgy, had a tired smile and slightly sloped shoulders, as if wearing the effects of a difficult life. Still, her eyes sparkled. Beside her and more than a head taller was her son, very handsome and slick without looking slimy. Seated in front was the sister, with beautiful long black hair permed in soft curls.

"And this was taken..."

"The same year. Rique's four years older than me; he's getting his masters. Sabrina's actually my age."

"Not too much like family, I'd wager." Sachiko pointed to the photo of Sabrina and Joshua in formal dress that was on the opposite page.

"Her prom. And we dated for a little while that summer, but—" He shrugged and pointed back to the portrait. "She really is more like a sister. Anyway, this is Rique, my best friend, and my other mom. I call her Momarosa."

"Rosa? Is this where your 'thing' with roses comes from?"

He blinked at her, gave a surprised laugh. "As a matter of fact. Rique's father, well, let's just say that even when he was in jail, Momarosa had restraining orders against him. He's dead now; killed by another inmate. When they were married, though, he used to make her take all the thorns off the roses in her garden. Said he liked his flowers beautiful and safe. Not just safe. Defenseless. He liked her that way as well.

"Anyway, I was maybe ten, and Rique and I were playing in his room when we heard this awful scream. So we run to the living room and she's standing there with this look of terror on her face, and on the floor is a box of roses. She starts yelling at Rique in Spanish to get the suitcases and pack for himself and Sabrina. Rique sees the flowers and runs to the closet. Then he hands me a paper sack and tells me to toss the roses in it. That's when I saw the thorns were torn off. Weird, you know?

"So we pile into the car, and she starts driving. All around Pueblo, just taking turns at random. She's crying, Sabrina's crying, Rique's swearing. I'm just quietly freaking out! Then we stopped at the police station and she lays on the horn until a cop comes out. He finally escorted us to my house. It was about an hour before she could calm down enough to tell us what happened. She thought he'd gotten out and was coming after her— she'd turned him in, apparently.

"Turned out, he'd had a fellow inmate who'd been released send them as a sick joke. I'd pretty much forgotten the incident, but I guess the emotional memory was still there."

He gave her a chagrined smile.

She bit her lip thoughtfully. "And now that you've confronted this memory, are you going to freak out over thornless roses?"

He shrugged. "I doubt it."

"All right, then. You're forgiven. Next page."

They looked at photos of his house, of the view from his bedroom window—a wide expanse of beige and green prairie with deep blue mountains suddenly rising from the horizon against a sky that shaded from clear summer blue to an almost white powdery blue. One mountain towered above the rest, snow covering its peak. Pikes Peak, he told her.

There were photos of their land in the mountains near Westcliffe, a more rugged terrain than she was used to with lots of rock outcroppings and cactus mixed in with wildflowers, pine and Aspen trees. He had a photo of his horse, a sturdy Morgan he'd acquired through a 4-H program.

"Do you ride?" he asked.

She shook her head. "I'm not a fan of horses."

When they got to photos of the band, she laughed. "Whose...car...is that?"

Joshua and four other guys including Rique were posed with their instruments on and around a brilliant yellow El Camino. On the tailgate was a well-known painting of the Virgin Mary in a pink dress and a blue robe, surrounded by gold.

"Rique's. I thought my parents were going to kill him—he used the graduation money they gave him to get that paint job. That's Our Lady of Guadalupe on the back. She's the patron saint of the Americas, and his chosen patroness, too. This is Carl with the blond hair and guitar; he plays bass and hand drums when we do stuff with more Native American influence. Leon is our percussionist. Austin plays just about any wind instrument you can imagine, but usually saxophone and flute. He's been teaching me a little of the saxophone. This is actually our professional photo—we've used it on flyers, and even had some posters and T-shirts done. Here—"

He turned the page, to more photos of them around the car at different angles. She could see in them that in addition to the icon, the car was decorated with a line of chili peppers running along the side.

"There's no losing that in the parking lot."

"Yeah. It's a lowrider, too. Got the bouncing shocks. Fun, fun car. Here's one of our gigs. A Halloween party the city sponsored at the Events Center. They had three bands, so we got to play and have some fun, too."

Along with some long shots of them on stage, there were photos of them in costume at the party itself. One was Joshua in a Renaissance peasant's outfit with his arms around a tall, thin, woman whose costume consisted of angel's wings and a red bikini and hot pants. She had a halo on her head but had sculpted her hair with red gel into two horns. She had one hand on his chest and the other low and to the back of his hip.

"A fan?"

Joshua snorted. "LaTisha. My Ex."

"What, wife?" She meant it teasingly, but he answered with vehemence.

"No. Thank God it never got that far!"

"That bad, huh?" She looked again at the photo. There was something very captivating about her, very sleek and sensuous, but kind of disturbing, too, like a cross between a panther and a snake. There was something possessive about the way she had her arms around him...

Think I'll just hate her now, Sachiko decided. She didn't realize she'd spoken aloud until Joshua laughed.

"I'll give you Rique's e-mail; you can join his anti-fan club. All my friends hated her. I kind of neglected a lot of people as well as things like my studies. I just really—our relationship was pretty...intense. What was good was incredibly good; what was bad...The costume really says it all: LaTisha was heaven and hell."

He looked at the photo with a half grin, half grimace, a little wistful.

Silence fell between them.

Sachiko broke it. "You're not on the rebound, are you?"

"No. I admit, I have a few unresolved issues to work out, but I haven't been pining or looking for love or anything. In fact..." He shut the book and kicked it under the couch, then turned to face her. "My plan had been to spend a quiet summer of hermit-like introspection and work. But then you had to come along with those exotic eyes and beguiling grin."

"Aw, did I wreck your widdle pwans?" she teased as he pushed her back against the cushions.

"You're forgiven." A moment later, he purred, "I like your ideas better."

Many, many moments later, she pulled away and leaned against his shoulder with a happy sigh. As before, they were playing by what she'd jokingly called "good Catholic boy rules." He'd even resisted her attempts to ease off his shirt, though she did manage to unbutton it part way. She caressed his smooth chest. He had one hand behind his head and the other was playing with her hair.

"Can I ask you something?" she asked.

"I love to be kissed right here," he answered, pointing to the hollow of his shoulder.

"I'll remember that," she said caressing the spot. "But my question is more serious. Ydrel said you told Isaac that it was okay to die, and you, you made him agree?"

He stopped stroking her hair. "Is he upset about it?"

"No, not really. But I am. How could you do that?"

For a moment he didn't answer. She waited, afraid to look into his face, wondering if she should have waited until another day to say anything, or even at all.

You know how upset he was about Isaac. Why'd you break the moment just to upset him again?

When he did speak, he didn't sound upset, just a little apprehensive. "Let me up, would ya?"

She slid away, and he sat up and reached under the couch, again pulling out his scrapbook. He flipped to the back. "This is my grandpa Jebediah, my mom's dad."

She leaned over to look at the photos, taken when Joshua was different ages: a portly, smiling man with just a hint of gray holding an infant with Joshua's mom leaned over him; a much grayer and heavier man passing out Christmas presents; finally, a drastically older and thinner man in a chair with a young Joshua standing beside him. The man had a blanket over his knees, although Joshua was in shorts and a tank top, and although they tried to hide it for the photo, Sachiko's nurse's training let her spot the IV.

"He died just after my tenth birthday. We never really knew quite what he had, just that his body would go nuts: one day, he couldn't eat enough; the next week, a cracker would make him vomit all day long. He had these awful, awful hemorrhages. He was in and out of the hospital for a few months; the doctors finally said there was nothing they could do and he had maybe a few months to live. They recommended a nursing home.

"But we couldn't. So we brought him home, and some hospice workers came and helped us. Anyway, he just got worse, and it got more and more painful for him. And my mom. I mean, even as an adult, she was always his little girl; if something needed to be done, she'd call him as easily as my dad. He almost died a couple of times, but just kept hanging on.

"Anyway, after one especially bad hemorrhage, my mom went downstairs to put the towels in the washer and call the hospital to see if there was anything we could do, anything, and I was with him. He was shivering so hard, and he was too weak to speak, but he just looked at me, he was so—"

He stopped, squeezed his eyes shut and mashed his lips together. She wanted to throw her arms around him and comfort him, but she still didn't understand how this applied to Isaac, so she waited, silent but sympathetic. Finally, he spoke, in a quiet almost childlike voice.

"I told him it was okay, that Dad and I would take care of Mom, and he could die. He didn't have to hurt anymore. I told my grandpa to die.

"And he smiled at me, and tears fell from his eyes, but he just smiled. Then he died."

Suddenly, he stood up, spilling the book onto the floor. He strode to the kitchen and pulled a can of soda out of the refrigerator. Only after he'd popped the can and downed half its contents in a long series of swallows did he return, picking up a box of tissue on his way. Smiling ruefully, he handed one to Sachiko and took one for himself. Only then did she notice she was crying, too. They blew their noses and giggled.

"So," he said, his voice stronger. "Isaac. Obviously, he wasn't in the same way as grandpa, but I could tell he was hanging on. I'd talked to him before, when he was lucid; he knew what Ydrel was doing, how he got caught up in the awful memories he was reliving. How he tried to save him from those memories. I think he was scared Ydrel might try to, I don't know, follow him into death. I know: that's ridiculous—"

"No. No, I understand what you mean. He got so caught up in those fantasies, like he was living what was in Isaac's mind."

Joshua smiled with relief. "Exactly. I didn't want to mention that to anyone; they might think I'm buying into Ydrel being psychic or something. But also, I recognized the look Ydrel had. I'd seen it in my mom. I'd worn it. So I said what seemed needed to be said. But Isaac needed to hear Ydrel's release, too.

"I tried to explain some of this to Ydrel, but I really didn't want to get into everything with my grandpa there. I mean, I was a mess for months afterward, didn't want to be near anyone older than my parents. My mom did Meals on Wheels—I'd have a fit whenever I had to go with her. I still can't talk about it easily. Obviously."

Now Sachiko set the book neatly on the floor and wrapped her arms around him. "Thank you for trusting me enough to tell me," she whispered.

He sniffled and shivered. "Sachiko, I—"

"What?"

"Nothing."

"All right, then." She pulled him back until they were again in their original position, reclined on the couch, her head nestled into his shoulder, his hand stroking her hair. "Finish your story."

"Finish?"

"Yes. You were a mess, wouldn't even feed old people!" she teased him lightly, then asked, "So what happened?"

"Confession, actually."

"You told your dad what happened?"

"No, my First Confession. I told a priest. Man, I was scared. The only thing that made me go through with it was that I wouldn't be able to explain to Momarosa why I couldn't get my First Communion.

"But the priest told me he couldn't absolve me because I hadn't done anything wrong. I didn't kill my grandfather. I didn't even make him die. I just gave a scared old man strength to complete the last journey God had for him. So I cried a little, and we prayed for Grandpa, and I confessed all my other bad behaviors, and in addition to the usual prayers of penance, he asked me to volunteer in a nursing home. It turned out to be very healing for me."

"Did the priest ever tell your parents?"

He pulled back to give her a funny look. "This was *Confession*. Total confidentiality, remember? I'm not sure I'd have ever confessed again if he'd told my parents. And believe me, I've needed confession."

"What? A good Catholic boy like you?"

"I wasn't so good last year. I had a lot to confess before I left home this summer."

"Because of LaTisha?"

For a moment, he didn't answer, but he continued to caress her hair, so she knew he was thinking rather than being upset. Again, she waited silently, letting her fingers trace little circles and designs on his chest, listening only to his heartbeat. It was wonderfully comfortable, and she was even getting a little drowsy.

She'd almost thought he wasn't going to answer, when: "LaTisha was the catalyst, but not the cause. That's what I'm trying to work out, I guess. But that's another deep, emotional story and I'm tired of deep emotional stories! Next week is your turn!"

"No promises. Do you want me to go so you can get some sleep?"

He laid an arm around her waist before she could rise. "Who said anything about being sleepy?" he asked in a low voice that sent delicious shivers along her spine. She smiled up at him.

They kissed.

Chapter Twenty-Six

When Roger barged into Ydrel's room early Saturday morning, Ydrel was showered and dressed and sitting on his made bed, reading.

"I assume His Majesty wishes to see me?" he asked in a dignified voice.

"Get moving," Roger snarled.

Ydrel rose without argument to precede him out the door. Again, his stomach was bothering him—something that was happening with increasing frequency—but he was not about to show any weakness in front of the orderly.

As he passed through, he glanced at Roger. "There's something different about you today. Are you sober?"

"Shut up!" But even though the orderly muttered obscenities under his breath, he did not, as he might have before, try to "accidentally" bump Ydrel into a door.

That would make Sachiko—and others on the staff—both happy and sad: happy that Roger was no longer abusing patients; sad that he didn't get pushed over the edge and do something that would get him fired. Ydrel wondered if there was some way he could manage both until he got to Malachai's office.

"Reporting as ordered, sir," Ydrel smiled sarcastically as he sat, laced his hands behind his head and leaned back in the chair, studying the psychiatrist closely.

He was in the usual pose: leaned back slightly yet with perfect posture in his oh-so-grand leather office chair, his elbows resting lightly on the arms and his hands steepled. He was pushed away from his desk and turned at an angle, so he didn't fully face the desk, or the client across from it, yet his face was turned and tilted slightly. The perfect picture of caring professionalism.

Still, Ydrel had seen and heard about little slips in his façade. Perhaps Roger wasn't the only one being thrown off center by their "upstart young intern."

Let's see if we can keep him off-center. "You know, it's not healthy for you to be spending so much time here. You ought to find yourself a woman or something."

"Thank you for your advice, but my concern is for you."

"Thanks, but I'm not interested in women right now. Maybe when I'm out of here and in the real world."

Now Malachai regarded him with a pitying smile. "I think we still have a great deal of work before you're ready to be released."

"So, that's why you're here? Got a deadline, Dolfus?" He emphasized Malachai's much-hated given name, and the pseudonym under which he wrote about Ydrel for the psychic phenomena magazines. "I don't have any new tricks for you. In case you hadn't noticed, I've had a rough week."

"I would think after your 'session' with Joshua, you would have a great deal to share. I've reviewed his summary tape; the use of ley lines in particular is quite interesting. Tell me: are you able to tap into their power as you've implied?"

"You don't find it ironic that on the one hand, you're pressuring me to perform tricks like some psychic monkey, and on the other, you're trying to disabuse me of the notion I'm psychic?"

Malachai got up from his chair and went to sit down on the coffee table in front of Ydrel. He leaned forward intently. "Can it be you've misunderstood me all these years? I have always believed you have paranormal abilities. Have we not tried to study them in order that you can better control them? I'm actually pleased young Joshua has been able to help you, although it's a blow to my pride that I did not come up with such simple, obvious ideas as his. But you still hold delusions and attitudes that keep you within these grounds."

It had been years since Malachai had crossed the barrier between him and Ydrel that the desk represented. Suddenly, the young client found himself off balance. He sat up cross-legged in the chair and wrapped his arms around himself protectively. "Like what?" he asked guardedly.

"These visitors that call you from consciousness, for one."

Visitors? "It was Joshua that taught me how to deal with Tasmae when you couldn't."

Again, that compassionate, pitying smile. "Ydrel, Joshua has a one-size-fits-all philosophy of psychiatry that, while naïve, is effective in certain cases. He doesn't truly believe you are psychic, but he lets you pretend it's the source of all your troubles; that's why his methods work as well on Tasmae as on real people.

"Now, I know you have paranormal abilities. I have pushed you to explore those abilities; sometimes, as this week, I've pushed too far. I underestimated Mr. McDougal's psychosis and overestimated your ability to defend yourself. I am sorry. Yet, perhaps this turned out to be a good thing? After all, it gave Joshua a chance to teach you some new and better techniques—from fantasy novels, I presume?"

Despite himself, Ydrel nodded.

"But that's the key, isn't it, Ydrel? Fantasy. Joshua believes in your psychic abilities no more than he believes in Doleson's aliens."

"Does it matter? If it's working, who cares whether he believes or not?" Yet the ache in his heart told Ydrel the truth—he cared.

Malachai looked down and sighed. "Ydrel. Ydrel, it does matter. Joshua's 'objectivity' isn't objective at all, because it's ignoring the root causes of your troubles, even how your past is influencing you. It doesn't matter to him because he sees what he's doing as working. It's very mechanical; in essence he's an engineer, tinkering to make his project function as best it can.

"But I know you. And I know the fact of some of your abilities, like your ability to receive and internalize other's thoughts and emotions. But I also know your emotions. You've been very lonely here, very isolated. It's no secret; that's one of the reasons we brought Joshua here. But before that, hasn't your Tasmae filled that need?"

"What? All she did was call me away and demand information! There was no friendship. Besides, I didn't ask for her. She called *me*. You think I've enjoyed playing oracle?"

Ydrel almost stood up, he was so suddenly angry, yet Dr. Malachai stayed as he was, sitting quietly on the table edge.

"But you were performing a valuable service. You were needed. And let's think about this rationally: She is an otherworld creature with incredible powers to contact minds across time and space. Why would she call upon a teenage boy for military information?"

He sank back into the chair. "She didn't know what I was," he whispered. "She said God brought us together." *Yes, God. Go ahead; smile that patronizing smile.*

But he didn't. "And you moved heaven and earth to fulfill what you perceived as your duty, let yourself be called away, even at awkward moments...Have you noticed how that pattern has changed since Joshua's arrival?"

"He told me to how get her to ask permission first!"

"I know. And have you found at times you're able to refuse—or maybe not even hear her call?"

He didn't wait for Ydrel's reply; Ydrel supposed the sullen look on his face was answer enough.

"More and more your attention has been focused on your new friendship, and you've had less and less need for your Tasmae. She's beginning to fade; with some work, we may be able to rid you of her forever.

"But you need to understand that she is, indeed, an illusion. And in the meantime, we need to investigate what true abilities you do possess. This is even more important now that you've discovered how to tap into power outside yourself. Think about how just your receptive abilities, uncontrolled, have hurt you. What could another ability, like telekinesis, do to someone else?"

Ydrel already knew what his abilities could do. He shuddered and wrapped his arms around his knees. He could feel Dr. Malachai looking at him intently. He didn't meet his gaze. Could Malachai be right? Was Tasmae really just an illusion, a way for him to feel needed? Then, what about the Master—was he just an illusion he could get rid of?

"Ydrel?"

Did he want Tasmae to be a delusion—even if it meant being free of the Master?

"Ydrel, what do you say?"

I need time. I need to think. "But I don't have anything for you," he whined miserably. "I spent a day manic, then I was attacked, and I went catatonic and then Isaac died, and, and—" The tears he hadn't been able to shed now came flowing to the surface. He buried his head in his knees. He felt a gentle hand on his shoulder. He tried not to flinch.

"Why don't you just tell me about these ley lines you've found? Then you can spend the next few days privately trying to focus this new power. Tuesday, we'll see what you can do."

Sachiko awoke Saturday morning to the tantalizing smells of freshly brewed coffee and bacon. The sizzling of the bacon made a soothing counterpoint to the whirr of the fans. Drowsily, she rolled over.

Then she realized she was still on Joshua's couch. The couch he used for a bed.

She sat up suddenly, pulling the thin cover up to her chest, her face burning with embarrassment. Then, as she awoke more fully, she felt a different sort of embarrassment as she realized she was still fully clothed. Nothing had happened last night except that she'd fallen asleep.

She rubbed her cheeks, glad her back was to the kitchen. When she thought her face was back to its normal color, she turned around. Joshua was at the stove, his back to her. He had on clean shorts and a T-shirt and looked like he'd already had a shower.

"What time is it?" she asked.

He turned and smiled. "Good morning. It's about 10:00. I was just about to wake you. I've got breakfast ready."

He tilted the pan so she could see the scrambled eggs before he put them into a platter next to the cooked bacon. "How do you like your coffee?"

"Cream and sugar. I'll fix it. Why didn't you wake me earlier?"

She stood up and stretched. In the middle of the stretch, she caught a glance of him staring at her. He had a funny kind of smile on his face. "What?"

"Nothing, really." At her glare, he rolled his eyes and went to fetch the coffee. "All right. I was just admiring how beautiful you look, but I know that's cliché—"

"You're right. And you didn't answer my question." She sat down and loaded up her plate as he poured her coffee. She placed a forkful of scrambled eggs into her mouth.

He took a seat on the next side of the table and started into his own breakfast.

"Well?" she prompted.

"I woke up early, and you didn't even move when I got up. You just looked so sweet sleeping there, I didn't have the heart to wake you, so I left you a note and went to work on the garden some while it was still cool out. When you didn't notice that I'd left, or when I returned, I went ahead and showered and started breakfast. I figured you needed the sleep."

She did feel rested, but that didn't quell her annoyance. "Well, we're still way behind schedule, especially if we're going to Newport today. It's going to take me an hour just to drive home and shower."

"So shower here. I'll be good; I'll even go work on the garden some more and you can lock the door if that'd make you more comfortable."

"And what am I going to wear? This is the only clean outfit I've got, and it's wrinkled. So are my jeans and T-shirt. What would my parents think?"

"You could spritz them and toss them in the dryer for a few minutes. That'll take the wrinkles out."

"Do you have an answer for everything?"

"Matter of fact." He grinned, and she couldn't help but grin back.

He did go to work on the garden some more while she showered, though she'd told him it wasn't necessary to leave. She even took his advice about the dryer, and in half an hour she was clean and dressed.

She took one of her books to the garden to read. She had seen the old swing under the maple tree in part of the cleared area, so she studied while he worked, looking up on occasion to remark on something she'd read or to admire the way his muscles moved as he pulled weeds and trimmed back plants grown wild. He had his shirt off and his dark skin glistened with sweat.

"You're going to need another shower by the time you're done," she commented.

He grinned impishly at her. "Will I have to lock you out of my house?"

She pulled herself up into a dignified pose. "I am a nurse," she said loftily. "I'm sure you don't have anything I haven't seen before."

He just smiled slyly and did a slow arm curl. "It's not what you have; it's how you package it."

"Oh, please!" She shut her book and stood. "I'm going in. It's hot out here."

"Thank you."

"The weather, you loon!" But she had to admit to herself that at least part of the heat she felt had little to do with the sun. It took her a while once she got in to turn her mind back to internal anatomy and surgical procedures.

She was just really getting into the chapter on Cesarean Sections, acting it out while she visualized the procedure and said each step aloud when Joshua came in. Even though he'd been the one to teach her to review that way, she stopped, a little embarrassed. He didn't seem to notice.

"You're right. It's too hot out there. Want me to drill you?"

She glanced at her book. "Actually, I'm doing surprisingly well with the visualizing; I'm really remembering a lot that way. But you have to promise not to watch me—it's too embarrassing, know what I mean?"

"Okay. I'm going to grab a shower now. What should I wear to meet your parents?"

"Change into whatever for now. If we're taking Dragonfly, you'll need to change into jeans, anyway. No one rides my bike without helmets and leg coverings. Got to protect that packaging, after all."

"I love the way your mind works." He laughed and leaned over to kiss her. He smelled like sweat and earth and green growing things. She put one hand on his bare chest as the kiss deepened.

Oh, I could get used to this... "Go clean up!" She gave him a playful shove.

Ten minutes later, he flopped onto the couch next to her, clean and dressed in a muscle shirt and cut-off jeans shorts and sporting a new earring. This one had a silver triangle set into a gold circle with a small diamond at its top point. Sachiko did a double take. "Is that what I think it is?"

"Vulcan IDIC. I can change it if you think it'd bother your parents..."

"Are you kidding? My dad may be retired Navy, but he's a big-time Trekker. Question is: does your mom know about it?"

He laughed. "My mom bought it for me. I'm going to take my laptop to the table and check e-mail while I eat. Want something?"

"Not if we're going to my parents'. They own a restaurant, remember?"

"Well, I'll be hungry again by then. You know what they say about teenage guys."

"They're insatiable?"

"That, too. Also, we can eat like there's no tomorrow."

She started to say something, realized how he'd twisted what she'd said in the first place and threw a pillow at him as he made his way to the refrigerator. Still, she had to admit that for all his flirtations and double-entendres, he'd pretty much given her the time and space she needed to study. In fact, she'd done better studying here than she normally did alone in her apartment.

It's so comfortable here. I'm so comfortable here, she thought.

She turned to watch him building a Dagwood-style sandwich. His body was moving to the rhythm of some song, although he neither whistled nor hummed, probably in deference to her studying. Suddenly, her stomach gave an uneasy lurch. He was only there for the summer; should she let herself get this comfortable around him?

Worry about that later, she scolded herself. For now, study. Cyst removal. Let's go.

An hour later, she stretched and shut her books. It was just after two, but she'd actually accomplished more than she'd expected. "I'm at a good breaking point," she said to Joshua, who was sitting at the table with his laptop and an empty plate. "Shall we?'

"Let me just finish this."

"What are you working on?" she asked as she walked up behind him and leaned over his shoulder.

Quickly, he shut the computer.

"Sorry," she said, backing away. "I didn't know it was private. I'll just get my stuff together." She turned to go, but he stopped her with a touch on the arm. She turned, a little puzzled, but didn't say anything.

He regarded her for a moment, his lips a thin line, one finger tapping the top of his computer tensely. Then, he unfolded it so she could see the message on the monitor, forwarded, apparently, from his father:

Subj: (NLPAssociation) Eye Movements in Psychic Phenomena?
That son of yours sure comes up with some stumpers! If I didn't know you, I'd think this was a joke.

I've never heard of any studies of the phenomena you mentioned, neither among mental health patients nor academic studies. I'll do a search, as you requested. Be patient.

In the meantime, your observations were certainly fascinating—I'd like to hear more if you can manage it. However, tell him to be careful about who he shares this with. He's still young in his career—does he really want to be associated with something as fantastic as ESP?

Regards,

"You're posting Ydrel's case on the Internet?" She didn't know whether to hit him or storm out.

He spoke quickly before she could do either.

"No! No, I just sent a description of an anonymous psychic I'd observed. For all anyone knows, it's a carnival sideshow performer I'm talking about. And it's posted onto a closed e-mail group for NLP Association members. My dad looked it over before he sent it. I, I just—"

He stumbled to a halt.

"I'm listening." She crossed her arms; her expression, like her tone, was closed. But at least she didn't turn away. That was the best she was going to do.

He took a breath. "Okay. One of the main precepts of NLP is if you want to know what's happening in the mind, look at the eyes. For example, think about the last time you saw snow outside your apartment window."

He caught her off guard, but grudgingly, she dredged up a memory. "Uh..."

"Your eyes flicked up and left—standard visual recall. Now imagine purple snow in a mountain valley...Up, right. Visual construction. Now, sometimes, people's motions vary, but always, it's the same in general—when the brain is at work, eyes move one way for vision, another for hearing, still another for feel; one side for recall, one for construction, or imagining. And it's different from when the brain is taking in input, like you're looking at something. It's not something you can consciously control. It's a reflex—"

She wanted an explanation, not a lecture. "What's this got to do with Ydrel and your email?"

"I'm getting to it! Ydrel, when he's being...well, 'normal,' follows the usual pattern. But when he's having a, um, psychic experience, his eyes are all wrong from what you'd expect if he were making it up—but not if he were remembering or actually experiencing what he says he's experiencing.

"Like when he said McDougal was making him manic: if he himself were manic, his eyes would have been doing one thing, and I know what that should be—I've seen it in others before. And I know his usual patterns. If he were just pretending, his eyes would have done another. It would have been obvious, at least to me. I'm not bragging or anything; it's just training.

"But his eyes were, well, wrong. Ydrel's pattern is visual-tactile-verbal; anything he comes up with, real or imagined, should follow that pattern. But when he was acting so odd and blaming it on McDougal, his pattern changed to verbal-visual—and anything tactile, he had to make it up. Later, I talked to McDougal—guess how he thinks."

"Verbal-visual?" She felt her anger shifting into skepticism, and she turned to lean against the table to better watch him than the computer.

Encouraged, Joshua went on. "Bingo! Plus, his eyes kept bouncing, for lack of a better word. It was like his cognitive processes were fighting for control. And his pupils were pinning."

"Were what?"

"Pinning—pinpointing. Contracting. Birds of prey do it under stress; Ydrel does it when he's 'going psychic.' If you look, you'll see it. Anyway, that's another reflex." He sighed. "It's beyond my experience. So I thought I'd ask the people in the field with the real experience, find out what they have to say. Who knows? Maybe there are other people out there who have the same kind of pathos. So far, all I've got is, 'weird stuff, Josh.'"

"Have you talked to Edith about this?"

"Sort of." His voice tensed, reminding her how young he was. "'Ko, I'm not sure she takes NLP seriously, or me, for that matter. Plus, she'd want to talk to Malachai about it, and I can tell you exactly what *he'd* have to say."

He glanced down at the computer and closed the program. "If I hear something that makes sense of this, I may broach the subject; but for now, I'd rather keep it private. And I swear to you," he stood and set his hands on her shoulders, "that I will say nothing that even hints at Ydrel's identity, or even that I'm talking about a patient and not some side-show act."

She felt the last of her anger melt under his sincere and guileless gaze, but she wasn't ready to give in so easily. "I don't want him hurt."

"Neither do I. He's already got enough people discussing his quirks and treating him like some kind of interesting case study."

She raised an eyebrow at him.

He looked away. "I'll go change."

Chapter Twenty-Seven

He came out of the bathroom silently, dressed in jeans and a polo shirt. She had on her riding leathers and jacket; without a word, he took her bag for her and held open the door. Outside, she gave him the extra helmet she had for passengers and showed him how to adjust it, and turned on the mike so that they could talk to each other on the ride. He answered only in grunts.

She wished she hadn't seen his email—or at least, not when she had. His explanation hadn't been enough to banish her anger. She found herself only talking to him to give him instructions on how to lean and keep balanced as they made their way to I-138. He held her tightly, but she could tell it was more from nervousness than affection.

Once on the highway, though, he relaxed and finally spoke. "You're right. My motives are different, but I'm doing exactly what everyone else has done to Ydrel. Even if nobody else knows who I'm talking about, I know."

He paused to take a breath. "Trouble is, I've already asked, and I do want to know. I've been trying to decide what to do about it, and the best I can come up with is to tell him what I've done and ask him how he feels about it. If he says it's okay, I pursue it; if not, I'll just let it go—treat it like it was an idle observation."

For a moment, she couldn't speak past the lump in her throat. "Do you know how wonderful you are?"

Now his arms tightened around her affectionately. "You're the wonderful one. I'm still new at this. Thanks for being my conscience. But I'm still not saying anything to Edith. I think that'd just open up a big can of worms."

"Agreed."

With that settled, the tension around them immediately lightened, and they spent the next few miles in companionable silence, enjoying the ride and the view. This close to the coast, the traffic was far thinner than in Providence, even at the height of tourist season. The highway was lined with thick woods and a scattering of evergreens and tall brush, occasionally broken by walls of jagged rock where a hill had been chipped away to make room for the highway.

Joshua sighed contentedly. "It's so lush along your highways. You almost feel like you could step off the road and get lost in the forest."

"What, it's not like that in Colorado?"

"Not where I'm from. The Front Range is mostly arid prairie, low round hills at most. The mountains, now that's a whole different story. Rugged, tall trees, lots of pine and aspen. 'Course, you *can* step off the road and get lost. Here, you walk a hundred yards and end up in someone's backyard—Oh, wow!"

They had come to the first of the two bridges that would take them to Aquidneck Island. Sachiko loved crossing the bridges and seeing the fancy condos and well-kept colonial homes that bordered the gray-blue bay, and hundreds of private sailboats offshore.

She felt Joshua's arms tighten around her waist and saw through her rearview mirror that he was looking more down than out and across the water.

"'S'matter, mountain man? Nervous about bridges? Are they so different than mountain passes?"

"Mountain passes have mountain on one side and trees and slope on the other. No long fall into the watery depths."

She thought about teasing him, but noticed he was now eyeing the bridge that paralleled the one they were on, which had replaced it. The old and decaying structure of steel, like an erector-set creation, had never been fully torn down. She supposed it would make anyone nervous. The one they were on was really as much a suspended highway as a bridge; to her, it was no different than driving on the mainland—except the traffic was better, as was the view. And speaking of view...

"Look ahead."

"Oh, wow. That's something. Really."

That "something" was the Newport bridge: a four-lane, two-and-a-half-mile suspension bridge leading onto Aquidneck Island. Sachiko always thought of it as a more graceful version of the Golden Gate—light green cables swooping upward, supported in two arches by structures that made her think of cathedral doors in their shape and grandeur. The highway fanned out from two lanes to five as they came to the toll booth.

They slowed to a stop for a moment so that she could toss a token into the basket and guided the Harley back into traffic as the highway again merged into two lanes. She could feel his arms and his knees tense.

"So do you think Ydrel's psychic?" She broached the subject as much to distract him as to satisfy her own curiosity. She knew how she felt—there was no way Ydrel could have known about her desperate suicide attempt or the reason for it if he didn't have some paranormal abilities. She'd been too adept at hiding things. No one at work had known about her relationship with Randall, and her parents had thought things were at least stable and satisfying for her. They'd been surprised to hear about her break-up, though she suspected that they had been somewhat relieved...

She realized she'd lost some of what Joshua was saying and struggled to pick it up. "Say again?"

"I said, it's kind of like believing in alien life: it's fun to think about, but I'm not sure we're ready for the reality. I mean, aliens sound cool until they come at you with vastly superior weapons and totally different ethics. And would you really want telepathic abilities? There's a funny Tom Smith song about a guy who can read minds and how it wrecks his relationship with his girlfriend. I mean, would you want to know what I'm thinking all the time?"

That was a loaded question, and she told him so. "I think there are some interesting twists in that mind of yours, but point taken. Ignorance can be bliss."

"Exactly. If what Ydrel's told me is true, being psychic has caused him a world of hurt. And if it's true, how many other people out there are suffering from the same problems, but without the benefit of the care that his money can buy? So what would be better—if his troubles are the result of a psychosis or if he truly is a fledgling psychic?"

He paused, and she grunted neutrally. She wasn't sure which situation she preferred.

"Frankly, I'd rather operate under the assumption that it doesn't matter. Whatever the cause, the real key is getting him to deal with it enough to function in society."

"You're sidestepping." Over the bridge and onto solid land now, she took the highway to its end. It curved past a huge casino with a walled-in parking lot. Flags flapped atop the wall, each decorated with the symbol of a suit of cards. Soon after, they were in narrow streets and older homes.

"Yeah, I know. I'm not ready for ESP, I guess. I love these old houses. Everything in Pueblo West is so new."

"Here we are." She turned right and drove a block, past old homes-converted-to-businesses. On the corner lot was her family's restaurant and home, a large deep red three-story house with evergreen trim. The wrap-around porches held tables swathed in red and white checkered tablecloths. Red and white umbrellas poked above the low hedge in the yard. Above the awning was a large sign in red and black letters:

Japperwoppy
The Finest in Italian and Japanese Cuisine
Sushi * Japanese Steakhouse

"That's an unusual name," Joshua commented.

"Dad loves Lewis Carroll and puns," Sachiko said, then laughed. "We actually had some people try to boycott the place—said the name was racist. They had camera crews and everything. Dad trotted out the whole family—sometimes, I think half my family works or has worked here—and calmly explained in three languages that this was a family business, and almost everyone in the family was an immigrant, first or second generation Italian or Japanese, and as such, we could name our restaurant whatever we darn well pleased. Then they set up a buffet for the boycotters and had a party. CNN picked up the story and we had so much business that year! I was in nursing school, but I still had to come help out sometimes."

Sachiko drove through the customer parking lot—which was small and nearly full despite the mid-afternoon hour—and parked near the side of an old garage. They stowed their helmets in the saddlebags and she pointed her fob at the bike. The lights flashed and it chirped.

Joshua laughed. "You're kidding! They have alarms for motorcycles?"

"You have any idea how much this thing cost? Look." She pointed to an engraving on the top of the gas tank: *Equipped with GPS tracking. I will find you. S. Luchese.* Joshua laughed again.

"Believe me, mister, on this coast, that's almost as good as the alarm. C'mon. We have to go in by the front for you to have the full effect of the place."

Feeling like a teenager, she took him by the hand and led him around to the main gate.

Ydrel stepped out of the bathroom in shorts, toweling dry his hair. For a moment, he enjoyed feeling chilled in the air-conditioned room, but he knew soon enough he'd feel too warm again. He'd been sweating all morning, too hot and queasy to eat, and had finally retreated to a cold shower. It had helped, but only temporarily. Already, he was starting to feel the heat. He draped the towel over the chair with a sigh.

Maybe I should go to the nurses' station, he thought, then just as quickly discarded the idea. What would he do, whine that it was hot and his stomach hurt? Besides, walking seemed like too much effort.

Then he felt the familiar scritching inside his head. Relieved, he lay down and allowed the Miscria to call him away from the heat and pain.

"Thank you!" Ydrel stretched out on the spongy moss, luxuriating in its coolness. He didn't care if it was an illusion; at least he was comfortable.

"I've been thinking," Tasmae began without preamble.

Ydrel laughed. "Funny. I've been trying not to think." He'd spent the morning burning through some of the novels Joshua had lent him in an attempt to drive Malachai's comments from his mind. For the moment, though, he made himself forget the psychiatrist. It was wonderfully cool here.

He relaxed, responding automatically to her questions without giving much conscious attention to them, or to his answers. Sometimes, he didn't think he was replying so much as letting the information flow out of him, as it used to before he knew what—who—the Miscria was.

That was fine by him. It just felt so good to be away from his body.

"But how do I build a bomb?" she asked.

"I'm not sure," he murmured drowsily. Maybe he could nap here a while? "Since standard gunpowder doesn't work on your world, we'd have to find something else that'll explode. I'd have to do some research..." He sat up. "Wait a minute! No!"

"No, what?"

"Look. Up until now, the stuff I've researched has been relatively harmless: sword smithing is more art than weaponscraft to us, and military history is, well, history. If I start trying to figure out how to make a bomb, they'll tag me as dangerous and really lock me up for life! Forget it!"

"We need to know," she replied.

He folded his arms over his chest. "*Forget* it."

Her eyes widened in surprise, then narrowed in intensity as she spoke into his mind. *I am the Miscria, the Seeker of Change. I call the Ydrel, the Oracle of Change. Ydrel Mentor, Ydrel Guide. You must answer my call. Ydrel brings the tools we need—*

The pull of her words made him dizzy, and he felt his resolve weakening. After all, they really needed him, depended on him. Who else took him so seriously? Maybe he could figure out something...

"No!" Ydrel shouted and mentally shoved against Tasmae's rhythmic litany. "You don't have any idea what I go through on Earth. I am a prisoner! I am locked up in a pretty little cage with a pretty little courtyard to run circles in and a library to tell me about a world I'm not allowed to be a part of! Then they watch me and test me and monitor me and if I do anything outside their idea of safe, they question me or drug me!

"Do you know that they tell me you're just an illusion? Then Joshua comes along and says it doesn't matter if I just act 'normal' but Malachai says how can I ever be normal if I believe you're real and I—"

As suddenly as his anger had come, it fled, leaving him empty with despair. He pulled his knees up to his chin and laid his head on them. Even here, his stomach was hurting again. He wrapped his arms around his legs, a tight ball of misery. He grabbed at his hair and pulled, as if expecting one pain to erase the other.

"Ydrel."

Although he didn't look up to see her, he could hear the forcefulness of her voice, feel the strength of her thoughts. He felt her hands firm on his shoulders. He could even smell her: the scent of earth and sweat and fresh air and some flower he couldn't name.

"Ydrel. I. Am. Real."

He didn't know if the thought comforted or frightened him. He shivered.

Once they entered the restaurant, Joshua found himself besieged by handshakes, kisses to his cheeks, and respectful bows. Sachiko's father, a compact man with swarthy skin and a nose that matched Sachiko's, led them to a side room with a long table set for ten. He indicated a seat near the door to Joshua, then sat down across from him. Sachiko sat beside Joshua, with her mother across from her. One of the waiters followed them in and took their drink orders and waited.

"You got any food allergies?" Vincenzo Luchese made it sound like a challenge.

Bemused, Joshua shook his head.

Vincenzo glanced at his employee. "Bring us what's good."

Sachiko rolled her eyes once the waiter left. "It's all good, and you know it," she scolded. "You drive Peter nuts when you do that!"

Her father shrugged. "Keeps him on his toes."

Sachiko turned to her mother in exasperation. Chiyo shrugged, though her Mona Lisa smile and the glint in her eyes told Joshua she found it amusing. A family joke, then, or a habit the family had made into a joke.

He bumped Sachiko's leg with his and grinned at her. Her annoyance melted and she grinned back.

Before anyone could say anything more, people—relatives, Joshua guessed by their similar looks and restaurant attire—came in to meet him. And to assess him, he thought. After about the fifth cousin, Joshua decided he'd have to ask Sachiko for a cheat sheet on the Luchese/Oshiro family tree. Several brought drinks with them and settled themselves at the table.

With the drinks and the appetizers came questions. Joshua admitted to considering psychology a plausible career, but that he wanted to pursue his dream of becoming a rock star first. "I know it's a longshot—"

"Yeah, but you have major talent," Sachiko interrupted.

Her words made him feel the same way he had when she admitted she'd found him good-looking. He cleared his throat and said to the table at large, "I have drive, too. And our band is awesome. We've got to give it a try. Besides, this is the time in my life to take chances like that. I'm not sure it's the kind of career I'd want once I'm a husband and father."

His eyes strayed to Sachiko, and he caught her looking at him. She turned her attention to her drink, but he could see the slight blush on her cheeks. For a moment, he forgot everyone else in the room.

Then her father hummed agreement. "That's good thinking. I'm going to check on the food. Come on, Joshua. I'll show you the kitchen."

"Sure," Joshua rose and excused himself, earning some snickers from her cousins, but an approving look from Sachiko's mother.

Her father led him along the wall of the main dining room and into the kitchen. Joshua barely noticed the linen-draped tables with candles; his gaze landed on the black-lacquered grand piano in the corner.

"That's a beautiful piano!" He wondered if his voice reflected the longing and envy he felt.

Vincenzo tossed up one hand dismissively. "Meh. Sachiko's uncle bought it for her, but she hated piano. We have a pianist, comes in on Sundays and special occasions. You like? You play for us later. So what do you know about restaurants?"

I don't want to join the family business, Joshua thought, then chided himself. For pity's sake! They'd just met. He probably just wants to show off the kitchen—or let me meet more relatives.

"Not much, sir."

Vincenzo waved his hands dismissively. Joshua wondered if he talked with his hands so much when he was in the Navy. He opened the swinging doors and waved for Joshua to enter the kitchen. "It's like music— or psychology. You need talent, drive...and presentation doesn't hurt, either."

He led Joshua down the aisles, talking a little about how restaurant kitchens differed from ones in the home, describing a little about their cuisine, introducing or re-introducing him to the staff/family. Joshua relaxed.

"So what do you know about knives?" he asked as they came to a magnetic strip on the wall holding a dozen blades of different sizes.

"Uh, don't use the same knife for vegetables as for meat?"

He nodded approval, then pulled down a large butcher's knife and thumbed the blade idly. "Every knife in the kitchen as a specific purpose. This one has two. I call her 'Veritas.'"

Oooo-kay. "Why—?"

Suddenly, Sahicko's father closed the distance and brought the blade up to Joahua's throat. Joshua yelped and leapt back, hitting the metal counter and causing the pans and bowls on it to clatter.

"What are your intentions for my daughter?" he demanded.

"I love her!" Joshua squawked. His voice cracked at the end.

Around him, someone snickered, and another said, "Geez! Ease up, Vinny."

He glanced from his face to the knife and saw that it wasn't as near his throat as he'd thought. Not that he was taking chances. He stayed still.

"Vinny" spoke with deliberate slowness. "You hurt her, and..."

"I don't ever want to hurt her. She's the most incredible woman I've ever met."

Her father looked hard into Joshua's eyes a few more moments, then pulled away.

Joshua released the breath he was holding and slumped, bracing himself on the counter. "Veritas, huh?" he asked as he took some slow breaths to regain his composure.

"You don't swear much, do you?" was all Vicenzo said as he returned the knife to its place. "I like that. You going to be okay?"

"I don't know. Am I going to get threatened with an iron skillet next?" The words were out of his mouth before he could stop them. What had he gotten into?

Then he heard the approving laughter. Someone said, "I think he'll fit right in," and he realized he'd just passed some kind of test. He hoped it was the last.

Vincenzo smacked his face twice, lightly, like Joshua had only seen done in the movies. "Come on. Bet you've never seen the inside of a restaurant freezer. So, does she know yet?"

"No. Not yet. It's only been a couple of weeks."

"You hear that?" he called to the room at large. "He's a smart boy. Nobody do anything stupid and mess this up."

Joshua imagined him adding "for my son." Yes, he'd passed with her father.

Now he just had to win her.

Ydrel's encounter with Tasmae had left him so upset, he'd staggered to the bathroom and thrown up. He'd half-hoped that someone was listening and would come to his aid, but no one came. He made his way back the bed with difficulty and lay down to stare at the ceiling and brood.

Malachai must review the audio himself or have some kind of program that flags certain words or voices or something. Do they have stuff like that? Wonder if Joshua would know? Still, ironic that the one time I'd like someone to check on me, no one bothers to show.

I should sleep, he concluded, but the pain his stomach and the command of the Miscria had robbed him of slumber.

Teach her to build a bomb! That would get me locked up in Maximum "Care" for sure! Though maybe tonight, that wouldn't be such a bad idea. Maybe the air conditioning works there.

First, he'd been too hot; now, he shivered under the covers. Maybe he should call the nurse. Maybe he was sick...

Of course, I'm sick! Sick of being monitored like a felon, sick of being too afraid to even tell someone my stomach hurts!

Sick of being made to fight someone else's war...

A tear slid down his cheek, and he lay there, shivering and crying, until at last sleep overcame him.

"Mmmm, that sends the most delightful shivers down my spine." Sachiko sighed.

"Why don't you come inside and I'll see what else I can do to make you tingle," Joshua murmured in her ear.

"I wish I could." She leaned against his chest. They'd stayed with her parents through dinner, then wandered through the touristy part of Newport before driving to the gazebo on Ocean Drive to watch the sun set. Now they were standing on his doorstep, wrapped in each other's arms. She never wanted to leave.

"But I really have to do some studying on my own. I hadn't planned on doing this today." She gave him a little squeeze. "It was fun, though."

He returned the hug. "I had a great time, too."

She snorted. "So much for paybacks."

"Oh, I wouldn't say that," he replied lightly, but before she could ask, he turned to the door. He stopped, his hand on the knob.

He asked, "Sure you don't want to at least get together in the morning? I could meet you for church—"

"Did my grandmother put you up to that?" she snapped.

He flinched.

Way to end a date, 'Ko. "I'm sorry. You were talking to her right before we left and— It's just that I haven't been to church in a very long time. It's kind of a sore spot between us." Suddenly, she felt awkward. What would he think of her now? And why should it matter so much?

But he took her hand, dispelling her fears with a touch. "That's all right. Just, if...you know, if you change your mind, the offer's good all summer. In the meantime, will you at least call me tomorrow? I don't want a single day to go by that I don't hear your voice."

She realized she felt the same way about him. "Deal. So, what did she say to you as we were leaving, anyway?"

"Oh, uh, she's going to pray *una novena a San Valentino.*"

Her jaw dropped. She wasn't sure which was worse—Grandma using him to get her to church or Grandma praying for their romance! "Oh, Josh! I'm sorry!"

"Why? I told her to add one to St. Joseph."

She raised her brows.

He got that funny expression on his face. He looked at their hands, suddenly shy. "To, uh, well, that I'd be worthy of you, I mean, if anything ever..."

She wrapped her arms around him and held him tightly. "I think it should be the other way around," she whispered. They kissed until she almost changed her mind about leaving, but she pushed away and dashed out to her bike.

As she roared off, it didn't occur to her to wonder why she was so happy.

Chapter Twenty-Eight

Ydrel found himself in the land of mists, disoriented, shivering, his sword in his hand and a cramp in his side. He turned slowly until he saw the Master.

"Let me go," he moaned. "I don't want to fight."

The Master didn't even answer, simply faded into the background as the monsters approached. Gray things, with depressions where the facial features should have been. Alien but weirdly familiar. This time, instead of their arms ending in blades, they had hands which held swords.

I can knock the blades from their hands, he thought. Then when I have a safe minute, I'm using all my power and leaving—

The sword disappeared.

"What?" he breathed, then felt the Master's command: YOU DO NOT NEED THIS PROP. YOU ARE THE ONLY WEAPON YOU NEED.

The monsters advanced.

"No!" he shouted to the Master. "I don't want to do this. I want to go home. Leave me alone!"

He cast about for a ley line. Were there such things in this world?

One of the creatures swung and he ducked. The others waited, but not from some cliché of honor. They were letting him warm up; soon enough, they would come at him at once, and not in some choreographed demonstration fight.

He couldn't find a line. Again he ducked another swing then stepped to the right just in time to avoid a blow. The movement made the stitch in his side flare.

"Just let me go!"

YOU KNOW WHAT YOU MUST DO TO LEAVE.

If only he had his sword. There was energy in it. Anything else? Not the sky, the fog, not even the barren ground.

But the monsters?

Energy flowed from living things, Joshua had said. His mother had poured out her energy to heal him once. Could he work it the other way around?

One jerked forward with a stabbing motion and he grabbed its arm. Instead of tossing it aside, however, he imagined himself a sponge, pulling, absorbing. When he felt the first energy, like cool water, he suddenly thirsted as he never had. He gritted his teeth, pulled on the energy, felt it swirl around him. It filled his head, dizzying and glorious.

When Ydrel came to himself, he found all eight monsters collapsed in the mist. Why were they there still? Always before, they faded when he'd struck the winning blow. He knelt and shook one, lightly at first, then harder.

GOOD.

He whirled and saw the Master, shining as if he'd absorbed the life energy of the beasts.

"Are they dead?"

The Master smiled at Ydrel with pride.

"Were they alive?" Ydrel demanded, even though he wasn't sure he wanted to know. "Were they real?"

AGAIN.

Suddenly, twelve monsters replaced the eight.

"Were they *real*?" he demanded. Had he done it again? Had he killed? A sob escaped his throat.

AGAIN.

"No!" He didn't care if he got lost, if he died. He was leaving this place. The creatures had sacrificed their life energies and he was going to put them to good use. Ignoring the advance of the new enemy, he closed his eyes and chanted. "I'm going back to my body. Back to the asylum. Back to Joshua and Sachiko and safety—"

One of the creatures scored on his side as he faded out of existence.

He jerked awake and just managed to stumble to the toilet in time to vomit into it. He sat on the cool tile, his back to the tub, gasping. He felt weak and shaky but full of frantic energy. His head was clamoring, and not even with the thoughts of others for once. His side was on fire. He scrambled at his shirt, pulled it up. The skin looked unbruised, but when he pressed on it, pain lanced through him.

He pulled himself to his feet using the counter and splashed cold water on his face from the faucet. He felt too hot, then too cold. He looked up into the mirror at his shadowed, pain-filled eyes.

Then he saw the not-quite-human monster standing in the tub, watching.

They'd followed him to the real world!

He ran out the door, through his room, and slammed into Joshua in the hallway.

"Whoa! You okay?" His friend backed up a step and caught his balance.

"Joshua! I have to talk to you!" He scanned the hall. Where had it gone?

"I need to talk to you, too. I need to apologize—"

Joshua's thoughts came at him in a flash, and he snarled with annoyance. "I don't care what your father's stupid organization thinks. It's not like they'd believe me. Do you believe me?"

"Ydrel, it doesn't matter what—"

"Yes! Yes it does!" He couldn't catch his breath. Was it pain or some kind of compulsion the Master had put on him? *They have to know now. If the monsters have followed, they have to know.* "Don't give me any crap about it not mattering what other people believe. I've been here five years because no one will believe me. And I'm going to die because no one believes me. Me, or someone else. He's going to make me a murderer or kill me trying!"

"What?"

The creature was in the hall, its eyeless face tilted in seeming curiosity. A mist swirled beside it, then solidified into a second beast. Ydrel stumbled over his words, but he had to convince Joshua, make him believe.

"He calls himself the Master. He calls me in my sleep. He makes me fight, makes me kill. Monsters, but they get more human each time. He wants me to kill. When I'm good, he...he rewards me. And when I don't fight, the monsters, they—"

"Ydrel, slow down. Have you told—"

"Are you stupid? They'd lock me up, say I'm imagining things. Did I imagine this?" He pulled up his sleeve, revealing the bruise where the monster had struck him. He heard Joshua's sharp intake of breath, but he couldn't see the expression on his face. The light was too bright. His head felt too light. He looked toward a shadowed doorway and saw another monster, faceless, waiting. A sob escaped his throat.

"They followed me, Joshua. To the waking world. They're waiting. The Master said if I ever told anyone, he'd kill me. Dammit, I need your help and I need you to believe me!" He scanned the hall, counting monsters. Three. Four...

"All right. I believe you. I'll help you, and if you need me to believe you, I will, but you need to do what I tell you, okay? Look at me." Ydrel felt the other man put his hands on his face and withdraw them almost as quickly. "Ydrel, you're burning up. How do you feel?"

"I'm cold," he complained. "I've been hot and cold all weekend, and my head's on fire and my gut's on fire, and they're just waiting to finish me off and I'm tired and cold and I'm scared and— You have to believe me!" He stopped before he could dissolve into hysterical sobs.

"All right." Joshua's voice was firm and authoritative, and Ydrel felt himself calm just a little. "The first thing we're going to do is get you to bed. You need something to drink and maybe something to eat—just soup, if you want, but you need strength in case whatever hurt you tries again. Have you tapped the ley line today?"

"I can't concentrate. I—"

"Try. C'mon. Can you walk?"

Slowly, but on his own, he made it to his room and into bed with Joshua keeping pace beside him. Joshua brought him a glass of cool tap water and made him drink it. He thought he would retch but managed to get it down.

The monsters hadn't followed, and he felt a moment of worry for the other people in the building. He reached with his senses, and found them near, focused on him and waiting. They'd wait—wait until his strength was back. Until he rested.

He needed rest.

He leaned back against the pillows.

"Good man. Now try to lie still. I'm going to get you some Gatorade, and I'll have Kelly come in and take your vitals."

He pushed himself up. "No! Don't tell anyone."

"You're sick, Ydrel. *Physically* ill. You need medicine and I can't prescribe it. You can't defend yourself if you're not healthy. You promised to trust me."

There were two monsters in the corner by his closet. Ydrel shut his eyes and lay back against the pillows, forcing down a whimper.

Joshua said more gently, "Tap your energies. I'll be right back."

As soon as he shut the door, Joshua let himself worry. Ydrel was definitely sick, probably delirious, but how much of his hallucinating was physical in cause? And even if it all was, would anyone here believe it was simple fever and not full-blown psychosis?

Let's take care of the fever first, he decided. If he's still talking about monsters later, we'll handle that then.

Kelly wasn't at the desk, but the other day nurse was. "Hey, Keith, could you do me a favor and check Ydrel's vitals? He's got a fever something fierce. And do you have any rehydrating drinks here, or should I go check at the kitchen?"

"For Ydrel or for you?" Keith asked as he pulled out the the thermometer and sphygmomanometer.

"Ydrel," Josh said. "He's got the chills."

"Why didn't he come to us?"

"You know how he is," Joshua forced his voice to stay casual, and was spared saying anything else by a loud crash. He and Keith traded looks, then ran for Ydrel's room.

The room was in shambles. Ydrel was standing on his bed, his eyes bright and desperate, head twisting as he looked wildly about him. Wherever his gaze landed, something happened. Keith gasped as a book flung itself off the shelf toward the closet. Ydrel shouted and whirled; the desk caught fire.

Joshua ran to the desk, grabbing a fallen pillow and using it to smother the flames.

"Ydrel, cut it out! You're going to hurt somebody," he called.

For a moment, the young patient focused on him. "Joshua, get out of here! Can't you see them? They followed me, they—" He shrieked and fell to his knees.

Joshua saw a bruise form at the base of Ydrel's neck. Keith ducked out of the room, dodging a glass that flew toward him and smashed on the wall beside the door.

"Stop fighting them," Joshua shouted. "Defense, Ydrel. Where are your shields?"

"They get past them," he sobbed. "These aren't thoughts!"

"Change them! Make them like armor. Do it!"

"I can't—"

"Concentrate! $E=mc^2$. Here!" Feeling rather stupid, Joshua forced himself to picture video game characters in combat armor and threw the image at Ydrel.

After a moment, things got very still. Keith came back in, followed by Dr. Caldwell. They looked at Joshua, but the intern shook his head slightly.

Madness Bound ✸ 319

"Ydrel?" he asked gently.

He was looking around the room, but his eyes were focused elsewhere. "They're...backing off. They can't get through."

Trying to sound as if it were an everyday thing, Joshua said, "Tie your armor to the line; that way, it'll stay with you. Can you do that?"

Ydrel nodded weakly. A moment later, he curled into a fetal position on his bed and lay on his side, crying. He offered no resistance as Keith took his vitals, but when he saw Dr. Caldwell, he shrank back, backing into Joshua who had sat down beside him. "Don't lock me away! Please! I didn't mean it! I—"

"Easy," Dr. Caldwell spoke gently, as if to a child. "No one's taking you anywhere. Keith says you're sick. Let's just find out what that's about, hey? Can you tell me what's wrong?"

"My stomach's on fire and my head's on fire and I'm so cold and they kept—" Ydrel bit his lip anxiously. "My stomach hurts."

"Okay. Can you lay down flat so I can check it out? I'll be as gentle as I can." With difficulty, he and Joshua eased Ydrel out of his curled position. Joshua sat at his head, brushing his hair out of his face, murmuring general reassurances. Ydrel complied docilely but struggled when Dr. Caldwell tried to pull up his shirt.

He pulled his hands away. "That's okay, Ydrel. I'll just feel around, shall I?"

As lightly as he could, he prodded his abdomen. Ydrel winced several times, but when he pressed to one side, Ydrel shrieked and passed out.

The physician ordered Keith to call for a flight for life and a surgical team to be ready at South County.

"I don't understand," Joshua said. "What's wrong?"

"His appendix," Dr. Caldwell spoke grimly. "I think it's burst."

Joshua leaned his head against the curved wood of the pew in the small hospital chapel. He'd accompanied Ydrel for the short flight to the hospital, told the team that met them the vital information Dr. Caldwell had coached him on, then filled out the admittance papers using the emergency file Keith had thrust into his hands as he'd boarded the helicopter.

Dr. Hoffman had called to tell him Ydrel's aunt and uncle were on their way from New York and would be there in about three hours, and that Edith and Dr. Malachai were heading down from Boston, and that he just needed to stick around for any reports from the surgeons. While he waited, he downed a Diet Coke from the vending machine and tried to bury his feelings of helplessness in a magazine. Then he realized there was one thing he could do. After getting asking someone to get him if there were any changes, Joshua had gone to the chapel to pray.

There he had been for at least a couple of hours. Twice, a nurse had come to give him an update on the surgery. The hospital priest had prayed with him and even heard his confession, before leaving him to go and tend to others. Edith and Dr. Malachai dropped by; in an act of compassion that both surprised and touched Joshua, the senior psychiatrist admitted that Ydrel had complained to him of a stomachache earlier that weekend, and he'd thought it an excuse to get out of a session. Then, he was alone again, praying or just kneeling quietly, hoping God would help him make sense of things he'd experienced in the last few weeks and especially what he'd seen today.

Ydrel had glared at the desk, and it had caught fire, spontaneously and without cause; he'd seen it. And when Ydrel had told him to duck, he'd felt something fly—it hadn't been thrown, it had *flown*—past his shoulder. He'd seen a bruise spontaneously appear on Ydrel's neck just after the boy flinched as if struck.

Could there really be something to his claims of being psychic, after all? And if he was telekinetic, what about the rest of his claimed abilities? And the monsters, and the Miscria? Was he delusional, or was he really what he claimed to be: a sane psychic overwhelmed by his paranormal abilities?

It doesn't matter, his training argued. *Either way, you treat him the same: accept what he believes at face value and give him the tools to interact with "normal" society in spite of it. It shouldn't matter.*

Then he thought about Ydrel's desperate plea, and the conversation he'd had with Sachiko on Saturday, and he knew that it did matter.

"Joshua Lawson?"

Joshua snapped out of his reverie and looked up at Ydrel's uncle. "Oh, hello, Mr.—"

"Douglas will do. May I interrupt?"

"No problem." Joshua stood up a little stiffly. "I was more thinking than anything. How's Ydrel?"

"Darrel is in recovery. They had to remove a portion of his intestine; there was some infection—gangrene, I think. He'll be here for several days, at least; we have to decide whether to put him in the psychiatric ward or see how he does in a private room in the post-op wing. That's what I wanted to talk to you about."

"Me?" Joshua's voice almost cracked. "Sir, I'm just an intern; I'm not qualified—"

"I may not get to visit as much as I'd like to, but I do keep very close tabs on my nephew," Douglas interrupted. "I have heard from nurses and psychiatrists about the improvement Darrel has made with your support and guidance. I know, too, for all his sarcasm at his party, he considers you a friend. Just a few minutes ago, he roused just enough to say three words: 'Josh, shields holding.' You probably know what that means better than I, but I do know that the last time he was sedated in a public hospital, he babbled deliriously. He couldn't hold onto a thought or even a personality. To see the difference—" Douglas's voice choked up with tears.

"Dr. Malachai and Dr. Sellars have been working with him for years."

"And they've done a fine job. But I'm wondering if they've done all they can for him. Darrel doesn't trust them, and I'll bet he doesn't tell them everything. He trusts you."

Again, the older gentleman paused, but this time he seemed to be trying to find the right words.

Finally, he said, "There are bruises and odd wounds all over Darrel's body. Fresh ones, not from that fight with the bastard they put in the room next to his."

Joshua picked up the insinuation. "Have you told Dr. Malachai?"

"I wanted to speak to you first. You're a new employee, a temporary one, and you have no lasting loyalty to the institution. I want to know: has Darrel mentioned anything to you? Is there anyone there you'd suspect of abuse?"

Here it is. Do I believe or not? "Sir, with one exception, I've never seen anything but the most professional and compassionate behavior there—and that exception was not physically abusive that I know of. But today...Ydrel—Deryl—told me he was being forced to fight monsters. I thought it was just delirium caused by fever, but later, I—I saw a bruise spontaneously appear on his neck. I can't explain it. And even so, he was flailing about pretty violently, so maybe he did it to himself somehow? I really don't know."

"Is that why you told him to stop fighting and make his shields like armor? Keith, the nurse, told me. He said you calmed him better than anyone ever has."

Joshua shrugged. "The kind of psychiatry I learned from my father is to accept the client's reality and teach them to cope with it on their own terms."

"Your father's a psychiatrist? I'd like to talk with him sometime about his practice. In the meantime, Darrel has a few days' respite here. I'd like to see him spend it in a regular room. Do you think he's up to it? Don't worry; I won't tell Dr. Malachai about this conversation. I do want your opinion."

Feeling both nervous and elated, Joshua replied, "I think he'll do fine."

Chapter Twenty-Nine

"Hey, there," Joshua leaned on the counter and smiled at Sachiko. It felt good just to see her.

"What are you doing here?" She looked up from her paperwork to regard Joshua suspiciously, then quickly amended, "Never mind. How's Ydrel? We got the surgeon's report, but..."

"He woke up for a couple of minutes before I left. He seemed very...grounded. He was even joking about going to extremes to get out of here. Anyway, I'd left my car here, so Ydrel's uncle got me a ride back. A limo. I could get used to that."

He leaned a little further over the counter to snatch up some M&Ms from the bowl Monique kept on the desk. When he looked at Sachiko, he felt a flutter in his stomach. He though he saw a flicker of something intimate in her eyes, but then her expression cooled into neutrality.

"It's seven-thirty. Shouldn't you be heading home?"

"Got some stuff to do, but it's okay. I make up for it on the weekends. I had a great weekend."

He winked conspiratorially at her, and her mask of severity crumbled. She dropped her eyes and shook her head with a chuckle.

"Oh, sure, laugh, Sachiko!" Monique scoffed as she came out from the back room. "You've been grinning like the Cheshire cat all afternoon. I thought it was supposed to be *Spring* fever?"

Turning his smile to the other nurse, Joshua started to sing "Summer Loving."

Sachiko rolled her eyes, but then Monique asked in song to hear more.

Joshua backed off with a laugh. "I've heard it's not a good idea to talk about your personal life at work."

"A wise policy," a deep voice said from behind him. Startled, the trio looked up at Dr. Malachai as if they were children caught playing hooky. From the stern expression on the senior psychiatrist's face, that was exactly how he regarded them.

" Joshua, I understand that Dr. Sellars has assigned you to stay with Ydrel most of the day, since he will not be in the psychiatric wing?"

"Yes, sir."

"Then may I suggest that you spend more of your time here working on the assignments you have pending, and less of it flirting?"

"Yes, sir." Biting back his mirth, he waggled his eyebrows at the nurses and headed down the hall back to the offices.

"I'm sorry, Dr. Malachai," he heard Monique say. "I was teasing him. He apparently met someone, and he's smitten."

Joshua slowed his pace, lingering to catch Malachai's response. "I would appreciate it if you did not encourage him. Boyhood crushes do not belong in the workplace. Ladies."

A few moments later, Joshua heard Malachai's retreating footsteps.

Sachiko hissed like a cat once Malachai was gone. Monique laughed.

"Now you see why I leave my personal life at home," Joshua heard Sachiko say.

He sighed and headed to his little office.

"Hey, what are you doing here?"

Joshua entered Ydrel's room with a huff. "Why do people keep asking me that question?"

He pulled up a chair and flopped into it, dropping his backpack to the floor. "If you must know, I'm here in my newly assigned role as the world's most highly paid babysitter."

Ydrel smiled but winced. "Please don't make me laugh."

"Sorry. How are you feeling?"

"Physically, like death warmed over; which, I'm told isn't too far from the truth."

"It was close. And otherwise...?"

Ydrel didn't look at the intern as he answered. "It's...different...here. There's more physical pain, and the anxiety is more...focused? Based on reality? I don't know, but it's not what I'm used to."

"And it impacts you differently," Joshua concluded for him.

"Oh, yeah! I woke up in the middle of the night, feeling pain that I'd never felt before and being overwhelmed with worry. The night nurse wanted to give me something, but I told her I wanted to try to 'meditate' first, and when she left, I worked on my shields." Now Ydrel leaned back against the pillows, a little more relaxed, and smiled. "What would you call that? Tweaking the harmonics? Modulating the shields?" Before Joshua could answer, however, Ydrel called out, "Come on in!"

A heavyset nurse entered, pushing a wheelchair with a teenage girl. The girl had a cast that ran from fingers to elbow and wore an uncomfortable-looking back brace.

The girl grinned and waved with her good hand. The nurse smiled at them. "I didn't know you had company; we were going to come back later. How'd you know we were there?"

Ydrel put fingers to his temples and said in a mysterious voice. "I am psychic. I see all." Then, grinning at them, he added more normally, "And I have unusually good hearing. So who's this?"

"Darrel, meet Clarissa. She was in a gymnastics accident a couple of days ago—"

"And I'm bored out of my skull! It sucks to be still all the time," she finished. "So what happened to you?"

"Appendix burst. And it's Ydrel. My real name's D-E-R-Y-L, but my aunt and uncle insist on spelling it the conventional way, so I'd rather be called Ydrel."

"That's cool. You look like you were in a car wreck," she said, eyeing his bruises critically.

"That's from when the monsters attacked me." Ydrel spoke matter-of-factly, and Clarissa rolled her eyes. When he saw the nurse's knitted brow, however, he added sheepishly, "I got kind of delirious from fever." Her face cleared, and she nodded understandingly.

Ydrel cast a quick glance Joshua's way and received an approving smile. So far, so good.

"Well," the nurse said brightly, "I'll leave you kids alone to get acquainted. Clarissa, I'll come back for you in a while."

"That's all right." Joshua stood up. "I can get her back to her room. Joshua Lawson."

"Hi."

"Joshua is from Colorado," Ydrel chimed in. "He's a psychiatrist and healer and a rock star."

Joshua snorted. "I'm an intern at a mental health facility in South Kingston, and I play in a band at home."

"Matter of time. So you're a gymnast? Any good normally?"

Fortunately, she laughed. "Better than you must be at fighting monsters."

"Oh, I'm amazing. I was way outnumbered. So what do you do?"

She told them about doing floor work and the uneven bars and how she fell wrong on the dismount and shattered her wrist badly enough to require surgery. Her doctor, an overly cautious man by her thinking, was also worried about the possibility of back injury and was keeping her braced and under observation for a few days. Ydrel told her about the appendicitis and how the doctors said he almost died on the table. Then she pulled out a deck of UNO cards from her pocket and they played.

Through it all, Joshua kept a back seat in the conversation, making mental notes about Ydrel's behavior so that he could report it to Edith. Ydrel actually did a remarkable job of keeping the conversation off himself and lacing what little he shared with jokes and modifiers so that even though he never lied, the truths he told didn't seem disturbing—or disturbed.

About half an hour into the game, his eyelids started to droop, and he yawned. "I'm sorry. I'm so sleepy all of a sudden."

"After what you've been through, I don't blame you," she said.

True to his word, Joshua wheeled her to her room and rang for a nurse to help her back into bed. Before he left, she said, "Tell Ydrel to call me if he wants to talk or play or whatever. He's kind of weird, but it's cool."

Ydrel was asleep when he returned, so he settled down with a case study until Ydrel's aunt and uncle came in. They chatted briefly, and when Ydrel awoke, Joshua again retreated to a corner to give them some time with him. He was struck by how much more comfortable the three seemed in the new surroundings, as if the institution itself had caused their tensions.

Joshua lost himself in the study, half-listening more for emotion than content, and just as he was finishing writing the last of his comments, Ydrel's uncle touched his shoulder.

"He's asleep," he said quietly. "We're going to sneak out for some lunch. Want us to bring you back something?"

Joshua's stomach gave a growl of approval. "Yeah, that'd be great." He started to reach into his pocket, but Douglas stopped him.

"Don't worry about it. Think you can last until we get back?"

"Oh, yeah. I have some snacks in my backpack, just in case."

They left, passing Sachiko in the doorway. Joshua rose from his chair, smiling. "Hey, there."

"How's he doing?" she asked quietly, but before he could answer, she had already picked up the clipboard at the end of his bed. There was something about her flipping through the chart with such keen interest while dressed in her riding leathers that both touched and amused Joshua, and he had to admire her a moment before he answered.

"He just fell asleep a few minutes ago, actually. Have a seat. Want a Power Bar?"

"No," she set the chart back on its peg. "I can't stay. Tell him I'll call or try to come by later or something." She glanced from Ydrel to him.

Now he saw the tension that was deepening the laugh lines at the edges of her eyes. "What's wrong?"

"Oh, my teacher, in his incredible wisdom, has taken another job and is cutting the class short. Friday's midterm is now the final—"

"What? Can he do that?"

"Apparently. The administration has given their okay, and anything we haven't covered will *just* come from the book." And she exploded into words Joshua didn't understand, though the intent was clear.

"Hey, it'll be all right." He pulled her into a quick embrace. "This is your third time in this class, so you're ahead of most everyone."

"But I fall apart on tests. Every time in this class—"

"I do know a lot about test taking. Seriously, it's the only reason I passed last semester at all. And it really seems like your problem is with the test, not the information."

For a moment, she looked like she was actually angry at him for being so rational. Then she laughed and pulled away, wiping her eyes. "Sure. But we study."

Madness Bound ☙ 331

"Promise. Meet you after work?"

"I've got the days off to study, so just come over whenever." She gave him a quick peck and left.

She's so perfect. Why couldn't I have waited for her? Then I wouldn't have to prove myself. What was so great about LaTisha that I let so much go for her? Stupid, hormonal idiot. Joshua sighed and tried to shake off his unease by reminding himself that if he hadn't gotten into such trouble with LaTisha and school and—well, and everything, really—he probably wouldn't have accepted a job clear across the country and would never have met Sachiko in the first place.

Still, he was relieved when Ydrel woke up wanting to talk. When Ydrel's aunt and uncle returned shortly afterward with food for Joshua, and Edith arrived as well, Ydrel immediately insisted that the intern be allowed to leave for a long lunch.

"You can stay a couple of hours, can't you, Edith? I think Josh has something he'd like to do in town."

Edith obliged, and Joshua didn't make even a token protest.

Chapter Thirty

Two hours later, Joshua pulled back into the parking lot of the hospital, singing to the radio. He waited until the end of the song before turning off the engine. He'd had a great afternoon—and all he'd done was grade Sachiko's practice tests and get a chaste, preoccupied kiss when he left.

I've got it so bad, he told his reflection in the side mirror. His reflection smiled back in agreement.

He hummed on his way down the hall, but his happy thoughts died away when he entered Ydrel's room and saw the grim faces within.

Ydrel was sulking, his face a mixture of anger and depression he'd seen only once before, at his birthday party. Edith sat in one of the hospital chairs, looking from Ydrel to her hands, her mouth turned down in a frown and her eyebrows furrowed. Malachai, meanwhile, lounged against one wall, his face stern and impassive. His gaze never left the boy on the bed.

Joshua cleared his throat, and all eyes turned to him. "What's up?"

Ydrel drew himself up to speak, looked at Malachai, and deflated back into his sulk. Edith and Malachai glanced at each other. He raised his brows in that permission-giving way of his.

She spoke. "Joshua, would you come with me for a moment?"

They found an empty room. Edith regarded him with a look of anger and disappointment that made him feel guilty without knowing why. She gazed at him for what seemed ages while he fought the urge to squirm.

"I understand Ydrel had a visitor today?" She barely made it sound like a question.

"Well, yeah, he had several. His aunt and uncle. Sachiko Luchese, though he was asleep when she dropped by—oh, you mean Clarissa?"

The narrowing in her eyes told him exactly what she meant, but he pushed ahead anyway. "Neat kid. She was here for a couple of hours in the morning. The three of us played UNO, but she and Ydrel did most of the talking. I wish you had been there to see how well he—"

"And where did you get the idea that Ydrel was allowed to fraternize with unauthorized visitors?"

"One of the nurses brought her by. I thought—"

"The nurses have been reminded of the potential danger of Ydrel's fragile mental state. You, however, should have known better. You were told to keep Ydrel company and to keep an eye on him, not to start a party in his room."

Anger took over Joshua's mouth. "The nurse brought Clarissa. It wasn't my idea. But to be frank, I thought it was a good one. 'Bout time someone started treating Ydrel as a regular kid. I thought that's what you wanted, too. I know that's what his uncle wants!"

"And just how would you know that?" Edith demanded.

Ten minutes later, his ears ringing with the warning that she would personally drive him back to Colorado if he admitted another unauthorized visitor or consulted with a patient's family behind her back, Joshua accompanied Edith back to Ydrel's room. As soon as they entered, Ydrel pinned the psychiatrist with such a look of betrayal that Joshua felt her freeze.

Malachai watched intently.

Jerk. How much of my getting chewed out is thanks to you? If you think I'm going to let you see me upset, you have another think coming.

"Sorry, dude," Joshua shrugged. "Looks like we're going to have to cancel the party."

Ydrel blinked, then smirked. "That su—stinks. I was looking forward to a beer."

The tension was broken. Edith slipped easily past Joshua and gathered her purse and briefcase. With some quick admonitions to get well, which Ydrel didn't bother to acknowledge, she and Malachai left. Malachai pointedly shut the door behind them.

Ydrel glared at it with almost tangible hatred. "Bastard."

Joshua felt an uncomfortable stirring in the air, one recently familiar. "Uh, don't set fire to anything, okay?"

Again, Ydrel blinked and looked away. "Wouldn't give him the satisfaction," he muttered. "You okay?"

"I'll live. You?"

Ydrel continued to glare at the door. "Didn't I tell you? Malachai's going to do his best to keep everyone convinced that I can't function in the outside world. And for all that she brought you into my life, I don't think Edith believes I can, either."

"Edith's scared for you," Josh replied, but he couldn't deny what Ydrel said, either.

Ydrel leaned back against the pillows and lowered his bed. He hissed through his teeth as he squirmed to get more comfortable.

"When's the last time you had a pain killer?" Josh asked.

"This morning. I was waiting until my aunt and uncle left to ask for another, then Malachai came, then Clarissa dropped by to talk and...Well, might as well get used to not talking to anyone but nurses and interns." He pressed the call button by his bed.

"You're not Catholic, are you?"

For once, Joshua caught him off guard. Ydrel's eyebrows furrowed. "What's that got to do with anything?"

"I met the hospital priest. Neat guy. So, if you were interested, I could see if he can visit and perform the Anointing of the Sick for you. It's his job, after all. Or I can see if there's a Christian chaplain who does hospital visits. I mean, it's no replacement for a beautiful girl...Oh, don't look at me like that. I'm in love; I'm not blind!"

"You're pretty religious, aren't you?" Ydrel asked abruptly.

"God and my faith have gotten me through a lot."

"I'm not sure I can believe in God anymore." Ydrel spoke quietly, his face turned away from the intern. "Too many people talk about 'God's will' and how God gives them the right to hurt other people. Taking their land. Killing."

"That's not God. That's human nature. Religion is a useful scapegoat for people who want power or don't want to get along with their neighbor. God gave us some pretty simple rules: don't kill, don't steal, don't covet. Jesus said just love God and your neighbor."

Then he smiled, thinking of his reaction to Malachai just an hour earlier. "The hardest kind of simplicity."

"Should you ever kill? What about self-defense? What about Hitler?"

"Guess it depends: are you a martyr, or a suicide? That's a sin, too. Hitler...Hitler should have been laughed into anonymity. Once he became so powerful, though, I don't know. I can't think of any other way to have stopped him for certain. And there is such a thing a just war, you know."

He wanted to ask why the sudden and intense concern but couldn't figure out a way to ask without sounding psychiatric. He waited, hoping Ydrel would open up

Instead, Ydrel asked, "Does this Anointing of the Sick stuff work for non-Catholics?"

"God is there for everyone, regardless of their specific beliefs."

"Do you think the priest might stick around afterward and talk to me? He's staff, after all, right? okay, then—as long as it doesn't get you fired or anything."

Ydrel opened his eyes in the dark room and glanced at the red numbers of the digital clock. 1:05. He picked up the phone before it could ring.

"Is the coast clear?" Clarissa asked.

"She's talking to her boyfriend," he told her. "We've got about an hour before she decides she'd better walk around, and everybody else feels pretty peaceful."

"I'll be right there!"

Ydrel brought the bed fully upright, then used a little telekinesis to bring the hairbrush from the table to his hand. He wasn't quite sure why he was concerned with his appearance, except that Clarissa was the first normal non-psychiatric person he'd talked to in years and he wanted to keep a good impression.

Of course, if I'd wanted to do that, I probably should have let the phone ring at least once before answering it.

Clarissa entered the room, and the thought was lost. As soon as the door was shut, she pulled off her robe. Underneath, she wore jeans and a T-shirt, and no back brace. She walked with athletic grace and plopped on the bed beside Ydrel and sat facing him.

"So the back's okay?"

"A little twingy, but I've got an appointment with the chiropractor. Better than the brace. But never mind my back. How did you know to pick up the phone when you did?"

She was smiling at him, her eyes so curious. Her mind so open.

He shrugged. It wasn't like he'd thought up a convincing lie, anyway. "I'm psychic. Truly. That's why I was committed."

She raised her brows, impressed. She believed him!

"Psychic? That is way cool!"

"No," he mimicked her tone, "that totally sucks." But for once, he smiled as he said it. She believed him!

"Come on! You can read minds!"

"And I always know what people think of me."

"What about empathy? If you can actually experience what other people feel—"

"Then I get overwhelmed in a crowd. Or, if the person is a strong projector, I lose track of what emotions are actually mine."

"Fine, then. Telekinesis!" she challenged.

"You don't want to see what I did to my room in my delirium. I don't know how I managed not to hurt anyone."

She leaned back. "Okay. You win. Sucks to be you."

For some reason, that made him laugh, and a lock of hair fell into his face.

She reached out to brush it back gently. "Anyone ever tell you, you have gorgeous hair?"

"No. Usually I get asked why I keep it so long."

Other than the priest, who had held his hand briefly before he left, and Joshua, who occasionally laid a hand on his shoulder, no one touched him for non-medical reasons. He hoped she wouldn't stop.

She didn't. Instead, she toyed with it in a very pleasant way. "Tell 'em girls dig it."

"Oh, I don't even want to open that can of worms."

She pulled back her hand. "Oh! Are you...?"

"No," he groaned. "I mean, I don't know. I— My abilities hit me just as I hit puberty. In an all-boys boarding school. Then in various mental hospitals. I've experienced plenty of other people's feelings, but I've never had a chance to explore my own. I told you it sucks to be psychic."

She returned to caressing his hair, slower, more deliberate moves that felt nice in a different way. He liked that, too. "But you have a handle on that now? You can block others out?"

"Yes..."

She kissed him.

Her kiss was gentle and it sent warm shivers along his spine that he enjoyed very much—until he remembered when he'd had those feelings before. He pushed her away. "Don't."

"What's wrong?"

"It's just—" He couldn't tell her about the Master, how the only time he'd ever felt like this was when he'd been made to after he'd killed something. "I—What's the point? I mean, you get to go home tomorrow, and you'll see your friends at the gym and tell them about this great adventure and how you kissed this crazy psychic guy. And me, I have to go back to—"

He stopped, seeing her eyes water with tears. He felt ready to cry, himself.

"I'm sorry. I didn't mean for it to be that way. I just thought—I'd better go." She turned.

Ydrel caught her hand in a sudden firm grip. When she turned to protest, he pressed a hand over her mouth and jerked his head toward the door.

They listened to the footsteps stop just before his threshold.

"Don't wanna go back," Ydrel whined in a sleepy little-boy voice, as he moved his legs to make it sound like he was tossing and turning. "I don't." Then he gave a snorting kind of snore and sighed. Under his hand, he could feel Clarissa trying hard not to laugh.

He thought hard toward the listening nurse: *Poor baby. Best to let him sleep as well as he can.*

A moment later, he heard the footsteps continue on. They waited. Gently, Ydrel removed his hand from her mouth and twined it into her hair.

"She's back at her station. Clever idea with the pillows, by the way; she thought you were still in bed. Clarissa, I'm sorry. I know that's not how you meant this, and it's really important to me that we part as friends. Besides..."

Now he smiled and gently caressed her hair, "who knows when I'll get the chance to kiss a beautiful girl again. You really are beautiful."

He pulled her toward him.

After a few minutes, the warmth and tingling overcame the fear and he reached up with his other hand to stroke the back of her neck. She set her hand on his chest.

Then he felt a familiar, urgent scritching in the back of his mind. The Miscria. With a sigh, he pulled away, but just enough that they were still touching forehead-to-forehead and nose-to-nose.

"Made up your mind?"

"Yeah." Again that persistent scritching. Urgent. Almost desperate. He sighed ruefully. "Sucks to be me."

"Get well and get out." She gave him one last kiss and tossed the robe back on, checking the hall carefully before scuttling back to her room. He stared at the door for a long time, not sure whether to laugh or to cry. Finally, he gave himself to the Miscria's call before he really did dissolve into tears.

"Where have you been?" The strength of Tasmae's projected anger rubbed against his raw emotions like sandpaper on a sunburn. He snapped back with projected anger of his own.

"I was sick. I've been in the hospital! I almost *died*! For pity's sake, it's only been a couple of days. Give me a break—"

"Days? Six weeks!" Confusion mixed with anger, echoed and enhanced by his own.

"Weeks? But, how—"

"Almost—died?"

Suddenly, a maelstrom of images and emotions accosted Ydrel's mind: *Anger. Fear. Confusion. Responsibility so heavy it pulled him down.*

His knees buckled. "Tasmae, stop."

I am the Miscria. An older woman smiles down on her. "Tonight you shall be ordained; then we will complete your training. You have the strongest talent yet, but there is much I must teach you." Her teacher at banquet, raising her cup, falling back, an arrow through her chest.

He felt a wave of grief so fierce it made him retch.

"Tasmae, please stop!"

I am the Miscria. Half trained, half brilliant. The Ydrel confuses. The Ydrel refuses. Others begin to doubt her ability to lead. She begins to doubt herself. People, friends, fighting and dying because she cannot lead. Because she has failed.

Thick waves of worry obscured his vision.

"Tasmae!"

I AM THE MISCRIA! The Ydrel says wait. The Ydrel says no. The Ydrel does not come. I call, and he does not come. I am forsaken. We are forsaken. The world pulls itself apart; invaders, demons, fall from the sky.

Desperation overwhelmed him, so strong that he could barely tell his own feelings from hers.

"Get out of my mind!" He tried to throw up his shields, but they were ripped away.

"I AM THE MISCRIA! Do not leave me!"

"STOP!" With desperation of his own, he pushed himself away from her.

He awoke bolt upright in the hospital bed, his scream still resonating off the plain walls. His sore body protested the sudden movement with a pain that made him gasp. For a moment, he welcomed it. It was his, not some projection of another's. Not Tasmae's.

Tasmae! Had she followed him? Was she lurking in the shadows the way the monsters had? His eyes searched the dark room.

Footsteps he'd barely registered ended at his door and the lights snapped on, making him blink.

"What is it, Ydrel? Did you have a nightmare?"

"Don't call me that! My name is Deryl." And, despite the pain it gave him, he leaned his forehead against his bent knees and burst into tears.

Chapter Thirty-One

Joshua returned to the hospital at six in the morning, ready to take another long shift as the world's highest paid babysitter. He was already anticipating four o'clock when Edith said she'd have someone come to relieve him and stay with Deryl until the client fell asleep. Sachiko had her final that afternoon and had promised to come by right after to commiserate or celebrate. He'd told her that they'd be celebrating, and he already wanted to go home and get his place in order.

This time, he'd brought his computer and small keyboard to the hospital with him; Rique had some changes to one of the songs they were going to audition with and wanted Joshua to work the transitions. He had his headphones so he could work it whenever Ydrel slept.

He found out from the nurse that they'd given Ydrel a sedative around two that morning, so he had a couple of quiet hours to work until Kate showed up to visit.

"Douglas is taking the opportunity to meet with some of his clients," she said, as she sat down beside her nephew and took his hand. "How is he?" she asked.

Joshua shrugged. "Guess he had a rough night, but nothing major."

Ydrel stirred and opened his eyes with difficulty. "I'm okay," he answered.

"Good morning, Darrel."

"Deh-rill. D-E-R-Y-L. If I let everyone call me Deryl from now on, will you at least spell it right?" He closed his eyes and was asleep again before she could answer.

Kate released his hand and pulled Joshua into the hallway. "What do you think?" she asked him.

Joshua thought the whole situation was stupid, but he replied, "I think he has the right to his own name."

She sighed and looked away—accessing a memory, Joshua noted. "Our grandfather was named Darrel. Our father was always furious that my sister insisted on the unusual spelling. Said it just encouraged unusual behavior. So when Darrel came to us, we thought..."

"With all respect to your father, unusual spellings are pretty commonplace nowadays."

"I know," she said. "We'd just hoped..." They heard footsteps approach and saw Douglas approach. Joshua went in to check Ydrel—Deryl, now—while Kate talked to her husband.

He found Deryl drowsy but again awake. "When's breakfast?"

Joshua checked the clock. "Half an hour or so. How are you feeling?"

"Not so well. Groggy." He lolled his head toward the door. "My aunt's crying."

"Good tears, I think. Do you remember what you said a couple of minutes ago?"

"I remember," he replied neutrally, then said no more until his aunt and uncle entered the room.

"So...Deryl?" his uncle ventured, pronouncing it correctly. "D-E-R-Y-L?"

Deryl smiled and held out his hand to them.

Deryl didn't volunteer why he'd decided to change his name, and his aunt and uncle seemed afraid to pursue it, so they spent an awkward half hour avoiding the subject until the nurse came in with Deryl's breakfast. Douglas declared that Kate needed nourishment, too, and they left with a promise to return later that evening.

Joshua waited until Deryl had finished most of his meal and was picking at the crumbs. "So? What's the story?"

"I'm not the Ydrel anymore. The Miscria—Tasmae—she's gone." He tossed down his fork, shoved the tray away, and told him about their meeting, and the argument, and how he had been overwhelmed by her thoughts and emotions.

"I couldn't breathe. I could barely keep track of what was me. I couldn't make her stop. So I ran. Back to here. To...*reality*. And I've got my shields up so tight that I feel kind of blind or deaf and I wouldn't be able to sense her Call if she put the weight of her world behind it."

Ydrel—Deryl now—stared miserably away for a minute, then glared at Joshua.

"Well?" he snapped. "Aren't you going to congratulate me? I did it. I've rid myself of this Miscria illusion, cold turkey, left her high and dry. Aren't you going to say you're proud?"

Joshua pulled up a chair so he could look at the boy directly. "No, and I'm not going to make you feel guilty, either. You've been at her beck and call for five years now? You've answered all her questions to the best of your ability. Maybe she needs to be pushed out on her own, find her own answers."

"She was so scared," he whispered. Joshua could see his eyes tightly contracted. Accessing memories not his own.

"It's scary on your own sometimes. Lonely, too. But sometimes, it's the only way to grow."

◇——◬——◇

Joshua looked up from his keyboard and checked the clock on his living room wall. It was almost six. Sachiko should have finished her final an hour ago. Why wasn't she here yet? Why hadn't she called?

The place was clean; the take-out he grabbed from a nearby restaurant waited in the oven; a small cake from the store sat on the counter. He'd showered, shaved, put on his best shorts and a Hawaiian shirt, and made a new CD of music. After this crazy week, he couldn't wait for a couple of hours alone with her doing something other than studying.

Where is she?

He called her phone again, got no answer, then to distract himself, dialed the hospital and asked for Deryl's room. He'd been feeling pretty bad all afternoon, and the doctor had diagnosed him with a post-op infection.

"He's asleep," Danika, the orderly assigned to watch him for the evening, answered. "Nodded off after he ate. He seems to be doing better."

"K. Thanks for being there tonight."

She laughed, "I'm getting paid overtime to sit around and read my novel. I didn't have any plans tonight."

He did—or at least he thought he did. He hung up and glared at the clock: 6:13.

"C'mon, 'Ko. At least call me."

He had put the CD into the player when he heard the familiar growl of a motorcycle. He turned on the music, then bolted to the door and threw it open. "Well?" he shouted down to her.

If she heard him, she gave no sign; she grabbed her backpack and trooped up the stairs silently, her helmet still on and the sun visor blocking her face. Joshua backed up a pace to let her in, shutting the door behind her and waiting apprehensively as she stripped off her riding gear. When she pulled off her helmet, she was smiling radiantly.

"Ninety-eight!" she shouted and leaped into his arms. Joshua caught her, cheering. They smothered each other's faces and necks with kisses, their words tumbling over each other's:

"He graded them as we finished, so—"

"You did it!"

"He said my essay was the best he'd ever read—"

"I'm so proud of you!"

"He thought I should go into gynecology, what a joke—" She leaned her head back to laugh and he kissed her neck. Her skin was as silky as her hair.

"You're incredible!"

"I'd never have passed without you." She pulled away just enough to look at him, and the adoration and desire on her face did more to him than any of her kisses.

"Sachiko, I... I didn't do much."

"Yeah, right." She kissed his mouth.

The kiss kept going longer and deeper until he was very aware of her body pressed against his, her legs around his waist, her weight totally supported by him, his hand on her—

They had to sit down. Fast.

Still holding her, still kissing, he backed up until he bumped against the bed. (*Couch, Joshua, Couch!*) He started to sit, but she pushed against him until he fell back with her over him, her tongue doing amazing things inside his mouth, her hands reaching under his shirt. On the CD player, Ricky Martin was singing, "Do you really want it?"

"Well?" she whispered.

He did. Oh, he did.

They had to stop.

He did not want to stop.

She shifted position in a way that set every nerve in his body screaming.

They had to stop!

"Sachiko!" He managed to twist his head away from her, push her back just a little. "Ko, honey, please. I love you, and I really think it's best if we don't do this!"

"What?" She pulled back from him, her body taut, her voice cold.

Joshua, with his blood ringing in his ears and his body screaming its own protests, didn't notice. "It's just that I've let things go too far too fast before and it was a disaster and—"

"What did you say?" Her demand came out staccato, yet he still didn't notice.

"I said we should stop, wait."

"Before that!"

Slowly, he collected his wits. "I...I love you?"

Sachiko closed her eyes, her expression one of such pain, disappointment and even fear that it drove all thoughts of lust from Joshua's mind. "What is it, honey?"

"Don't call me that!" She pushed away from him and went to gather her things.

"Huh?" Joshua leapt off the bed—couch!—and reached for her.

She swung around, nearly hitting him with her helmet. "Look. I don't know what game you're playing, but those words have a very specific, very special meaning to me!"

Josh jumped back defensively. "Me, too!"

"Yeah, right." She slammed the door behind her.

Joshua stood slack-jawed and blinking until he heard the Harley's roar. He dashed out the door, calling her name, but she was gone. He went back in, slammed off the CD player, and threw himself on the couch, his mind a jumble.

Ten minutes later, he reached across to grab the phone.

"Sachiko, honey? Listen, I—I have no idea what just happened. Please, please call me when you get home and explain this to me. I want to make this right. I—" He hung up before he could sound any more pathetic. Finally, he took a shower, dressed in more professional clothes, left another phone message for Sachiko, and headed to the hospital. Maybe Ydrel—Deryl, now, Deryl—could explain what he'd done wrong.

He walked into Deryl's room to find Danika reading aloud from her historical romance while Deryl dozed. Joshua hesitated at the door, but Deryl opened his eyes.

"I'm awake. Hey, Danika, I'll bet Josh can watch me while you go get something to eat."

Danika gave Joshua a puzzled look but set her book-mark in her book and got up.

"If you read that, you have to tell me what happens!" Deryl called after her. Once the door was shut, he raised his bed so he was sitting. "All right, what happened with you and Sachiko?"

Joshua flopped into a chair and told him a somewhat edited version of the story. Deryl didn't look so well, and anyway, he didn't need all the more...personal...details. When Josh finished, Deryl turned his head drowsily toward his friend, blinked owlishly, and started cussing.

"Hey!" Joshua snapped. "I came here for help, not to get chewed out."

"Not you. Ma—her ex. Didn't Sachiko tell you?"

"I know she's had a bad experience. What about it?"

Deryl sighed in exasperation. "Don't you two talk? Or do you just suck face whenever you're alone?"

"Have you got anything useful to say?" Joshua replied stonily.

"Useful...useful..." Deryl's focus faded. He shook his head. "You have to talk to her about him. About, all of it. Otherwise, things'll get bad between you two."

"Worse than now?" Joshua asked sarcastically, but Deryl turned to him, his voice urgent, his eyes contracted to mere pinpoints.

"Yes, worse! And she has to be there. It's important she be there, or my baby might die, and Tasmae—and she won't be, unless you are and you're together and...and..." Suddenly, his eyes dilated back to normal, and his expression glazed. "What was the question again?"

For a moment, Joshua wasn't so sure, himself. "What does Sachiko's jerk of an ex have to do with her walking out on me?"

Deryl rolled his eyes in that familiar way that said Joshua was missing the obvious. "He's a master manipulator. Everybody thinks he's such a great guy. Even Sachiko. Did. Wrapped around his little finger. Stupid, evil, son of a—"

"So? What's that got to do with me?"

Deryl sighed. "Guess what his favorite words were?"

"I don't know. I—" Then he knew. He groaned.

Deryl spoke in a controlled, mature tone, a lot like Dr. Malachai's most professional voice. "'I love you, Sachiko dear, and I think it's in our best interests if we—' Funny how *we* always meant *she*."

"But I *do* love her, and I *do* think it's best we wait. How do I convince her I'm sincere?"

Deryl didn't seem to be listening. "She took all the risks, made all the sacrifices. Gave him everything. She even..." He shut his eyes and was silent. Joshua watched him morosely for a few minutes, then sighed. He'd have to figure it out himself.

Deryl's eyes snapped open suddenly. "What would you risk for her?"

Caught by surprise, Joshua answered, "Anything."

"What would you sacrifice?"

"Short of my soul, everything."

"Prove it."

"How?" But Deryl's eyes had shut again, and this time he snored slightly. A short while later, Danika returned, and Joshua left. He drove to Sachiko's apartment to see if her bike was there—it wasn't, so he headed home.

How could convince her of anything if she wouldn't talk to him outside of work, when she had made it clear their relationship was to remain secret at work?

Then he remembered just what she'd said about that: "Unless we're engaged or something, and then you can sing it in the halls, for all I care."

By the time he got home, he had the beginnings of a plan. He bounded the steps to his apartment and went straight for the phone. "Rique! Don't kill me, man; I know I promised, but—you've got to help me write a song."

Chapter Thirty-Two

"Earth to Sachiko!" Monique waved her hand in front of the computer screen. "C'mon, girl, can that log actually be that interesting?"

"I'm just trying to catch up on the weekend," she replied evenly.

"Me, too. So I'll ask again: Did you do anything?"

"Almost." Almost got drunk. Almost started a bar fight.

Almost called Joshua a dozen times.

She'd finally called Liz for advice.

"He says he loves you," Liz had said. "He wants to wait, he wants to 'do it right'? Not to mention he's sweet, smart, and drop-dead gorgeous! What? Are you out of your mind or something?"

Maybe she was. She didn't know. She didn't know anything anymore, it seemed.

She sighed.

"Oh, oh." Monique sat down next to her. "How'd you do on your test?"

"Ninety-eight," she replied listlessly.

"Oh. So you broke it off, then, huh?"

"Broke what off?" Joshua's voice interrupted, making Sachiko jump. Why wasn't he with Ydrel? Why did he have to show up now?

"What are you doing here?" she demanded.

"Last time I checked, I still worked here." He tried to reply blandly, but irritation crept into his voice.

Monique jumped in. "If you'd actually been reading those logs, you'd have seen Joshua has done the impossible. He got Ydrel to drop that alien fantasy of his."

Joshua looked pained. "I didn't do anything. He—"

But Monique continued as if he hadn't spoken, "And don't mind Sachiko. She broke up with her boyfriend. He couldn't take the heat of her success."

"What?" He stared at Sachiko, open mouthed and wide-eyed.

Sachiko huffed, her annoyance building toward anger. "She's guessing. Erroneously!"

"Then tell us," Monique urged. "We're your friends."

"Or, if you'd rather just talk to Monique," Joshua offered.

Why does he have to be so nice about it? She wanted to strangle him!

"Look, I appreciate the sentiment, but there's nothing to discuss. It's just... Congratulations on Ydrel—Deryl." She broke off before she said anything more and turned her attention to the open log on the computer screen.

She hadn't known. She'd been so caught up in her own misery, she hadn't even visited Ydrel in the hospital.

How had she let this...this kid, get to her?

"Yep," Joshua said knowingly.

Despite herself, she glanced at him from the corner of her eye.

He had his arms crossed, and his lips pursed in a thoughtful way. He nodded.

"Men are scum," he said with such mock seriousness that she had to bite back a smile.

Monique snorted. "How would you know?"

Now he stood hipshot and batted his eyes at the nurse. "Oh, girlfriend, I have so been there!"

As Monique exploded into giggles, he leaned across the counter and spoke softly to Sachiko. "Are you sure it wasn't just a misunderstanding? Maybe he's sad and confused and really wants another chance?"

She wanted to tell him she was sorry. She wanted to tell him it wasn't his fault. She wanted to tell him. Everything.

"Don't you have work to do?" she growled.

His expression hardened into anger and hurt. She didn't care. She couldn't care.

"Matter of fact," he muttered, then turned his attention and smile to Monique. "I really came here to find out where Mr. Doleson is. I haven't seen him, and his room's empty."

"Didn't Dr. Hoffman tell you? That's right—he had to take his daughter to the dentist today. Mr. Doleson was released this morning. Outpatient status. His wife came up over the weekend and they were talking about moving to California and starting over. He wants to produce a new talk show, like Geraldo, but with only positive things—people married for 50 years, kids who do charities, that sort of stuff. He was talking about it all last week. In fact, I think he left you something."

She rifled through the papers on the desk until she found a large envelope. "Dr. Hoffman didn't think you'd be here until this evening, so he left it with us."

"Dr. Sellars is with Deryl over lunch." Joshua tore open the envelope.

As he stood silently reading, Sachiko made her escape.

"Whoa," Joshua breathed as he looked over the note Mr. Doleson left. The card read "Thank you" in gold foil. Inside was a handwritten note:

Joshua,

I'm going to do like we discussed and forget about them watching and just do my best to show them the best in humanity. Thanks for putting things into perspective—that's what I plan to call my new show: Perspectives.

For moment, Joshua couldn't speak. When he did, his voice was choked with emotion. "That's...way cool." He smiled at Monique, then turned to share his joy with Sachiko.

She was gone.

Monique sighed at the empty chair. "I hope she makes up with this guy. Fast."

"Me, too."

Deryl's infection cleared quickly, and it was decided he could return to SK-Mental. He was moved while sedated, and Edith asked Joshua to be with him when he awoke in his old bed.

"Was it a dream?" Deryl murmured thickly, looking around at the familiar surroundings.

"No. It was all real."

Deryl rolled over and defiantly snatched the raggedy old bear from its spot on the end table, clutching it to him. He turned his back on Joshua and closed his eyes.

He remained that way the rest of the day, and into the next.

Naturally, he was on the agenda at Friday's meeting.

"I attempted to talk to him." Edith sighed. "All he would say was that he felt like a zoo animal."

Good for you, Joshua thought, taking a sip of his latte to hide his grin.

He nearly choked when Dr. Malachai grunted and asked, "Then, we're seeing a return of the paranoia?"

"I hadn't thought of that," Edith admitted. "Zoo animals are under constant display. I was thinking of the paradox of being in a place of relative safety and relative confinement—it's not the first time he's referred to this facility as a cage."

"Which animal?" Dr. Bartlebort asked. "It could be a statement of his feelings of power—or lack thereof—"

"Or it could just be an accurate statement of how he's been treated," Joshua cut in. Part of his mind advised him to quit while he still had a job

But his mouth didn't take the hint. "Think about it: How do you transfer a zoo animal? You catch him unawares, tranquilize him, and next thing he knows, he's waking up in a new place. Sound familiar?"

"We thought it would be easier on him—" Edith started.

Joshua raised his hands in defense and answered as gently as he could. "I'm not making any comment about the motives."

Then he turned to Malachai. "I'm just an intern. But don't you think that there are times when a patient's words have objective validity?"

"More NLP?" the senior psychiatrist asked languidly, and Joshua knew he was in for it even before he heard what came next. "I think this is something we can discuss further—after the meeting, of course."

Joshua left Dr. Malachai's office later with his ears burning. He was unsure who he was angrier at: Malachai, Deryl, or himself.

He'd put a lot of blood, sweat and tears into his plan to win back Sachiko: Rique had not only refused to help him, but had chewed him out and threatened to kick him out of the band; his parents had said they'd support his decision, but suggested that it could mean living at home and working at Carl's Jr. next year.

He was tired from staying up late working on the music and emotionally drained from trying to act normal around Sachiko at work, which was even tougher since she was working double shifts to pay back the nurses who'd covered for her while she studied for her exam. It didn't help that Edith had taken his comments, which he really intended for Malachai—the one who arranged the whole transfer farce—to heart.

Must be why Malachai likes her so much as a partner, he grumbled to himself as he headed to Deryl's room.

Let him fire me, he thought defiantly. As long as they don't take away my key until Saturday.

He paused at Deryl's door to release his tension and negative feelings, then went in.

The room was dark, so he made a beeline to the curtains, pulling them open with a single sharp movement. "Wake up, Ling-Ling!"

"What?" Deryl growled, squinting at the intern. He was curled up in bed, his hair stringy and unkempt, his arms curled around his stuffed bear.

"Wake up, Ling-Ling. You know, that famous panda at the San Diego Zoo or somewhere?"

Rather than pulling up a chair, he grabbed a pillow off Deryl's bed and set it on the floor so he could sit at eye level with him. "You have any idea how spun up everyone is over your 'zoo animal' statement?"

"Oh?" A smile tugged at the young man's lips.

Suddenly, Joshua understood. And something in him snapped.

"You little—" He bit off the words that were coming to his mouth. "I nearly got fired for defending you this morning and you were just playing head games with the psychs?"

"What else have I got to do?" Deryl demanded sullenly.

"You know, this song is getting really, really old. 'Boo-hoo. Poor me. I have a filthy-rich aunt and uncle who love me, people who care for me—and even some who care about me. I have three full meals a day, plenty of entertainment, safety, security—'"

"Imprisonment!"

"You ever seen a real prison? I have. For that matter, I'm willing to bet a third of the population of earth would be willing to trade your pampered imprisonment for their impoverished freedom."

"Fine! They can have it!" Deryl sat up.

Joshua stood. "Fine! Get better and make a space available!"

"Go to hell!"

"I can't. But let me tell you: Life stinks, but it don't get any better if you lie around with your head under the covers. Now, I'll admit, you've been handed a bigger share of crap than a lot of people, but you also sabotage yourself."

"Who asked you?" Now Deryl was standing on the bed, clutching the bear so tightly in his fury that the seams were threatening to pop. Around him, the air seemed to thicken and intensify as if with static electricity.

Joshua, caught in his own fury, barely noticed. "No one. This is free advice from a lowly intern. You made a lot of progress this summer—I'm not the only one who's said that, either. But your little sulk has set you back. If you want to get out of here, you'd better stop thinking like Ling-Ling and start acting like Shamu!"

He stormed out, making a turn just as Descartes flew through the doorway and slammed into the wall.

Joshua, meanwhile, almost slammed into Sachiko.

"What was that all about?" she demanded.

"I think your father would call it 'wall-to-wall counseling,'" Joshua snapped, and shouldered past her, not bothering to see if she was looking after him.

She did, in fact, turn to watch him storm down the hall, her arms crossed, not sure if she was miffed or bemused.

Neither of them saw Deryl's old toy slide, as if pulled by invisible strings, across the hall and back into Deryl's room.

Chapter Thirty-Three

When Joshua was stopped at the foyer Friday morning, he was sure the security guard was going to hand him his walking papers and a box of his stuff, but the guard simply wanted to inspect the items he was carrying in. He opened the synthesizer case and scrutinized the keyboard, then unzipped the garment bag to reveal Joshua's change of clothes—the same suit he'd worn to Sachiko's party, professionally laundered and pressed.

"New therapy?" the guard asked, raising an eyebrow at the bouquet of flowers. They were oriental lilies again, with a few roses tucked in.

"If you're around at six tonight, stop by the first level nurse's lounge," Joshua said, but inwardly he groaned. His unusual methods were starting to become a source of merriment with the psychiatric staff. Or had the guard heard about his argument with Deryl yesterday?

"And I'd really appreciate it if you didn't tell anybody about this—it's kind of a surprise."

"Mmm-hmm," the guard replied. He gave Joshua a minute to juggle his other luggage, then handed back the bouquet. "Good luck."

Floyd met him just in the lobby with a cart covered by a sheet, under which they hid everything but the suit. As Floyd wheeled it away to a safe place, Josh headed to the locker room. There, he stored the suit in his locker, pausing only to smile wryly at the poster taped inside the locker door—a photoshopped picture of Joshua in a mind-meld with Mr. Spock from the old Star Trek. In large, 50's-movie lettering, it read, "Joshua Lawson—Psychic Psychiatrist!" At the bottom was the caption, "I feel your pain." He was pretty sure Dr. Hoffman had made it and taped it to his locker.

For a day, Joshua had left it up, with an addition of his own: a sticky note saying, "I Want to Know What You're Thinking," but now it resided inside his locker door. He thought about putting it back out with a new caption, but he didn't have the will.

Sometime today, he would have to talk with Deryl. He was looking forward to that about as much as he was looking forward to seeing Sachiko before six.

The day, however, turned out surprisingly good. He worked on case studies—he suspected Malachai was loading them on him to keep him away from live patients—until Floyd knocked on his door.

"Edith is looking for you."

He gathered up his papers and headed to her office, not knowing what to expect. When he opened the door and saw Deryl's aunt and uncle seated on her couch, he stopped dead in his tracks. Kate, Deryl's aunt, looked like she'd been crying.

"What did you do to our nephew?" Douglas asked.

He couldn't help himself; he glanced at the clock. Seven hours. *Please, oh please, God, let them let me finish the day.*

"I'm sorry. I—I lost my temper. It was unprofessional of me, I know, I just, I really—"

Kate stood suddenly and threw her arms around him, cutting off any further reply. "You dear, you angel," she said, her voice heavy with emotion.

He threw a confused look to Edith, saw her biting a back a smile at his chagrin. "You haven't seen him today, have you?" she asked.

"Uh, no." He disentangled himself from Deryl's aunt, who apologized, murmuring something about pregnancy hormones. "He's okay? I'm not fired?" The last slipped out before he could stop himself.

"Go see for yourself. But if you ever yell at a patient again, you will find yourself using your psychiatric skills to convince people to 'Biggie Size' their order." Her smile belied her stern threat, and he paused only long enough to drop off his file and shake Douglas' hand before heading back down the hall to Deryl's room.

The door was slightly ajar. On the doorknob was a long, hanging sign: *Mad genius at work—Enter at your own risk*. He peeked at the other side: *Do Not Disturb—I'm disturbed enough already*! He recognized it as one of the gifts Clarissa had given Deryl at the hospital, passed to him via a nurse and with the approval of Edith and his uncle and aunt. He pushed open the door and again stopped in his tracks.

The room wasn't just clean; it was immaculate. Even the posters gleamed in the sunlight that streamed through the open window. The bed was neatly made, with the bear sitting defiantly in the middle of the evenly placed pillows. Stuff had been rearranged on the shelves; the books on military tactics and history were gone, replaced by the schoolbooks and paperbacks Joshua had lent him, as well as the first Harry Potter book. *Clarissa's doing?* Joshua thought. *I wonder if Deryl's got Malachai pegged as Snape or Voldemort?*

Deryl sat at the desk, dressed in a clean shirt tucked into his jeans, his hair shining and combed and gathered into a leather tie-back—yet another gift from his new friend. He was writing steadily, but turned when he heard Joshua enter.

"'Bout time," he greeted the intern. "Did you have a nice morning hiding in that cubby hole you're calling an office?"

Joshua had long since given up asking how he knew these things. "It works." He did his best to sound casual, as if the sudden change was nothing unexpected.

Deryl rolled his eyes. "Do I need to add references to this report? I'm not sure I learned how."

"We'll hit that next time. It's really just a matter of form."

He realized he still hadn't fully entered the room, but Deryl saved him the trouble by getting up and stretching, though gingerly, in deference to his stitches.

"Want to go for a walk? I'm getting tired of sitting around."

Outside in the commons, away from monitoring devices or prying ears, Deryl confessed, "I don't know whether to be angry at you or thank you."

"Let's just forget it, then. It's been a rough week for both of us. So you've decided to Sha-mooze the staff?"

Deryl gave him a sour look. "And I'm the one who's locked up. You were right. If I want to get out of here, I have to do it by the book. Speaking of which—or, thinking of which, in this case—he's Snape; I've got someone more vicious in mind for Voldemort."

He laughed at his own private joke, then said, "So, you ready for tonight?"

Now Joshua sighed, a gusty release of nervous energy. "Yeah. As long as my voice doesn't crack and she doesn't throw flowers in my face, I should be fine. You going to be there?"

"In the background. I don't want anyone distracted by the presence of a patient." For the first time, he set a reassuring hand on Joshua's shoulder. "It'll be all right. She loves you. She's just afraid to admit it. Oh— but get her a cappuccino. She'll need it."

Sachiko glanced at the clock opposite the nurses' station and stifled a groan. Almost 6:00. *Two hours to go.* She stretched to relieve the tightness in her neck. Thank heavens Jared was coming to relieve her early tonight. She needed sleep. The last time she'd worked double shifts was as an ER nurse, where the constant emergencies kept her awake and active while on duty, and able to crash hard once she got to bed. The more sedate schedule here just seemed to drain her yet left her too keyed up to get to sleep when she got home.

It's not just that, and you know it, she growled to herself. She'd lain in bed looking at her phone, aching to call and apologize but not knowing how or what to say, begging for it to ring and for Joshua's voice to be on the other end. After that one subtle attempt to get her to open up at work, he'd pretty much stayed away from her. When he did speak to her, he was cool, professional, and always in the company of others.

Serves you right. "Let's keep our relationship out of the workplace." We know where we got that crap, don't we? She rubbed her eyes until the tears that threatened to surface subsided.

"You gonna make it?" Monique asked lightly.

"No." Sachiko heaved herself to her feet. "I'm going down to the cafeteria."

"You can't!" Monique's voice held panic. She didn't look at Sachiko so much as past her and down the hall.

"Monique, I'll only be gone for a few minutes. I'm tired, I'm achy, and I've had a rotten week. All I want to do is stretch my legs and get a—"

"Cappuccino?" concluded a warm voice behind her. She spun and caught her breath.

There was Joshua, dressed as he had been for her party—the night of their first kiss—right down to the earring. He leaned against the counter, and there was no mistaking the gorgeous, come-on look in his eyes. In one hand he held a Styrofoam cup.

Her peripheral vision picked up Floyd behind him with a covered cart, and others nearby, but for a moment her mind didn't take them in.

"Uh, yes, as a matter of fact. Thanks." She reached for it, but he pulled it away teasingly. Then, with a courtly gesture, he invited her to sit in the chair they'd wheeled out of the conference room.

He was so close to her, smiling in a way that made her insides melt. She wanted to run. She wanted to drive him away with some cutting remark. She wanted to throw her arms around him. She didn't move.

He waited, his eyes locked on hers. About twenty people had gathered. Were they here to celebrate her test? That'd be just like Monique—or Joshua.

"Please?" he asked quietly. "Trust me?"

She squared her shoulders, brushed back a stray lock of hair from her face, and took the drink. With as much dignity as she could muster, she sat in the proffered chair. Floyd had set a small table beside it for her coffee, and she set it there after a large swallow.

Joshua pressed a button on his synthesizer and a romantic, upbeat tune she didn't recognize began playing. He took a bouquet of flowers off the cart and leaned in close to place them in her arms.

"Careful of the roses," he said in a soft voice meant only for her. "They have thorns." Then he backed up and began to sing, a song she hadn't heard before.

When Dr. Malachai saw people heading toward the nurses' station, he dismissed it as coincidence. Surely if anything important were happening, he'd have been informed. Then he heard the music and Joshua's singing and, with a practiced gait that took him at almost a run without making him seem in a hurry, headed over to see—and stop—the young man's shenanigans.

He'd gotten just close enough to see the backs of the crowd and make out Joshua's words, when Deryl suddenly appeared, blocking his way.

Barely acknowledging the client, he stepped to the left.

Deryl followed, again blocking him.

He stepped right. So did Deryl.

"You owe her," the young man said clearly and slowly, his tone hinting at hidden knowledge and open resolve.

Dr. Malachai gave Deryl a smile, which the boy mocked. With a bland expression, gritting his teeth, he stayed still and silent.

At first, Sachiko thought Joshua was just apologizing, singing about how someone else had said he loved her and broke her heart, but his "I love you" was true from the start. How he found the other part of his soul in her eyes.

As she sat there, torn in her own conflicting desires, he knelt on one knee, pressed a small box into her hand and sang,

I don't want a passing romance, gone as summer went

I want a lifetime's love, I want a holy covenant

I'll give you my moments, my days, my 'till death do us part

Roses should have thorns, but I promise through the years

Whenever you feel pain, I'll kiss away your tears

If you'd

Trust my heart

Believe my words

A love like ours could rock this world

It's a scary road to ride on, but the place to start

Is to trust my words

Believe my heart

Believe my words

Trust your heart

He stopped singing and she could only stare, shell-shocked. She knew she looked like an idiot, but she couldn't make herself move, make herself believe this, this...wonder...was happening. The music came to a close. She could hear people shifting restlessly. Still, she didn't move.

He smiled a timid smile and squeezed her hand over the box. "Just think about it," he said, giving her an out. "I'll be in the break room."

He got up, took three steps back as if she were royalty, then turned and strode down the hall. Floyd followed, rolling the cart that held the synthesizer.

As soon as they rounded the corner, it was as if a spell had been broken. Sachiko was able to breathe again, and everyone crowded around her. She ignored them, staring at the little burgundy box in her hands until Edith ordered everyone to give her room.

"Do you want to go to my office alone for a few minutes?" she offered.

"No, no, I just…" Her voice trailed off. She was still staring at the box.

"Well, open it!" Monique urged.

When she saw the simple, battered but shiny silver band inside, threaded through a silver chain, every wall of ice she'd erected melted at once, crashing down like an iceberg in the warmth of spring.

Someone behind her said, "I don't get it."

"It's his great-great-grandfather's ring." Somehow, she managed not to choke on the words. Her breathing was fast and shallow and she couldn't understand why she didn't just break down crying. Or why she didn't want to.

Edith laid a hand on her shoulder, and she jumped as if zapped.

"I have to go talk to him," Sachiko said, and hurried down the hall.

As soon as he got to the break room, Joshua gave up all pretenses of composure and made a beeline for the soda machine.

God, oh, God, please don't let me have made a fool of myself for nothing. The image of her face haunted him. He'd imagined a lot of reactions over the last week, from her throwing her arms around him in joy, to throwing the flowers, ring and all at him in fury, but he hadn't anticipated the way she just stared at him like he'd grown another head. *Please, if nothing else, let her understand I was sincere.*

He didn't realize how his hands were shaking until his third unsuccessful try at shoving a dollar into the slot. Floyd carefully took the bill, pulled it straight and inserted it into the machine. He hit the button and even popped the tab before handing Joshua his Diet Coke.

Joshua tried to smile his thanks, but his desperation must have been showing—the older orderly laid a reassuring hand on his shoulder. "It's goin' to be all right. You were righteous. She was just surprised."

"She wasn't the only one," came a voice from the doorway. They turned to see Dr. Malachai. He stood in what was probably meant to be a casual pose, but it was ruined by his stern expression.

Here it comes, Joshua thought. He took a large sip of his soda.

"Floyd, I'd like a few words in private with our young intern, if you don't mind." The tone of his voice said it hardly mattered if the orderly did mind.

Nonetheless, Floyd turned to Joshua, a question in his eyes.

"Thanks for your help, man," Joshua held out a fist. Floyd tapped it with his. Then, with a nod to the chief psychiatrist, he left the two alone.

For a long moment, Malachai stood with the room between them, regarding Joshua with a not-quite-challenging stare. Joshua stared back, leaning against the machine. Malachai's presence was actually a relief, in a way; it gave him something to focus on other than Sachiko's expression. In the back of his mind, he could hear the familiar theme from the shootout scene of an old Western. *I'm not blinkin', pardner.*

Malachai broke the silence. "Have a seat, Mr. Lawson."

The chief psychiatrist pulled up a metal chair and sat in it, leaning back in a practiced, nonchalant way. Joshua sat with elbows on the table and eyes on his soda. He didn't feel like playing psych games. *Just get it over with.*

"Well, it would seem we have a similar taste in women."

So you were *making the moves on her at that party!* It was not what Joshua expected, and the words were out of his mouth before he realized what he was saying: "Had your shot, sir."

To his surprise, Malachai laughed, acting for all the world like they were just two guys discussing chicks. "And this is your shot, I suppose? Embarrassing her and yourself in front of people who may one day become your colleagues, just to satisfy your flair for the theatrical?"

Oh, don't hold back. Tell me how you really feel. "Sachiko understands."

"Even after seeing her reaction, you believe that? How well do you really know her?"

Joshua was starting to tire of Malachai's superior attitude. He gave the older man his most knowing glare. "Enough."

Malachai cocked a brow. "And it doesn't bother you, being Catholic and all? I'd have thought—"

Joshua didn't want to hear anything from *him* about the woman he loved. "The past is the past. I'm the present and I want to be the future."

The psychiatrist threw his hands in the air, the way Josh's mother sometimes did when she was exasperated. "As you wish. But are you sure you're not making a rash decision? After all, this isn't the first time you've rushed into something that later turned out to be disastrous."

Surprise must have shown on Joshua's face, for he hastily added, "Your father told me about LaTisha Dane before you arrived here. He was concerned and asked that I keep an eye on you. I didn't feel the need to mention it—and yet, here we are."

Joshua was suddenly thankful for Sachiko's discretion at work, and glad that he'd already told his parents all about her and his plans. But he didn't like Malachai thinking his feelings for Sachiko were anything like those he'd had for LaTisha.

He leaned back, matching the other's posture and superior attitude. "Sir, I take it you've never been married? Engaged? Truly in love?"

"Are you implying that I wouldn't understand?" Malachai's smile twisted sickly for a moment. Joshua chose to ignore it.

"It'd make it easier to explain. With LaTisha, I was, well, obsessed, really. I let things slide because I just wanted to be with her, because I felt so good around just her. It was kind of like a drug, really. I felt more of a man, but I was becoming less of a person.

"With Sachiko, it's like a part of me I didn't know was empty is suddenly filled. Being near her, even at work, is the best part of my day, but I'm also just driven to do more and better in everything else, whether it concerns her directly or not. I'm more of a person, and more of a man, because of her."

"And if she doesn't feel the same about you?"

The pain and fear of that thought, now voiced, pierced him, and he had to stop before replying.

He covered as best he could by taking a large gulp of Diet Coke. "Then I'm still better off for having known her, and I hope that this experience helps her realize that she deserves someone who'll risk everything for her; that she's worthy of true, enduring love."

"Poetic. But interesting you should mention risk."

'Bout time. Just act natural.

When Joshua didn't react, Malachai continued, again with exasperation, "What are we to do with you, Joshua? Your work has been acceptable, particularly considering your youth and inexperience, but your professionalism on the job...Do you realize in the month you've been here, you've dressed down the orderlies, flirted with the nurses, allowed an unauthorized person access to a client, and acted as if you were the peer of the people who should be your mentors?"

I've also been instrumental in the recovery of one client and the progress of another, sat death watch for a third, been hit with a chair protecting a client, and created a training video on an innovative method that—who'd have thought it?—works, he thought angrily, though he didn't say anything. It'd only sound defensive if Malachai was going to fire him, and boastful if not. Instead, he sipped his soda and waited for the hammer to fall.

"And now this scene. Tell me, what would you do in my place?"

What Joshua really wanted to do was roll his eyes and snarl, "Will you stop the cat-and-mouse games and just fire me already?" Instead, he just waited, infuriatingly calm and guileless.

Again, it was Malachai who broke the silence. "It would be...impolitic to fire you at this time. Besides, I'm not sure how I'd explain the double blow to your father; he is trusting me with you, you know. However," his voice took on a serious edge, "any more unconventional behavior, and I will have no choice but to terminate your employment. Do you understand?"

"Yes, sir."

He waited until his boss left the room before muttering what he really felt: "Bastard." Now he'd have to go to confession again. He was really starting to despise that guy.

He tried to take a drink of soda, discovered that the can was empty, and slumped. How long had it been since he'd left Sachiko at the nurses' station? He could only have been talking to Malachai for a few minutes, but it seemed more like an hour. He pulled himself up enough to fold his hands in prayer. *St. Valentine? I didn't do a novena or anything, but if you could put in a good word...?*

He almost jumped to see Sachiko next to him.

Madness Bound ✪ 375

"A girl's got to be careful what she says to you," she said without preamble, she said as she pulled up a chair.

It took him a moment to realize she'd remembered her comment from their first weekend together. He wasn't sure how to respond. She was right beside him, so close he could lean a little and touch her shoulder with his, but she didn't look at him. She held the ring box, closed, in her hands. Her expression was tense, her mouth a tight line.

He couldn't look at her. He turned away, started to drink, realized again that his soda was empty, and stared at the can as if it could reveal some secret.

"So...Did you write that yourself?"

"Yeah. I know, the lyrics were kind of corny, and they don't really scan—"

"No! No, it was beautiful." For a moment, he caught her swift glance through his peripheral vision. Then she was staring at the box again, turning it over in her hands. "It's just, I don't think you've realized the trouble you've made for us."

"Sachiko, I—"

"No, hear me out. First, Monique is not going to give us a day's rest. She'll want to know every detail of our relationship from here on out, and you only have to deal with it for the summer. And I'm betting she's not the only one. Then, there're my parents—I don't think you appreciate what an ordeal a Japanese-Italian wedding is. Not to mention grandmother when she finds out her novenas have been answered—"

"They have?" Joshua did not believe his ears. "She will—it is—I mean, you will? We—"

Sachiko burst out laughing. "Oh, shut up and help me put this on, will you?"

Joshua, hastening to comply, hands shaking with relief and suppressed adrenaline, fumbled with the chain and nearly dropped the ring.

"Hey! Be careful with that! It's a priceless heirloom, you know!"

"Sorry. But what do you expect, leading me on like that?" Gently, he placed the chain around her neck and fastened the clasp.

"Warned you about paybacks." She looked down at the ring resting between her breasts. She clasped it, giggling, and spun into his waiting arms.

Their kiss was restrained—they were at work—but after a long week apart, it was very sweet. She pulled away before he could lose himself in it. Still, he held her in a tight embrace and reveled in the comfort and warmth of her body.

He kissed the top of her head. "Want me to stick around until ten?" he asked.

"Actually, love—"

Love. That word sounded so wonderful! "Say that again!"

She pulled away enough to look him in the eyes. "Joshua Abraham Lawson, I love you."

Chapter Thirty-Four

Deryl grinned to himself and used his thumb to blend the shadows on the sketch of Joshua proposing to Sachiko. After sticking around the hallway to make sure Sachiko ran to Joshua, he'd retreated to his room. They had to come by here before heading to Japperwoppy, where her optimistic family had planned the engagement party.

A knock on the door told him he'd overestimated the time they'd need to accept the congratulations from the staff—or maybe they were anxious to share the news with him? He felt something in him release and relax, and he had to close his eyes a moment before he shouted, "Like you have to knock!"

"Protocol must be followed," Joshua replied as he and Sachiko entered. "Where were you?"

"I found myself a good vantage point." He turned the sketch for them to see but pulled it back when Sachiko reached for it. "No way! I'm not done. You guys came here earlier than I'd expected—but come on! Where's the ring?"

Sachiko plopped on the bed beside Deryl and pulled out the chain for him to see. He glanced from the simple silver band to Sachiko's sappy smile, then to Joshua, who held up his empty hand with a shrug. But he, too, had a happy, love-struck grin, and Deryl could feel the stretching in his own cheeks. How long had it been since he'd smiled so much?

Impulsively, he threw his arms around Sachiko. "I'm so happy for you!" he whispered.

"I'm still not sure I believe it," she whispered back.

"Trust him." He gave her one more squeeze and released her. With a small giggle, she wiped her eyes. He found he had to take a deep breath, himself. "Oh, hey. Your clothes are hanging in my closet. Why don't you go get changed while I tell your fiancé what will happen to him if he ever hurts you?"

"Fat chance of that. Wait—my clothes?"

Joshua pulled out the suit bag and handed it to her. "Your mom got them from your apartment for me this afternoon. She said either way, you'd want to come by the restaurant tonight—"

"My parents know?"

"Honey, your dad's one scary dude! Of course I went to him first!"

Her eyes widened, then she glowered. "He stuck that butcher's knife under your chin."

Joshua hesitated, then nodded. "Veritas. Day we met. Didn't stop me."

"Arrgh! It's like prom all over again!" Sachiko threw her arms into the air, snatched the suit bag and headed to the bathroom, griping in Italian about overprotective fathers.

"She's got a temper. It runs in the family," Deryl warned.

From behind the door, Sachiko yelled, "I heard that!"

Joshua smirked. "I can handle it."

"How'd you handle Malachai?"

Joshua responded with a snort, and Deryl realized that whatever mix of scolding and innuendo the Chief

Psychiatrist had used had gone right past him. Deryl glanced at the picture he was drawing, and again that wave of well-being washed over him. Was this joy? Yet, he also felt a funny kind of emptiness...

He rubbed at the base of his skull, as if the pressure could fill it.

"You okay?" Josh asked, taking a seat in the same chair where just a few weeks ago, they'd faced each other off about his "friendship assignment."

"Been quite a summer," Deryl offered in lieu of an answer.

"Summer's not even half over. You okay?"

"I... Well, don't tell Malachai, but for the first time in a really long time, I feel... I'm not sure. Hope? I'm going to get out of here." A laugh escaped him, and he pressed his fist against his mouth to stop it. "I actually believe I'm going to get out of here."

Joshua just smiled—a little sternly—and nodded, but Deryl could feel the joy coupled with victory that poured from his friend like the heat of the sun. "Well, it's about time. But we've still got a lot of work to do to convince the rest of the staff before you can come to my wedding."

"Ha! I'm not waiting that long. End of summer. We leave together. Deal?" Deryl held out his hand.

"Deal." Joshua took it, then pulled him into a quick hug.

"I think my mother knew what I was going to answer, ya know what I mean?" Sachiko stood at the door in a sapphire dinner dress and matching heels. She did a little spin and the skirt swirled around her knees.

The joy that emanated from Joshua took on a different tone, one that made Deryl uncomfortable and...not jealous, but envious of his friend's good fortune. He ducked his head and turned to his sketch to keep his friends from noticing.

"I think you look great," Joshua told her.

"Thank you, but what does Mom think we're going to do?"

"Dinner with your fiancé isn't enough?"

She laughed. "All right. I got your point. Hey—you!"

Now that the moment had passed, Deryl was able to grin at her.

"You want me to bring you some *diakufu* on Monday?"

"Please! I mean, if your mom's made any—"

Sachiko snorted. "I have the feeling that's not the only thing she's cooked up today."

When the door had closed behind them, Deryl turned back to his sketchbook. For a while, he just sat, his eyes resting on the drawing, feeling nothing, or perhaps feeling too much.

He flipped back to an earlier page, let his fingers trace the lines of Tasmae's profile. That empty ache sharpened, and he swallowed hard. He forced himself not to think about how he'd left her, about her terror at losing him; otherwise, he'd go running back to her before he was ready. He could not go back to her yet. He had to be healed. Strong. Sane.

"But I'll come back to you," he whispered. "I promise. Just hold on for me."

Please Leave a Review

Please take a few minutes to leave a review. It only takes 20 words to share with others what you like and don't like about the book. It helps readers and helps with Amazon ratings which makes author and dragon happy.

Subscribe to My Newsletter

If you want to keep up with my adventures, books, and classes in person and on print, sign up for my newsletter. You'll get a free ebook with a story about Deryl before the asylum! https://fabianspace.sub-stack.com/subscribe

Acknowledgements

Madness Bound started out as a story I wrote back in 1986 in part out of spite. My science fiction literature professor didn't understand the analogy I was making in my midterm paper, so I decided to write a story for the final instead. He liked it and asked if I'd write the novel. I spent a year working on it, and in fact enlisted my roommate and her friends to help. Sadly, friends go separate ways and their names fade into the past, but I will never forget the encouragement and interest they showed.

The book utterly failed to interest a publisher, so I put it aside, went into the military, got married, had kids...When I felt ready to resume writing, I dusted it off, re-read it and realized the publishers had shown much wisdom! It was lame, especially the main character.

However, I liked a lot of it, so I ripped it apart, drove the main character insane (poor Deryl) and rebuilt it as a trilogy. That was a fun year, and I have to thank my husband for putting up with me not going to bed until all hours because I just had to write the next line.

Peter Stampfel at DAW was the first to get the new book, and sent me a very encouraging note that I still have. While DAW didn't take the book, he did give me the impetus to write the second in the trilogy.

Fast forward to 2010, and Dragon Moon. Gwen Gades loved the book, but hated the title (which was

Asylum Psychic.) She held the contract hostage until I had a better title. I went to my great friends at The Writers Chat Room (writerschatroom.com) who brainstormed with me until we came up with Mind Over... *Mind Over Mind* was the first; then *Mind Over Psyche* and *Mind Over All.* I couldn't squeeze the Joshua/Sachiko wedding in, and some readers complained, so I completed the set with *Hearts Over Mind.*

Gabrielle Harbowy, editor at Dragon Moon, did an awesome job with the edits, not just making or recommending changes but explaining to me why she was suggesting them. She not only made the book better, but she made me a better writer.

Jeanne Litt checked over the book to make sure I had reasonably portrayed the practice of neuro linguistic programming. Not only did she make sure my intern Joshua did his job well, but she had waited nearly a decade from the time I asked her to the time I actually sent the manuscript. How kind is that?

In 2023, I got the rights to the *Mind Over* trilogy back, just as an editor friend was telling me how much she'd loved the books. Thus encouraged by Rebecca Martin, I decided to republish them. I was never sold on the title, especially Mind Over Psyche, so I asked my friends at the Catholic Writers Guild for suggestions. Mark Baker came up with Madness of Kanaan: *Madness Bound, Madness Unbound, Madness of Worlds*, and *Madness of Love.*

So much love and adventure went into this book. Thanks again to all my supporters and to the gracious God who led me to this calling.

There's More Fun in FabianSpace!

DragonEye Series
Murder Most Picante
If Wishes Were Dragons
Nun of My Business
Christmas Spirits
Greater Treasures
Siren Spell
Good Intentions
Idol Speculations
Plus short stories

Science Fiction
Space Traipse: Hold My Beer Series
The Old Man and the Void
Dex's Way
Discovery
The Rescue Sisters short stories

Neeta Lyffe, Zombie Exterminator
Zombie Death Extreme!
I Left My Brains in San Francisco
Shambling in a Winter Wonderland